Also by Barbara Delinsky

Lake News
Coast Road
Three Wishes
A Woman's Place
Shades of Grace
Together Alone
For My Daughters
Suddenly
More Than Friends
The Passions of Chelsea Kane
A Woman Betrayed

The Vineyard

A NOVEL

Barbara Delinsky

SIMON & SCHUSTER

NEW YORK • LONDON • TORONTO

SYDNEY • SINGAPORE

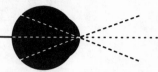

This Large Print Book carries the Seal of Approval of N.A.V.H.

SIMON & SCHUSTER
Rockefeller Center
1230 Avenue of the Americas
New York, NY 10020

10 9 8 7 6 5 4 3 2 1

Library of Congress Cataloging-in-Publication Data

Delinsky, Barbara.
  The vineyard : a novel / Barbara Delinsky.
    p. cm.
  1. Wine and wine making—Fiction. 2. Family-owned business enterprises—Fiction. 3. Single mothers—Fiction. 4. Rhode Island—Fiction. 5. Remarriage—Fiction. I. Title.

PS3554.E4427 V56 2000
813'.54—dc21   00-037311

ISBN 0-7432-0426-3

Acknowledgments

DOING RESEARCH for a book has the potential for reward on several levels. I was fortunate in the course of writing *The Vineyard* to be on the receiving end of both information and enthusiasm. Without these, *The Vineyard* wouldn't be quite what it is.

For information on grape growing and the workings of vineyards along the southern New England coast, my thanks go to Anne Samson Celander, Susan and Earl Samson, and Joetta Kirk of Sakonnet Vineyards in Little Compton, Rhode Island. For help with crises in such vineyards, I thank Bob Russell of Westport Rivers in Westport, Massachusetts.

My thanks to Cecile Selwyn for sharing the latest thinking on dyslexia and its treatment; to Carol Baggaley for information on birthing kittens; to Daisy Starling for things Portuguese; and to Jack Williams for his thoughts on hurricanes of the dry variety.

All the above know their fields well. I am solely responsible for any errors made or variances taken in the name of literary license.

For their support, their expertise, and their energy, I thank Amy Berkower, Jodi Reamer, Michael Korda, Chuck Adams, and Wendy Page.

As always, with love, I thank my family.

The Vineyard

One

ON WHAT HAD BEGUN as just another June day in Manhattan, Susanne Seebring Malloy returned to her Upper East Side brownstone after lunch with friends to find a saffron yellow envelope in the mail. She knew it was from her mother, even without the vineyard logo in the upper left corner or her mother's elegant script in the address. Between the Asquonset, Rhode Island, postmark and the scent of Natalie's trademark freesia, there was no doubt at all.

Susanne stepped out of her Ferragamos and curled her toes in dismay. A letter from her mother was the last thing she needed. She would look at it later. She was feeling hollow enough as it was.

And whose fault was that? she asked herself,

irrationally annoyed. It was *Natalie's* fault. Natalie had lived her life by the book, doing everything just so. She had been the most dutiful wife Susanne had ever seen—and she had been Susanne's role model. So Susanne had become a dutiful wife herself. By the time the women's movement had taken hold, she was so busy catering to Mark and the kids that she didn't have time for a career. Now the children were grown and resented her intrusion, and Mark had staff to do the small things she used to do. She still traveled with him sometimes, but though he claimed to love having her along, he didn't truly need her there. She was window dressing. Nothing more.

She had time for a career now. She had the energy. But she was fifty-six, for goodness sake. Fifty-six was a little old to be starting a career.

So where did that leave her? she wondered, discouraged now as she took the new catalogues from the mail and settled into a chair by the window overlooking the courtyard. It left her with Neiman Marcus, Bloomingdale's, Hammacher Schlemmer, and a sense that somehow, somewhere, she had missed the boat.

She should ask her mother about *that,* she thought dryly—as if Natalie would sympathize with boredom or understand restlessness. And even if she did, Natalie didn't discuss problems. She discussed clothing. She discussed wallpaper. She discussed bread-and-butter letters on engraved stationery. She was an expert on manners.

So was Susanne. But she was fed up with those things. They were dull. They were petty. They were as irrelevant as the bouillabaisse she had cooked yesterday before remembering Mark had a dinner meeting, or the cache of hors d'oeuvres and pastries she had prepared in the past six months and frozen for the guests who never came anymore—and speaking of food, if Natalie was sending her the menu for the vineyard's Fall Harvest Feast, Susanne would scream.

Ripe for a fight, she pushed herself out of the chair and retrieved the yellow envelope from the hall table. Mail from her mother was common. Natalie was forever sending copies of reviews of one Asquonset wine or another, and if not a review, then a personal letter of praise from a vintner in California or France—though Susanne wasn't interested in any of it. The vineyard was her parents' pride and joy, not hers. She had spent decades trying to convince them of that. Lobbying efforts to get her involved, like most else in her life, had grown old.

But this envelope was different. It was of the same heavy stock that Natalie favored, but its color—deep yellow with dark blue ink—was a far cry from the classic ivory with burgundy ink of usual Asquonset mailings. And it wasn't addressed to Susanne alone. It was addressed to Mr. and Mrs. Mark Malloy in a calligrapher's script that, too, was a deviation from Asquonset style.

Uneasy, Susanne held the envelope for a mo-

ment, thinking that something had been going on
with Natalie the last few times they talked. Her
words had been optimistic ones, focusing on how
Asquonset was recovering from Alexander's
death, but she had seemed . . . troubled. More than
once, Susanne sensed there was something Natalie
wasn't saying, and since Susanne didn't want to be
involved in vineyard business, she didn't prod. She
simply decided that being troubled was part of the
mourning process. Suddenly, now, she wondered
if there was a connection between this envelope
and that tension.

Opening the flap, she pulled a matching yellow
card from inside.

PLEASE JOIN US
FOR A CELEBRATION OF OUR WEDDING
LABOR DAY SUNDAY AT 4 P.M.
THE GREAT HOUSE
ASQUONSET VINEYARD AND WINERY

NATALIE SEEBRING AND CARL BURKE

Susanne frowned. She read the words again.
Wedding?

Stunned, she read the invitation a third time,
but the words didn't change. Natalie remarrying?
It didn't make sense. Natalie marrying *Carl?* That
made even *less* sense. Carl Burke had been the
vineyard manager for thirty-five years. He was an

employee, an earthy man of meager means, nowhere *near* on a par with Alexander Seebring—Susanne's father—Natalie's husband of fifty-eight years, dead barely six months.

Oh yes. Susanne knew that Carl had been a big help to Natalie in the last few months. Natalie mentioned him often—more often of late. But *talking* about the man was one thing; marrying him was something else entirely.

Was this a joke? Not likely. Even if Natalie were a comic, which she wasn't, she wouldn't do anything as tasteless as this.

Susanne turned the card over, looking for a word of explanation from her mother, but there was none.

Reading the words a fourth time, having no choice but to take them as real, she was deeply hurt. Mothers didn't *do* things like this, she told herself. They didn't break momentous news to their daughters in a formal invitation—not unless they were estranged, and Natalie and Susanne weren't. They talked on the phone once a week. They saw each other every month or so. Granted, they didn't confide in each other. That wasn't the nature of their relationship. But even in spite of that, it didn't make sense to Susanne that Natalie wouldn't have forewarned her about Carl—unless Natalie had forewarned her, in her own evasive way, through those frequent mentions of Carl.

Perhaps Susanne had missed that, but she certainly hadn't missed mention of a wedding. There hadn't been one. For all outward purposes, Natalie was still in mourning.

Susanne read the invitation a final time. Still stunned, still disbelieving, she picked up the phone.

IN THE FOYER of a small brick Colonial in Washington, D.C.'s, Woodley Park, a yellow envelope identical to the one his sister had received lay in the heap on the floor under the mail slot when Greg Seebring arrived home that same afternoon. He didn't see it at first. All he saw was the heap itself, which was far too big to represent a single day's mail. He had been gone for three. He guessed he was looking at mail from all three, but where was his wife?

"Jill?" he called. Loosening his tie, he went looking. She wasn't in the living room, kitchen, or den. He went up the stairs, but the two bedrooms there were empty, too. Confused, he stood at the top of the banister and tried to recall whether she had anything planned. If so, she hadn't told him. Not that they'd talked during his trip. He'd been on the go the whole time, leaving the hotel early and returning late, too talked out to pick up the phone. He had felt really good about catching an early plane home. He had thought she would be pleased.

Pleased, indeed. She wasn't even *here*.

He should have called.

But hell, she hadn't called him, either.

Feeling suddenly exhausted, he went down the stairs for his bag. As soon as he lifted it, though, he set it back down and, taking only his laptop, scooped up the mail. Again, it seemed like too much.

He wondered if Jill had gone to see her mother. She had been considering that for a while.

Dumping the lot on the kitchen counter, he hooked the laptop to the phone and booted it up. While he waited, he pushed junk mail one way and bills another. Most of what remained was identifiable by a return address. There was an envelope from the Committee to Elect Michael Bonner, a friend of his who was running for the U.S. Senate and surely wanted money. There was one from a college friend of Jill's, and another postmarked Akron, Ohio, where Jill's mother lived, perhaps mailed before Jill had decided to visit. There was one with a more familiar postmark and an even more familiar scent.

Lifting the yellow envelope, he pictured his mother. Strong. Gracious. Daffodil-bright, if aloof.

But the vineyard colors were ivory with burgundy. She always used them. Asquonset was her identity.

The envelope had the weight of an invitation. No surprise there; partying was Natalie's specialty. But then, Alexander Seebring had loved a

big bash, and who could begrudge him? No gentle-
man farmer, this man. Many a day he had walked
the vineyard in his jeans and denim shirt alongside
his manager. If not that, he was traveling to spread
the Asquonset name, and the hard work had paid
off. After years of struggle, he had Asquonset
turning a tidy profit. He had earned the right to
party.

Natalie knew how to oblige. She was in her element directing caterers, florists, and musicians.
There had always been two festivals at Asquonset
each year—one to welcome spring, one to celebrate the harvest. The spring party had been
skipped this year, coming as it would have so soon
after Al's death. Apparently, though, Natalie was
chafing at the bit. She hated wearing black—didn't
have a single black dress in her wardrobe, had actually had to go out and buy one for the funeral.

So, barely six months later, she was returning
to form. Greg wasn't sure he approved. It seemed
wrong, what with her husband of so many years—
his father—still fresh in his grave, and the future of
Asquonset up in the air.

Natalie wanted Greg to run it. She hadn't said
that in as many words, but he had given her his answer anyway: *No. No way. Out of the question.*

He wondered if she had found a buyer—wondered, suddenly, whether this party was to introduce whoever it was. But she would have told him
first. Then again, maybe not. He had made his feel-

ings about the vineyard more than clear. He was a pollster. He was on the road working with clients three weeks out of four. He had his own business to run, and he did it well. Making wine had been his father's passion. It wasn't Greg's.

Not that he was exactly an impartial observer. If Natalie sold Asquonset, there would be money coming in, half of which eventually would be his. In that sense, it behooved him to check out a potential buyer. He didn't want his mother letting the vineyard go for anything less than it was worth.

Dropping the envelope on the counter, he pulled up the laptop and typed in his password.

But that envelope seemed to command his attention. Curious to know what Natalie had in mind, he picked it up again, slit it open, and pulled out a card.

PLEASE JOIN US
FOR A CELEBRATION OF OUR WEDDING
LABOR DAY SUNDAY AT 4 P.M.
THE GREAT HOUSE
ASQUONSET VINEYARD AND WINERY

NATALIE SEEBRING AND CARL BURKE

He stared blankly at the card.

A wedding? His mother and Carl?

His mother and *Carl?* Where had *that* come from?

Natalie was seventy-six. Maybe she was losing it, he thought, shaking his head. And what about Carl? He had to be a few years older than that. What was in *his* mind?

Carl had been at the vineyard forever. Alexander had considered him a friend. But a friend wouldn't snatch up a man's widow less than six months after his death, any more than a man's widow would turn right around and marry the nearest thing in pants.

Understandably, Natalie would be leaning on Carl more, now that Alexander was gone. Greg hadn't thought anything of the fact that lately she was mentioning Carl more often. In hindsight, he realized that those mentions were always in praise. It looked like Greg had missed the point.

Was it romance? *Sex?* Weren't they a little old? Greg was forty, and losing interest fast. Sex required effort, if you wanted to do it right. So maybe they didn't do it the way *he* did. Hell, he was embarrassed thinking of his mother doing it at all. But . . . with Carl? Carl was an old *coot!*

Maybe he was a clever one, though. Maybe he had his eye on the vineyard. Hadn't he retired and passed the reins on to his own son? That supposedly had been Alexander's doing, but Carl had been vineyard manager too long not to have a say in who took over. So maybe Carl wanted Simon to have the vineyard. Maybe marrying Natalie was his way of ensuring it.

Greg had to call Natalie, but Lord, he hated doing that. What could he say—*I don't want the vineyard, but I don't want Simon having it either?*

Maybe he should call Susanne first. She saw Natalie more often than he did. She might know what was going on.

Lord, he hated doing that, too. Susanne was sixteen years his senior. They shared a mother, but they had never been close.

Swearing under his breath, he loosened his collar button. He didn't need this. He needed a vacation, actually had one planned. So going to Asquonset on Labor Day weekend was out of the question. He was going north, all the way to Ontario for a fishing trip. Already had it booked.

Not that Jill was pleased. Given a choice, she'd take Asquonset. She liked it there. At least, he thought she did. Hard to say lately. She was going through something. She had been quieter than usual. Could she be having a midlife crisis? he wondered. At *thirty-eight?*

He didn't want to think about his wife falling apart, but it beat thinking about Natalie marrying Carl. He would deal with them later. Crossing the kitchen, he opened the door to the garage. Jill's car was gone, which meant it was probably parked at the airport. Definitely visiting her mother, he decided. Then he had a thought. Hoping for a glimpse of what was bugging her—thinking that the letter from her mother might hold a clue—

knowing that he could always say he had accidentally slit it open along with the rest of the mail—he opened it and pulled out a neatly folded sheet.

"Dear Greg . . ."

Dear Greg. It was not from his mother-in-law to Jill. It was to him. He looked quickly at the address. Not to Jill at all. To *him. From* Jill.

Feeling a sudden foreboding, he began reading.

IN A GARAGE STUDIO behind an old white Victorian on a narrow side street in Cambridge, Massachusetts, Olivia Jones was daydreaming at work. She did it often. It was one of the perks of her job.

She restored old photographs, a skill that required patience, a sharp eye, and a steady hand. She had all three, along with an imagination that could take her inside the world of almost any picture. Even now, as she dotted varying shades of gray ink to restore a faded face, she was inside the frame with a family of migrant workers living in California in the early thirties. The Depression had taken hold. Life was hard, food scarce. Children worked with their parents and grandparents, hour after hour, in whatever fields needed picking. They began the day dirty and ended it more so. Their faces were somber, their cheeks gaunt, their eyes large and haunting.

They sat close together on the porch of a weathered shack. Moving around them, Olivia went inside. The place was small but functional. Bedding lay against nearly every wall, with a woodstove and a few chairs in the center. The air held the smell of dust and hard work, but there was more. On a heavy table nearby sat a loaf of fresh-baked bread, aromatic and warm. A stew cooked on the woodstove. One shelf held an assortment of cracked pottery and tin cups and plates. There would be clinking when the family ate. She could hear it now.

Returning to the porch, she was drawn in with an open arm, reconnected to this group as they were connected to one another. Everyone touched—a hand, an arm, a shoulder, a cheek. They were nine people spanning three genera-tions, surviving the bleakness of their lives by tak-ing comfort in family. They had nothing by way of material goods, only one another.

Olivia was thirty-five. She had a ten-year-old daughter, a job, an apartment with a TV and VCR, a computer, and a washer and dryer. She had a car. She had a Patagonia vest, L.L.Bean clogs, and a Nikon that was old enough and sturdy enough to fetch a pretty penny.

But boy, did she envy that migrant family its closeness.

"Those were hard times," came a gruff voice by her shoulder.

She looked up to see her boss, Otis Thurman, scowling at the photograph. It was one of several that had been newly uncovered, believed to be the work of Dorothea Lange. The Metropolitan Museum in New York had commissioned him to restore them. Olivia was doing the work.

"They were *simpler* times," she said.

He grunted. "You want 'em? Take 'em. I'm leaving. Lock up when you go." He walked off with less shuffle than another man of seventy-five might have, but then, Otis had his moods to keep him sharp. He had been in something of a snit all day, but after five years in his employ, Olivia knew not to take it personally. Otis was a frustrated Picasso, a would-be painter who would never be as good at creation as he was at restoration. But hope died hard, even at his age. He was returning to his canvas and oil full-time—seven weeks away from retirement and counting.

He was looking forward to it. Olivia was not.

He kept announcing the hours. Olivia tried not to hear.

We're a good team, she argued. *I'm too old,* he replied.

And *that* was what intrigued her about this migrant family. The old man in the photograph was grizzled enough to make Otis look young, but he was still there, still productive, still part of that larger group.

Things were different nowadays. People burned out, and no wonder. They were up on the high wire of life alone with no net.

Olivia worried about Otis retiring, pictured him sitting alone day after day, with art tools that he couldn't use to his own high standards and no one to bully. He wasn't going to be happy.

Wrong, Olivia. He had friends all over the art community and plenty of money saved up. He would be delighted. *She* was the one in trouble.

She had finally found her niche. Restoring old photographs was a natural for someone with a knowledge of cameras and an eye for art—and she had both, though it had taken her awhile to see it. Trial and error was the story of her life. She had waitressed. She had done telemarketing. She had sold clothes. Selling cameras had come after that, along with the discovery that she loved taking pictures. Then had come Tess. Then brief stints apprenticing with a professional photographer and freelancing for a museum that wanted pictures of its shows. Then Otis.

For the first time in her life, Olivia truly loved her work. She was better at photo restoration than she had been at anything else, and could lose herself for *hours* in prints from the past, smelling the age, feeling the grandeur. For Olivia, the world of yesterday was more romantic than today. She would have liked to have lived back then.

Given that she couldn't, she liked working for Otis, and the feeling was mutual. Few people in her life had put up with her for five years. Granted, she indulged him his moods, and even he acknowledged that she did the job better than the long line of assistants before her.

Still, he genuinely liked her. The eight-by-ten tacked to the wall proved it. He had taken it last week when she had shown up at work with her hair cut painfully short. She had chopped it off herself in a fit of disgust, irritated with long hair in the sweltering heat. Immediately she had regretted it. A barber had neatened things up a bit, but she had gone on to work wearing a big straw hat—which Otis had promptly removed.

Bless his soul, he said that he liked her hair short, said that it made her look lighthearted and fun—and then he proceeded to catch just that on film. She was standing in front of a plain concrete wall, wearing a long tank dress, toes peeking from sandals, hair boyish. Feeling exposed and awkward, as unused to being on that side of the camera as she was embarrassed about her hair, she had wrapped her arms around her middle and tucked in her chin.

Otis had used light, angle, and focus to make her look willowy rather than thin, spirited rather than self-conscious. He had made the shiny strands of that short, sandy hair look stylish, and the maroon polish on her toenails look exotic. He had made her brown eyes large in a delicate face. Somehow, he had made her look pretty.

When her eyes slid from that photograph to another tacked nearby, her smile widened. Tess was with her in that one, nine years old the summer before. They were dressed as a pair of dance hall girls in a Dodge City saloon in the days of the wild, wild West. Otis had condemned the picture as the lowest form of commercial photography, but they'd had a ball dressing up. They talked about going for an Elizabethan look this summer—assuming they could afford another weekend at the shore. Money was tighter now, without child support. The reality of that was just sinking in.

Jared Stark had let her down in every imaginable way. He was supposed to have loved her. Barring that, he was supposed to have loved their child. At the very least, he was supposed to have helped keep that child sheltered and clothed. So, what had he done? He had *died*.

A timer rang. Setting aside the anger that had displaced grief, Olivia silenced it. Tess was the love of her life, and school was nearly out for the day. Recapping her inks, she washed her brushes and carefully placed the maybe-Lange photographs in the vault. She neatened the office, filled her briefcase with paperwork to do at home, and opened the door in time to greet the mailman.

Otis's personal letters and bills went in one pile, those addressed to the studio went in another. Among the larger pieces there was a supermarket flyer, a mailing from the American Institute for Conservation of Historic and Artistic Works, and the week's *Time*. At the bottom of the pile was a large manila pack.

One look at its sender and Olivia felt a wave of

pleasure. The mailing label was ivory with a burgundy logo that depicted, in a single minimalist
line, a bunch of grapes spilling from a wineglass.
Beneath it was the stylized script—so familiar
now—that read *Asquonset Vineyard and Winery,
Asquonset, Rhode Island.* The address was handwritten in the more traditional but no less familiar
style of Natalie Seebring.

Holding the large envelope to her nose, Olivia
closed her eyes and inhaled. She knew that freesia
scent now as well as she knew the handwriting. It
was elegant, conjuring images of prosperity and
warmth. She basked in it for a minute, then crossed
to the large table where the last batch of Seebring
photographs lay. They were from the early fifties
and had needed varying degrees of repair, but they
were ready for return. Now there was a new pack.
Natalie's timing was perfect.

Olivia had never met the woman, but she felt
she knew her well. Photographs told stories, and
what they didn't tell, Olivia easily made up. Natalie had been a beautiful child in the twenties, a
striking teenager in the thirties. In the forties she
had been the blushing bride of a dashing soldier,
and in the fifties, the smiling mother of two ador-
ing children. According to her photographs, she
dressed well and lived in style. Whether a parlor
with an exquisite Oriental rug in the foreground,
an elegantly upholstered settee at midrange, and
original art on the wall behind, or a garden sur-

rounded by lush shrubbery that screamed of color even in black-and-white, the backgrounds of the pictures she sent were entirely consistent with the image of a successful wine-making family.

No downtrodden migrant crew this one. Of course, these pictures didn't have the artistic import of one taken by Dorothea Lange, but Olivia had followed the growth of this family for months and was totally involved. The appeal here was prosperity and ease. She had fantasized about being a Seebring more times than she could count.

Her own story was light-years different from anything she had seen in the Seebring pictures. She had never met her father. Her mother didn't even know who he was. Olivia had been the product of a one-night stand on a liquor-blurred New Year's Eve in an alley off Manhattan's Times Square. Carol Jones, her mother, had been seventeen at the time.

Feminists might have called it rape, but months later, when Carol finally realized she was pregnant, she was rebellious enough and defiant enough to tell her parents it was love. For those pious folk, the pregnancy was one defiant act too many. They disowned her. She retaliated, predictably rebellious and defiant, by leaving home with nothing of her heritage but her name—Jones.

A lot of good that did Olivia. There were pages of Jones listings in every telephone directory. There were pages and *pages* of them in New York.

And now, not only couldn't she find her grandparents, she couldn't find her mother either. Moving from place to place herself, Olivia had left a trail of bread crumbs to rival Hansel and Gretel, but no relative ever came looking. Apparently, no relative cared—and it was their loss. Olivia might be no prize, but Tess was. Tess was a gem.

Unfortunately, the loss went two ways. This gap in her history meant that Olivia and Tess went without extended family. It was just the two of them—just the two of them against the world. That wasn't so bad, though; Olivia had come to terms with it. She could cope.

It didn't mean she couldn't dream, of course, and lately she dreamed she was related to Natalie Seebring. Being grandmother and granddaughter was pushing it a little, but there was a woman in some of the early Asquonset pictures who, given a marginal resemblance to Carol, could be Olivia's grandmother. Olivia hadn't seen the woman in any of Asquonset's postwar pictures, but there were easy explanations for that. She might have been a WAC who had fallen for a serviceman and ended up in New York. Her husband might have been a rigid military type who wanted things done his way, or he might have been irrationally jealous, forbidding her contact with her family. Hence, her absence in photographs.

But if she was Natalie's sister, then Natalie would be Olivia's great-aunt. Even if she were only a cousin, the blood bond would be there.

Olivia glanced at the clock. She had to go get Tess. Time was growing short.

But the lure of this new package was too great to resist. Opening the clasp, she peeked inside. The scent of freesia was stronger now. She pushed aside a cover letter and saw several dozen photographs. Most were eight-by-tens in black-and-white. Under them was a bright yellow envelope.

Curious, she pulled it out. Otis's name and address were on the front, written not in Natalie's freehand but in a calligrapher's script. She was giving a *party,* Olivia decided—and immediately vowed to go as Otis's date. She didn't care if people snickered behind their hands. She wanted to see Asquonset. She wanted to meet Natalie.

She laid the invitation on Otis's desk with his personal mail—then quickly took it back and returned it to the mailer with the pictures. He wouldn't be in again until tomorrow. She liked the idea of having the invitation in her own house for a night.

Tucking the package into her briefcase, she checked the office a final time, then let herself out and locked the door. Natalie's new batch of pictures would be the treat she gave herself that night when everything else was done.

Savoring the anticipation, she half walked, half ran through narrow streets hemmed in by tightly packed houses, trees, and parked cars. The June air was stagnant and warm. She arrived at Tess's school in a sweat, a full ten minutes late.

Most of the children had gone. A few stragglers remained on the playground, but they were immersed in themselves. Tess stood alone at a corner of the school yard with a shoulder weighted down by her backpack, one foot turned in, her glasses halfway down her nose, and a desolate look on her face.

Two

FIGHTING A SINKING HEART, Olivia kept her voice light. "Hi, sweetie." She gave Tess a hug, which was barely returned, and smoothed aside a mass of unruly brown hair.

"You're late," Tess said.

"I know. I'm sorry. I got hung up on something as I was walking out the door. How was your day?"

Tess made a gesture that might have been a shrug, but it was lost when she started off down the street. Her legs weren't long, but they moved fast. Olivia had to step to it to keep pace.

"Tess?" she coaxed.

Still that defiant silence.

"Hard day?"

"The worst. I'm dumb. I'm just dumb."

"No, you're not."

"Yes! I'm the dumbest one in the class."

"No, you're the *smartest* one in the class. Your IQ is out of sight. You're dyslexic, that's all."

"That's *all?*" Tess cried, stopping dead in her tracks. Her freckles were bright red against the pallor of her skin. Her wire-rimmed glasses magnified a pair of big, brown plaintive eyes that were suddenly filled with tears. "Mom, she made me stay in from recess again because my paper was a mess. My handwriting stinks. She can't read it. And my spelling stinks. And even if it didn't, I didn't do what she told us to do. I didn't hear her right, so my hearing stinks, too!"

Olivia took her daughter's face in both hands. "Your hearing does not stink! You hear every word I say, even when you're not supposed to because it's *adult language.*"

Tess tore her chin free and resumed her march. Olivia was beside her by the time they turned the corner and strode along for several more blocks until Tess eased up. This time, when she put an arm around the child's shoulder and drew her close, Tess didn't resist. They turned right onto one street, then left onto another.

"Kind of like a maze," Olivia remarked when they made another sharp turn. She was hoping for a smile.

Instead, she got a glum, "Yeah, and we're rats."

"So, what's the reward at the end?"

Tess didn't reply. And then they were home.

They lived in an apartment attached to a small brick house that, in its heyday, had belonged to one of the would-be elite of Cambridge society. The fact that it was sandwiched more closely to its neighbors than a house belonging to the true elite would have been was hidden by a thick stand of trees. Those trees also prevented neighbors from seeing when the owners closed in the screen porch, added a small bedroom and bathroom, and put the space out for rent.

Olivia wasn't the first tenant by a long shot. The galley kitchen was vintage fifties, and the bathroom little better, but she had loved it on sight—loved the character, the quaintness, the charm. One look at walls of ivy-covered brick and a flagstone walk flanked by mountain laurel in bloom and, even before seeing the inside, she knew she had to live there.

Only after they moved in did she realize how tiny the place was, not necessarily the best buy for the money. But it was done, and it did have character, quaintness, and charm. She set Tess up in the small bedroom, which she painted with a soft blue sky and a forest of floor-to-ceiling trees. She used a sleep sofa in the living room for herself. The sofa was flanked by a pair of lobster traps standing on end, each holding lamps. An old wood trunk on a dolly—both painted sea green, like the lobster traps—served as a clothes chest and was easily rolled away at night. An overstuffed easy chair sat

to the side, large enough for Olivia and Tess to
share for bedtime reading. An antique, early-
American table with matching chairs—Olivia's
birthday gift to herself the year before and the in-
spiration for hours of imagining who had owned it
before them—stood in the kitchen end of the room.

They no sooner opened the door this day when
the phone began to ring. Their eyes met, their ex-
pressions knowing and vexed.

"It's Ted," Tess said.

"Uh-huh."

"We're ten minutes late. I bet he's been trying
that long."

"Uh-*huh*."

"He's probably frantic about something," the
child advised, scornful in a way that Olivia would
have considered disrespectful if she didn't know
Tess was so right.

Ted was always frantic. He was a high-strung,
type-A personality, an impulse buy on Olivia's
part, picked up at the checkout counter of a bookstore. In hindsight, she should have known he was
trouble from the fact that he didn't smile once during that initial encounter. But he looked her in the
eye, which was more than many men did, and
talked readily, as some men did not. He was even
interested in what she was reading and why.

Naturally, she initially thought his intensity
was infatuation. He brought flowers, took her to
dinner, rented movies. He phoned her so often that

she finally suggested he not call her at work. By that time she had realized that he wasn't infatuated at all, but was simply approaching their relationship as neurotically as he approached the rest of his life. They had been dating for five months, and now the end was near.

Olivia had to hand it to herself. She had a knack for picking losers. Not that she wanted to. Not that she planned to. Typically she fell for one feature—say, great eyes or a sexy voice—and it wasn't always physical. She had fallen for Pete Fitzgerald because he could cook. He cooked Irish, Italian, and Jewish. He cooked Greek. He cooked the lightest Russian blini she had ever eaten. Out of the kitchen, though, he was a dud.

When the phone continued to ring, she snatched it up. "Hello?"

"Hi," said Ted. "Just checking in. It's been a hell of a day here—one meeting after another—like this is a plan to change the whole world for eternity when all it is is a five-year plan for one puny little company that'll probably go under before the first year's done anyway. Why are you late getting home?"

"Things backed up," Olivia said, rolling her eyes to make Tess laugh, "but listen, I can't talk now."

"I know how *that* is—haven't had time to do anything for *me* since first thing this morning—I swear I've been talking that whole time—I'm probably not good for much more myself—I'll call you back in ten minutes."

"No. Tess and I have stuff to do. I'll call you later."

"Well—okay—I'll be here for another hour, then at the gym for an hour—but that is *assuming* the machines I need are free, which is a *big* assumption—meatheads monopolize the free weights for hours—I mean, I'm no ninety-eight-pound weakling but they sneer at me and I run—so just in case it takes me longer than an hour, why don't you try me at home at eight?"

"I'll try. Gotta go." She hung up the phone, exhausted. Ted had that effect.

Tess's chin quivered. "Mrs. Wright sent a note."

"Oh, dear." Ted was quickly forgotten. Olivia took a deep breath. She could only hope that the note had been in a sealed envelope.

"I tore it up."

"You didn't."

"Tore it up and threw it away."

"Oh, Tess. I need to see it."

"You don't. She's just one teacher. She doesn't know everything."

So. Sealed envelope or not, her daughter knew something of what the teacher had written. "Where is the note?"

Tess looked away, defiant.

Olivia caught Tess's chin and gently turned her back. "Where is the note?"

She looked at the ceiling. Her jaw remained set.

Sighing, Olivia released her daughter's chin and stood back. That was when she saw the torn corner of something protruding from the front pocket of Tess's jeans. She pulled out one portion of the note, then a second and third. On the small square of counter beside the stove, she put the pieces together.

"*Dear Ms. Jones,*" the note read. "*We truly do need to talk about what to do about Tess for next year. I know that the thought of having her repeat the year is unpleasant, but ignoring my notes doesn't help the situation.*"

Ignoring what notes? Olivia thought with a sense of dread.

"*You and I need to meet. The final decision on next year's class assignments is being made on Monday. If I don't hear from you before then, I'll go ahead with my recommendation that Tess stay in fourth grade a second year. Yours truly, Nancy Wright.*"

Olivia's mind was spinning. Tess had been tested and diagnosed. She had tutoring at school three times a week. As of Olivia's last meeting with both teacher and tutor, the child was showing a slight improvement in spelling. But she continued to fail tests either because she misread the directions or because she miswrote her answers. She couldn't read. It was a terrifying problem. *She couldn't read.*

The tutor claimed it would get better in time.

Olivia wanted to know how much time. Tess seemed to be falling further and further behind the others in her class. She liked learning and retained what she learned. When Olivia read to her, she was responsive and smart. One on one, she was capable of understanding complex concepts. On her own, though, she lacked the tools to access those concepts.

Three half-hour sessions a week with a tutor wasn't enough; Tess easily could use twice that number. What she really needed was a whole special school, but that was a pipe dream. So Olivia did what she could, helping with homework. She also tried to get the teacher to be more kind, although Tess wasn't aiding her own cause when she failed to deliver letters that the woman sent home.

"Don't yell at me," Tess begged. "I didn't bring the other notes home because I know what she wants to do. I can see it in her face whenever she looks at my papers. I was thinking that if I tried harder it'd get better and she wouldn't look at me that way, only she still does."

Olivia pulled Tess close and held her with a sudden fierceness. She understood. In fact, she *agreed*. She hadn't wanted Tess in Nancy Wright's class in the *first* place. The woman was a stickler about directions, and following directions was one of the hardest things for Tess to do. She panicked. She rushed. She lost her place. She guessed. The other fourth-grade teacher was far better with learning-disabled children, but as the principal had dryly informed Olivia, she couldn't take *all* of them in her class.

For the life of her, Olivia didn't understand why Nancy Wright hadn't called when her notes weren't answered. A phone call would have been far more appropriate in the first place. Putting a child's failings on paper and then sending that paper home with the child seemed cruel.

Olivia couldn't begin to estimate the damage that had been done to her daughter's self-esteem in the last year. Granted, it might have happened with any teacher. Tess was at that age. Much more of the same, though, and she wouldn't only need a tutor—she would also need a therapist.

What to do? Olivia had the name of a tutor who would work with Tess through the summer, but tutors cost money, and the electronic transfer of funds that had continued for several months after Jared's death had ceased abruptly with his parents' verdict that Tess wasn't Jared's child.

That Tess wasn't Jared's. The charge still stung.

"But she *is*," Olivia told the lawyer who had sent the letter informing her of the family decision.

"Can you prove it?"

Of course, she could. Tess was there in the flesh!

But Olivia had watched *The Practice*. She knew how lawyers thought. Lawyers wanted DNA tests.

"My client was cremated," this one said. "His ashes were scattered over the Great Smokies. Unless DNA tests were done before, you'll have a hard time proving it. His family won't hand anything over for testing. You'll have to take them to court."

Olivia vowed to do just that—for all of two minutes. Then she came to her senses. She couldn't put Tess through a paternity battle. Besides, it took money to win money.

So the Stark connection was severed. It was another sad twist to an already sad saga, because it wasn't about money at all. It was about love. Olivia had loved Jared. He was a brilliant man, a scientist who was forever writing up treatises on seemingly obscure things, like the correlation between eating carrot greens and the ability to identify birdcalls at night. He claimed that what he did was crucial to mankind, and Olivia remained a believer even when he lost interest in her. She hadn't planned on getting pregnant. When it happened, she saw it as God's way of telling Jared to stay put. He didn't. The man was long gone by the time Tess was born, but paying child support for nine-plus years had been his own free choice. He had taken it on without complaint.

Olivia had hoped that his family would give that fact some weight. She had hoped that they would want even some small part of the son they had lost. Apparently they did not.

So here was Tess, badly in need of help. Olivia would take out a loan to pay for more tutoring if she felt the child would go for it, but that wasn't what Tess wanted. She wanted tennis camp, had her heart *set* on tennis camp, *had* to go to tennis camp because two of the popular girls in her class were going, and she saw it as her one chance to excel. She had never played tennis before, but she was a good little athlete, and if she really tried, then anything was possible.

Not that Olivia had the money for tennis camp. Not that she would have the money for *food,* if she didn't find another job. She had sent résumés to dozens of museums in the hope that one would want an in-house restorer. To date, she had received six rejections. She supposed she could always go back to selling cameras, but she had hated doing that. She loved taking pictures and did it almost on instinct. Teaching others how to do it was something else. Olivia had neither the patience nor the vision. Her mind worked differently from most people's. Tess hadn't come upon dyslexia by chance.

What to do?

She had an idea. Tipping up her daughter's head, looking into that beautiful little freckled face framed by long brown curls—a legacy of the father who hadn't wanted to know her—Olivia fell in love for the gazillionth time. "Want Chinese for dinner?"

Tess's eyes lit up. "General Gao's?"

Olivia nodded. "But only after homework."

"I'm starving *now.*"

Olivia opened the refrigerator and poured a big glass of milk. "This'll tide you over. The sooner you start on your homework, the sooner we can go."

Tess took the glass. "I have to read twenty pages."

"Twenty?" Twenty pages was daunting for a ten-year-old dyslexic. "Of what book?"

Tess held it up—a geography text.

"O-kay," Olivia said, trying not to sound discouraged. "Why don't you start while I change? We'll do what's left together." She picked up the mail and sifted idly through it on her way to the closet. Halfway there, she turned and sank into the sofa. In her hand she held a letter that had no return address, only a Chicago postmark. It was enough.

Her heart started to pound. Okay. The handwriting looked different. But it had been four years since her mother had written. All sorts of things might have happened to explain the change. The woman might have broken her wrist and be wearing a cast. She might have lost one arm in an accident. She might have had a stroke. She might . . . just might be so nervous about writing to Olivia that her hand was shaky.

Olivia ripped up the flap and immediately swallowed down a sharp disappointment. Her last letter was inside the envelope, unopened. She unfolded the note with it and read, *"To whoever's writing these letters—you keep sending them to this house, but there's no Carol Jones here. Don't write again. She isn't here."*

Olivia bent forward and hugged her knees. This address was the most recent she had, so either her mother had moved right after mailing the last letter or had mistakenly put down the wrong return address—"mistakenly" being the important word. Olivia refused to believe it was deliberate. She refused to believe that her mother didn't want any contact at all. Granted, her last letter had been short and noncommittal, but she hadn't told Olivia to get lost. She had never done that. She simply had gone off on her own a week after Olivia's high school graduation. As she saw it, at that point her obligation was fulfilled. Other mothers felt that way. It wasn't so bad.

The bottom line, though, was that if Carol hadn't received her recent letters, then she didn't know where to reach Olivia now, either. So maybe she was trying. Maybe she, too, was mailing letters and getting them back. Olivia had had the post office forward mail from her old apartment to this one longer than they usually allowed, but that time had long expired. What to do now?

The phone rang. Tess started to rise, quick to do something other than read, but Olivia snapped upright, pointed her back to the chair, and went for the phone herself.

"Hello?"

"Just me again—I'm getting ready to leave here and head for the gym—I probably won't be home until eight, and then there's the news on CNN, and by the time I've had something to eat it'll be late—but I need to know if tomorrow night's a go."

Olivia pushed a hand into her short hair and held on. "Tomorrow night?"

"The North End Bistro." It was a new Italian restaurant, open barely a month. He had heard good things about it and was rushing to get there, as if it would close if he didn't go soon.

Olivia figured that if the restaurant closed so soon, it wasn't worth eating at. "I can't, Ted. Weeknights are hard. I've told you that." Tess needed homework supervision. Besides, Olivia came home from dates with Ted feeling competitive and tense. Nothing about him was laid-back. Nothing.

"They don't have a reservation open on a Saturday night for three weeks—that's how popular this place is—I'm telling you, Olivia, now's the time to go."

Suddenly irritated, Olivia said, "If it's that popular, it'll be here in a month. Make reservations then, Ted. Tomorrow night's bad."

"Okay—okay—I'll hold the reservation just in case you change your mind—so call me later, will you?"

"Let's talk in a day or two."

"But what about the North End Bistro?"

She fought for patience. "I said no."

"You said you might change your mind."

"You said that. *I* said I couldn't make it."

"Sounds like you're in a lousy mood—Otis must've been in a snit again—what an ornery son-of-a-B he is—good thing he's retiring—a few more years with him and you'd be a basket case—so listen, I'll call you later."

She took a breath. *"No,* Ted. Good Lord, give me a *break!"*

"Hey—don't get upset—jeez, look at the time—I have to go—much later and the meatheads will have taken over the gym—they spend their evenings there—lifting is their idea of culture—I'll call you tomorrow." He hung up before she could argue.

Olivia stood for a moment wondering how she could get through to the man, when Tess said, "Maybe he's dyslexic. He doesn't hear, either."

"You hear," she scolded. Heading off to change clothes, she was struck with a sudden attack of self-pity. Between a school crisis, a maternal rejection, and Ted it had been one hell of an hour. She deserved a prize for valor.

Doing an about-face, she returned to the front door and brought her briefcase back to the sofa. The minute she opened it, a hint of freesia escaped. She took out Natalie Seebring's envelope and held it for a minute.

Don't let me down, Natalie Seebring, she thought and, for the second time, opened the clasp. Leaving the cover letter and the yellow envelope addressed to Otis inside, she drew out the pictures and laid them on her lap. Slowly, savoring each, she studied one after the other.

She knew the cast of characters by now. There were pictures of Natalie and her husband, and of Natalie, her husband, and the children. Some of the pictures included a new baby. A new baby! There was no sign of the older son in those. Sifting through, she saw no picture of the three children together at all. That was odd.

Then again, not so, she realized. This new baby was a late-in-life child, a little surprise born to two people still in love. The older son was probably away at boarding school, even college. Olivia imagined him at Harvard. She half expected to see a picture of him wearing football gear with the college letter on his shirt.

She didn't find one like that, but she did find a picture of the daughter at her wedding. There were pictures of Natalie's husband in the vineyard, with and without vineyard workers. Judging from the long sideburns worn by the men, this batch was from the sixties and seventies. There were also construction photos. It looked as though a new building was going up at the vineyard—an on-site winery, said the construction sign. She couldn't wait to see the building when it was done.

Olivia was relaxing already. She had never visited a vineyard, but everything she had seen in the photographs of this one spoke of prosperity, easy living, lots of sunshine, sweet grapes, and goodwill. She couldn't wait to see photos from the eighties and nineties, imagined scads of grandchildren hanging over the porch of the Great House, stacked in rows with their parents on the wide stone steps, lined up around picnic tables for the vineyard harvest.

These latest photos wouldn't need much repair. There were a few stains, a few spots where the emulsion had bubbled. There were several corner folds that had caused cracks, and some prints that were curled or bent. The largest problem—always the case in her work—was fading, but it was easily solved by copying the photo onto high contrast paper and enhancing the image with filters. Only in rare instances, such as the Dorothea Lange print, was handwork involved. Natalie's pictures wouldn't need that. By and large they entailed more preservation than restoration. Olivia would be treating the set archivally. Natalie had been firm about that. She wanted her pictures to last forever.

Wondering what she planned to do with them, Olivia fished out the cover letter. It was on Asquonset letterhead, a full sheet of ivory paper with the burgundy logo in the upper left corner. Like the address on the mailing label, this letter was done by hand, written in letters that flowed as Olivia imagined Natalie's voice would do.

"Dear Otis," she wrote,

> Enclosed please find the next install-ment of photographs. I continue to be amazed at the miracles you have worked on the older prints. These ones are newer. I'm afraid that's a wine stain in the corner of the one of my daughter's wedding. I wish I could say that the wine was from the wedding. If that were the case, we might have left it there for sen-timental reasons. But, no. It's a recent stain—my fault, I'm afraid. We were about to launch our new Estate Cabernet when I was sorting through these prints. My hand isn't as steady as it once was. Better wine than scotch, I suppose, given what we do for a living.

Olivia smiled. Natalie had a sweet sense of humor.

> We're nearing the end of my collec-tion of photographs. There will be a final package, which I hope to put in the mail next week. As I stated at the start of this project, my goal is to have all photo-

graphs returned to me by the first of August. That will give me a month to put them together in the fashion I want.

With regard to that fashion, I have a request. It occurs to me, with the time at hand now, that I'm going to need help with this next part of my project. Summers are busy at a vineyard, and there's so much else going on in my life that I fear I won't do justice on my end to the fine job you've done with my prints.

There is text to accompany the photographs. I've been writing it in bits and snatches, and it's been therapeutic. But six months isn't very long to put together a life story. My bits and snatches need organization and editing, and there are whole other parts that I haven't touched on yet. So I'm looking to hire a summer assistant. I need someone who is computer literate but who has an eye for art.

Olivia sat up. I have an eye for art, she thought.

I want someone who is organized and neat and pleasant to be with. I need a curious person, someone who will ask questions and dig around and get me to say things I might otherwise keep to myself.

I'm organized and neat, Olivia mused. I'm pleasant to be with. And curious? I have a *gazillion* questions about the pictures I've restored.

I was thinking of hiring a college student, perhaps an English major, though I fear most have already flown wherever it is they fly for the summer. I'm placing an ad in Sunday's paper, but I would far rather work from a personal recommendation. You've done such a wonderful job with my photographs, Otis. You've been prompt and professional. I'm hoping that you may have Cambridge friends of like mind, certainly ones with an artistic bent, no doubt a few who are also good with words.

Ooops. A tiny glitch there. It wasn't that Olivia was *bad* with words. Not exactly. She just had to work harder than some people to get them up and running. Was she truly dyslexic? She had no idea. She had gone through school prior to the days of testing and labeling. According to those involved, she was simply a slow learner. But she did learn.

She did get things done. It might take her awhile, but the finished product was just fine.

Natalie's offer got even better.

> The Great House here at Asquonset has plenty of room to spare, so I can offer room and board, along with a handsome stipend. Time is of the essence. I welcome any recommendation you can make.
>
> My thanks, and best wishes,
> Natalie

By the time Olivia set down the letter, her thoughts were racing. Spending the summer in Rhode Island would be her *dream*—and she could do it, she could. Okay, so she wasn't a fast writer—in fact, she was actually something of a *struggling* writer—but she could work nights and weekends to make up for it. She could do what Natalie wanted done. She knew she could. Didn't she do all those things for Otis?

Otis. Oh, dear. Otis wanted her to work through the end of July. She couldn't just quit. She owed it to him. He was a friend.

But Otis was *retiring*. After July, he wouldn't be her employer at all. He was abandoning her. Okay. Not abandoning her. Setting her free. So what if she left a few weeks earlier? What harm would that do? He had stopped taking in new work. All that was left was to finish the old. She could work extra hours until she left, and he could get the rest done after that.

Tess would love Asquonset. The vineyard lay midway between the Asquonset River and the Atlantic, and she would love both. She would love the tennis court right there on the grounds— Olivia had seen it in photographs. Tess would love the Great House. And Natalie—she would *adore* Natalie. Natalie was the quintessential grandmother. She was the quintessential *great-*grandmother.

Room and board in the Great House. Olivia would die for that.

And a handsome stipend, too? She wondered how Natalie defined that. If the stipend was truly handsome, it might go a long way toward hiring tutors for Tess. A truly handsome stipend would come in really handy.

Jared was gone for good, and Olivia's mother remained among the missing—these two harsh facts of life were now softened by Natalie Seebring's invitation.

All right. So it wasn't *exactly* an invitation. But the end result was the same.

I want that job, Olivia thought.

Three

OLIVIA SLEPT FITFULLY. She wanted the Asquonset job, wanted it with a passion that grew as the hours passed. It wasn't the most realistic thing to set her heart on, she knew. There were scores of people more qualified than she, people who could write easily and had formal training—not that she doubted she could do the job. She *could*. She was *sure* that she could. And where there was a will, there was a way. Besides, she had something the others lacked: she already loved Asquonset. Plus, thanks to the photographs, she knew the people and even part of the story.

But would Natalie choose her?

When she finally slept, Olivia dreamed that she got the job. She was still at it the next morning, daydreaming while she got Tess dressed and fed and out of the house. Even as she walked with the briefcase and its precious contents under her arm and her daughter by her side, her thoughts were miles away.

The air was still, the Cambridge streets narrow and close. By the time they reached the school yard, she was fantasizing about open fields and ocean breezes.

"Mom?" Tess looked up at her—beautiful Tess, the top of her head chest-high to Olivia, her hair neatly combed, her freckles soft on her freshly scrubbed face, her slim body still prepubescent. Her glasses were clean and perched high on her nose. She looked to Olivia positively angelic—except for her expression, which fell somewhere between timidity and distaste. "What do I tell Mrs. Wright?"

Mrs. Wright. Lord. Olivia had forgotten about that—repressed it, no doubt. Tess's school problems were an ongoing ordeal. The night's escape to Asquonset had been sweet.

Tell her we have a solution, Olivia thought, quickly back in the midst of the mess. *Tell her you'll be having a tutor* five *days a week this summer. Tell her I want you moving into fifth grade with the rest of your class. Tell her, sweet child, that next time she wants to reach me, she should get off her duff and pick up the phone.*

"Tell her," Olivia said with restraint, "that I'm calling her this morning to set up an appointment. I'll meet with her whenever she wants."

"I'm not staying back."

Olivia pressed a two-fingered kiss to her daughter's nose. "I know."

Tess grabbed the fingers and held them away. "I don't care if the kids *do* think I'm stupid. If I stay back, it's like someone's saying they're right."

Olivia wanted to cry. She had never wanted her child to know this kind of pain. "Someday," she said, vehement now, "those same kids will be asking *you* for answers."

Tess stopped walking. "When?"

"When the nuts and bolts of reading take second place to understanding the material."

"What do you mean, nuts and bolts?"

"The pieces. Like words. Punctuation."

"And grammar? I hate grammar. I can write sentences. Parts of speech are easy to *use*. What's hard is having to *name* them. I don't see why I have to do that."

"You have to name them because it's a requirement of getting into fifth grade." The school bell rang. "Go on, now."

Tess looked worried. "My stomach hurts."

Of course it did. She was about to go off all alone. What she needed was a best friend. She needed someone in the school yard who would run over to her when she arrived. Other children were huddled with their friends. Olivia wanted that for Tess. She was a sweet child. She was sensitive—and pretty. But she wore thick glasses and she struggled in class, which made her the butt of jokes. It was enough to break Olivia's heart.

"Just think," she said now. "Only two weeks more." And then Asquonset? Asquonset might break the cycle. Daily tutoring might help. The ocean air might help. Tess would be sailing with children who had no way of knowing she couldn't read. If they accepted her, if she made a friend or two, if she had a positive experience for a change, it could make the difference.

"Am I going to be able to take tennis lessons?" Tess asked.

"I'm working on it."

"I am *not* having a tutor."

"If you don't have a tutor," Olivia bartered, "then you can't do tennis."

"Then if I have a tutor, I *can* do tennis?"

Olivia was caught. "We'll see." She pointed at the door of the school.

Tess scowled at the pointing finger. Shifting her backpack, she trudged off.

"Hey," Olivia said, her tone gentle now.

The child stopped, turned, and ran back, gave her a fast hug, then turned again and ran toward the school.

Feeling a swell of love, Olivia watched until she blended in with the other students climbing the steps, but the door was no sooner shut on the last of them than her mind shifted south. She saw another door, one she knew well from photographs. It was a screen door leading from Asquonset's Great

House to an awning-covered patio. That patio overlooked the vineyard, row upon row of trellised vines growing taller and fuller as summer progressed. Olivia could just hear that screen door squeaking open and slapping shut, squeaking open and slapping shut, squeaking open and slapping shut. It was an enchanting sound.

She wanted that job. She *needed* that job. Worrying about Tess was a full-time chore—testing, tutoring, meeting with teachers, trying to help her out at home. It was a drain, but she wouldn't do any differently. Tess was the best thing that had ever happened to her—and the child was trying, she really was. She was working her little butt off to compensate for the problem.

Boy, they had earned a summer off, she and Tess. Working for Natalie wouldn't be like working for Otis. It wouldn't be like working at all.

OTIS WAS IN RECOVERY, better than yesterday but still a little off—this much was apparent to Olivia when he came in the door. "We're out of fixer," he said without a hello. "I asked you to put in the order."

Olivia came out of her chair. "I did." She held Natalie's package to her chest. "It's on the storage shelf out back."

"We need it for the Brady prints. I told you I wanted to do the copy work today."

"It's there. Otis? I have to show you something." The timing wasn't right. He was not going to be receptive. But she couldn't wait. She had to act on this now.

He walked past her to his desk on the far side of the room, and began flipping through yesterday's mail.

Olivia followed him and held out the package. "This came, too."

He scowled at it. "What?"

"It's from Natalie Seebring. More photographs. But there was a letter with them. I think you should read it."

"If she doesn't like what we did, she can stuff it," he said, but he held out a hand. "Show me the thing. I have work to do."

She gave him the letter and waited impatiently while he read it. His expression remained dark. The timing wasn't only *not* right. It was *awful*. But if Asquonset was going to happen, if she was going to beat out more qualified applicants, she needed the elements of enthusiasm and speed.

Otis finished the letter, flipped it over, and looked at the blank back, then flipped it front again. He gave Olivia a long look. She held her ground. He read the letter again. By the time he had finished the second reading and looked at the page for a while, she could tell his mood had mellowed.

"I know what you're thinking," he said with a touch of what sounded like sadness, and Olivia felt suddenly disloyal. Otis was her employer and a friend.

"Well, you're retiring," she reasoned. "Seven more weeks and I'm out of a job, and anyway, you've stopped taking new work. We can finish what you have in two weeks. We can. Really." When he was silent, she added, "If we don't, I could come back for a day or two."

"That's not the point. The point"—he held up the letter—"is that this is only a summer job. You need something full-time."

"But nothing else has come up. I'll keep looking. I can do it from there. This just buys me a little time."

He frowned, brooding. "That's not the point either, I guess. There's something else. I've been watching you work on the Seebring job. You've become attached to it."

"I just love old photographs." They were rich. They conjured a time when life was simpler and more romantic.

"These more than others. Why?"

She was embarrassed. "I don't know."

"Yes, you do. Natalie has you wrapped around her little finger."

"That's not true. I've never even met the woman."

"Not that I blame you," Otis went on. "She had me wrapped around her little finger once, too, so I know how that is."

Olivia was startled. "You knew her?" She had assumed that Natalie was simply another client drawn to the studio by its reputation. Then she remembered the yellow envelope with Otis's name on the front. Horrified, she pulled it from the large manila envelope. "I'm sorry. This was tucked in with the photographs. I didn't open it."

Otis did that himself and pulled out a yellow card. He was barely ten seconds reading it when he began to smile. It was a sheepish smile that lingered, even when he rapped a fist to his heart and rolled his eyes. "Shot down again."

"Excuse me?" Olivia asked.

"She's remarrying. Once upon a time, I fancied it would be me."

Olivia was doubly surprised. This was a whole *other* twist on Natalie knowing Otis. But then what Otis had said registered fully. "Remarrying? Where's Alexander?" Granted, Olivia hadn't seen photos from the last decade, but it had never occurred to her that Natalie and Alexander weren't still together. That was part of the image.

"He died."

Olivia gasped. "When? *How?*"

"Six months ago. Heart attack."

Olivia pressed a hand to her chest. "I'm so *sorry.*" She had never met the man, yet she felt his death as if he were an old friend. He had played a part in nearly every Natalie story she had created. Now he was dead, and there was a new man in Natalie's life. It was a lot to take in.

"When were you and she together?" she asked Otis.

"A long time ago. And it was more my initiative than hers." He tapped the invitation. "Obviously."

Olivia was still trying to process the abrupt shift in her image of Natalie. She was trying to conjure up the face of a man who wasn't Alexander, but kept coming up blank. "When is the wedding?"

"Labor Day, which coincidentally is her deadline for this work."

That quickly, Olivia resumed her quest. "She needs help meeting it. She's in a bind. I can help."

Otis sighed. "Again, I have to ask about the source of the attraction. I know what it was for me. Natalie thought I was an artist. She loved my work. But that isn't what's appealing to you."

"She just seems nice—you know, a grandmotherly type."

His voice grew chiding. "She isn't your grandmother, Olivia."

"Of course not."

"Of course not," he mocked. His eyes were bloodshot this morning, but they remained knowing. "You're chasing a dream, my girl. You imagine spending the summer at the ancestral home with a grandmother who takes care of everything, but Natalie isn't that way. Natalie takes care of Natalie."

Of *course* he would say that. Natalie had shot him down. He wouldn't be normal if he wasn't a little bitter or hurt.

Olivia, though, saw only generosity in Natalie.

Granted, she had no way of knowing how a new husband might affect the picture. But marriage or not, the facts didn't change. "She's offering room, board, and a stipend. A *handsome* stipend, she says."

"Her definition of 'handsome' may differ from yours."

Olivia didn't blink. "Maybe, maybe not. I need that money, Otis."

"But this isn't a career move," he complained. "It's just for the *summer.*"

"I *know* that," Olivia said, desperate to convey her belief that it was the right thing to do. "That's what's so *perfect* about this. I've thought it all through, Otis. Really I have. I can finish up here and get out of your hair. I can let you retire without a guilty conscience, because I'll be in another job that I want. I don't even have to give up my apartment. I can sublet it for the summer, and then I'll have it if I want to come back here in the fall. Tess finishes school in two weeks. We can pack up and be in Rhode Island the next day."

"How do you know Natalie'll want Tess?"

"What's not to want? She says it herself in that letter—there's plenty of room at Asquonset. Tess is one little girl. She'll be nearly invisible. I'll find a tutor. I'll give her tennis lessons. I'll hire a teenager to be with her while I work. Between the river and the ocean, there's plenty for a little girl to do. Natalie's used to grandchildren. I'll bet they're swarming all over the place. She may even have *great*-grandchildren by now." Olivia had another thought. "Tess could baby-sit the great-grandchildren. For *free.*"

Otis looked unimpressed. "I don't think there are any great-grandchildren. As far as I know, there aren't even any grandchildren running around. They're grown and on their own. Why do you think she has extra room in that house?"

"Because it's so *big,*" Olivia said. "And those grandkids may be on their own, but summer's when they come back to visit. Asquonset is an incredible summer vacation place."

"How do you know that, Olivia?"

"I just know." Her gut told her so. Granted, her gut had been wrong in the past, particularly where men were concerned. But this was different.

"Maybe you're tired of Cambridge."

"No."

"You've been here longer than you've been anywhere else."

"Because my job here was so good," Olivia argued. "But my boss is retiring. Pulling the rug right out from under me."

"So you're dumping him first, that it?"

She shot him a quelling look.

"What about Ted?" he asked.

"Ted is not in this picture."

"Have you told him that?"

"No. I don't exactly have the job yet."

"But you want it."

"Yes."

"For the money."

"For Tess."

"What if the money's no good?"

Olivia wasn't worried. A "handsome stipend" had to be at least good, and even if it wasn't, room and board counted for something, not to mention nearness to the ocean and the use of a tennis court. The change of scenery alone was worth something.

Otis pushed a pad of paper and a pen her way. "Write down what you want."

"What I think she's paying?"

"What you want. What'll make the effort worthwhile."

Olivia couldn't do that. Anything she put down would be too much. She would be embarrassed.

"Okay." Otis pulled back the pad. "I'll do it." He wrote down a sum that was roughly twice what he would have paid her for the summer if he hadn't been retiring. While she stared at the figure, slightly stunned but already thinking of what that much money would buy, he picked up the phone, drew Natalie's letterhead close, and punched in her number.

"What are you *doing?*" Olivia cried in alarm. She had the sudden vision of his ruining the whole thing with an ill-placed word.

"Saving a little breath. Let's see if we're in the same ballpark."

Olivia nearly stopped him. She didn't want to know—if knowing meant the end of the dream.

But the call went through before she could react, and Otis was suddenly greeting Natalie like the old friend she apparently was. There was a minute of warm conversation—talk about the pictures that were done, the ones newly arrived, the upcoming wedding. Again, Olivia mentally tried to pair Natalie up with a suitable groom, but Cary Grant was the only face she saw, and he was long dead.

Otis asked Natalie for details about the assistant she wanted.

Hugging her middle, Olivia watched that pad of paper as he wrote down the answers to his questions. *Typing and editing skills. Writing from notes. Mornings with Natalie, afternoons alone Monday through Friday; weekends free. Living accommodations in a separate wing of the house. Food included. Pets? No. Children? Yes. Stipend?*

Olivia held her breath long after Otis had written the answer. Natalie was offering twice what Otis had guessed. It was a windfall for someone like her—an incredible amount by *any* measure. She pressed her fingertips to her mouth to keep glee in check.

Otis seemed likewise stunned. He asked Natalie to repeat the figure, and tapped the paper with his pen to confirm that the amount he had written was correct.

Olivia heard bits of the remaining conversation, things like "very generous . . . yes . . . history lesson . . . clear the air," but the words sailed past her. Excited beyond belief, she had let her thoughts loose in a new direction. Up to that point, she had been thinking about money for a tutor. What Natalie was offering opened a whole other door.

By the time Otis hung up the phone, Olivia had pulled out the bottom drawer of her desk and taken a booklet from her personal stash. Returning to Otis's desk, she put it down for him to see. It was the catalogue from Cambridge Heath, a private school that was known to cater to the learning-disabled children of local college professors.

Olivia wasn't a college professor—not by a long shot. She had never even been a college student, having graduated from high school by the skin of her teeth and gone straight to work. She considered herself an artist now—Otis's description, long before hers. That was how she billed herself on the job queries she had sent out. She guessed that any school in the Cambridge area would have a handful of parents like her.

Besides, Tess *was* the daughter of a college professor. Hadn't Jared been on the faculty of UNC at the time of his death? That had to count for something.

And if not, there were other schools. In fact, she realized excitedly, there was a school like Cambridge Heath in Providence. Providence was an up-and-coming city. Olivia had sent résumés to museums and art galleries there. Providence was only a short distance from Asquonset. It would be nice to be near Natalie when the summer was done.

And, of course, there was the possibility that if things worked out at the vineyard, the summer job might evolve into something else—permanent gal Friday, social secretary. It was very promising.

Not that she was counting on all that, but it never hurt to dream.

Otis picked up the book and thumbed through, turning to the pages with Post-its. There he read what Olivia knew by heart. Yes, he could tell she had been dreaming. She had been dreaming far longer than she had known of Natalie Seebring.

"Well, this is fine," he said dryly. "You'll be able to afford this school for one year. Then what?"

Olivia refused to be deflated. "Either Tess will get a scholarship or I'll take out a loan, but she has to *be* there first. Otherwise, I'm a nobody. I don't have connections. The state says Tess is getting everything she needs in public school, but she hates it there. There's a good teacher for next year, but I have no guarantee she'll get that one, and the teacher she had this year has set her so far back emotionally that the teacher she gets next year will have *twice* the job to do—and that's *assuming* I can convince them to promote her." She put a firm hand on the catalogue, feeling determined as never before, now that what she wanted so badly for Tess was within reach. "Tess needs to be in a school like this one. Don't you see, Otis? I need this job. It's our *chance*."

But there was still a major hurdle to cross. It was all fine and good to talk about the job, all fine and good to think about private schools, all fine and good to think that maybe, just maybe her luck was turning—but Natalie still had to hire her.

"I can make it happen," Otis said, which was what Olivia was thinking herself.

She nodded, then waited, barely breathing.

"I want the money for you," he said. "It's the other that worries me. The dreaming."

"I'm not dreaming. I'm going after this job with my eyes wide open."

"And you wouldn't love to be part of that family?"

"Of course, I would. Who wouldn't? But I'm not a Seebring. I'll never *be* a Seebring."

"As long as you understand that."

"I do, Otis. I *do*. You said it—this is a summer job. It's a bridge between your job and . . . something else. If it turns out to be fun, I'll have good memories, but that's not the best part. The *best* part is that my daughter will have something she needs but wouldn't otherwise have. I want that for her, Otis. Wouldn't you, if she were yours?"

Four

TWO WEEKS LATER, wearing new white shorts and
sneakers, and a green and a blue blouse, respec-
tively, Olivia and Tess set off for Rhode Island.
They left behind a law student delighted with her
summer sublet, a retirement-bound photo restorer,
and, at curbside, a perturbed Ted.

"He has his hands on his hips," Tess reported,
looking through her side mirror. "Why is he so
angry?"

Olivia refused to look back. She made a practice in life of not doing that. Once a decision was
made and a course of action set, the only way to
look was ahead. That said, she was sad saying
good-bye to Otis and felt a twinge of regret on
leaving the apartment. What she felt leaving Ted,
though, was pure relief.

"He's not angry," she told Tess. "He's hurt. He wanted us to spend the summer here with him."

"Doing what? Riding the *swan* boats? That's all Ted thinks I *do*. It wouldn't occur to him that I like to shop."

It hadn't occurred to Olivia, either. In their household, shopping had always been more functional than fun. But Olivia had an image of what people wore summers in Asquonset—especially summers of parties preceding a wedding—and it wasn't what hung in her closet. She didn't want to embarrass Natalie, and the fiancé might be even *more* fashionable. He was still a big question mark. Olivia had pictured a wine baron from the vineyards of France, until Otis said that his name was Carl Burke, at which point she ruled out France. The name was Irish. Since she hadn't ever heard of any Irish wine families, she made him the Irish American head of a California vineyard. She imagined a dignified, elegant, classy man. Men like that surrounded themselves with dignified, elegant, classy people.

Since that circle would temporarily include Tess and her, Olivia loosened the purse strings and took Tess to the stores. Suddenly the daughter who wore nothing but T-shirts and jeans was a whole new creature. She tried on colorful shorts and halter tops, short skirts and sundresses—not only tried them on but *modeled* them—and she looked adorable in everything, because she was smiling.

In different clothes, she was a different person. Olivia didn't need a psychiatrist to tell her the meaning of that.

Asquonset was a new beginning, and she had Otis to thank. She hadn't even had to go for a personal interview. Natalie had hired her on his word alone.

Ted was appalled. "But don't *you* want to see where you're going? Okay, so you've seen photographs, but they can't tell you what you need to know. Photographs don't tell the truth. She's *clearly* sending ones that show the place at its best—that's how it's done."

Olivia didn't think that arguing was worth the effort. Ted's pessimism was pure sour grapes. He refused to see that their relationship was ending, and continued to talk about calling her each night, meeting her for dinner midway between Cambridge and Asquonset, even driving down to visit. She tried to put him off gently with pleas of needing to get to know the job, of finding out how demanding it would be. When he didn't take the hint, she was more blunt. She was feeling stifled, she said. She needed space.

Even then he didn't listen. Ted didn't hear what he didn't want to hear, and that was his problem. But Olivia wasn't letting him rain on her parade. She refused to let him disparage Asquonset.

"The pictures I've seen aren't marketing photographs," she informed him. "They were taken before anyone even knew what marketing *was*. Some of them are snapshots from a Brownie camera. They're the real thing."

Otis had confirmed it. When pushed, he had confessed to being at Asquonset a number of times. Had he ever met Carl Burke? He didn't recall it, but he did recall the Great House. He said it was even more beautiful than the photographs—quite a concession from a man who had been spurned.

Besides, Olivia and Natalie had talked on the phone. Natalie had no problem with Olivia's lack of a college degree. She liked what Olivia had done with the Asquonset pictures and claimed that the letters she had written on Otis's behalf showed sufficient writing skill. She liked that Olivia asked questions while they talked, and insisted that being organized, personable, and devoted—as Olivia had been to Otis—was more valuable to her than formal credentials. Finally, she said that she had learned to trust her gut and that her gut spoke of a rapport between the two of them.

Olivia's did the same. Over the course of three conversations, she came away with the conviction that Natalie wanted to hire her as much as she wanted the job. The skeptical part of her nature didn't know whether rapport had been the deciding factor, whether Natalie was feeling guilty at having shafted Otis so many years before, or whether she simply wanted the hiring over and done. Olivia did know that talking with Natalie was easy, much as she imagined it would be to talk with a good-natured grandmother. Natalie was easygoing and enthusiastic. She was flexible. She was eager to please.

The best part, though, was that she seemed delighted by the prospect of having a child around.

"And you believe that?" Ted had asked with a snort.

If this man wasn't already history with Olivia, the snort would have clinched it. Tess was her pride and joy. She resented his suggestion that the child was a bother to anyone. "Yes, I believe it. She's gone out of her way to make things come together for us. She found us a tutor. She found us a tennis teacher. She even made arrangements for Tess to take sailing lessons at the yacht club."

"Did you interview the tutor? For all you know it could be a high school kid wanting a few extra bucks—same with the tennis teacher—and if she absolutely *has* to sail, she can do it with my parents in Rockport."

If nothing else, I'm thankful for sparing her that, Olivia thought. She had met Ted's parents. Taking them to a restaurant had been a nightmare of complaints—spotted stemware, poor service, food that was undercooked, overcooked, or misordered. They were as uptight as their son. Olivia didn't want her daughter anywhere near them.

"And take the mother angle," Ted charged,

pounding the last nail into his own coffin. "How can you cart your child off without scoping out the place you're carting her to—for that matter, how can you take off for the summer when you don't have a job for the fall? If it was me, I'd be staying right here, pounding the pavement. And if you don't care about it for your sake, that's okay, but you ought to be caring for Tess's sake. Responsible mothers don't do this—it isn't smart."

Isn't *smart?* Olivia, already sensitive enough about not having a college degree in a town where most people had three, was offended.

"Tell you what," she snapped. "When you have kids, you can do what *you* think is smart. For my kid, I'll do what *I* think is smart."

And she was doing just that. Some of Ted's arguments might have had merit if she hadn't felt such conviction that what she was doing was right. It was a feeling she'd had from the minute she first read Natalie's letter.

Besides, trust was a big issue, and in this instance it went both ways. If Natalie could hire her sight unseen, Olivia could accept the job the same way.

THEN CAME THE DREAM. The first part was real— growing up in a Vermont town that catered to a ski crowd from New York, the only child of a woman who herself was little more than a child. Olivia was raised by neighbors until she was old enough to wear a key around her neck. By that time, Carol Jones was working with a local realtor and interacting closely with that ski crowd from New York. In her dream, Olivia relived the nights at home alone, afraid of the dark, afraid of the angry sounds coming from the landlord downstairs, not knowing where her mother was, and fearing she would never return.

The second part of the dream was the interesting part. In it, Carol Jones returned one morning not with a paramour, but with her own mother.

Olivia had never met her grandmother. She had been told that the woman was dead, which was the easiest thing for Carol to say, but Olivia kept the flame alive. During the loneliest of those childhood hours, burrowed in her hideout in the corner of a dark closet where she felt safe, she concocted dozens of stories to explain a grandmother's absence. Likewise, she imagined a dozen different reunions.

In this dream, the grandmother who came from nowhere one sunny day was a woman of means. She had spent years looking for her daughter—her headstrong, rebellious, pregnant daughter—who had run off to spite her parents, and then had been too frightened to return. One private investigator after another had given up on the job, but the grandmother had stuck with it. Now, all these years later, her perseverance had paid off. Thanks to an old photograph of Carol that had been painstakingly restored and looked exactly like Olivia, the older woman had tracked her down.

That sweet, stubborn, at long last successful grandmother had Natalie Seebring's face.

OF COURSE, it was only a dream. Thinking about it, though, as her aged Toyota carried them south, Olivia took it as an omen. Her excitement grew.

Unfortunately, so did Tess's anxiety. The questions came one after the other in steady succession. "Where will we live?"

"In the Great House. There's an empty wing of the house. We'll be there. I've told you this, Tess."

"Empty? Like, haunted?"

"It's okay. They're nice ghosts."

"Mommm."

"No ghosts, Tess. No ghosts."

"How old's the man she's marrying?"

"I don't know."

"What if everyone there's old? Old people don't like kids."

"They do, as long as the kids behave."

"What if I get on their nerves anyway? Who else is at Natalie's house?"

"Please, Tess. Not Natalie. Mrs. Seebring."

"You call her Natalie."

"Not to her face, and besides, I'm an adult."

"Does Carl live there?"

Olivia sighed. "It's Mr. Burke, and I don't know whether he lives there or not."

"Is there a cook? A maid? A *butler?*"

"I don't know."

"I don't think I'll be very good at sailing."

"Of course you will."

"Did you call Cambridge Heath?"

"Yes. They're processing your application." Olivia had talked to the admissions officer just that morning. Not trusting that something wouldn't be lost, she had a folder with her that contained copies of Tess's application and medical records. A second folder contained brochures from Braemont, in Providence, and schools in three other New England cities, all of which had museums where Olivia might find work. A third folder contained copies of her résumé and of the letters that she'd already sent. She planned to send a follow-up letter with her summer address. It was as good an excuse as any to remind them that she was alive and looking for work.

"What if I don't get in?" Tess asked.

"If you don't get in," Olivia rationalized for the umpteenth time, "it'll only be because there wasn't an open spot in the fifth grade. Right now, the class is filled. They're expecting a dropout or two over the summer."

"Why would someone drop out?"

"They move. Their parents take jobs in other parts of the country."

"What if they don't?"

"If they don't, we'll apply for next year."

"Then what'll I do *this* year?"

If they moved to a different city, there would be another public school, with the possibility of a better teacher and a better program for someone like Tess. If not, Olivia just didn't know. Her conference with Nancy Wright hadn't gone well. *It's the demographics,* the woman had claimed with more than a little arrogance. *Our student body is ahead of most. We can't hold all of these children back while we cater to a few who lag.* Olivia had had to go to the principal of the school and lobby hard before they finally did assign Tess to a fifth-grade class, but it was clear that they did so reluctantly and that they would hold Olivia responsible for the move. If something went wrong, they said in so many words, the school wouldn't be to blame.

And that, in a nutshell, was the problem with the school Tess was attending. The mentality was adversarial—them against us. There was no sense of partnership, no sense of working together for the good of the child. The process had left Olivia more convinced than ever that Tess needed something different.

OLIVIA WAS FOCUSED on that thought when they turned off the highway and, following Natalie's directions, headed down the local road. She was wondering what would happen if she screwed up and couldn't do this job. Writing letters was nothing compared to writing a book. Her computer would check spelling and grammar, but it wouldn't express ideas and connect one with the next.

The truth? This job was a reach for her. If she lost it in a week, there would be no summer by the sea—no iced tea on the veranda, no picnics, no sailing. There would be no hours of being lost in the past. There would be no glowing reference from Natalie, no California connections from Carl, no good word put in to a powerful friend who might know someone on the board of directors of a museum that had an in-house restoration department. If Olivia screwed up, there would be no stipend, and without that stipend she could kiss good-bye the dream of sending Tess to Cambridge Heath.

So maybe it was irresponsible of her as a mother to have raised the child's hopes. But how not to? Tess had had to be interviewed and tested. Olivia couldn't have submitted an admissions application for her without her knowledge.

They passed a plaque marking the Asquonset town line. The inside of the car grew still. Olivia was as terrified as she was excited; she imagined that Tess felt the same.

The road was flanked by low-growing shrubs and the occasional large maple or oak, but the few houses strewn about looked run down. There was a rusted piece of farm equipment at the start of a dirt path, and a broken-down truck in a field just beyond. If Olivia didn't know better, she would have thought she was in a dying town.

But she did know better. There were neatly mowed fields in the distance beyond the truck, and grazing in its midst, a pair of elegant horses. Besides, according to the Asquonset Web site, the vineyard was thriving. Last year it had produced sixty thousand cases of wine, up from fifty-five thousand the year before, and the estimate for this year was even higher. Asquonset wines were hot up and down the East Coast. Estate labels were being served in the best restaurants, more moderately priced labels were being snapped up for home use, and all of that stood to increase if Natalie's upcoming marriage merged two big wine names. No, there was nothing dying about this operation. A little chipped paint on the outskirts of town wasn't getting her down.

More to the point, she wasn't about to judge a book by its cover. She had wasted far too much energy in her life doing that. She had fallen for Jared's brains and Ted's intensity, for Damien's singing voice and Peter's baklava. Not a one of the four had offered much else in terms of a relationship.

Now Olivia had new clothes, a new job, and a new town. This was a new day. She was turning over a new leaf.

• • •

ASQUONSET CENTER materialized just when Natalie's directions said that it would. It was little more than a crossroads, with a sandwich shop on one corner, Pindman's General Store on another, a Cape cottage that appeared to house a lawyer, a psychiatrist, and a vet on the third corner, and a private home on the last. All four buildings were variations on the wood-frame theme, with the sandwich shop low and long, the general store narrow and tall, and the cottage and private home somewhere in between. All four were yellow and painted none too recently—although the faded look struck Olivia as being deliberate. A couple emerging from the professional office looked well dressed and content, as did a pair of little boys sitting on the general store steps. American flags flew proudly. Mailboxes were neatly numbered. A FedEx delivery truck approached from Olivia's right. The driver honked and waved at a group of twenty-somethings sitting on picnic benches outside the sandwich shop.

Deliberate, indeed, Olivia thought. The center of town had age and a cultivated charm. She suspected that there were wonderful stories to be told about the origin of Pindman's or the various incarnations of the professional building; and the sandwich shop had eternal-gathering-spot written all over it. She would be back with her camera to photograph this corner, and more than once, she guessed.

The road began to climb, taking them past a

small brick building with a *Town Hall* sign and an oversized garage with a *Fire Department* sign. They crested a gentle rise that held a pretty white church. Its steeple was luminous in a pale blue sky, but what caught Olivia's breath was the view of the ocean beyond.

"Look!" she cried.

Tess said, "I'm hungry. Aren't there any restaurants here?"

"There's the *ocean.*" But the view was already gone, obstructed by a stretch of thicket, and then the road dipped again, heading inland. Olivia was ebullient. "This is going to be so good." She rolled down the window and felt a wash of warm, salty air.

"I have to use the bathroom," Tess announced.

"Hold it. We can't be two miles from the vineyard."

"But there's *nothing* here," Tess remarked, and she was right. At that minute, Olivia saw only scrub forests and barren fields.

Then the vineyard came into view—not the vineyard, actually, just the sign, but the effect was the same. It was bold and bright, startlingly vivid in a world where all else seemed muted. No single minimalist line here. This bunch of grapes spilling from a wineglass was painted in glorious color, and instead of having the expected burgundy letters, the vineyard name was embossed in gold.

Heart pounding, Olivia turned left onto a narrow road covered with pebbles that crunched under her tires. The road undulated inland, alternately climbing and leveling, brightening with fields of young cornstalks, darkening under forests of cedar and birch.

"Where's the house?" Tess asked after a minute.

Olivia was waiting, watching, wondering the very same thing. They crested another rise, and the fields changed. There were low stone walls running along the side of the road now, and though the greenery here grew in rows as neat as the corn, it was low to the ground.

Olivia had done her homework. "Those are potatoes," she told Tess. "The Seebrings grow both—corn and potatoes."

"I thought they grew grapes."

"They do now, but they didn't always. Potatoes came first. They were the cover during Prohibition."

"What does *that* mean?"

"During Prohibition, people weren't allowed to sell wine. For all official purposes, Asquonset supported itself growing potatoes and corn."

"But they did grow grapes and they did sell wine?"

"Much less than they do now, but yes."

"Then they were criminals."

Olivia didn't want Tess *thinking* illegal, much less asking Natalie about it. "Well, Prohibition was very unpopular. More people were against it than for it. That's why it didn't last very long. It was a bad idea from the start. Put down your window, Tess." She inhaled as Tess complied. "Smell that?"

Tess sniffed. "I smell dirt."

"It's earth. It's earth that's fertile and moist."

"If there's poison ivy here, I'm in trouble."

"You won't get poison ivy. I brought your medicine. You never get it when I bring the medicine."

Tess didn't respond to that. She was sitting as far forward as her seat belt would allow, scanning the road again. "So, where's the *vineyard?*"

Five

OLIVIA GUIDED THE CAR around a turn to a patch of farmland that at first glance looked simply scrubby and low. Then she noticed posts, wires, and a pattern of plantings. Exhilarated, she declared, "Right *there.*"

As the car cruised slowly closer, a world of neatly trellised vines became delineated, tidy rows of gnarled canes and branches with pale green canopies, sides trimmed and guided for maximum exposure to the sun.

Some rows had signs. *Chardonnay,* read one. Farther on, another read, *Pinot Noir.*

Olivia got goose bumps. It didn't matter that the hard little BBs growing on the vines in June only remotely resembled grapes. After ogling

Asquonset on paper for months, she felt as if she were in the company of celebrities.

No. That was not the right analogy, she realized. Celebrity was shallow. The feeling here was almost religious. Driving more slowly up that pebbled road, flanked by descendants of the vinifera that had been producing precious European wines for hundreds of years, she felt a hush. And the awe seemed mutual. She imagined that the vineyard had parted to let them through and would close up again once they passed.

"What do the signs say, Mom?"

"They're the names of grapes. Must be by section. That was Pinot Noir on your right. You know which side that is."

Tess often confused them. This time, she didn't. She pointed right, then switched sides. "What's that one?"

"Riesling," Olivia read and gasped. "Oh my."

A man had risen between two rows of vines.

"Who's *he?*" Tess asked.

"One of the workers, I guess."

"Where'd he come from?"

"He must've been crouched down in there." Standing now, he was taller than the highest trellis by more than a foot. She saw auburn hair, sunburned skin, broad shoulders, a maroon T-shirt with the arms ripped off and a tear under the neck band. He wore dark glasses, but he was clearly looking their way.

"Why was he crouched down?"

"He was working."

"Why is he staring at us?"

"Not staring. Just looking. We're strangers. He's curious."

"Mom," Tess murmured out of the corner of her mouth, "why are you slowing *down?* He does *not* look nice."

No, in fact he didn't—but Olivia hadn't realized that she was staring, or that she had slowed. Facing forward, she accelerated gently.

"I hope they're not all like him," Tess said once they were safely past. "He doesn't want us here."

"Why do you say that?"

"His face said it."

Olivia thought his face was pretty compelling. Somber and intent. But compelling.

"So, where's the house?" Tess asked.

"It's coming."

"We'll be at the river soon," the child warned. Bless her, she had studied the maps and remembered Olivia's narration. She knew that if the ocean was behind them, the river was ahead. Yes, Olivia thought, she is smart. What she lacked was a sense of distance, which had more to do with inexperience than dyslexia. She didn't realize that driving slowly, climbing and twisting, they had crossed barely a quarter of the peninsula that the Seebring family owned.

Then the Great House appeared. It rose with

surprising suddenness, and actually had been there all along, but was so neatly framed by trees at the very top of the hill that it had been hidden for a bit. Then again, Olivia may have been so taken by the sight of the vineyard that she had missed it. The Great House looked different from the photographs she had restored. It appeared nowhere near as large or as bright in person. The first floor was clad in large slabs of stone held together by mortar, deeply shadowed where a sloped roof covered the porch. The second floor wore wood, weathered gray by the sea air. The two blended into one hard, craggy face.

It hadn't been like that in pictures. Bottom and top had seemed gentle and distinct. For a second, Olivia had the horrible thought that she had created something in the darkroom that hadn't existed at all—worse, had created something in her *mind* that hadn't existed at all.

All right, she reasoned. Without a point of reference, perspective was often lost in photographs. In the case of the pictures of the Great House, she had relied on the trees. But trees could be larger or smaller. If Olivia had imagined them larger than they were in real life, the Great House would have seemed larger as well.

And then there was the age factor. The Asquonset she had worked with was many years younger than this one. Some things were bound to be different. But the windows were the same—large, handsome, multipaned casement windows angled open. The peaked gables were the same. The shingled roof was the same.

The face the house wore might be craggy and hard, but its eyes were open, its brows raised in curiosity as they approached. With clouds floating in wisps above the roof and the vineyards spilling beneath it, Natalie Seebring's Great House was still an impressive sight.

Driving that final short distance, Olivia allowed herself a final dream. She pictured pulling up at the door and having a beaming Natalie run out, followed by a flock of household staff, lining up on the walk, eager for introduction.

Olivia pulled up in the semicircle at the end of the stone walk and parked the car. A low stone wall marked the crescent. A nearby flagpole flew the American flag on top and the Rhode Island flag beneath it.

She sat for a few seconds, waiting. The front door was a wood-framed screen, much as she had imagined, but it remained empty and dark.

Climbing out, she rounded the car. Taking Tess's hand, she went up the walk. Her heart was in her throat. So much was at stake here.

The front steps were stone, five in all, and wide. They climbed them, crossed the darkness of the porch, and peered inside.

"Is anybody home?" Tess whispered.

Olivia put her ear to the screen. "I hear voices."

"Talking about us?"

"I doubt it." If she was wrong, they were in trouble. From the sounds of it, there was an argument going on.

She knocked softly on the wood frame of the screen door. The distant voices were joined now by the jangle of the telephone.

They had come at a bad time. Given her druthers, Olivia would put Tess back in the car, drive out to the main road, waste five or ten minutes, then rearrive. It was a foolish thought, of course. It would be ridiculous to turn back now. Besides, they had already been seen by the man in the vineyard.

Mustering courage, she pressed the doorbell, an ivory button encased in a swirl of wrought iron. The chime was resonant. The voices inside stopped. Seconds later, the sound of light footsteps approached. Seconds after that, Natalie Seebring appeared.

When she saw them and smiled, Olivia felt a wave of relief. Everything was going to be all right. Natalie was here—and even thirty years older than in the last photos Olivia had seen, she was lovely. She was of average height and slender, in neat jeans and a polo shirt with the vineyard logo on the breast pocket. But Olivia was most drawn to her face. Her skin was dewy, only barely made up, lightly creased but soft and sweet. Her hair was thick and white, gently shaped to her jaw, faintly windblown, feminine but not prim. She stood straight and agile, wore her age with pride and style, and exuded command.

Olivia was immediately in awe.

Still smiling, Natalie opened the door and, amid the faintest scent of freesia, waved them inside. Olivia was just as delighted with what she saw there. The front hall was large and predominantly green. It had an Old World feel to it, with lots of dark wood interrupted by several murals. The staircase made a gradual turn, with a landing every five or six steps. A big orange cat sat on the first landing. A smaller black-and-white one sat halfway to the second.

Olivia could tell the instant Tess spotted the cats by her excited little catch of breath.

"You're just in time," Natalie said. "There's a war going on here. I need reinforcements."

The words were barely out of her mouth when a woman entered the hall. She looked barely sixty. Her gray dress said she was the maid.

"Mrs. Seebring, that's your daughter on the phone."

"Olivia, Tess, this is Marie," Natalie said, rolling the *r*. "She has worked at this house since she was old enough to hold a job. That's thirty-five years. Now, suddenly, she decides she wants a career change? I don't think so."

"It's time," Marie said, extending a piece of paper that Olivia guessed to be her notice.

Natalie drew her hands back out of reach. "I won't take that. You're upset with the change, is all. But I need you, Marie."

Marie shook her head.

"At least wait until after the wedding," Natalie begged.

"I can't," Marie said and handed the paper to Olivia, who took it out of sheer surprise. "Mrs. Seebring's daughter is on the phone. The woman has been trying to reach her. Would you please make her take it?" She turned and walked off.

"*Marie,*" Natalie protested.

"I have wash to do."

"I don't *care* about the wash," Natalie called, but the maid was gone. She sighed and gave Tess a more tenuous smile. "Guess we lost?"

Tess nodded. "Are these your cats?"

"Yes. That's Maxwell on the landing and Bernard halfway up."

"They're both boys?" Tess asked, then gave a small cry and bumped into Olivia when a third cat brushed her leg.

"That's *Henri,*" Natalie said, giving the name a French twist. "No need to be afraid."

Tess knelt to pat the cat. This one was a black-and-gray tiger. "I'm not afraid. I just didn't see him coming."

"Neither did I," Natalie said. "He showed up here one day looking half starved, and I couldn't turn him away."

With Tess momentarily content, Olivia was acutely aware of the telephone button blinking red on the mahogany table by the stairs. "We can wait here, if you want to take that call."

"I don't," Natalie said. "My daughter isn't any more pleased with me than Marie is. None of them understands. As far as they're concerned, I'm an old piece of cotton candy that should just be sweet and pink. They don't credit me with having a mind."

"The phone, Mrs. Seebring!" came Marie's distant call.

Natalie pressed two fingers to her temple. Her eyes met Olivia's.

"Would you like me to take it for you?" Olivia asked.

Natalie's relief was instant. "Please. Introduce yourself. Tell her that I can't talk now."

Delighted to be of use so soon, Olivia crossed to the phone. In an upbeat voice, she said, "This is Olivia Jones. I'm Mrs. Seebring's new assistant. I'm afraid that she can't take the phone—"

"Assistant?" an upset voice cut in. "What kind of assistant? And why *can't* she take the phone? I'm her daughter. I only want a minute."

Olivia looked at Natalie, who held up her hands, shook her head, took a step back.

"I believe she's outside," Olivia said into the phone. "Can she call you back?"

"Of course she can. The question is whether

she will. She's avoiding my calls. Olivia Jones, you say?"

"Yes."

"When did you start working for my mother?"

"This is actually my first day."

"Do you know what's going on?"

"Uh, I'm not sure that I know what you mean."

"The wedding."

"Yes. I know about that."

There was a pause, then a beseeching, "She needs to rethink this. It isn't right. My father's been dead barely six months."

Olivia didn't know what to say to that. She was a newcomer. She was an outsider. "I think you ought to talk with your mother about this."

"That's easier said than done. This is a woman who couldn't tell her own daughter that she was re-marrying. She knows that what she's doing is wrong. It's an embarrassment."

From the far side of the room, Natalie said, "She can't accept that I have a heart that beats, and beats hard. I'm supposed to be old and dried up."

Olivia hadn't covered the mouthpiece quite fast enough.

"I heard that," Susanne charged. "She's stand-ing right there, but she's too cowardly to take my calls. She knows that she shouldn't be doing this, not after everything my father did. He built that vineyard. She wouldn't be there today if it weren't for him. Look, will you give her a message?"

"Yes."

"Tell her that her family isn't going to that wedding. My brother and I are sick about this. She was supposed to have loved her husband." There was a tiny pause. "What did you say she hired you for?"

"I'm helping out in the office."

"Oh dear. Someone else left? They're dropping like flies. They don't like what she's doing either. Are you another one of her strays?"

Olivia was mildly offended. "Excuse me?"

"She takes them in, you know. Some work out. Marie has been there forever. Others are one-week wonders. She goes by gut instinct. Did she tell you that?"

"Yes. But I'm not a stray. I've spent the last five years doing photo restoration work under Otis Thurman. I left his office to come here."

"That's very nice, but I'd like you to listen for just a minute. Please don't speak. Just listen. We're worried that Natalie is either fading mentally or that she's being brainwashed by Carl. We don't know how else to explain this marriage. So I ask you—beg you—to keep an eye on her. If you sense that either of those things is happening, will you call me?"

Olivia's loyalties instinctively lay with Natalie, but she wasn't getting into a fight with Susanne. "I'll try," she said.

"Thank you. I appreciate that. Please tell my

mother that I'll call again next week. Oh, and welcome to Asquonset."

Olivia hung up the phone and turned to Natalie.

The older woman looked sheepish. "I'm sorry. I'm afraid I've dragged you into the middle of my hornet's nest."

Olivia wasn't sorry in the least. Barely five minutes there and she felt part of the household. "She sounded upset."

"She is. She doesn't understand."

"But if you've explained it to her . . ."

A guilty look stole over Natalie's face.

"You haven't?" Olivia asked, startled. "Maybe if you did . . ."

Natalie looked torn, as though she desperately wanted to do that but for the life of her couldn't. "It's easier said than done. She idolized her father, as did her brother, Greg. And that's wonderful. I wanted that. I worked to make it so." She studied the wall of books, seeming suddenly tired. "So now there are misconceptions that need clearing up. How to do that without speaking ill of the dead?" She kneaded her fingers. "Family dynamics are like nothing else in life. You set a pattern early on, and it's nearly impossible to change. I've always had trouble talking to my children—talking *openly* to my children. Some things are hard to discuss. Some things are more easily said to a stranger."

"Like me?"

Natalie didn't answer at first. She put a hand on Tess's head, seeming to take comfort as Tess stroked a loudly purring Henri. "I hope so."

"And it all has to do with the wedding?"

"Oh, no. It has to do with more. Lots more. But the one common thread is Carl." She looked up toward the door through which Marie had gone, and her face brightened. "Ah. Two more boys. The big, mangy one on the left is Buck. He's a Maine coon, dropped off at Pindman's last fall by a tourist who couldn't stand his howling in the car a second longer. The tall, lean one is Simon. He's my vineyard manager. Simon, say hello to Olivia Jones and her daughter, Tess."

Olivia looked up to see the man from the vineyard—apparently not just any old worker, but the vineyard manager, no less. Well, he certainly was tall, she decided, although she wouldn't have said he was lean from that earlier chest-and-above glimpse. She could see the whole of him now, though. His waist and hips, covered by loose work shorts, were lean indeed, as were his legs, which were as dirty as his work boots and the gray socks that protruded from the top. His sunglasses sat on the top of his head, half lost in all that auburn hair, but his sunburned nose was the only touch of warmth on his face. His eyes were a midnight blue and cold. His jaw was shadowed.

Natalie's vineyard manager. This could be a problem, Olivia thought as she glanced at Tess, who was staring at Simon. Although the child didn't seem frightened, she made no effort to move away from the hand Natalie had placed on her head. There was safety in that hand. Olivia could feel it even from where she stood.

Simon nodded first toward Tess, then Olivia. *He doesn't want us here,* Tess had said. Olivia didn't know if it was that or if the man was simply tough.

"He's the dark, silent type," Natalie said with fondness, even pride. "Like his father. Speaking of whom . . ."

"He's in the shed," Simon said in a voice that was dusty and deep. "He says he'll be over in a bit. I'm heading up to Providence."

Natalie's smile faded. "Oh dear. There's a problem."

"I'm not sure. I saw something on the reds that may be the start of mold. I want a second opinion."

Natalie explained to Olivia, "It's been a wet winter and spring. We were hoping that the sun and wind would dry out the vines." To Simon, she said, "I was planning on your joining us for dinner."

Olivia thought she saw a wry twist at the corner of his mouth, but his eyes held Natalie's and his voice remained respectful. "I'm sorry. I can't tonight." With only the briefest glance at Olivia, he turned and left. Buck followed him out.

The phone rang.

Natalie sighed and said, "Since the business

phone doesn't ring here, that will most likely be my son. Susanne calls him to complain the minute she hangs up with me."

Olivia gave the phone a quick look. "Shall I?"

"Please."

She lifted the receiver. "Seebring residence."

"Is this Olivia Jones?" asked an authoritative voice, and for a split second Olivia feared she had unknowingly committed a crime and been tracked down by the FBI—or, worse, by *Ted*.

But it wasn't Ted's voice. Besides, she had barely *arrived*. Nonetheless, such a call would be typical Ted. Perhaps he was using a friend as a foil?

"Who's calling?" she asked guardedly.

"Greg Seebring. Is this Olivia?"

She relaxed. Natalie was right; Susanne must have given him her name. No crime committed, and even better, no Ted. She was free. "Yes, this is Olivia."

"I'm Natalie's son, and let me tell you, I don't have the time to make this call. I have problems of my own right now, but my sister is driving me nuts because our mother is driving *her* nuts. I just want to tell you this. Natalie is behaving oddly. This marriage is inappropriate and untimely. I suspect that with Dad gone she's just needing someone else to lean on, and the nearest one for that is Carl. It could be that there's a Burke conspiracy to take over the vineyard, I don't know yet, but if so, it won't work."

Olivia had been thinking merger, as in an amicable union of two powerful families. She didn't have to be a finance expert to know that a takeover could be hostile. "Perhaps," she said, "you ought to talk to your mother."

"I don't have time for that. I also don't have the *energy* for it. My mother and I function on entirely different levels. I just want *you* to know that *we* know what's going on, and that if you do anything to aid and abet the Burke cause, we'll consider you part of the conspiracy. Good God, you may be anyway. Did Carl hire you?"

"No, and I know nothing of what you're talking about."

"Honey," he said with a dark laugh, "I deal with political animals day in, day out, and one thing I've learned is that when they insist they know nothing, like you just did, they know plenty. I'm wise to the situation. Consider yourself warned. Give my regards to my mother." He hung up.

Replacing the handset, Olivia wondered for the first time about the exact nature of the hornet's nest Natalie had mentioned. One vineyard taking over another was serious stuff. The family could be torn apart. Natalie could move to Napa. Asquonset could fold. Olivia could be implicated in a lawsuit that could drag on for years.

"He's angry," Natalie said.

Her voice put Olivia's speculation on hold. "I think he's worried." That sounded gentler.

"But not worried enough to get on a plane and fly up here," Natalie charged. "Did he mention his conspiracy theory?"

"Um . . . in passing."

Natalie's eyes grew sad. "This should be a happy time," she said and for a brief moment succumbed to the sadness. Then she drew herself up and regained visible resolve. "It *is* a happy time. Come, I'll show you around. Then I want you to meet Carl."

Six

PRECONCEPTIONS LINGERED. Olivia had already seen that the Great House wasn't as large as she had imagined it to be, yet the interior startled her. Through all these months and so many pictures, she had envisioned room after room, alcove after alcove, sofa after settee after Louis XVI chair, with the ghosts of guests mingling, eating, talking, sleeping. What she saw in reality was smaller and simpler—exquisitely decorated, with designer furnishings and every modern convenience, but far more casual than formal.

Undaunted, she amended her thinking from grand and large to charming and small. There would be no indiscriminate galas in this place. Visitors would be carefully selected. Parties would be intimate.

The first floor consisted of a dining room and kitchen on one side and a living room on the other. Branching off the living room were a parlor and a den. "These were intially bedrooms," Natalie explained. "When the family grew, we added the second floor."

That second floor housed four bedrooms. The door to one was shut, but Natalie showed them the others, one more beautifully outfitted than the next, again in an inviting and livable way. The best, though, was yet to come. At one end of the hall was a narrow staircase. It led to an airy room that looked out from the back of the house over rolling vineyard-covered hills. It was Natalie's personal office, replete with a cat named Achmed.

"Achmed?" Tess echoed, heading straight for the cat.

"He's Persian. My vet thought he'd be a dignified addition to her office, but he wreaked havoc with the other animals. That's why I told you no pets. Bring a dog in here, and fur would fly. Achmed is a temperamental son-of-a-gun. Takes to you, though, Tess. Look at that."

Tess was on her knees, on eye level with the Persian, which sat straight and tall on a brocade footstool and didn't seem to mind at all the small stroking hand.

"He stays up here," Natalie said. "Doesn't mix with the hoi polloi down below. Achmed. The name seems to fit, don't you think?"

"I *do*," Tess said appreciatively.

"I call this my loft," Natalie told Olivia. "We'll be working here."

Olivia was as charmed with the setting as Tess was with the cat. Skylights and a computer were the only modern concessions. The desk was of dark wood, the two side chairs were upholstered wing-backs, the sofa was of thick velvet, and the walls were shelved with a vintage collection of books. The lamps were brass with aged shades. The carpet was faded and fringed. Even Achmed had an air of age.

Time stood still in this room. Olivia couldn't imagine a better place to write a tale of the past. The place even *smelled* old, in the richest possible sense. She easily could have stayed here for the rest of the afternoon.

But Natalie had other ideas. Assuring Tess that there would be more cat time later, she led them back to the second floor, down the hall, and off through a short corridor to the new wing. This, too, was smaller than what Olivia had envisioned. Rather than many rooms with a central gathering area, even a minikitchen, it was a mere three bedrooms built over the back patio. What these rooms lacked in size, though, they oozed in quaintness. They were simply but beautifully appointed—bed, easy chair, bureau, and dressing table in each—not too much, just enough. The window dressings were floral to match the comforters on the beds. The carpets were a solid color and plush.

One of the rooms stood alone. The other two were connected by a large bathroom. These were the two Natalie guided them toward.

"I want the blue one," Tess whispered excitedly, tipping her head back to eye Olivia through her glasses.

Olivia was so delighted that the child seemed pleased with Asquonset that she would have given her whichever room her little heart desired. She actually preferred the other room, herself. It was green, which was her favorite color, and it was slightly larger than the blue room. Best of all, there was a window seat, from which the view was breathtaking. Past the awning below, she saw the tail end of the back patio, bordered by vibrant-colored flower gardens and paths. She could see the spill of vineyards down the hill to the far woods and—the pièce de résistance—off in the distance, a hazy view of the ocean.

Forget Natalie's office. Olivia would have been content to spend the rest of the day on that window seat.

Again, Natalie had other ideas. She had arranged for the daughter of one of the office workers to take Tess exploring. The girl was thirteen, with a mass of long blonde curls, a halter top and jeans, and full smiles for Tess, who seemed immediately to respond. As soon as the two set off, Natalie directed Olivia back up to the loft.

She took a picture from the desk, one that

Olivia hadn't seen before. It was small and grainy, a black-and-white snapshot of a young boy resting against the edge of a horse-drawn cart filled with barrels. The boy wore a shirt that was dirty and thin, and overalls that were torn at the thigh, faded at the knee, and so lengthened at the shoulder straps that the bib reached only midchest. Even then, the pant legs were short enough to show dirty socks and worn leather shoes.

Olivia had lived through enough old photographs to guess that this one had been taken during the Depression. The clothes were the same, the bleak background, the boy's somber expression. He looked to be thirteen. He was probably ten. Hard times did that, she knew.

Then Natalie began to speak. Her voice was so clear, the flow of her words so smooth that Olivia could see the narrative of the book taking shape even then.

Have you ever tried to pin down your earliest memory? I've tried often over the years, because I wanted mine to be different. Sometimes I pretend that it is. Sometimes I remember being four years old, hearing the silence between my parents and feeling the tension. But I can't visualize an actual scene. I can't see myself standing in one particular spot or looking at one particular thing.

I should have been able to do that at four, even at three. You probably can. But the upheaval in our lives was so total in the days following Black Thursday that those earlier details were wiped out.

I repressed them. I did. The remembering was too painful. We had been rich. Suddenly we were poor. Any recollections I have of that early silence and tension are simply a reconstruction of what I later learned to be fact.

My earliest memory—the one that I can conjure up in living color, right down to the time, the weather, and the clothes I was wearing—took place when I was five, on the day when we moved to Asquonset.

"You were *five* when you came here?" Olivia asked.

"Yes. Five."

"Then *your* family was the one that owned Asquonset?"

Natalie smiled. "Ah. You thought I married into it. No, don't be embarrassed. You aren't alone. Alexander has always been the public face of Asquonset, so people assume that he was here first. Let it be the first of many misperceptions that my story will correct."

Another certainly had to do with financial

means. *We had been rich. Suddenly we were poor.* Even after working on those early pictures, Olivia hadn't put poverty into the tale. She was in the process of mentally shifting to a riches-to-rags-to-riches angle when Natalie went on.

Nowadays, moving from city to country is in vogue, but in November of 1930, in that tier of society whose underpinnings were tied to the stock market, it was a sign of failure.

My father had owned a bank. It was one of the many that collapsed after the crash. Could he have saved his? Oh, he tried. He sold our house in Newport. He sold the Pierce-Arrow. He even sold our family heirlooms. But the bank had issued too many loans to too many speculators. Besides, we had been buying on margin, too.

The losses caused by the crash were just too large. My father sold the house in New York, the car, even my mother's diamond ring, all to pay off debts so that we could start again free and clear.

Try to imagine his pain. He had failed people who had entrusted their money to him. Many of them had been personal friends. Some sold their houses and any possessions of value, as we had.

Some were seen on breadlines. Others suffered worse fates. I remember the hush that came over the dinner table, years later, when one name or another was mentioned. My parents had lost more than one friend in the days immediately before and after the crash, men who had chosen suicide over suffering the humiliation, the embarrassment, the pain of total ruin.

My father suffered all three. Not only had he failed his friends, but he had failed his family. We had had money, but it was gone. The farm was all that remained. We left the city in disgrace.

She stopped talking. Her expression was pained, her eyes faraway.

"And you were able to feel it?" Olivia asked softly.

Natalie was slow in answering, slow in returning from that place so long ago. "The disgrace? Yes. I felt it." It was in her voice even now, a self-consciousness that hadn't been there before. Her eyes didn't meet Olivia's.

"Did people *say* things to you?"

She studied her hands. "I don't know. I was either too young to understand or too young to remember. My brother never mentioned anything specific. Maybe I blotted it out."

"You had a brother?"

"Yes. Brad was four years older than me."

"Yet you inherited the vineyard."

"Brad opted out early on," Natalie said and grew silent again.

Olivia wanted to ask more, but she wasn't sure if this was the right time. Natalie had explicitly said curiosity was a must for the job. But at what was clearly a painful moment?

The silence felt right. She sensed that Natalie needed it. Indeed, after several minutes, the older woman returned to the photograph of the boy and seemed to find new strength.

My parents were terrified. They didn't say it. They didn't say much at all as they packed us up and moved us out, but looking back all these years later, I can imagine what they felt. Our world had radically changed. Life as we'd known it was done.

My brother, Brad, who was nine at the time, was the one who, much later, re-created for me the cold, dark November day when we left New York. We took the train to Providence as we had so many other times when we went to the house in Newport. Those other times, we had been headed for vacation, wearing new clothes, carrying valises crammed with more new clothes, and we were met at the train by our driver in the latest-model car. This time, our clothes were older, our valises and trunks filled with the last of our earthly possessions, and we passed up the first-class Pullman car in favor of coach. We were met in Providence by one of the few employees my father still had.

His name was Jeremiah Burke. My father had brought him from Ireland several years before to grow our potatoes.

The farm was my father's hobby back then. It was the place he escaped to when he wanted a break from the rest of his life. He had been known to return to New York with dirt under his nails, and he took pride in it. Hobby or not, he liked doing things well. Even in this, he was competitive.

Hence, Jeremiah Burke. Jeremiah not only knew about growing potatoes, but he knew about farm management. Within months of his arrival, my father put him in charge.

In addition to a lyrical brogue, Jeremiah brought with him from Ireland a wife and a child. The three of them had lived until then in the stone farmhouse that was about to become our home.

That drizzly November day, Jeremiah picked us up in the old work truck that he used on the farm. Though he had cleaned it as best he could, it still smelled of dirt. To us it was a foreign smell, a rough smell, adding one more unknown element to the fear we felt that day.

We piled our trunks in the back and ourselves in the front. In later years, my brother and I would automatically climb into the bed of the truck. On this day, though, as my brother told it, we were packed in the front, one child each on the lap of a parent, with Jeremiah at the wheel. If the crowding caused discomfort, we were too numb to feel it. Even my father, who had once been so gregarious, was dead quiet.

We headed south out of Providence. When the paved road ended, we jolted over rutted dirt roads, but I remember neither that nor our actual arrival at Asquonset. Brad said the place was dismal, and I'm sure it was. We were used to luxury. Asquonset was anything but.

"I cannot imagine that," Olivia chided. "You're being polite."

"No. Really. It's such a beautiful place."

"Now."

"Even the land. I imagine it would be beautiful without a single building on it."

Natalie smiled. "Good girl. I've chosen the right person. Your heart's in the right place. We just have to fine-tune your view of reality. I may not remember my very first view of this place, but I certainly do remember the ones after that. 'Beautiful' was not an adjective that I would have used to describe Asquonset back then."

The Burkes had moved into a smaller cottage on the property, leaving the stone farmhouse for us, and my father had done his best. Those pieces of furniture that we hadn't sold had been shipped ahead and were in place in the living room, kitchen, and bedrooms. Jeremiah's wife, Brida, had scrubbed the house and made it shine as much as a farmhouse built in the 1870s could shine, but it was as different as night and day from the home we had left in New York. As was the custom in the country, the ceilings were low so that the fire could more easily heat the damp, cold air, and we did have indoor plumbing. We were lucky in that. But the place was small, closed in, and dark, totally alone on its windy hill.

It was a metaphor for our life.

Natalie stopped talking. Her eyes were far-away as she moved her hand ever so lightly over the photograph.

"Who *is* this boy?" Olivia asked.

The older woman looked up with a start. It was a minute before she found herself and smiled. "This boy?" She raised the picture. "This boy is my very first distinct memory."

It was late afternoon on the day of our arrival in Asquonset. I was outside in fields that had yielded their crop of potatoes six weeks before. I'm not sure how I got there. I doubt my parents would have wanted me out in the rain. I suppose that they were unpacking at the house and didn't see me leave.

I must have been desperate to escape. Between their personal gloom and those low ceilings, I imagine that I felt choked.

The fields were bare, plowed clear of everything but rain and earth. I walked as far and as fast as I could, but I was frightened enough of the place to keep the farmhouse in sight. It was small and distant. But it was there.

I'll never forget it. I wore a little hat, just as I would have if I'd been in New York. It was made of felt and had a tiny turned-up rim and straps that went under the chin. It was no match for the rain. With each step my hair grew wetter, until it hung in sodden strands around my face. I was wearing T-strap shoes that had been white that morning. They had been scuffed during the trip from New York, but out there in the field, they were quickly covered with mud. I bent to wipe them clean. When I straightened, the hem of my coat had mud on it, too.

The coat and my dress were pale blue. They were the best of my old clothes that still fit. Horrified, I tried to brush the mud off, but the smear spread. The more I brushed, the worse it got. My stomach began to hurt. The sense of loss went far beyond my clothes.

Then I saw Carl.

She was lost in the snapshot, which she held now as though it were gold.

It took Olivia a minute to make the connection. *"This* is Carl?"

"It is," Natalie said with a contented sigh.

"He was *Jeremiah's* son?"

"Why the surprise?"

Why the surprise? The scenario Olivia had dreamed up was suddenly all wrong. "I just—just assumed that Carl was a newer acquaintance. I thought he was from somewhere else."

"Well, he was, if you count his being born in Ireland. But he was a toddler when his parents brought him here. He was Seamus then. Somewhere along the line, people started calling him Carl. He doesn't have any of the brogue that Jeremiah did."

Geography wasn't the half of it. Olivia was talking about social status. She had pictured Natalie marrying someone very upper crust. Not that she could say that without sounding like a snob, which, Lord knew, she wasn't. But this being a fantasy, she had imagined a prince.

"I pictured him as a longtime wine person," she said with some tact.

Natalie smiled a sweet smile. "Ah, but he is. He's more of a wine person than anyone else I've met in the last seventy years. Not that I knew it that first day. It was a while before I learned what was being grown on the far side of the hill. Remember, this was 1930. Prohibition was still in effect. We didn't talk about growing grapes or making wine, and we surely didn't talk about selling what we made. We weren't supposed to be doing what we did."

Olivia couldn't get over the idea that Carl Burke had been a hired hand. The more she looked at his picture, though, the more familiar he felt. She had seen his face before. It had been in some of the pictures she had restored. He had been a grown man then, but the eyes were the same. They were calm to the point of impassivity, feeling more familiar to Olivia with each minute that passed.

"What about that first memory?" she asked. "What did he say out there in the field?"

But Natalie had lowered the snapshot. Her eyes were on the door and had taken on a special light. Olivia followed her gaze. Recognition was instant.

Carl Burke was a good-looking boy who had grown into a good-looking man. He was approaching eighty now and had earned the right to be craggy and slouched. But he stood tall, and if being craggy meant having a shock of silver hair, a ruggedly handsome face, and an air of dignity, Olivia was all for it. She might have fallen in love with the man on sight herself, if he hadn't been taken already.

Natalie reached for his hand. "Carl, come meet Olivia." Seeming eminently pleased with herself, she drew him forward. "Carl Burke . . . Olivia Jones."

"Welcome," Carl said. His voice was quiet. Taken alone, it would have been dispassionate. Taken with the warmth in his eyes, it was—*yes*—kind and very definitely sincere. "I just met your daughter. She's a little sweetie."

"And Olivia just met your son," Natalie injected with pride.

Olivia frowned. "His son?"

"Simon. Downstairs in the hall."

Oh dear. Simon. The vineyard manager. The man with the midnight blue eyes. "He's the dark, silent type," Natalie had said with fondness. "Like his father."

Olivia had simply assumed that the Seebrings took pride in hiring families. Not having heard Simon's last name—and believing Carl to be royalty of sorts—she hadn't made a connection between the two men. Suddenly, though, it made perfect sense. It also explained Greg Seebring's remark about a Burke conspiracy to take over the vineyard.

Olivia saw the resemblance now as she looked at Carl. Father and son had the same quiet eyes. Granted, Carl's were warmer than Simon's, but neither man looked sly.

Of course, Olivia had thought Ted was interesting. She had thought Jared was responsible, and that anyone who could cook as well as Peter had a homing instinct. She had been wrong on all counts. She might well be on this one too.

"I'm sorry," she told Carl awkwardly. "I hadn't realized that Simon belonged to you. I guess I'm not too quick on the uptake today."

He brushed aside her apology. "Did he show you around outside?"

Natalie answered. "He didn't have time. He was heading for Providence. He thinks we have a problem with mold."

Carl made a frustrated sound. "The weather's ripe for it." He turned to Olivia. "Farming is never easy." He gestured toward the door. "I brought your bags over to the wing. Didn't know which went in which room, though."

Olivia had been planning to get their luggage herself. "You didn't have to do that."

"Yes, I did. We want you here. I'm doing my part to get you securely installed before anything changes your mind." He said the last with an odd gravity and turned to Natalie. "We lost Paolo. He's leaving with Marie." Both names were spoken beautifully, with just the hint of an accent that didn't seem Irish at all.

Natalie hung her head. After a minute, with a resigned sigh, she told Olivia, "An operation like ours requires a fair amount of large equipment. In addition to helping out Simon, Paolo is our in-house mechanic—*was* our in-house mechanic. I wasn't joking when I mentioned a hornet's nest. We're having something of a house revolt here."

Olivia looked from one face to the other. "All because of the *wedding?*"

Natalie moved closer to Carl. Their hands met, linked, found an unobtrusive spot behind Natalie's back, but Olivia noticed. Any romantic would. It was a sweet gesture, the sign of a sharing of strength, and all the more meaningful for its privacy. Olivia was touched.

"It isn't only the wedding," Natalie said. "It's

Al's death. He courted these people. He gave them flowers on their birthdays and handed out Christmas bonuses. Me, I was the taskmaster. I told them what needed to be done. If a floor was mopped once and felt sticky, I had it mopped again. If the silver had tarnish on its back side, I wanted it repolished. I've never been one to like leaving a job half done. Unfortunately, that ruffles feathers sometimes. So Alexander was the one who did the stroking. He applied salve after I cracked the whip. He was the good guy, I was the bad guy. They felt that they lost their best friend when he died."

"And now she's marrying me," Carl picked up. "Some of them feel betrayed."

"They don't understand what we feel," Natalie told him.

"Well, they *should*," he insisted with more fire than Olivia had yet seen. "These people aren't strangers to affairs of the heart. Paolo was mooning over Marie for twelve years before she took notice, and Anne Marie, the receptionist in the business office, just announced that once her divorce is final, she's marrying her high school sweetheart from thirty years back."

Natalie's eyes widened. "Is she leaving, too?"

"No, but she could be sticking up for us more than she is—not that it would help much, what with the business office being apart from the rest."

Natalie explained to Olivia, "Asquonset has three divisions. The vineyard produces the grapes.

The winery turns the grapes into wine. The corporate staff gets the wine into restaurants and stores. Since the corporate offices are housed way over on the far side of our land, the staff there is isolated." She took a tired breath. "Our accountant just left, but we saw that coming. He was a longtime friend of my late husband and has been threatening to retire for years. The others on the corporate side are newer and younger. They live in local towns and work nine to five, with four weeks' paid vacation a year, health care, retirement funds, and so on. They won't leave. Nor will anyone at the winery. Success begets loyalty, and we've been very successful. Our wine maker has built a name for himself in viticultural circles in part because of the freedom and money we give him to work with. So *he* won't leave."

"The problem," Carl picked up, "is with employees who've been here awhile. Some, like the accountant, are reaching retirement age and would be leaving anyway. Others not so. But it has to do with what Nat said before. They loved Alexander. He was the guy who doled out everything good. If you were to ask them, they'd say he was the one who hired them in the first place."

Natalie scowled. "He did no such thing. I advertised, I interviewed, I hired."

Carl touched her cheek and said a soft, "We're aware of that. They aren't."

She was that easily diffused. Letting out a

breath, she said, "Yes. The problem in a nutshell." Her eyes found Olivia's. "There was never cause to make it clear. My husband needed the stature more than I did, so I let him have it. Unfortunately, that's backfiring on me now. They all saw Alexander as father of the vineyard. They loved him. They felt loyalty to him. That loyalty goes on. Like my children, they're offended that I'm remarrying so soon."

Carl added a quiet but potent, "And so low."

"Well, they are *ignorant,*" Natalie declared.

"Ignorant or not, they're leaving us in the lurch."

Olivia asked, "How many have left?"

"Paolo's leaving brings it to four," Natalie said.

"Four, out of how many in all?"

"Thirteen. The vineyard operation has Simon, his assistant, a general field hand, and Paolo. We have two full-time people at the winery—the wine maker and his assistant. There are four in the office—an accountant, a marketing director, a sales administrator, and a receptionist. And three here at the house—a maid, a cook, and a groundskeeper. The field hand went first. He'd been nursing a grudge against Carl since Carl brought in a woman to a position above him."

"The grudge worsened when Simon took over as manager and the field hand stayed a field hand, instead of moving up," Carl said.

Natalie resumed the count. "Soon after that, we lost the accountant. Now Marie and Paolo." She raised wary eyes to Carl. "Do we expect more?"

"Joaquin is grumbling." Again spoken with style, in this case a gently lyrical Wa-*keen*.

"Joaquin," Olivia echoed, marveling at the beauty of the names.

Natalie's smile held surprise. "You did that *well*. The name is Portuguese. Our staff has always been heavily Portuguese, what with their numbers being so large, so close by, just over the Massachusetts line. Joaquin is the groundskeeper, but he's truly a Jack of all trades. His wife is our cook." She grew fierce. "Carl, *keep* him. If he goes, Madalena goes. I can't do without my cook, not right before the wedding." Suddenly defiant, she drew herself up and returned to Olivia. "But it's their loss. With or without them, Asquonset is solid. We have Carl to thank for that."

Carl's cheeks grew ruddy. "Come on, Nat."

"Carl and Simon," she amended, no less vehement for splitting the credit. "The vines are stronger every year. Production is up. The grapes are more balanced. Our wines are steadily gaining recognition." She sent Carl another wary look. "Is Simon right? Is there a problem with the Pinot Noir?"

"There may be."

"Then he isn't just running away?"

"Oh, he is," Carl granted with a small smile. "But he may have a valid excuse."

Olivia was wondering what the big man was running from when Natalie faced her with a flourish. "There you have it. Our staff is depleted, the vineyard is wet, and my children are sure to make more trouble before the summer's out. You, my dear, are not only my memoirist, you're my personal buffer. Are you up for it, Olivia Jones?"

WAS OLIVIA UP FOR IT? Was she ever. She wanted nothing more than to return to Natalie's first distinct memory, anxious to get the memoir fully launched. But Natalie had to see about hiring a new maid, not to mention giving a pep talk to Madalena and Joaquin.

So Olivia spent the rest of the afternoon unpacking. She emptied Tess's bags and then her own, filling closets and drawers with what they had brought, but their new clothes were nowhere near as exciting as the shirts Natalie had pulled from a carton before sending her off. Half were T-shirts, half were polo shirts, half in Olivia's size, half in Tess's. Some were burgundy with ivory print, some the reverse. All had the vineyard's logo and name.

Slipping one on with her shorts, Olivia looked in the mirror. She rolled the sleeves and adjusted the blousing at the waist. Leaning closer, she finger-combed her short hair and was about to pinch color into her cheeks when she realized that it was already there. She stared at herself a minute longer. Short hair and all, she didn't look bad.

Wearing the T-shirt with pride, she went off in search of Tess.

Seven

SUSANNE WAS UP AT DAWN, which was early indeed in June. She was baking brioche for breakfast, or so she reasoned at four-thirty, as she slipped into a robe and crept out of the bedroom, leaving her husband in a deep, jet-lagged sleep.

He had returned the night before from five days of nonstop meetings on the West Coast. In the hope that they would have dinner together, Susanne had bought the fixings for his favorite veal dish. Then the plane was two hours late taking off, and it was after ten before he walked in the door. He did try to eat, but she would have been blind not to see that he was doing it only to please her. Taking pity on him, she sent him into the den, where he sat with his favorite symphony on the stereo, for a few hours of decompression.

Susanne had sat with him until her eyes started to close. She didn't know what time he'd come to bed, only that he was there when she had woken for the first time, at two.

In the kitchen now, she heated milk, butter, and sugar, added yeast, eggs, and flour, kneaded the dough, and set it aside. She split a fresh pineapple, sliced its fruit, and returned it to the shell in an artful arrangement that included cantaloupe, kiwi, and banana. She whipped up Mark's favorite sour-cream coffee cake, tossing in blueberries and raisins for good measure.

She punched the brioche dough down. While it rose again, she cooked fresh asparagus, washed arugula, and beat eggs for a frittata. She arranged plates, silverware, mugs, linen napkins, and flowers on linen place mats at the kitchen's granite island. She rearranged the flowers once, then again.

She formed the brioche dough into individual portions and fit each into its own mold. She ground fresh coffee. Changing her mind about the linen place mats, she exchanged them with woven ones and added raffia ties to the napkins. She scrubbed her work counter, washed and dried everything in the sink, and then scrubbed that, too. She removed the coffee cake from the oven and put in the brioche.

She brought in the morning paper, read as much of it as she wanted in the fifteen minutes that it took to drink a cup of coffee. She wiped out the refrigerator until the brioche was done, brushed her hair and teeth, washed and moisturized her face, then sat at the granite island and waited for Mark to wake up.

By the time he joined her, it was after nine. She had been up for five hours and felt it. He, on the other hand, looked refreshed, sleep-mussed but handsome. Neither thinning gray hair nor ten extra pounds around his middle could change that. It struck her, amidst all else on her mind, how much she had missed him and how glad she was to have him home.

He gave her a long hug that said the feeling was mutual. "Mmmm. I don't know which smells better, you or whatever that is you're baking."

"It's either Dior or brioche," she said against his raspy jaw. "Take your pick."

"I'll take Dior and a cup of coffee for now." Loosening his arms, he drew back only enough to search her face. "You were up early."

"I tried not to wake you."

"You didn't, but I'm smelling more than perfume and brioche. From the looks of this kitchen, you've done a day's work already. I'm afraid I won't be able to eat half of what you've cooked. Couldn't sleep?"

She gave a diffident shrug.

"Bad dreams?" he asked.

"If only they were dreams."

"Uh-oh. Still Natalie? I thought you were going to talk with her again."

"She won't take my calls."

He arched a brow but remained wisely silent.

"Okay," Susanne confessed, "so I said things I shouldn't have that first time, but what did she expect, popping this marriage on me that way?"

"You told me that she'd been mentioning Carl a lot before that."

"Mentioning Carl. Not mentioning love or romance, and certainly not mentioning marriage. Marriage was totally out of the blue. I'm her daughter. I was hurt."

"Did you tell her that?"

Susanne sighed. "Not the way I should have, but when I call now, someone else always answers the phone. She's hired a new assistant who is disgustingly bouncy."

"A corporate assistant?"

"A personal one," she said and added a drawled, "Apparently, her social life is that busy."

Mark gave a soft meow.

Susanne dropped the drawl, though she wasn't apologizing. "Marie is leaving, and she says she isn't the only one. So part of me is pleased that I'm not alone in being upset by this marriage. The other part feels that the Asquonset I know is . . . is slipping away."

"You've always claimed not to care," he reminded her gently.

"I don't. I just feel bad for Dad."

"More than he can feel himself. He's dead, Susanne."

"Yes. He is. It's like Natalie was just waiting for that."

"I don't think so. She was a loyal wife."

"Maybe she wasn't. I never thought she'd re-marry. Maybe I don't know about the other, either."

"You do know," Mark chided.

Yes, Susanne supposed that she did. But that didn't forgive what Natalie was doing now. "She bided her time until her husband died and not a minute longer." She felt a moment's satisfaction when Mark didn't deny it.

But immediately he said, "Why don't you take a drive up?"

Her satisfaction faded. "To Asquonset? I can't. I have things to do here."

"What things?" he asked, holding her gaze.

She didn't answer. None of what she had to do was important—they both knew that. She was at a crossroads in her life and didn't know what path to take, but going home—going back—was at the very bottom of the list.

"Mother doesn't want me there," she reasoned. "We'll only fight."

"Maybe you'll talk."

"Mother talk? Mother *talk?*"

"Well, you two have to communicate *somehow* before the wedding."

"Why? I'm not going."

His hands unlocked and slipped away. Moving around her, he helped himself to coffee.

Cupping the mug, he leaned back against the counter. "I think that would be a mistake."

"Greg isn't going."

"A double mistake, then. She's your mother. Boycotting her wedding will cause a permanent rift."

"The wedding is the thing causing the rift."

He didn't answer, just stood there nursing his coffee. Finally he asked, "How old is Natalie?"

"Seventy-six."

"How old do you think she'll live to be?"

The question startled Susanne. "*I* can't answer that."

"Does longevity run in her family? Heart disease? Cancer?"

"Why are you asking this?"

"Because Natalie is approaching that age where she may be wondering how much time she has left. She may be thinking that she can't afford to do things that people in their thirties, forties, or even fifties consider 'proper.' "

"You *condone* this marriage?"

"No, but I can't condemn it, either. She's coming from a different place from you and me."

Susanne folded her arms. "She's in good health. She'll live another twenty years. At *least.*"

"Spoken by the daughter who wants that to be so, but what's the point for you, if you cut yourself off from her?"

"She's the one doing the cutting. She's making a choice."

"Seems to me you're the one making the choice. *She* wants her children and grandchildren in her life. That's what the invitation was about."

"But . . . an *invitation,* Mark?"

He let out a long breath. Setting his mug on the counter, he approached her and stroked her arms. "She tried to tell you, but couldn't quite get it out. Sweetheart, that's her way. It always has been. She's more formal about things than you are, just as you're more formal about things than *our* daughter is. Maybe it's generational. Maybe it isn't. Either you can condemn her and live with the consequences of that, or you can swallow your pride and drive on up there. You do have the time, Susanne . . ."

GREG WAS UP nearly as early as Susanne, watching daylight steal over Woodley Park from the small balcony off his bedroom. One after another, his neighbors' rooftops were touched by pale gold. The paleness would deepen in no time. Washington was in for another hot day. He could feel the humidity even now. It was thick, slowing everything down.

Or so he explained standing there for as long as he did. If life moved at its normal pace, he would be on his way to work. He was behind. He had been behind for three weeks now. His e-mail had piled up unanswered. Same with phone messages. His desk was covered with proposals to study, findings to analyze, correspondence to handle.

He could delegate—that was what his staff was for—but no one at the office could help him here at home, not with what he needed to do.

The place was neat and clean. He had done the laundry the night before, had folded it and put it away. Now he made the bed. He made breakfast. He read the paper cover to cover and gave his laptop a distracted glance, thinking all the while that he ought to shower and dress.

Instead, he remained in his boxer shorts, wandering from room to room, checking his watch. At nine he put in a call to Akron. His mother-in-law answered, just as she had each of the other times he'd called.

"Hi, Sybil. Is Jill around?"

There was a pause, then a cautious, "She's in the other room, but I'm not sure she wants to talk."

"She's my wife. She *has* to talk."

The line was silent.

"Sybil?"

"Yes."

He ran a hand around the back of his neck, hung his head, and sighed. "Okay. I was upset last time I called. I probably shouldn't have been so . . ."

"Imperious?"

"Yes."

Jill's mother was clearly skeptical. "And you feel differently now?"

Yes, he felt differently. He had run out of anger. What was left was harder to name. It wasn't anything he was used to feeling. "I miss Jill."

The tone of his voice must have conveyed something he couldn't put into words, because Sybil finally said quietly, "Hold on."

He held. And held. He imagined an argument going on in the other room. Jill really didn't want to take his call. He wasn't sure where that left them.

"Hi, Greg," she said in a chilly voice. "What's up?"

"You tell me," he said, then caught himself and added a more contrite, "Forget that. I want to apologize. I shouldn't have shouted at you the way I did last time."

"You're right."

"I was angry."

"That wasn't what I needed."

"I know." He was wandering again, holding the cordless phone. For a small house, the place seemed monstrous. Jill was at the same time everywhere and nowhere. "I miss you," he said. It had worked with Sybil. He wanted it to work with Jill.

It did, but in a very different way. She let loose. "Well, now you know how I've been feeling for the past five years. You run all around the country—

gone for days at a time—building the business, you say, but after a while that sucks, Greg. Marriage is supposed to be about you and me. There's supposed to be an *us* in it, only there isn't in ours. Our lives are about you—you and your business, you and your clients, you and your friends. There's always something else you have to do, other than me. Why in the world did you ever get *married?*"

Strange. He had never asked himself that question. Not once. Not once in five years had he regretted marrying Jill. That was such a basic fact of his life that he found her remark to be offensive. "I could ask you the same question," he shot back. "What kind of woman runs home to her mother at the first problem?"

"The kind who can't get through to you any other way."

"You're my wife. You should be here."

"Because I'm your wife? No. I should be there because we love each other."

"We *do.*"

"You can't even define what love is!"

He squeezed his eyes shut, rubbed the bridge of his nose, and swore softly. "Come on, Jill. Let's not go there again."

"I *need* to go there. Saying the words just isn't enough. I need to know what they mean."

She would. She was a woman. But he was a man, and his mind grew unfocused when confronted with words like "love" and "soul" and "eternity."

But possession was nine-tenths of the law. She was his wife. She had taken vows. "Fine," he said. "Come back, and we'll talk."

She didn't respond.

"Jill."

"I don't want to come back. I know what'll happen. One look at you and I'll cave right in."

He dared a small smile. "Because you do love me."

"Yes. I've never denied that. But it doesn't mean that I want to stay married to you. I can't live this way, Greg. It's too lonely."

Lonely. That felt familiar. Perhaps he was feeling that, too. "Come back, babe," he said in a voice that was heavy with emotion. "Come back and we'll talk."

She said nothing.

"Jill?"

"I'll let you know."

Eight

OLIVIA AWOKE NEARLY AS EARLY as Susanne and Greg, but while Susanne's sleep was disturbed by annoyance and Greg's by loneliness, Olivia's was broken by bliss. Dawn found her on the window seat in her bedroom, delighted to be at Asquonset.

In the west, the sky was the color of eggplant. In the east, it was a paler, softer mauve. The occasional cloud added texture and depth, more purple to the west, more pink to the east. A blanket of fog lay on the lowlands farthest from the house. Olivia fancied that the vines in that part of the vineyard were stealing a last few winks before facing the work of the day.

And that work? Making grapes. It had been the major point of discussion at dinner the evening before.

Dinner had been in the dining room, a welcome feast of a roast duck served on fine china by the husband of the cook. Only Natalie and Carl, Olivia and Tess had been there, a small, intimate group— a one-step-removed-from-family group. Olivia found it such fun to pretend.

Olivia and Tess had overdressed, of course. They had worn long skirts, bandeaux, and sandals—all new. Natalie and Carl had on the same clothes they had worn that afternoon, and though they had gone overboard telling Olivia and Tess how nice they looked, Olivia took it as their first lesson of the evening about Asquonset life. It was casual, unpretentious, and focused on work.

The second had to do with wine. It was served, but only sparsely. No one at Asquonset really drank; they merely tasted. This night's sampling was of a three-year-old Estate Riesling, a sweet white wine that went well with duck. There was sniffing, gentle swirling, then sniffing again as the bouquet was released. Even Tess took part in the ritual, though her wineglass was filled with Asquonset Little Bunches, a snappily labeled grape juice that was actually one of the vineyard's biggest sellers.

The third lesson concerned the weather. Carl talked about it at length, and this was no small talk. The weather could make or break a vintage, and the weather this season had been far from optimal. Spring had come late and been too wet. Still, the vines had bloomed, and what Carl called, with some reverence, the "grape set" looked good. But the weather remained iffy. They needed sun more than one day out of four—if not, he explained, the year's yield wouldn't ripen and grow sweet.

Holding Tess's hand, squeezing it now and again to keep her focused, Olivia had listened closely to every word. She had followed as best she could the talk about sugar and acid, about Brix levels, prophylactic spraying, and predatory beetles. Greater understanding would come this morning—Natalie was giving them a tour of the vineyard.

In anticipation of that, Olivia already had her camera loaded and ready. But she couldn't wait. On impulse, she opened the casement window and carefully removed the screen. Suddenly the morning air entered unhampered, cool and moist, fresh, sweet. It should have chilled her—she wore only a light nightshirt—but instead she was invigorated.

Taking up the camera, she photographed the sky, varying her settings to make sure she got the color and the clouds. She photographed that blanket of fog, which was lifting and thinning even as she watched. She photographed the vineyards below as, minute by minute, dawn embraced the vines. She photographed the patio beneath her window, where wrought-iron furniture was artfully placed and peonies were still damp with dew.

She was like a child in a penny-candy store, and the tempation was simply too great. Tiptoeing through the connecting bathroom, she peeked in at Tess. The child was sleeping soundly on a mound of pale blue linen, her face nearly buried in a jumble of hair. Olivia had watched her sleep often enough to know that she would be out for a while still.

Closing the door carefully, she crept out to the carpeted hall and slipped down the narrow staircase that led to the outside directly from their wing of the house. *Not that I expect a fire,* Natalie had assured them when she showed them where it was, but it served Olivia's present purpose well.

Only after she turned the handle and had the door ajar did she freeze, wondering if the house was alarmed. Most everything in Cambridge was, as was just about everything in most *every* city in which she had lived.

The thought of waking the entire house gave her a moment's pause. She would feel like a total fool.

But all was quiet. There was no alarm. The door opened without a squeak.

Heart pounding with excitement, she slipped out onto the patio. The flagstone was cool and damp, but the effect was bracing. Clearing the awning, she crossed to the edge of the stonework and stood, taking in the view, for a good ten minutes. The camera hung idly from her shoulder while her eye captured images as precious as any she might capture on film.

In time, she raised the camera. The view

through the lens, however, wasn't as whole as the one in real life. The camera couldn't capture the sound of birds waking up to the new day. It couldn't capture the crystal stillness of a dewy vineyard, or the gentle movement of clouds, or the smell of lilacs and damp earth, or the sound of a distant foghorn.

Enchanted, she returned the camera strap to her shoulder and went down the stone path that led away from the house. Low-growing greens framed it—a nubby tableau of juniper, cypress, and yew. Eventually they gave way to grass and the open space so precious to the vines, space that they needed to breathe. She had heard enough the night before to understand why.

Putting her shoulders back, she lifted her head, laced her fingers behind her, and filled her lungs with the morning air. In that instant, she felt strong. She felt confident that she could do Natalie's job. She felt proud of herself for having gotten herself and Tess to such an incredible place. She felt defiance toward all those who had given up on her in the past. She felt fresh and renewed.

"That's quite an outfit."

She turned with a start. Simon stood behind her, holding a steaming mug. His hair was damp, newly washed, but his beard was an even darker shadow than it had been, and his eyes matched. Or maybe it was just an effect. Perhaps the last trace of night obscured color. Or maybe it was the tight muscle of his upper arm, bare where his sleeves were torn out. Or those heavy work boots. Whatever, he looked menacing.

But Olivia wasn't being menaced out of her Eden. Nor was she playing the coy maiden. She had been caught outdoors in a perfectly respectable nightshirt. There was no harm in that.

She stood her ground. "You're not supposed to be here."

"I work here," he said with what was either a small smile or a twitch. "I live here."

She knew that was not exactly true. He had a place of his own several acres over, though Natalie did say that he was in and out of the Great House all the time.

"I meant," Olivia clarified her statement, "that you're not supposed to be up this early."

Those dark eyes didn't blink. "I'm always up this early. This is the best time of day to work."

"In the vineyard?"

"Sometimes. Today, in the office. I have e-mail to send. I need advice."

"About mold?"

"Fungus. Yes."

"It was confirmed, then?"

He nodded. "No surprise there. The season's been cool and wet. We need more sun."

"Looks like you'll get it today," Olivia said with a glance at the glimmer of gold that was starting to touch the tops of the trees.

He shrugged in a way that said maybe yes, maybe no, and took a sip of his coffee. His eyes held hers over the mug, which was a chunky ceramic thing that she imagined was his and his alone. He lowered it, holding it easily in one large hand.

Olivia would have gone inside to dress if he hadn't been blocking the way. She kept waiting for him to move on, but he continued to stand there, just where the path to the patio began, looking big and very male, with his weight on one lean hip and his eyes on hers. Well, she wasn't looking away. She refused to. If the game was about who would blink first, she could play as well as he.

Finally she won. After a long minute, his eyes moved off.

She felt oddly deflated. "Is something wrong?" she asked.

Gazing out at a distant point, he drank more of his coffee. Then he looked back. "That depends on you. If you're here for more than Natalie's project, there's definitely something wrong."

Olivia was indeed there for more than Natalie's project. She was there for the money, the sun, the fun, the escape, the possibility of finding a family connection. But Simon couldn't possibly know any of that.

"I'm sorry," she said. "I don't follow."

"If you're here to find a husband, you're barking up the wrong tree."

Olivia's brows rose. She nearly laughed, he

was so far off the mark. "A *husband*. If I wanted *that,* I'd be in a place full of people. Sorry. No. That's not why I'm here."

He didn't relent. "Natalie fancies herself a matchmaker. She wants to see me married."

Olivia had been slow in making the connection. Appalled now, she flattened a hand on her chest. "You think she's . . ." She wagged a finger between them.

"Yeah, I think she's . . ." He mimicked the motion.

"Oh. No. Definitely not." She gestured to that effect with both hands. "Natalie wouldn't do that. I'm not the kind of person people think about that way." She was thin and pale. She had a ten-year-old child, a history of romantic defeat, and hair that was too short and spiky to be the least bit alluring. Feeling self-conscious about all of it, she grew defensive. "Natalie has good reason to want me here, but it has nothing to do with you. Besides, you're not my type." She liked his legs, but she was done falling for a single feature. Nice legs did *not* a relationship make. Everything about Simon Burke was hard. "Abso*lute*ly not my type. And what's wrong with you that you can't find someone yourself?" It was not something she would have asked if he had been ugly or weird, but even above the legs, he was handsome in his way. Hard, but handsome.

"I'm not interested."

It was a moment before his remark registered. Then she blurted an involuntary, "Oh dear." She might have guessed it. "I'm sorry." Wasn't it often the case with the best-looking men?

He shot her a disparaging look, but it quickly yielded to something so lacking in emotion as to be frightening. "I was married. I loved my wife. She and our daughter died in a freak accident while they were sailing."

Olivia caught a breath and reversed her thoughts. She hadn't expected that. "How *awful*. I'm *so* sorry."

"Being sorry doesn't bring them back." His voice was flat. He wasn't criticizing her, but simply stating a fact. "Not a day goes by when I don't think of them."

"How long ago did it happen?"

"Four years."

"What were their names?"

"My wife was Laura."

"And your daughter?"

One eye flinched, the smallest sign of pain. "Does it matter?"

"Yes." Olivia was an expert at making up stories, but if the facts were there, she wanted them. She wanted names to put with faces when she thought about Simon.

"Liana."

She allowed herself to breathe. "Laura and Liana. Very beautiful."

"Yes."

"How old was Liana?"

"Six when she died." His eyes held accusation. "That would make your daughter just about the age mine would have been, had she lived."

Olivia couldn't imagine losing Tess. Couldn't *imagine* it. She knew also that if she were Simon, she would feel *excruciating* pain seeing Tess. "And *there*," she declared, "is ample proof that Natalie did not bring me here because of you. The coincidence is too much. She wouldn't have knowingly done that. It's too cruel."

"Cruel things can be done with the best of intentions."

"Not this time," Olivia insisted. "I'm here to work." She needed to believe that Natalie had picked her for her love of the past and the job she had done for Otis. Natalie hadn't asked about her history with men, which she would surely have done prior to fixing her up with her stepson-to-be. She hadn't even asked for a picture. "Do I look like Laura?"

"Not in the least."

"I rest my case."

He snorted. *"Make* your case, is more like it. She didn't *dare* get someone who looked like Laura."

Olivia had no idea what Laura had looked like, but in that instant she felt ugly by comparison. A wall came up. "Listen, this is all beside the point.

Even if you were interested, I'm not. I have challenges enough in my life right now, thank you."

"Good. Just so we understand each other."

"We do. Perfectly."

"As long as everything's out on the table."

"It is." But it wasn't, of course. She kept thinking about his wife and daughter, about the sudden horrific loss. "Were you with them when it happened?"

He didn't pretend not to follow. "No."

She wondered if he regretted that. "Could you have saved them if you were?"

"No."

"Was Laura a local girl? Someone you grew up with?" His childhood sweetheart? The one he had waited years for? The one he had built dreams upon? The only one he had ever envisioned marrying?

He looked suddenly annoyed. "Is there a point to these questions?"

"Just curiosity. How can you stay here after all that? Isn't it too painful?"

His annoyance faded as quickly as it had come. His eyes went toward the ocean. It wasn't visible from this spot, nor was there an echo of surf, but they both knew it was there.

"If it were me," Olivia said, "I'd go somewhere totally different." It was something she had done more than once, picking up and leaving places that didn't work for her anymore. The seven years she had spent in Cambridge was a record. She was definitely her mother's daughter.

And apparently, Simon was his father's son. "I've lived here all my life," he said. "I can't leave. The vineyard is who I am."

"There are other vineyards."

"Not like this one." He turned to leave, sparing her a final, disdainful glance. "If you learn anything this summer, let it be that."

SIMON RETURNED TO THE HOUSE to make himself breakfast as he always did, alone and in silence. Laura had loved the early morning silence, too. She had filled it with her appreciation of the dawn and of him, and he had never once, through all that stillness, felt alone. Now, and for the past four years, he had felt nothing but alone. Still, he treasured the silence.

This morning, though, he felt unsettled and not particularly hungry. So he refilled his mug with coffee and, with shaggy Buck in tow, set off for the shed.

The shed. It was an unassuming name for what was actually an impressive place, albeit in his biased opinion. Located on an open piece of land to the east of the Great House, it was large. What had housed a single tractor when Simon's grandfather had come to Asquonset in the 1920s was now four times that size and held not only a tractor but a hedger, a sprayer, a ripper, and miscellaneous small equipment. Moreover, with its long shingled walls and double-hung windows, it was more refined than a shed. What clinched it, though, was the second story. It had been added six years before, one of Carl's final dictates as vineyard manager. Under a gabled roof reminiscent of the Great House's, it now housed Simon's office.

That was where he headed. Setting the coffee mug on the desk, he fed the cat a handful of treats while he booted up the computer, then he read through his e-mail. There was plenty of it. He might have become something of a social hermit in the last four years, but he had friends in the viticultural world, colleagues with whom he was regularly in touch. Many were from his years at Cornell, now teaching at other universities and working at other vineyards. Others were contacts he had made at government agricultural agencies. Rarely did a week go by, for instance, when he wasn't in touch with the research station in Geneva, New York. He wanted to be on top of the latest thinking.

Grape growing was far from an exact science. There were too many variables. From vintage to vintage, grapes were like snowflakes—no two were ever alike. That factor made it interesting, made it *challenging,* particularly in Rhode Island. Grape growing here was different from what it was like in other parts of the world. The soil was different. The weather was different. There were also fewer vineyards here and, therefore, fewer colleagues with whom to compare notes.

At his computer now, with Buck rubbing against his leg, Simon weighed the advice offered by half a dozen friends in the field on battling *Botrytis cinerea*. It was one of the most common of the fungi that appeared in humid microclimates such as Asquonset's, and he had hoped for a consensus. But the suggestions ranged all the way from doing aggressive spraying to doing nothing at all.

Kicking back in his chair, he retrieved his coffee and stared out the window. From this height, he had as beautiful a view of the vineyard as any, but his eye went to the horizon, where a wavy line of gray marked the ocean. His chest tightened. His girls had breathed their last out there. It was a thought as dark as the clouds moving in. Clouds were the last thing he needed. The grapes finally were starting to dry, but the early morning sun wasn't anywhere near as strong as what it would be at midday, and from the look of those clouds, it would be raining by then. He didn't need the National Weather Service to tell him that.

He weighed his choices. He could apply another coat of sulfur dust, but he had done a routine spraying just the week before. Too much and the wine made from these grapes would smell foul. On the other hand, if he did nothing and the rot spread, he might lose the whole block.

No. Doing nothing wasn't an option.

What he really wanted to do was to ask his father. Even without a drop of formal education, Carl was the most knowledgeable person in Simon's circle of friends. He had read nearly everything worth reading about grape growing, and even now attended conferences when Simon backed out. Jeremiah Burke might have watched over the first grapes at Asquonset, but it was Carl who had put the place on the map. He understood why some grapes grew well here and some didn't, and had cultivated the former. He had instituted the trellis system that Asquonset still used, and was one of the first on the East Coast to tout integrated pest management as the most ecologically sound method of pest control. In his years at the helm, he had produced one remarkable vintage after another.

Carl would know what to do now. He was definitely the one to call.

But he was probably still sleeping. Probably sleeping with Natalie. She wouldn't let him formally move into the Great House until the wedding, but Simon had seen Carl slipping out a side door on more than one foggy dawn.

But hey, Simon wasn't finding fault. Carl had paid his dues. He deserved this pleasure. Besides, if sleeping with Natalie—if *marrying* her—lengthened Carl's life, Simon was the beneficiary. He wasn't ready for another loss so soon.

Four years. His chest tightened again. He rubbed the pain away with the flat of his hand.

Draining the last of his coffee, he set down the mug and came out of his chair. "Don't get up," he told the cat and stepped over its plump body. At the foot of the stairs he left a note on the large chalkboard for Donna Gomez, his assistant manager and—frighteningly—now his only other staff member. He was still reeling from the losses. Losing Paolo would be especially painful. He had liked Paolo. The man hadn't needed Simon looking over his shoulder. He knew grapes.

But it was done. Hours of trying to change the man's mind hadn't worked. He was gone, and Simon would survive.

The grapes were something else. Whether they lived to swell and sweeten was now entirely up to him. Actually, that wasn't true. It was up to God, but that thought gave Simon no solace at all. God could be cruel. It was up to Simon to do what a mere mortal could to thwart any malice that might be aimed at his grapes.

Heading for the Cabernet block, he began at the first of the forty rows and studied the tiny bunches of hard little peas that hopefully would grow into grapes. When he spotted upper leaves that threatened to block the sun, he gently worked them around the trellis. When he spotted lower leaves posing the same threat, he carefully removed them. There were no rules here. If he picked too few, the leaf canopy would shade the grapes and prevent them from getting the sun they needed to ripen. But leaves were crucial for photosynthesis, which turned carbon dioxide into sugar. If he picked too many, the sweetness of the grapes would be at risk. How many he picked and where depended on the variety of grape, its location on the vine, and the weather. It was strictly a judgment call on his part

Moving from one vine to the next now, Simon made that call gladly. He had been hand-leafing for as long as he could remember, and he loved the process. There was a rhythm to it, an art. The finished product had to feel right. It was an instinctive thing.

This morning he slipped easily into the rhythm, as much to escape the unsettled feeling in the pit of his stomach as to help the grapes. His boots anchored him in the moist soil. The creaking of the vines had a calming effect.

He didn't look at his watch as the morning progressed, didn't look at the thickening clouds, but worked his way slowly down one row and up the next. Buck materialized at one point, sat down, and watched. When Simon turned a corner into a new row, the cat simply crossed underneath. Simon found him good company, silent and undemanding.

Other than a brief pause when Donna tracked him down, Simon kept his mind on his work and his eye on the vines. One minute he was hunkering down, working in the area of the grapes, the next he was standing to train the vine around the first of three trellis wires. The topmost of the leaves were barely chest-high to him now. In another two months, they would be eye-high and on the upper-most of the wires.

He picked off a low leaf that grew just above a cluster of nascent grapes, studied the resulting configuration of fruit and light, then plucked off another. Satisfied, he moved to the next bunch.

"What are you doing?" came the voice of a child.

He looked up. Olivia Jones's daughter stood halfway down the row, staring at him through glasses that made her eyes look too large in com-parison to the rest of her, which seemed small, en-veloped by a neon green rain slicker. She had the hood up, but frizzy wisps of brown hair stuck out at odd spots.

Simon hadn't realized it was misting until he saw her push the back of her hand over her glasses.

"That makes it worse," he told her, wondering how she could see with her glasses all smudged. He gestured her away from the vines. "You're standing too close. The grapes need to breathe."

She took one step away, but no more. "You're just as close as I was."

"I'm working," he said and returned to his task, hoping she would take the hint and leave.

"If I was too close, then so's your cat."

"He's a cat. He's shorter than you, and he's not wearing a big raincoat."

"He's ugly."

Simon shot her a look. "Thank you. That was very nice." He studied his vine.

"What are you doing?"

He snapped off a leaf. "Pruning."

"What does that do?"

He snapped off another leaf. "It thins the leaf canopy."

"Why do you need to thin it?"

"If there are too many leaves around these grapes, they can't get the sun." He sat back on his haunches to study the cluster he'd cleared.

"It doesn't look very sunny to me. And those don't look like grapes." Her tone of voice made her sound like a spoiled little girl.

Turning around, he decided that she looked like one, too. Her eyes were hard. Her chin jutted out. "Trust me," he said. "They're grapes."

"Can I eat them?"

"Don't you dare."

"Why not?"

"Because they're sour and they're hard. If you eat them now, you'll have a bellyache and I'll have no harvest."

"I wasn't going to eat *all* of them," she said.

"Don't . . . eat . . . any," he told her, enunciating each word separately while he gave her a long, hard look. Incredibly, she returned it. He was thinking that she had some kind of gall—not entirely unlike her mother, he noted—when she turned and marched off in the other direction.

She didn't like him. Fine. He didn't like her either. He hadn't asked to have a child around. He certainly didn't want one wandering through his vineyards. He couldn't afford to be distracted—the quality of the year's vintage was precarious enough without that.

When his stomach growled, he glanced at his watch. It was nearly noon. Right about now, Madalena would be putting out a spread of sandwiches in the Great House kitchen. Anyone could stop by. It was a casual custom, one of the perks of life at Asquonset. He'd been grabbing lunch at the Great House all his life.

Today, he was in the mood for something different. He didn't care what. A grinder from the crossroads would be fine. Even a Big Mac from Huffington would do. Huffington was the next town over. He could handle the drive.

First, though, he needed therapy. Ignoring the mist, which was looking more like rain by the minute, he went back to leafing and trellising until he felt the knot inside him loosen. The vineyard did that to him, never failed. The rest of his world could be falling apart, but the vines were always there. Whether dormant or growing, shorter or taller, heavy with grapes or with promise alone, they responded to his touch.

When Donna dropped by after spending the morning with the Chardonnays, he sent her up to lunch without him. Likewise, he passed when Natalie called him on the Nextel that was hooked to the back of his belt. His hair grew wet. His shirt grew wet, sticking to his skin, but he worked until the sound of the vines and the smell of the earth had restored his equilibrium.

Then he returned to the shed, hopped in the pickup, and left Asquonset behind.

Nine

ONE WEEK LATER, Olivia was again up at dawn, perched on the window seat in her bedroom, her arms hugging her knees. One week later, she reminded herself. Hard to believe. Each day had been fuller than the last—and Natalie's book was slow in coming.

Was Natalie concerned? No.

"How can you write my story without knowing Asquonset?" she asked and proceeded to make one suggestion after another for things that kept Olivia away from the loft and work on the book. Olivia might have begun to fear that Simon was right—that Natalie hadn't brought her to Asquonset to write a book at all—if Simon had been around. But he was nowhere in sight during a walking tour of the vineyard or an introductory lunch at the yacht club. They didn't so much as pass his pickup during a driving tour of the town. And when it came to an afternoon at the movies with Natalie and Carl, he either wasn't invited or opted out.

The movie outing was on Saturday. Natalie and Carl were as into it, and as into fast food at an old-fashioned drive-in afterward, as were Olivia and Tess. How could Olivia not dream then? Of course, Natalie had ulterior motives for bringing her to Asquonset, but they involved returning long-lost kin to the vineyard—or so the dream went. Lord knew, there didn't seem to be any other young blood around. To Olivia's knowledge, neither of Natalie's grandchildren had called. Nor had any cousins or nieces and nephews. Carl had no family but Simon. And Simon's wife and daughter were dead.

The dream got a whittling down on Sunday, when Olivia and Tess were invited to services in the sweet, white-steepled church near the center of town. It seemed that several carloads of people from the vineyard went together each week. Olivia and Tess were invited along as part of the Asquonset family, in the broadest sense of the word.

Tess was mildly appalled. "We don't go to church," she whispered in dismay as Olivia ushered her off to their rooms to get dressed when breakfast was done.

"We do," Olivia replied. "Just not often. We haven't found a church that we like."

"But what am I supposed to *do* there?"

"Listen. Sing. Pray."

"What do I wear?"

"Your new sundress."

Tess sent her a pleading look. "Every other time I wear something new, it's wrong. I mean, there I am at the yacht club meeting the kids who'll be in my sailing class, and they're not wearing white shorts and sandals. They're wearing cutoffs and sneakers. I felt like a *geek.*"

"Fine. So now you're wearing cutoffs." With Asquonset shirts. Tess always chose one of those, Olivia noticed. "But this is church. You heard what Natalie said. People dress for church."

Olivia put on her own new sundress. She took care with her makeup and worked extra hard on her hair. Her appearance was a reflection on Natalie, and she wanted to look the part of the worthy assistant. Or cousin. Or niece.

Simon wasn't with the Asquonset group, or anywhere else in the church either, but this time Olivia's clothes were just right. She said an extra little prayer of thanks for that, plus an extra little prayer for sun and an extra little prayer for Tess.

Looking back over their first days at Asquonset, Olivia wondered if the last had indeed worked. Tess was nervous about sailing and she was dreading tutoring. There were some positive things, though. For starters, she had found four best friends in the cats that lived in the house. Like children at the playground, they were waiting when she came down in the morning, or came in from outside, or popped up to the attic office in search of Olivia. They followed her from room to room and jockeyed for her attention, Henri with greater stealth than the more in-your-face Maxwell and Bernard, and Achmed from his imperial perch in the loft. In turn she spent hours doting on each, rubbing heads, brushing backs, sketching their faces on her pad.

Cats weren't other kids, but as playmates they were better than nothing.

Another positive thing was tennis. Carl turned out to be the instructor, and Olivia couldn't have asked for a better one for Tess. He was patient and gentle. Since he was a known quantity to the child by now, he wasn't threatening, as a new teacher would be. He was also good at tennis.

"I had to be, living here all these years," he teased when Olivia remarked on it. "Alexander loved the game. He used to pull me out of the vine-yards to play when he didn't have a partner. Then Simon wanted to learn, having the court right here and all."

"Was he better than me?" Tess asked, tipping her head back and looking up through her glasses from under the bill of an Asquonset hat. She'd had a total of two lessons at that point and had easily missed more than half of the balls he had tossed at her racket.

Carl appeared to give it some thought. "No," he finally said. "You're better. Simon wanted to be all power and speed even before he learned to connect with the ball. He was all boy, swinging this way and swinging that, missing most everything in sight."

"I was missing stuff."

"Less at the end than the start. You're catching on. You're watching the ball, like I told you to do. You're coming to judge the distance between your hand and the center of the racket."

"And Simon didn't?"

"Well, it took him awhile." Carl leaned closed to Tess. "Only don't you tell him I said that."

So, on the plus side of the ledger for Tess were the cats, the Asquonset gear, and Carl. On the negative side was tutoring.

Tess didn't want it. She didn't want any reminder of weakness. She would have been quite content to spend the summer without opening a book, but Olivia refused to have that. The whole point in coming here was to be able to afford daily tutoring. Olivia knew there would be fights before each session, but she vowed not to be swayed.

That resolve was strengthened by the tutor herself. Sandy Adelson was the head of the special needs program at Braemont, the same day school in Providence that Olivia was eyeing for Tess. That was a major plus, as far as Olivia was concerned— an immediate *in,* should Olivia land a job nearby for the fall—but it was only the first of the pluses.

Sandy was the daughter of one of Natalie's oldest friends. She lived ten minutes from Asquonset. Something of a free spirit, she wore her gray hair straight, center-parted, and long; her halter tops were hand-crocheted and her jeans wildly embroidered. She was the least likely looking expert on learning disabilities that Olivia had ever met, but she was an expert nevertheless. She was also dedicated, if the hours she spent poring through Tess's files prior to their first meeting were any indication.

They held that first meeting on the patio, at a table under the awning. Olivia had vowed to be there, even before Sandy requested her presence. That was the first difference from past tutors; the second came barely five minutes into the session.

"I think," Sandy said, speaking straight to Tess, "that I'd like to try a new approach. I've had success using it with other students with visual discrimination problems like yours."

"I'm dyslexic," Tess corrected.

"Yes, but there are different kinds of dyslexia. Some kinds involve auditory processing. Yours involves a visual problem. You don't see letters and words the way you should. But unless you see them correctly, you can't spell them or write them or understand them."

"I just had my glasses checked. I can see fine."

Come on, Tess, Olivia scolded silently. *You know what she means.*

Sandy was unperturbed. "Physically, yes. Your

eyes see what's on the paper, but they don't interpret it in a way that your brain understands. We can correct that."

"How?"

"By giving you tools to help you see the correct way."

"Tools, like nuts and bolts? Or special glasses?" Tess asked, sounding bored.

Olivia had to bite her tongue to resist reprimanding her daughter.

Again, Sandy seemed unfazed. "Tools, like new ways to look at words. New ways to read books. New ways to study for tests. New ways to *take* tests."

"You can't do all that in one summer."

"I can come close." Turning to Olivia, she said, "There are learning strategies for children like Tess. Has she been taught SQ3R?"

Olivia blinked and shook her head.

"How about visual mapping?"

"No," Olivia said. "Her tutors have focused on reviewing what's been done in class."

"Without much success," Tess put in.

Sandy returned to her with a smile. "Well, maybe that's why. We have to be proactive, not reactive. We have to prepare you to succeed, not play catch-up after you've failed."

Tess didn't have a comeback for that.

"So one of the things we'll do is to preread the books that you'll be reading in the fall."

"Preread?" the child asked in dismay. "Like,

read now and then again in the fall? I don't think that'll help. I'm a terrible reader."

"You won't be once you learn how to do it the right way."

"But it takes me forever to read books *one* time," Tess tried.

"It won't, once you get the knack of doing it in a way that works for you."

"But how do I know what books I'll be reading in the fall, if I don't know where I'm going to school?"

Olivia explained the situation.

Sandy had answers here, too. "We'll get reading lists from the public school she's been at, plus Cambridge Heath and several other private schools. There will be overlap. We'll work with that book. Most of the ones assigned at this level are good for teaching visualization skills. We'll do vocabulary work from whatever book we pick."

Tess moaned. "I'm terrible at vocabulary. I can never spell things right."

"Really?" Sandy asked. She opened her bag and pulled out a book. "We use this one in the fifth grade at our school."

"*I* can't do fifth-grade work. I'm not *there* yet."

Sandy opened to a random page, put the book in front of Tess, and pointed. "Do you know what this word is?"

" 'Knee,' " Tess said.

"Ah. You saw the beginning of it—the *k-n*—

and guessed. This word does begin with *k-n* but it isn't 'knee.' "

"See? I'm not good at this."

Sandy put a calming hand on Tess's arm. Opening her bag again, she pulled out a notebook. She opened to a clean page, took a pencil, and neatly printed "knight" for Tess to see. "This is the word in the book. Look at both. Are they the same?"

Tess compared the two. She nodded.

"Knight." Sandy said the word and printed it again. "This isn't the kind of night that's the time of day when we sleep. It's a different kind of knight."

"A soldier," Tess said.

"Correct." She pointed with the tip of her pencil. "Look at it with these letters sticking up at the beginning and the end, like swords or lances. Now, I'm going to draw a line around these letters." She did it as she spoke. "I'll go up over the top of the *k* and down over the *n* and the *i* and the *g*. I'm going high again with the stem of the *h,* and a little lower with the *t*. We go down the side of the *t* with a little jag where the letter is crossed. We go down to the bottom now and start back underneath. I'm under the *h*. I'm going down deeper under the *g*, then back up and across on an even line under the *i* and the *n* and the *k,* then back up to where I started. There. It's boxed in. Look at that shape."

Tess leaned forward and looked.

"Run your finger over it," Sandy said.

Tess traced the outline with her finger.

"Can you feel its shape?" Sandy asked. "Feel those lances on either end, like the queen's guard?"

Tess nodded.

Sandy tore off the page. "One of the tutors said in his report that you can draw. Yes?"

Tess sat a little taller. She gave another nod.

Sandy put the old page next to a clean one. She handed Tess the pencil. "Draw me a knight."

"A knight? Any knight?"

"Any knight you'd like, as long as it's a soldier, like you said."

While Tess drew, Sandy sat back. She looked around the patio and out over the vineyard. She took a deep breath. She was clearly enjoying herself.

Olivia was thinking that in optimism alone she had it over past tutors, when Tess put down the pencil.

Sandy's eyes held instant appreciation. "Wow. You *can* draw. This is going to be fun. Now write the word under the picture."

Tess picked up the pencil and copied the word from the first sheet.

"Now draw a box around it, just like I did," Sandy said. "Take your time."

Tess drew the box. It had her own little flair at the corners—Olivia hadn't expected total conformity—but it followed the general line of the letters.

Setting the pencil aside, Sandy took that paper and the first one she had used, and turned both over so that Tess had nothing to copy. "Now write the word," she said.

Tess looked like she was about to argue. Then she picked up the pencil and correctly wrote the word.

"Well, there you are," Sandy crowed. "For that, you get to have tomorrow's hour with me under that big old fat tree over there on the other side of the vineyard."

"A *whole* hour?" Tess asked. "I only had half an hour at school."

"What I'd really like," Sandy said, "is *two* hours a day."

"*Two.*" Beseechful, Tess looked up over her glasses at Olivia. "This is my *summer.*"

"An hour, then," Sandy said with a conciliatory sigh. "That won't be too bad."

Tess breathed a sigh of relief.

SITTING IN HER WINDOW SEAT the next morning, Olivia smiled as she remembered the tutorial. Tess had been had. Sandy not only knew about learning disabilities, she knew about kids. If ever Olivia had been optimistic that they were in the right hands, it was now. Dealing with Tess's dyslexia was no longer adversarial. Sandy was on their side. Olivia felt less alone.

She put her chin on her knees. Asquonset was a

charm in that sense. She didn't care if Natalie's book did take longer to do. It would get done.

There was a movement below her, a figure approaching the end of the patio to survey the vineyard at dawn. It was Simon, right on time. As he did each morning, he held that mug of steaming coffee, though Olivia imagined it there more than actually saw it. The dawn light didn't illuminate much more than his overall shape.

Leisurely, she studied his legs, then those lean hips and the rising wedge of his torso. He had several layers of shirts on in the early morning chill, and they made his shoulders look particularly large. But she knew what those shoulders looked like with the sleeves of his T-shirt cut off. She knew how solid the muscle there was.

She sat still as she watched him. After that first morning, she hadn't gone outside. It was obvious she rubbed him the wrong way. Bumping into him seemed pointless. Besides, from here she didn't have to be coy. She could look at him all she wanted.

She would have five minutes to do it. That's how long he would stand there drinking his coffee, looking out over his realm. Then he would leave the patio, mingle with the vines on his way to the shed, and be gone from her view. He was definitely a creature of habit.

Sure enough, at the five-minute mark he shifted his stance in preparation for setting off. This day, though, he didn't leave. He turned his head slightly, as though he had heard something, and stood listening. In profile, she saw the tumble of hair on his brow, the line of his nose and his chin. Then he turned back all the way and looked straight at her.

He can't possibly see me, she thought. But she wasn't taking any chances. She held her breath, kept her arms around her legs and her chin on her knees, and sat perfectly still. At least, everything voluntary was still. Her heart, though, was beating faster, and there was a thrumming deep inside. *Caught with my hand in the cookie jar,* she mused, squelching a nervous laugh.

He can't possibly see me, she thought again, but it certainly felt like he had. She was trying to figure that one out when he faced forward again and set off to continue his daily ritual.

Ten

RAIN BEAT ON THE ROOF of the loft, where Natalie had spread out her photographs. Olivia recognized them as belonging to the very first batch Otis had received, now several months back. She didn't see her mystery woman. These pictures were from an even earlier time. They were primitive black-and-white shots, most of empty fields and dark buildings. Looking at one of the buildings, Olivia recognized the beginnings of the Great House.

"You have a good eye," Natalie remarked when she commented on it, but rather than elaborating as Olivia hoped she would, she simply stood studying the group.

Olivia followed her lead and stood beside her,

doing the same. The pictures were earthy and bleak, drawing her back to the time of the Great Depression. Within minutes, she was newly arrived at Asquonset, there with Natalie's family on that cold and rainy day in 1930.

Turning away briefly, Natalie took a snapshot from the credenza. It was the picture of Carl, the springboard to that first distinct memory.

He was dressed much like he is here, only that day in the rain he wore a brown wool cap and a loose wool jacket. He was standing in the field like he was planted in the ground, looking so much taller and older than me that I should have been terrified. He was a strange person in a strange place. To this day, I don't know why I didn't turn and run back to the house. He didn't smile. But there was something about him . . . something kind. I needed kindness that day.

"Are you lost?" he asked in a voice that didn't sound so old.

I shook my head.

"Scared?"

I shook my head again, then pushed the wet hair off my face.

"Well, you don't look happy."

I wasn't. I was cold and wet and lonely. "I want to go home," I said.

Carl glanced at the farmhouse. "No one's stopping you."

But that farmhouse wasn't home to me. It was just a faraway pile of stones. "Home to New York."

"I was there once. Don't care to go back. It's better here."

"Why?"

"There's air here. There's trees and water."

"All I see's rain and mud," I declared.

"Know what that mud is?"

"I do," I cried, thinking he thought I was a baby. "It's wet dirt!"

Carl remained placid. "Only on top. Underneath is what makes things grow. You don't get soil like this in other places." He squatted down and pushed a hand through the mud. "If this was packed tight, it wouldn't be any good. But see? It's soft. There's good drainage here. That's why we can grow what we do."

"I don't want to grow anything."

He stood and held his muddy hand out to be washed by the rain. "That's because you want to be in New York, but you aren't there. You're here."

"My friends are in New York."

"You'll make friends here."

"My school's in New York."

"The one here's okay."

"But I'm not staying! I'm going back to New York!"

"Did your parents tell you that?"

No. They hadn't. As the awfulness of that realization sank in, my eyes filled with tears. Struggling to hold them back, I started to shiver. I felt miserable.

"Those clothes are all wrong," Carl scolded in a way that suggested concern far more than criticism. I understood that only in hindsight, however. At the time, I was too young and upset to make the distinction. All I heard was—kindness.

"You need better things," he said. "You need pants and real shoes and a jacket like mine." Before I knew what he was up to, he had taken his jacket off and wrapped it around me.

I should have been appalled. The contrast between that coarse brown jacket and my soft blue coat was everything I didn't want. The jacket was old, and it was wet. But it smelled clean, cleaner now than I feared my muddy coat did. And it brought instant warmth.

"Come on. I'll take you home." He set off for the farmhouse, gesturing me along with a hand. It was the same one he had run through the mud. That quickly, the rain had washed it clean.

"Did you get all those things?" Olivia asked Natalie.

"All what things?"

"Pants. Real shoes. A jacket like Carl's."

Natalie lifted one of the pictures from the desk. It showed a group of young boys pulling potatoes from the ground. At least, Olivia had thought they were young boys when she had repaired a fold in the center of the picture. But there was a smugness now on Natalie's face that made her take a closer look.

"This is *you?*" she asked, pointing to one of the boys, who despite wearing the same jeans, shirt, and shoes as the others, suddenly didn't look like a boy at all.

Natalie confirmed it and identified each of the others. "Here's Carl. This is my brother, Brad. Carl and Brad were the same age. These other two boys were the sons of a neighbor. We gave them potatoes and corn in exchange for milk."

But Olivia couldn't take her eyes off the girl. She had already learned that Natalie's family had lost everything before moving to Asquonset. Knowing it was one thing, though. Accepting it was another. She had spent too long painting Natalie into a life of elegance and ease not to be shocked by what she saw here. "How old were you?"

"Maybe . . . seven."

"And you worked in the fields?" Olivia would never have imagined it.

"We all did."

"Weren't there laws against that?"

Natalie smiled. "Tell it to the family that grows what it eats. Actually, we were among the lucky ones. We didn't have a mortgage. In the early thirties, farmers' incomes dropped so far that even those who could feed themselves lost their farms. The price they were getting for their crops was so low that they couldn't pay their mortgages." She pointed to the neighbor's boys. "They lost theirs."

"What did they do?"

"My father bought them out. They worked the dairy for him."

"I thought your father was broke."

"Compared to our assets in New York, he was, but all things are relative. He bought the farms abutting us for next to nothing."

"But where did he get even that?"

Natalie picked up another of the photographs. It showed Jeremiah Burke sitting on an open wagon. The wagon carried the same barrels that Olivia had seen in the photograph of Carl.

"Wine?" Olivia guessed, delighted.

Natalie nodded. She studied the picture.

Olivia prodded gently. "Wine saw you through the Depression?"

"We didn't make much. We didn't have the

know-how. What you're seeing here might have been the season's entire yield, but prices for wine were higher than for anything else we grew. The black market saw to that. If Prohibition did nothing else, it made drinking the thing to do."

"Weren't you afraid of getting caught?"

Natalie's eyes filled with pain. "I swear, my father half hoped that he would. He never recovered from the crash. He had natural business instincts, like buying neighboring farmland, but he never got over the guilt or the shame of what had happened in New York. You can't see it from this picture—well, maybe you can if you look deep into those troubled eyes—but he was a broken man. Once he had been robust and outgoing, but look at how thin he is here. And we did have food. He just had trouble eating it. If he'd been punished for selling wine, he might have felt better.

"But people weren't getting caught," she went on. "The government couldn't begin to punish all the people breaking the law. The Volstead Act was designed to enforce Prohibition, but there were a ridiculously small number of agents appointed to do it, and an overwhelmingly large number of violators. So my father made his little bit of wine. The proceeds he got from selling it gave us seed money for the future. Literally. Prohibition was repealed in 1933. Our wine became less valuable then—it wasn't very good, in the final analysis—but my father had a vision. He brought in rootstock from Europe and began planting vinifera varieties."

She smiled sadly. "Poor guy. He struck out over and over again. One variety failed, then another and another. He didn't have much of a green thumb."

"But Jeremiah did. Didn't he help?"

"Jeremiah grew us potatoes and corn, carrots, beets, and parsnips. Grapes were something else, and we weren't the only ones having trouble. The Europeans were the experts at growing grapes, but their methods didn't work as well here. It wasn't until the sixties that Americans devised their own methods and finally entered the game. My father was gone by then."

"How sad."

Natalie rested a hip on the edge of the desk. "Yes. He really did start it all. I'm sorry that he didn't live to see how far we've come. Those times when we've had everyone here . . ."

"Who is everyone?" Olivia asked, given the lead-in. "How large is your family?"

"Not large. There's Susanne and Greg and their respective spouses. Susanne and Mark have two children. Both are grown. Neither is married. Melissa is a lawyer, Brad is a business consultant. Greg and Jill don't have any children yet. I don't know what they're waiting for. In my day, we had children younger. But times have changed. Jill isn't much older than you, so they still have time, by today's standards. That isn't to say that I'm not impatient. I'd love to have more grandchildren. But it isn't my decision to make." She shot a heaven-help-me glance toward the ceiling. "It could well be that Melissa or Brad will marry and give me great-grandchildren before Greg and Jill get around to it." Her eyes settled on Olivia. "What about you? Are your parents still living?"

Olivia shrugged. "Not important."

"It is. I like to know about the people who work in my house. Are they alive?"

"Oh yes," Olivia said, because she wanted to believe it. She even wanted to believe they were in touch with one another.

"Where?"

She dipped into one of her fantasies, such a familiar one that she half believed it was true. "San Diego." She pictured her father as a career navy man whose frequent relocation had kept him on the go. Now that he was a senior whatever, on the cusp of retirement, he didn't travel as much. He had a place on the beach in San Diego. For all Olivia knew, Carol might be there right now.

"Do you have siblings?" Natalie asked.

Still in the fantasy, Olivia nodded. "Four brothers. They're navy men, like my dad."

Natalie's eyes lit. "There's a navy base right here in Newport. Any chance one of them might have business there while you're here? Alexander was an old friend of the secretary of the navy. I'd be glad to make a call or two."

Olivia backpedaled. "Oh no. No need. Thanks so much, but that wouldn't work. I mean, I'm here because they're there. We have very different lives."

Natalie's face dropped. "You aren't close, then?"

"Well, we are," Olivia said, because the last thing she wanted was for Natalie to think she didn't value family if it turned out by some quirk of fate that they were related. So, even when it meant extending the fib, she let the fantasy run. "The thing is, I'm the baby. You only had one older brother, but I have four. They give new meaning to the word 'protective.' I was smothered. I couldn't breathe. They finally agreed to give me space."

"But what about Tess? Don't they want to see her?"

"They do. We go back now and again."

"Ah," Natalie said.

Olivia didn't know what that meant, but she wasn't waiting to find out. She needed to put distance between herself and the story she'd just told. "I want to know more about this," she said, taking up another picture from the desk. The children were several years older, on a tractor this time. Brad was on a fender, but Natalie was right up there in the driver's seat with Carl. She couldn't have been more than nine or ten and still looked boyish. The two boys were starting to look like men.

"You said Brad was your only brother. Did you have any sisters?" There hadn't been any in the car

when the family had left New York, but that didn't
mean they weren't living with another relative.

Natalie shook her head. "It was just Brad and
me."

Olivia wasn't discouraged. She had already decided that the mystery woman was either a cousin
or a friend.

She was about to ask about it when Natalie
took the photo of Carl, Brad, and her on the tractor
and slipped mentally away. It was a while before
she spoke.

> My situation was different from
> yours. My brother and Carl were pro-
> tective, but I didn't mind it at all. In
> turn, they didn't seem to mind when I
> tagged along. I was articulate, agile, and
> smart. What I lacked in strength, I made
> up for in speed and wits. The three of us
> went everywhere together. I was one of
> the guys.
>
> I don't know what I would have done
> without them. Asquonset was one new
> experience after another, and my parents
> were no help. They were stoic and stern.
> They directed us here or there and told
> us what to do around the farm, but they
> never laughed. They rarely even smiled.
> The concept of pleasure had been left
> behind in New York, along with all sense

of security. Add my father's shame to that, and things weren't good. The two of them lived each day as though they were fully expecting another crash.

They aged at double speed during those years. In no time, they were old. It was heartbreaking to see.

We were more resilient—me even more so than Brad. I was younger. My attachment to New York was more tenuous. Besides, I had found something that first day that New York didn't have. I had found Carl.

He became my idol. He was quiet and confident. Nothing ruffled him. He knew everyone and everything. No matter how new life was to me at Asquonset, being with Carl was like being in a familiar place. His confidence was contagious.

I started school and made friends, and those friends didn't know where we'd been. They only knew that we were better off than most, and we truly were. We ate three meals a day. Our clothes were more serviceable than stylish, but we never went without shoes. We went to the movies every Saturday afternoon. We could afford that. We couldn't afford to travel, but the idea of taking a train had lost its appeal. The newsreels were

all about the hungry and homeless riding boxcars. We were far from hungry
and homeless.

All things were relative, of course.
Asquonset was a dour place that grew
more oppressive the longer the Depression lasted. If our parents weren't sitting
stiff and alert in front of the radio, they
were poring through the tabloids in
search of bad news, and there was never a
lack. Banks continued to close long after
the crash. More of their friends went
under. My parents had been in the center
of the social scene in New York, and
either personally knew those people
mentioned in the paper or knew of
them. Unemployment continued to rise.
Shanty villages called Hoovervilles
sprang up to house the homeless. Soup
kitchens were inundated with the hungry.

Roosevelt was swept into office with
promises of a New Deal, but all my parents saw were pictures of the devastation
of the Dust Bowl. Though Asquonset remained fertile and moist, they feared we
were next. They read everything they
could about prevention, and had us out
in the most remote of our acres planting
grass and trees to anchor the soil. Long
after the economy began to improve,
they lived with the fear of relapse.

Brad was a casualty of that fear. When the gloom got bad enough, he left. He dropped out of school when he was sixteen and lied about his age to get a job with the Works Projects Administration. He built bridges and highways. He dug tunnels. He sent money home. But that was small solace for my father, who wanted him to be educated and ready for the time when good jobs returned. Moreover, in losing Brad, he had lost one of his most able-bodied workers.

Me, I had lost one of my two best friends. Same with Carl. So he and I grew even closer. If we'd been growing up together now, the four years between us would have been insurmountable. We'd have gone to different schools with different crowds and different activities. Back then, though, things didn't work that way. We did everything together.

Natalie stopped talking and smiled. They sat in the wing-back chairs now. Olivia was making notes on the pad of paper on her lap. Natalie's hands were folded gently.

Olivia waited for her to go on, but there was simply that sweet smile and the occasional nod. She was transported back to that long-ago world.

Olivia wanted to be there, too. "What were some of those things?"

"Oh, we went back and forth to school together."

"On a bus?"

"No-o." This was said with a chiding chuckle. "There were no buses. We walked."

"How far?"

"Three miles. We picked up others as we went along. Carl was like the Pied Piper. He was the tallest and the least talkative, but he had a certain"—she searched for the word—"a certain *charisma*. He never looked for attention, never wanted it, but people gravitated toward him. It was a classic case of the mystique of the one who is most aloof. Carl passed by, and people looked; and when they looked, they saw Brad and me, too. We were his sidekicks. It was because of him that we were accepted as quickly as we were."

Olivia was smiling along with her now, picturing the daily procession to school. "That sounds so neat."

"Neat?"

"Fun."

"Walking three miles through driving rain wasn't fun."

"But all of you doing it—following the Pied Piper—it's a wonderful image. What else did you do?"

"Do?"

"For fun."

"Oh, little things."

"Like what?"

Natalie gave a half shrug. "You know. What all kids do." She blushed. "Time hasn't changed some things."

"*Sex?*" Olivia asked in surprise, because she'd thought time *had* changed that—at least, in terms of age and savvy. When Natalie's cheeks remained pink, she said, "I'm sorry. That's private. I shouldn't be asking about it."

"I hired you to ask about private things. I won't necessarily tell all, but I want you to ask." That said, she had regained her composure. "The age factor did come into play there. When Carl was fourteen, I was only ten. When he was sixteen, I was only twelve. We weren't boyfriend and girlfriend. We didn't smooch in the back row of the movie theater."

There was a pause.

Olivia helped her out. "But you wanted it."

Still blushing, Natalie nodded. "Carl was the only one I could imagine being with. I used to dream about that."

Her voice stopped, but her facial expression continued to speak of beautiful things. Olivia watched her until she couldn't bear the suspense any longer.

"Did you dream of marrying him?"

"We danced together," Natalie said.

"You dreamed of that?"

"No. It was real. Dancing was big during the Depression. It was the cheapest form of entertainment."

Olivia knew something of that. "Did you and Carl do *marathon* dancing?"

"No. But we knew people who did. Some of them went on and on for months, some with good reason. As long as they remained on their feet, they had a roof over their heads, food, and the promise of prize money." She smiled. "No. Carl and I didn't do anything like that. But we'd seen enough of it on the newsreels to know some of the dance steps. Carl had a little crystal set—you know, a little radio. We'd go back behind the shed and find a little music, and we'd dance." Her eyes went wide. She had thought of something else, another good memory, judging from the excitement in her eyes.

"What?" Olivia asked.

Natalie looked at her, then looked away and laughed. "It's silly, really. But it was so nice."

Olivia laughed along with her. *"What?"*

"January, February, March—those are important months in a vineyard. That's when the vineyardist cuts back the vines. It sets the entire tone for the next season's growth. My father insisted on doing it himself in those early days. Our job was to collect the discarded canes. They would eventually be burned, but before that, we used them to build huts."

"Huts?" Olivia asked, entranced.

"Carl knew how to tangle the branches so that they would hold together. The finished product wasn't anything fancy, and since there weren't any leaves, you could still see out. But those walls cut the wind and the cold. They made a nice little place."

"And you danced there?"

"We did, indeed. Oh my. I'd be looking up at him, dancing the way I'd seen in those films. Carl wasn't much of a dancer. Still isn't. His feet wouldn't quite behave, but he had a way with those arms." She inhaled deeply and, mouth closed, hummed an ecstatic pair of notes.

Olivia didn't write down a thing. There was no need. She could see that hut clear as day, could see through the holes between those branches. The inside would be lit by a candle, illuminating two gently swaying bodies. She could hear a tinny echo of the big band sound, right down to the static of the crystal set. It was so incredibly romantic.

She sat back in the chair with a sigh. "Those were the good old days. I would like to have lived back then."

Natalie looked at her strangely, much as Otis had not so very long ago. "No, you wouldn't. Times were hard. The future was precarious. By the end of the thirties, war was in the air. You can't begin to know what that was like."

"But families were closer back then. They gave each other support."

"That doesn't mean they were happier."

"But life was *simpler* back then," Olivia insisted. "There are times I would give my right *arm* for less responsibility."

"Is that what you think we had?"

"I think that the division of labor was more defined. Men did the work, kids did the chores, women kept the house. Nowadays, it's all mixed up and overloaded."

Natalie gave her a chastening smile. "You have an idealized view of the past. You've made things more simple than they were. The division of labor may have been more defined, but the labor was harder. We didn't have the technology back then that we do today."

"Maybe not," Olivia said, standing her ground, "but technology has its limits. I don't care what claims a fabric softener makes about leaving clothes smelling like the great outdoors, there is nothing like the smell of sheets that have dried on the line."

"Well, I can't argue with you there," Natalie replied good-naturedly. "But I still think you're wrong about the other. Times weren't easier back then than they are now. They were—well, different, that's all."

OLIVIA DIDN'T BELIEVE Natalie any more than she had believed Otis. Life may have been physically harder in the thirties, but she would take physical hardship over emotional stress any day. Yes, the

thirties were still the good old days. Life was simpler. Needs were better defined and people more
honest. When survival was the issue, choices were
clear.

Survival was not the issue today, which made
choices more murky. Today, people left home and
wandered. They did different things. They wore
more hats. Olivia wore so many at the same time
that sometimes her head wobbled on her neck—
and each hat came with its own awful set of responsibilities. She knew what it was to feel alone
and overwhelmed when those responsibilities
clashed.

She hadn't expected that to happen to her at
Asquonset. She had expected that life under Natalie would be a throwback to those older, simpler
times. Certainly, she and Tess had been made to
feel cushioned in the days since they had arrived.

A throwback to simpler times? Life at Asquonset during the week that followed was to be anything but.

Eleven

EVEN HERE, Olivia wore many hats.

She was a mother—that never stopped. She was a chauffeur when Tess needed transportation to the yacht club and back; a teacher when she needed help with Sandy's assignments; a therapist when the child was down on herself, which was still far too often for Olivia's peace of mind. Where Tess was concerned, she was a maid, a laundress, even a cook, too.

She was a job hunter for herself, and a private-school hunter for Tess.

She was a fugitive when Ted called the business office and the receptionist, forewarned, put him off.

Not even as Natalie's memoirist were things

simple, despite Olivia's best intentions. She was organized. Natalie had given her an alcove in that heavenly third-floor loft, with her own desk and a computer, and Olivia had set up a filing system for her notes and the pictures that would coincide with them. At night she lay in bed envisioning hours in the quiet solitude of that office, fleshing out her notes and organizing Natalie's life story just as a renowned biographer would. Elaborating on the renowned-biographer theme, she imagined walking into the snobbiest of bookstores in Cambridge and delivering a reading to a house packed with the intellectual elite. She imagined being hired as the memoirist for other luminaries. She imagined doing the talk show circuit and being invited to lead a theme cruise.

Reality was less idyllic. Much as Natalie's narrative flowed, finding the exact words and their exact order was hard. Olivia could spend half an hour on a single sentence, and then it was usually at night. During the day, there was neither quiet nor solitude in the loft, what with the phone ringing all the time. Natalie was no shrinking violet, it seemed. She ran the marketing department at Asquonset, and was constantly getting calls about that. She got calls about the local voter registration drive, which she headed, and calls about the church bazaar, which she chaired. Between those calls were ones to do with the wedding. She had sent out over a hundred invitations, and although a response card was included, many people insisted on calling.

"They want dirt," she told Olivia, a tone of pique in her voice after she had taken two such calls in quick succession. "They want salacious little details—as if Carl and I have been carrying on for years—which we have *not.*"

Olivia had been wondering about that herself. "They don't come right out and ask it, do they?"

"Well, no. But that's what they're thinking. They're evasive—you know, say things like, 'You've been with Carl a long time, haven't you?' Or, 'It must have been a temptation having him near all these years.' Or, 'You're a foxy lady, Natalie Seebring.' "

"Do they *really* say that?"

Natalie pointed to the phone, indicating the call just ended. "This one said, 'We *always* suspected Carl was closer to you than he was to Alexander.' Well, I take *objection* to that. In the first place, I don't like the idea that they're talking among themselves. In the second place, the fact is that Carl was Alexander's right hand. He worked his heart out for the man. He covered for him constantly."

"Covered for him?"

Natalie erased the thought with the wave of a hand. "Not a day has gone by in the past two weeks when someone hasn't called wanting to gossip, but I don't have the time. I'm due over at the office in forty-five minutes. The company that does our ads is coming down from Boston to make a presentation for next spring's campaign." She looked bewilderedly at the photographs spread over her desk. They were the ones from the earliest days. Olivia had wanted her to identify each one with names and dates.

But that seemed secondary even to Olivia now. "Who have you invited to the wedding?"

"Mostly friends and business associates. I limited the list."

"Is there extended family? Cousins, maybe?" Perhaps even the mystery woman? Wouldn't that be a hoot? Seeing someone who looked like her mother—or like herself, or like *Tess*—would be an amazing thing!

"I have cousins, but it wasn't appropriate to invite them. We were never close. Alexander has a sister. I did invite her family and her—how not to, her being my sister-in-law all these years—but she sent back an immediate refusal. She's offended. Well, fine. We want this to be a small affair."

The phone rang again. She shot it a helpless glance, then looked to Olivia.

"Why don't I take it?" Olivia said and drew up a pad of paper. "I can easily enough keep track of yeses and nos."

"Would you mind?" Natalie asked on such a sweet note of relief that Olivia's heart swelled.

Of course I wouldn't mind, she thought. *This is what family is for.*

With a smile for Natalie, she picked up the phone. "Seebring residence."

"Hello. This is Lucy McEnroe." Olivia wrote down the name. "I'd like to talk with Natalie, please."

Natalie had taken one look at the name and given a single definitive headshake.

"I'm sorry," Olivia said, slipping with relish into the role of trusted insider. "She's out of the office for the day. This is her assistant, Olivia Jones. May I help you?"

Her husband has a restaurant in New York, Natalie wrote on the pad. *They stock our wines.*

"I just wanted to say hello to Natalie," Lucy replied. "Henry and I returned from Paris to find the invitation to her wedding. Well, *that* was a shock."

"Isn't it wonderful, though?" Olivia said, staring at the name of the restaurant as Natalie jotted it down. She had heard of it. Hadn't she just read something about it in *People* magazine?

"All things considered," Lucy mused as though she were considering it for the first time right then, "yes, I guess it is. Carl has been our contact with the winery for the past few years. He's a good man."

Olivia played on that. "It would mean *so* much to Natalie and him if you and your husband would come to the wedding. May I put you down as a yes?"

"Well, we're a little unsure. The Labor Day weekend is always a busy one for us. If the wedding is going to be huge, we won't have much time with Natalie and Carl."

"Actually," Olivia confided, "it's going to be fairly intimate. They've limited the list to those people who mean the most to them. You and your husband have been loyal friends. We all take great pride knowing that Asquonset wines are available at the Dome. It's such an important restaurant. Didn't I see that Prince Charles and the boys were just there?" The words were barely out of her mouth when she had the awful fear that she'd remembered wrong.

But Natalie was nodding in delight.

"You certainly did," Lucy confirmed, seeming as impressed as Natalie that Olivia had mentioned it. "We were thrilled. People eat up every little detail about those boys. How do you put a price tag on that kind of publicity?"

"You don't," Olivia acknowledged as she read Natalie's latest scribble. "I'm afraid we can't promise publicity like that at the wedding. Natalie has friends in the press, several of whom will be coming, but she's asked that they respect the privacy of the day. Whether they do is anyone's guess."

"You know," Lucy decided, "I think that we would like to come. Yes. We would. I've always loved Natalie, and that Carl . . . a gorgeous man, there. It sounds like it's going to be a special time. Consider this an acceptance. We'll plan ahead and get someone to cover the restaurant for us."

"*Y-E-S*," Olivia wrote on her pad. Ending the call as though Lucy were an old friend of hers, too, she looked at a grinning Natalie.

"Thank you," Natalie said. "You did that very well." When the phone rang again, her grin faded. "Oh dear."

But Olivia was into it now. She held up a not-to-worry hand, picked up the phone again, and said a jaunty, "Seebring residence." She listened for a minute, then put the caller on hold. "It's the caterer," she told Natalie. "He's wondering if you've chosen the menu from the list he sent."

Natalie pressed a spot between her eyes. "I was supposed to call him last week." The hand left her eyes. She extracted a folder from the desk drawer and set it open in front of Olivia. "I've checked what we want. It's early to be doing this—we can always make changes later—but this man is a *stickler* for getting something tentative down on paper. He's affiliated with Johnson and Wales, though. He's the best in the state. In truth, I could close my eyes and blindly point to ten things on this list, and every single one of them would be incredibly delicious. Would you be a dear and run through this with him, while I head over to the office? I think my notes should be clear."

HER NOTES WERE PERFECTLY CLEAR. Olivia went through the menu course by course, playing the role of the hostess, asking all of the questions she would want answers to if she were giving the party herself—and Lord knew, she had played *that* game often enough. It was great fun.

She had no sooner hung up the phone when it rang again. This time it was Anne Marie, the receptionist at the office, calling to say that an applicant for the position of maid was on the line and that Natalie had suggested she put the woman through to Olivia.

Olivia had never hired a day cleaner, much less a full-time maid. But some things were obvious enough. Taking the call, she asked about those, made notes for Natalie, and put them in a file marked MAID. She was readying to return to the photos of the early Asquonset years when Carl arrived.

"Let's take a walk," he said. "I'll show you the winery."

THEY DIDN'T ACTUALLY WALK, but took one of the golf carts used by the staff to shuttle from one part of Asquonset to another. "We cover sixty-five acres in all," Carl explained in a deep, slow, confident voice as he deftly steered the cart along the gravel road. Olivia could understand how Natalie had found that voice a comfort during her earliest days here. It flowed in a richly masculine way.

"Fifty are planted with grapes," he said. "A few

have corn and potatoes, but the rest are either forested or devoted to buildings." As he turned off onto a dirt path that wormed through the trees, he shot her an amused glance. "So here we go, riding through the forest, and you're wondering why in the devil we didn't put the buildings closer together."

Olivia smiled. "That thought did cross my mind. But what do I know about wine making? I'm sure there's a good reason."

"Good?" He was indulgent as they rounded a turn. "Actually, it's more for looks than anything else. Natalie wanted the Great House to be special. She wanted it to stand alone, up there at the top of the vineyard. She wanted people visiting to have a taste of what it was like when the vineyard was just a vineyard." He chuckled. " 'Course, it hasn't been 'just a vineyard' for years. But it's only in the last twenty or so that we needed more buildings. When that happened, Natalie took to the idea of having distinct activity centers. She feels that each one can have an importance all its own that would be lost if they were grouped together. So she put the business end in a converted garage by the road and the winery up here by the river."

"What about the shed?" Olivia asked. It was a three-minute walk from the house. No golf cart was needed at all.

"The shed's something else," Carl explained, keeping his eyes on the path. "Like the Great House, it was started way back when, then added to and added to. If we'd been starting from scratch, she might've given it more of its own space. But she says she likes seeing it. She says it's such a vital part of the vineyard that it has a right to be closer to the Great House."

He paused.

Olivia was admiring his profile, thinking how remarkable it was at eighty and what a delight to watch, when he said, "Speaking of the shed, I want to apologize."

"Apologize?"

"For Simon. He hasn't been particularly welcoming."

Olivia smiled and shook her head, gesturing that there was no problem at all. "He's worried about the grapes, and here we are with another damp day." The trees shielded them now, but above the leaves were clouds aplenty. "Besides, he's been fine."

"He's been barely civil," Carl remarked, holding the wheel now with both hands. "He could have joined us for dinner at least once since you've come. He could have been the one to take you through the vineyards. He *should* have done that, since he's in charge there now. I want you to know that it isn't anything about you. It's about him."

Olivia suspected that, yes, it was about her, too. Simon knew she was there. He looked up at her each morning now. Had she been more professional, more successful, more interesting—he might have sought her out.

Not that *she* was interested. She was definitely *not* interested.

But then there was the other. "He told me about his wife."

Carl looked at her in surprise. The cart slowed. "When'd he do that?"

"My first morning here. We were both outside. No one else was up." She hurried on, grateful for the chance to get it out in the open. "He said he was worried that Natalie had brought me here to be with him, and he wanted me to know that wouldn't happen."

The cart came to a stop. Carl looked appalled. "Did he *really* say that?"

"I told him that I didn't want it either, and I'd like to tell you that, too." She wanted it on the record, just in case anyone else had weird ideas. "I'm not Simon's type. I'm not what he needs. I'm not looking for a man *at all*. I'm doing just fine on my own. Between Tess and my work, I have plenty to keep me busy." Mindful that Carl was Simon's father, she added, "This has nothing to do with Simon, you understand, and everything to do with me."

Carl returned his eyes to the path. He set the cart moving ahead again, but his brows remained knit.

Olivia tried to soothe him. "I'm sure Simon's a wonderful man. He's smart. He works hard. I look out my window every morning at dawn, and there he is with his coffee at the end of the patio. He deserves the best after what he's been through. I can't begin to imagine what it's like losing two people you love like that."

"Three," Carl said.

The word hung in the air.

"Three?"

Carl took his eyes from the path only long enough for her to see their sad blue cast. "Simon lost three people he loved in that accident—Laura, Liana, and Ana."

"Ana." Olivia repeated the name as Carl had said it—*Uh-na,* with each syllable distinct. It was an incredibly simple, incredibly beautiful sound. "Ana. Who was she?"

"My wife. Simon's mother."

Olivia pressed a hand to her heart. It had stopped cold for a second, then begun to pound. After a minute, she blew out a breath. "Your *wife* was on the boat, too?"

Carl nodded. The movement was heavy with sorrow, a testament to the fact that Simon wasn't the only one who had suffered a loss—and suddenly a whole other chapter of Asquonset history opened up, one that Olivia hadn't given much thought to before. Her focus had been on Natalie, but Carl had to have had a life all those years as well. And Simon had to have had a mother.

"How *horrible,*" she said softly. "The memories must be just as painful for you as they are for Simon."

The golf cart continued slowly on. "I'm older. I can be more philosophical than my son. Ana and I had many good years together. She was a kind woman. She was an understanding woman. But she wasn't well. She had been diagnosed with cancer the year before the accident. She was having treatments. They were difficult. The doctors didn't give her much time. But she loved to sail. We all did." With a gentle smile, he grew silent.

"Simon, too?"

"Simon, especially. He taught Laura how to sail—and she was good at it. She knew how to handle that boat. She did everything right."

"Then what *happened?*"

Carl drove on for another minute before he spoke. "She knew how poorly Ana was feeling and thought that a ride on the bay in the sun would give her a boost. So she zipped the three of them into life jackets, raised the sail, and left the dock. Ana was happy. People who watched them leave said they could see that. She was propped up against the gunwale, with little Liana nestled in under her arm. It was a perfect day for a sail, just enough wind without much of a chop."

Olivia was looking at him, waiting for the next installment, when the cart emerged from the woods. The world around them brightened, a cruel irony in view of his tale.

Carl brought the cart to a stop. His hands fell to his lap. Eyes straight ahead, he took a deep breath.

"The sailing was so good that Laura went out farther than she might have done on another day, and there was nothing wrong with that. She wasn't the only one to do it. There were other boats around. They were taking advantage of ideal conditions, too." He looked at Olivia. "There was a speedboat—one of those big, long, powerful ones. Two men were on it, hopped up on something. Didn't even realize they were heading for our boat until they were nearly on top of it. They tried to veer off, but their judgment was so impaired that it had the reverse effect."

"My God," Olivia breathed.

"They cut the sailboat right in half, then sped off. Never did catch them."

"My *God.*"

"The coast guard says the force of the crash just tore everything apart. Even with life jackets on, they didn't have a chance. It was like they were on bicycles on a train track when a huge locomotive sped past." He let out a breath, then inhaled slowly and straightened. "Now why did I tell you all that?"

"Because I asked."

"It's not something we talk much about. Doesn't seem to be a point."

"But talking makes you feel better. Don't you think?"

He considered her point, then sighed. "What *I* think doesn't matter as much as what my Natalie thinks. She thinks it's important, which is why she hired you. You know about the situation with her family?"

"Yes."

"I've known Susanne and Greg since they were born. I always liked them. And they always liked me. They weren't snotty little rich kids, if you know what I mean."

Olivia nodded.

"They're feeling unsettled," he went on. "They weren't prepared. I've agonized over that."

"Did you and Natalie discuss how to break it to them?"

"For *weeks*. Natalie kept trying to broach it with them, but she never quite got the whole thing out. She was worried that they would react exactly the way they have. So we went back and forth, she and I. A personal visit. A phone call. Nat doing it. *Me* doing it. We finally took the way that was easiest for us. They can criticize us for it, but I'm not sure they would have taken the news well in *any* form. They're still dealing with Alexander's death."

Olivia sensed that he was right. "Natalie seems philosophical about their reaction."

"That's Natalie for you. She isn't one to bitch and moan. She accepts and moves on. She's a survivor. She's a *doer*. That's why she hired you." Looking at Olivia, he grew purposeful. "I want Susanne and Greg back in the fold, but I understand the problem. It'll be hard for them to see me one way after so many years seeing me another. You'll have to help them do that."

"I'll try."

"I'm not trying to take Alexander's place," he went on. "He was their father. I don't want to be that. All I want is to make their mother happy. That's all I've ever wanted."

"Did you love her, way back when you were kids?"

"Sure, I did."

"Why didn't you marry her then?"

"Because she married Alexander."

"But why didn't she marry you?"

"Hasn't she told you?"

"No."

"She will."

Olivia smiled. "You tell me now."

But he drew himself up and smiled. "Nope. That's not my job. Natalie's the storyteller. I'm just the guy who runs the winery." He hitched his chin forward. "Here we are."

Olivia looked up at a large gristmill. "Oh *my,*" she said in surprise. *"This* is the winery?" She had imagined something quite different.

Carl started up the cart. "It is," he said with pride and drove on until the dirt path ended in a paved lot. A road approached it from the other direction. He pulled up beside two parked cars, killed the switch, and stepped out. "I'd like to say that I run this end of the operation, but that'd be taking too much credit. I'm an old guy. I need my afternoon nap."

"That doesn't mean you can't run things," Olivia said, because Carl was as vibrant a man as she'd ever seen at his age. "You run this. Natalie runs marketing and sales. Simon runs the vineyard." With mention of his name, she pictured the man. The image was enhanced now by what Carl had said. "Do you think Simon works the kinds of hours he does so that he doesn't have to think about the accident?" From what Olivia had seen, he worked sunup to sundown, seven days a week.

Carl was at her side of the cart when she stepped out. He touched her elbow just lightly enough to get her walking beside him. "Maybe. But being vineyard manager is that kind of job. It's like parenting. Grapes need coddling 'round the clock."

They crossed the parking lot and started up the short stone path that led to the winery door. The name and logo were on a plaque, a smaller version of the sign off the main road, but Olivia only gave it a passing glance. "He must take vacations."

"Not in four years. What's he going to do—go to the Caribbean alone?"

"Doesn't he date at all?"

"He hasn't so far."

"But what does he do for *fun?*"

The older man thought about that. "He tends the grapes." He pulled the screen door open.

Olivia found herself in a semicircular foyer whose stone walls made it feel like a cave. The corridors that branched left and right were narrow but tall—a full three stories' worth of windows. As Carl guided her to a large wooden door in the center, he said, "Tending the grapes isn't a bad thing. It got me through many a hard time."

Olivia was about to ask what hard times he meant when, feeling a sudden drop in the temperature, she looked around and forgot the thought. They were in a cavernous room filled with huge stainless steel tanks. Each tank had dials and gauges on the front. Long ladders stood against several, stretching the twelve or so feet from the floor to the top of the tank. The floor was hard concrete.

Carl was a tour guide with an agenda. He led her past the tanks to the far end of the room, where he showed her the machine that crushed and stemmed the grapes. He explained that red wine was made by fermenting the grapes skin and all, while white wine was made from the fermented juice alone. He showed her the tubing that carried juice from the crusher to the stainless steel tanks, where the fermentation took place.

He led her into a second room, this one nearly as cavernous but filled with multiple tiers of oak barrels. In contrast to the harsh stainless steel and concrete of the fermentation room, this room was mellow. The light was dim. The barrels were neatly lined up and soft edged. The smell was of wood.

"We age the wine here," Carl explained. "The barrel, itself—how it's made, where it's from, how many seasons it's been used—plays a large part in the process. All those things affect the taste of the wine. The length of time the wine sits here is another variable."

That decision, it seemed, was made by the wine maker. His name was David Sperling, and his office was an enclosed laboratory-like loft high above the barrels. Olivia was introduced to him and to his assistant, either of whom she might have liked to talk with a while, but Carl moved her along to the bottling room. Here was state-of-the-art machinery, installed just the year before. Proudly, he explained how the sterilized bottles were moved in and out, up and down, down and around in the process of being filled, corked, and labeled.

Olivia was fascinated. By the time they reached the outside air again, she was ready to start over and go through the whole thing a second time. Carl looked pleased when she told him that, but he had afternoon plans that began with rescuing his intended from her advertising meeting.

"Another time," he promised.

It was just as well. The golf cart puttered back through the woods and had no sooner emerged from the dark and rounded the side of the Great House when Olivia saw Tess. She was sitting on the bottommost of those five broad stone steps, her body hunched into a knot.

Twelve

OLIVIA SAT DOWN on the step beside Tess. "Hi, sweetie. How was your morning?"

Tess answered with the quiver of her chin, quite a feat with her chin on her knees. Glasses halfway down her nose, she stared glumly out at the vineyard.

Olivia tucked a long brown curl back toward the French braid that was supposed to have held it in place. She wondered if Tess was discouraged by something specific, or if it was just more of the same. "How was Mrs. Adelson?"

"She's fine, but I'm not. I'm not getting this, Mom."

Ach. More of the same. Harder to take, perhaps, with a new strategy and such high hopes. "You will. It just takes time."

"She says totally different things from the tutors at school."

"I know that. She and I have discussed it." Olivia tried to catch Sandy alone whenever she could. She was feeling guilty for letting the past tutors do so little and wanted to be—to use Sandy's word—proactive. "But everything she says makes sense, Tess. Mrs. Adelson may be just what you need."

Tess lifted her head, turned it, and stared at her like she'd lost her mind. "Do you *know* what visual mapping means? First there's a *story* map. Then there's a *character* map. I mean, I could spend a year doing each one, Mom. It takes *forever* to map things out."

"Now it does. That's because it's new. Once you get the knack of it, it'll be easy and quick. It'll become second nature. You like the book, don't you?" They were reading *A Wrinkle in Time,* by Madeleine L'Engle. It was on three of the five book lists that they had checked, and Sandy was thrilled. She had worked with it many times before and said that it was perfect for visualization training.

Tess murmured a begrudging, "Yes."

"And just think about the head start you're getting on the other fifth-graders."

"But then I have to read the book a second time when school starts. I *hate* reading."

"That's only because it's a struggle. Once

you're done with Mrs. Adelson, it won't *be* such a struggle. You may even enjoy it."

Tess looked up through her glasses in a way that rendered her eyes all the more woeful. "But what if I go to a different school? What if I go to one that doesn't even read this book?"

Sandy Adelson's school read it. Olivia was starting to think about applying for Tess to be admitted there. Cambridge Heath hadn't yet made a decision, they had told her when she called the day before. Nor were there any job nibbles . . . *anywhere*. She could easily turn her focus to Providence, could prod the places she had already contacted and send résumés to others. She could map out a thirty-mile radius of the city and send letters to everything within that distance.

"If that happens," she reasoned, "you'll have learned how to do visual mapping, so you can apply it to the books that you *do* read." Wrapping an arm around the child's shoulders, she gave a squeeze. "Come on, Tess. Anything that's good is hard. But in time it gets easier and easier. Mrs. Adelson says you're one of the smartest kids she's ever worked with—and she's been working with dyslexics for twenty years."

"Yeah, well, she can't help me with sailing. I looked at the book they gave us, Mom. I can't figure that stuff out."

Of course, she couldn't. That *stuff* included things like "head stay," "bowsprit," and "traveler," all of which fell under the title "nomenclature." Tess couldn't get past the title to the others.

"Did you try to visualize it?" Olivia asked. "Did you try to see 'nomenclature' as names, like 'shirt,' 'shorts,' 'shoes'?" She pointed to each as she said it.

Tess gave an aggrieved sigh. "Parts of the boat. That's what you said. But I can't visualize them if I don't know what they are."

"We went over the diagram."

"It's just a *picture.*"

"You're upset. Getting upset doesn't help."

"Those *things* don't *mean* anything to me."

"That's only because you're not familiar with sailboats, Tess. Once you put the name with the part in real life, you'll know what it is. They said they'd be working on that this afternoon, didn't they?"

"Yes, but most of the other kids already know it."

Olivia guessed that was because the other kids either were from families that belonged to the yacht club or had grandparents who had been taking them sailing since they'd been old enough to talk. "O-kay. Then this is what I think you should do." Here it was—a basic lesson in socialization. "Let the teacher talk. Let the other kids talk. Ask questions. Learn from what they say."

Tess looked doubtful. "What if they ask *me* something? What do I *say?*"

"If it has to do with the parts of the boat, just

say that this is the first time you've ever been on a boat."

"But it isn't. We went whale watching. We went on a sunset sail up in Maine."

"Not the same, Tess. Come on. You know that." She glanced at her watch, then at the patches of blue that had appeared in the sky. "Have you had lunch?"

"Yes."

Olivia hadn't, but she could live without lunch. It was twelve-thirty. She had to drop Tess at the yacht club at two, then hurry back here to do the work she'd been hired to do.

But first things first. "We're getting some sun. Let's make pictures."

"Of what?"

"Grapes. I snap, you draw." She tipped her head. "Yes?"

"Can I snap, too?"

"Only after you've drawn."

"That isn't fair. Using the camera's faster than using a pencil. Why do you always get the easier part?"

"Because I can't draw for beans," Olivia said. Hooking an arm around Tess's neck, she popped a kiss on the child's head. "Let's *do* it."

THE AIR WAS SIGNIFICANTLY WARMER by the time they fetched the camera, the sketchbook, and a piece of charcoal, the last being Tess's choice in lieu of a pencil, her little bit of control over the situation. That said, she went along willingly, as Olivia had known she would. Tess liked to draw because she did it so well, which wasn't to say that her fear of sailing class was eased, but at least she was distracted from it.

Olivia turned her face to the sun and breathed in the scent of warm leaves and drying earth. She forced herself to relax, forced herself to believe that Tess would grow up to be a literate, fully functioning, self-sufficient adult.

"Let's go," Tess said.

Olivia opened her eyes. She looked around. Between Natalie's tour and her own study of the vineyard map, she knew what was where. Simon would be working with the most worrisome of the grapes. Given this region in general and this summer in particular, those would be reds—either Cabernet Sauvignon or Pinot Noir.

She pointed in the other direction, toward the Riesling block, but hadn't gone more than five paces when she did an about-face. It made perfect sense to locate Simon first. Then they would know exactly what to avoid.

"Which *way,* Mom?"

"*This* way." She walked along the road until she reached the Pinot Noir fields, picked a random row, and started down it. The dirt underfoot was loose. It looked to be newly plowed. The vines

reached the first tier of the wire trellis, with the occasional leaf now growing higher. The grapes
themselves were larger than they had been when
Olivia and Tess had first come, but they were still
sad, nutty-looking little bunches. Simon was
nowhere in sight.

Tess ran up beside her. "The light isn't right
here. It's too flat. You always say that it's better
with early light or late light."

"Yes, well, this is the time we have, and it's
midday. See, that's where you're the lucky one.
You can draw in whatever kind of light you want."
Just ahead of them, a small bird flew away from a
spot under the leaves some two feet off the ground.
Within seconds, another followed.

Olivia stopped walking. She studied the spot
where the birds had been. Slowly, she moved in.
"It's a nest," she said softly. "Do you see?"

Tess was fast in the lead, creeping forward. She
stopped several feet from the nest and crouched
down. "Look," she whispered in delight when
Olivia came down beside her.

The nest was small and perfectly round, a
miraculous creation of dried grasses and sticks.
More miraculous, though, were the little beaks
moving amid tiny balls of fluff.

"Three babies?" Olivia whispered.

"Four," Tess whispered back. She scooted
away, pulling Olivia with her, and let go only when
they were a good six feet from the nest. She sat

down in the dirt. "If we stay too close, the parents will be afraid to come back, and the babies will die." She opened her sketch pad.

Olivia watched her for several minutes. She never failed to be amazed how a child with a visual discrimination problem that made reading so difficult could so easily reproduce a visual image freehand. But Tess did it. These drawings might lack the fine shading and nuance that would come with maturity, but she reproduced shapes of remarkable accuracy and scale with uncanny skill. Her drawings could be as simple as that minimalist line of grapes in the Asquonset logo, but they captured the subject—and with feeling.

This by a child who, as a toddler, had had trouble putting the round puzzle piece in the round hole; a child who, to this day, couldn't do a jigsaw puzzle if her life depended on it; a child who loved to learn but found reading to be pure torment.

Tess had been right. The light was too flat for making interesting photographs of the grapes, so Olivia photographed Tess. The child was adorable, sitting there on the ground with her legs folded in and her hair curling out. Her gaze went back and forth from the bird's nest to the paper. When her glasses slid down, she pushed them up with the heel of her hand. The charcoal moved easily, almost lyrically.

Olivia caught Tess's concentration. She caught deliberation over one line drawn, and the change of mind over another. She caught excitement when the baby birds' parents returned to the nest. She also caught startled awareness, then abject horror when Tess looked up and saw Buck.

"Oh no, Mom," the child cried softly and scrambled to her feet. "The cat'll get the birds." She stole forward, passing the nest, putting her little body between the big Maine coon and the chicks. She held out a hand to Buck and crooned, "What a nice cat you are, what a *nice* cat you are." Dipping its mangy head, the cat rubbed her hand. "Good boy. *Good* boy. Know something? I think there's more to do on the other side of this field. Wanna show me? Come on, Buck. Come on, kitty."

The cat followed her as she moved away, crossing down the row of vines. Olivia photographed the two of them until Buck suddenly made his body low and long and scooted under the vine to the next row with his scruffy tail in pursuit. Up for the challenge, Tess shot Olivia a wide-eyed look before taking off down the row, whipping around the end, and disappearing.

Olivia grinned. With the camera strap on her shoulder now, she followed at a saner pace. She couldn't see Tess above the vines, but the occasional squeal was a tip-off to where she'd gone. Olivia followed the sounds, walking along the end of the block, looking down one row after another in search of the pair.

She was nearly at the last row when she found them, but a regrouping had taken place. Buck was now with Simon, who wore dark glasses and a sheen of sweat. He was on his haunches, working with the leaves nearest the grapes. Tess stood alone at the end of the row.

Olivia came up behind her, thinking that now that they'd found him, they should make tracks, but Tess seemed firmly rooted. Apparently the game wasn't done.

Simon gave the two of them little more than a glance. Aside from its brevity, which suggested their irrelevance in his life, it was neither here nor there.

"Are you pruning again?" Tess asked.

"Yes," he said without looking her way.

"Is that all you ever do?"

"No."

"It's all *I* ever see you do."

"That's because you're off playing while I work."

"Not playing. Studying."

His hand hovered midair before settling on a leaf and gently removing it. "Fine. You're studying."

Tess stepped closer to the grapes. Bending at the waist, she peered at the little bunches of buds. "These are still pathetic. When do they start looking like grapes?"

Simon shot Olivia an annoyed glance. She held up her hands and shook her head. He was a big boy.

He could take care of himself. Besides, she had been wondering about those little bunches herself.

He studied the vine for a minute before removing another leaf. "August."

"Why so long?"

"It takes them that long to grow."

Tess took another look at the cluster nearest her. "Are you sure they're *grapes?*"

He stopped for a minute and mopped his forehead with his arm. His voice was tight. "Yes. I'm sure they're grapes."

"It was a legitimate question," Tess charged.

Simon looked at her then. "That's a big word, 'legitimate.' Too big for a little girl like you. You shouldn't use words you don't understand."

"I understand it. I'm not dumb."

Olivia couldn't see Tess's face, but she sure knew that voice. It was defensive. They were walking on thin ice here.

The cat felt it, too. He was looking from Simon to Tess and back.

Olivia was wondering if she should speak up and diffuse things when, calmly enough, Tess asked, "What else do you do?"

Simon moved on to the next vine, first reaching up to guide the highest leaves around the trellis. "I use a ripper on the ground you're standing on."

"A ripper?"

"A machine that furrows the dirt and aerates the soil."

"Why do you need to do that?"

He sighed. "The more holes there are in the dirt, the better it breathes. Of course, your standing there clogs them all up again. You're undoing my work."

For a minute Tess didn't move. Then she took a large, flat-footed step that brought her right up to the nearest vine.

"Tess," Olivia cautioned, but Tess was on a roll.

"How do you know what leaves to pick?" she asked Simon.

Simon sent Olivia a warning look, put his hands on his hips, and looked back at Tess. "I just know."

"How?"

"It's instinctive."

"I'll bet you're just saying that. I'll bet there aren't any rules. I'll bet you just pick off whatever leaves you want." In the blink of an eye, she reached out and tore off as many leaves as a hand could get in one clutch.

"Tess!" Olivia cried and came forward this time.

By the time she reached the child, Simon was there, too. His expression was dark. "Thank you," he said, taking the leaves from her hand. He held them up. "Do you know what you just did?"

Tess tipped back her head to meet his gaze. Her face was pale, but she didn't cower. "I pruned your vines."

"You just tore the life and guts away from this fruit."

"I don't think she meant—" Olivia began, but Tess cut her off, jutting her chin toward Simon.

"*You* do it."

"Not like that, and not as many. It's an art. But you wouldn't know that. You think you're pretty smart, but you're not."

"Simon, please don't—" Olivia tried, but he cut her off.

He was glaring at Tess. "Oh, are you *ever* not. What you just did was thoughtless and mean. What you just did was *stupid.*"

Tess stared at him, breathing hard, fighting tears. About to lose the battle, she turned on a heel and headed back the way she had come. "You're the one who's mean," she called back. "I don't care if you hate me." She whirled around again. "I wouldn't *want* you for my friend."

"Well, that's good," he called, "because it ain't gonna happen. Want friends? Try a smile. Bet you don't know how to do that, smart little girl."

"Simon," Olivia begged.

"I know how," Tess said, rigid with fury, "but I wouldn't waste it on you. You're mean—and—and you smell and you're lousy at tennis—and—and—and—your cat is *fat!*" She whirled around and stalked off.

Swearing softly, Olivia started after her. She hadn't gone far, though, when she turned back to Simon. "That was incredible," she said in dismay. "Just *incredible*. I mean, I can excuse her because she's a child, but you'd think you were one, too, the way you stood there bickering with her."

Judging from the belligerent look on his face, he wasn't ready to back down. His eyes were still dark, his jaw square and hard. "Did you see what she did? These grapes are my responsibility. How'd you like it if she tore up some papers and ruined three days of *your* work?"

"She didn't know she was doing that. Maybe if you'd explained what you were doing instead of being so *superior,* she would have responded more rationally."

"I don't have time to explain every little thing I do. In case you haven't noticed, this is a business I'm running."

"Oh, I noticed. How could I not? You work all the time. It's no wonder you have zero social skills." She put a hand over her face, then took it off and held it up. "Sorry. That isn't the issue here. The issue is Tess."

"She's a hateful child," he said and started to turn away, but Olivia wasn't about to leave it at that.

"No," she replied, leaning forward with fury, "she's a child with a problem, just like you are. Yours is eternal grief, terminal self-absorption, maybe even a martyr complex—I don't know. Hers is dyslexia. She's ten years old, and she can't read. She just finished a nightmare of a school year with a teacher who belittled her and kids who made fun of her, and yes, she should smile more, but how do you make a child do that when she feels like scum? She thinks she's dumb because she tries and tries and can't get more than a C, and she wears glasses, so she thinks she's *ugly.* She came here with a big self-esteem problem. I was hoping the summer would give her a break. You just single-handedly blew away that hope."

She glanced at Buck, who was staring at her with startled eyes. "She's right. Your cat *is* fat."

With that, she went off in search of Tess. She jogged back down the rows the way they'd come, turned at the end of the block, and let anger propel her up the road toward the house. All the while she searched the fields, but there was no sign of a little girl with a green Asquonset T-shirt and faded denim shorts. In a matter of seconds, Olivia feared that Tess had run into the woods, lost her way, ended up at the river, fallen in, and drowned.

She stopped running, suddenly short of breath. "Tess?" she called, frantic now. *"Tess?"* She shaded her eyes and scoured the horizon. *"Where are you?"* She would call the police. She would call the fire department. She would ring a bell. An alarm. Surely they had one at the Great House.

She had just set off in that direction when she spotted something green that didn't match the rhododendrons. It was Tess, sitting with her back to the world, in the midst of the shrubs in front of the Great House.

• • •

SIMON SPOTTED TESS at the same time Olivia did, and though her legs moved faster, his were longer. He overtook her when she was still thirty feet from the child, and slowed only marginally.

"I'll talk to her," he said.

"Not unless you've grown up in the last two minutes," Olivia warned in a voice that was low but tight.

He deserved the dig and knew it. But realizing that was solving only half the problem.

Stepping in front of her, he forced her to stop. "I'd like to talk with her."

Olivia's eyes flashed. "If it's to ease your guilt about behaving badly, don't bother. She knows there are uncaring people in the world."

He felt the force of her anger, flashing in her eyes. Even if she hadn't spoken, he would have gotten the message.

"I'm not one of them," he said.

"How do I know that?"

"You'll have to take my word for it. I made the mess, so I should clean it up."

He held her eyes, thinking that she ought to look like a boy with that hair but that she didn't. Then her fierceness eased, and it was even more true; when she allowed even an ounce of weakness to show, she was downright feminine.

Was it weakness? Or was it vulnerability? Or even confusion? He wondered.

Whatever, she looked like she wanted to believe him but wasn't sure she could. And she was right to be that way. There were plenty of uncaring people in the world. Only, he wasn't one of them. He really wasn't. At least, he didn't want to be.

"Please," he said.

The fierceness returned in a look that said she would have him *by the balls* if he made things worse. The message was so pointed—so *lewd*—that he nearly laughed. Fortunately, he knew better than to do that.

He approached Tess quietly. When she shot a look over her shoulder and saw him there, her eyes flew to her mother, then back. Her body tensed. She slid a foot under her thigh in advance of rising.

He struck quickly, keeping his voice low. "I'm sorry. I was wrong. I shouldn't have said what I did."

Tess stared at him.

"I was upset."

She didn't move.

"I should have explained why I do what I do with the leaves. There is a reason behind it all."

Tess clenched her jaw.

She wasn't making it easy for him, and he deserved her resistance, too. But it wasn't easy. He wasn't experienced in dealing with ten-year-old children, much less in groveling.

"I'm used to working alone," he said, hoping she might understand that.

"It's me," Tess said, and suddenly it was there

on the surface, just as Olivia had said, an issue of self-esteem. "You just hate me."

He felt terrible. "I don't hate you."

"You've never said one nice thing to me. Never once."

"I don't hate you. How can I hate you? I don't know you."

"I annoy you. You take one look at me and you think about every awful thing in the world."

"No," he said. "I take one look at you and I think about my daughter. She died four years ago. I miss her."

He hadn't planned to say that, couldn't believe that he had. Tess was a child. She wouldn't understand death. And if she asked how Liana had died? He couldn't mention a sailing accident. *Couldn't* mention that. If he did, she would never step foot in a sailboat.

Olivia would never forgive him. *Natalie* would never forgive him.

But Tess was looking less harsh. At least she was listening.

"That doesn't excuse it," he told her. "The things I said were mean and untrue. I was punishing you because I don't have her. It was wrong of me. I'm sorry."

He sent Olivia a tentative glance, wondering if he was botching it, looking for a sign but seeing an expectancy instead, like she was waiting for him to say more.

What in the hell more was he supposed to say?

He wasn't good at this. He would have been a lousy father.

Putting his hands in his back pockets, he faced Tess again. "Well, that's it. I just wanted to apologize." Feeling awkward and more inadequate than he had ever felt in his life, he cut his losses and left.

He didn't look back, not even when he knew that Olivia's eyes were on him. He didn't want to see those eyes. They made him *feel*.

He kept walking toward the Pinot Noir fields, kept walking until he was immersed in the scent of the vines, until he heard the soft creaking of the only creatures that he did know how to raise. He was good at this. He would stick with it for a while.

Thirteen

"JILLIAN?"

"Yes?"

"This is Olivia Jones. How are you?" Jillian Rhodes was the law student subletting Olivia's Cambridge apartment

"Fine, thanks. Your place is great. I just love it."

"I tried earlier. There was no answer. They must be working you too hard."

"They don't think so," the young woman said, "but I shouldn't complain. They're paying me well. How are you and your daughter doing?"

"We're fine, thanks. I was wondering what's come in the mail."

"I have it in a pile. Hold on." There was a clatter. Olivia's mind's eye saw the handset drop the length of its coiled cord and bounce against the kitchen wall. It was as good a diversion as any from the suspense of wondering what was in that pile.

"Here we go," Jillian said. "I sent you the bills."

"I did get them."

"What's left is mostly junk. There's a slew of catalogues. There's a bunch of credit card applications. Are you waiting for something special?"

"Something from a school called Cambridge Heath?"

"Uh, no. Nothing here like that."

"Then from a museum?" Olivia asked. "Or an art gallery?"

There was a pause. Then, "Here's a postcard from an art gallery in Carmel. It's an advertisment for a show."

"No, this would be a business letter."

"Nope. Sorry."

Two down. Olivia swallowed her disappointment. "What about a personal letter, something handwritten, maybe from the Midwest or the West, or even from the South?" Who was she kidding? She had no idea where her mother was. The woman could be right across the bay in Newport, for all Olivia knew!

"No," Jillian said. "There's nothing here like that. There's one that looks like it's handwritten, only I just wet it and the ink doesn't smudge. Amazing what solicitors do now. There've been some phone calls, though. From the same man. Serious voice, urgent sound. He wants to know how to reach you, but he won't leave his name."

Olivia sighed. "That'll be Ted. He knows I'm here, but he doesn't have my direct number. When he calls the central office, they refuse to put him through."

"What should I say next time he calls here?"

Tell him to get lost, Olivia wanted to say. *I told him we were done. Have I had second thoughts? No. Do I miss him? NO!*

But dumping that on Jillian would be a cowardly thing to do. Olivia figured that at some point, she was going to have to call Ted herself.

"Just keep putting him off," she said. "Whatever you do, don't give him the number I gave you. That's only for emergencies. Call me if someone named Carol Jones calls. Call me if Cambridge Heath calls. Call me if someone calls me about work. That'd be the museum or gallery."

"Gotcha," Jillian said.

"HI. THIS IS OLIVIA JONES. May I speak with Arnold Civetti, please?" Arnold Civetti was the curator of a small museum in New York that had a large collection of photographs. Otis said that the man had been toying with the idea of hiring an in-house restorer for years, and that maybe with the right person presented to him on a platter he would do it. Olivia had sent him a résumé early on in her job search and had received an immediate "Thanks, we'll let you know, don't call us, we'll call you" kind of letter. Three months had passed since then.

She was tired of waiting. Didn't the squeaky wheel get the grease?

"I'm sorry," said a male voice with a slight British edge, "Mr. Civetti is out of the country."

"Can you tell me when he'll be back?"

"I'm afraid he's gone until after the Fourth. Is there anything I can do for you in the meantime?"

Ideally, he would have said, *I know your name quite well, Ms. Jones. Mr. Civetti mentioned it to me over the phone just last week. He has been in Europe for three months, or he would have been in touch sooner, but he is* very *interested in talking with you. We do indeed have a position for some-one with your qualifications. I have Mr. Civetti's appointment book right here in front of me. Shall we set up a meeting?*

"I do photo restoration work," Olivia said. "I've trained under Otis Thurman." She paused, but there was no reaction to the name. "Since Mr. Thurman is retiring, I'm looking for a new posi-tion. I sent Mr. Civetti a letter last spring. I was wondering if he's given it any more thought."

"We farm out our work."

"Yes, I know. I've actually done some of it that you farmed out to Otis. He was under the impression that Mr. Civetti was considering hiring someone full-time."

There was a brittle laugh. "Oh, I doubt that. Our funding is tighter than ever."

"Then perhaps he would consider me for freelance work." It wasn't ideal. She needed health insurance for both Tess and her, and buying it outside a group would cost a fortune. If she put together enough freelance jobs, though, she could swing it, she supposed.

"Do you have a studio?" the man asked.

"Yes." Otis would let her use his in a pinch. She knew he would.

"And the name of the studio?"

"Jones and Burke," she said off the top of her head. She certainly couldn't use Jones alone. It was common and boring, totally unmemorable. Jones and Burke sounded fine. Actually sounded a little British. Even a little *familiar*. Why was she picturing leather pocketbooks with two-toned flaps?

"You know," the semi-Brit said, "I'm looking through the file as we talk, and I can't seem to find your résumé. Perhaps you could send us another. Include a list of some of the jobs you've done. I'll pass it on to Mr. Civetti, and he'll give it a look."

"I'd appreciate that."

"My pleasure. No need to call again. We'll give you a jingle if we need your services."

• • •

"HI. THIS IS OLIVIA JONES. Is Laura Goodearl there?" Laura Goodearl handled acquisitions for a museum in Montpelier. She didn't do hiring, but she was connected to Otis. He said that she would know if there was photo restoration to be done.

"This is Laura."

"Oh. Hi. I wrote you last month about the possibility of doing some work. I'm Otis Thurman's assistant?"

"Otis." Spoken with a smile. "What a nice man he is. My dad was an artist. He and Otis were friends. How is he?"

"Getting ready for retirement."

"Which is why you're looking for work. We do have a few things coming in, but they won't be here until October. Do you want to send me a résumé?"

Olivia already had. She had also sent a change-of-address notice. "Sure," she said, trying not to feel blown off. "I'll put it right in the mail."

"And give me another call, maybe at the end of September, just to remind me that you're there, okay?"

Olivia promised she would, but she hung up the phone feeling discouraged. "A few pieces" weren't terribly promising. If there was work here, it would be freelance and small. She was done at Asquonset by Labor Day. With Natalie's handsome stipend earmarked for Tess's education, she was going to need living expenses.

• • •

"OLIVIA JONES, PLEASE."

"This is Olivia."

"Hi, it's Jillian Rhodes. I just thought you should know that the same man called again last night. He said it was very, very, *very* important that he talk with you."

Oh, Olivia could hear it. It was quintessential Ted. "I'm sorry about that," she told Jillian. "He shouldn't be bothering you like this. I guess he figures he has a better chance of wheedling the number from you than from the secretary here. I'll give him a call." She paused. "Anything in the mail today?"

"Not anything you want."

"Oh. Okay. Thanks, Jillian."

"TED."

"*Olivia.* How *are* you—did you *know* I was just thinking about you—it couldn't be coincidence that you're calling now—this is *perfect* timing—I just got in from working out—dinner will be done in the microwave in forty-two seconds—forty-one— forty—so it'll be like we're having dinner together."

Olivia kept her voice calm. "Ted," she instructed with care, "I want you to stop calling."

"I only called once."

"Please. Don't lie."

"I'm *not*," he insisted and let out a breath. "All I wanted to do was say hello. Why wouldn't you take my call?"

Olivia wasn't in the mood to argue about how many calls there had been. "Because there's no point. We're not dating anymore."

"That was one of the reasons I wanted to talk with you—this weekend's the Fourth of July—I'm thinking of driving down."

"Ted. Listen to me. We're not dating anymore."

"But we're friends—that hasn't changed just because you're there for the summer—we're best friends—we talk about everything."

"You talk. I don't. I don't want you calling, Ted."

There was a small pause, then a startled, "You sound serious!"

Olivia was wondering how she could make it any clearer when he said an annoyed, "God *damn* it, you've met someone else—it happens to me every time I meet a woman I like—you need to tell me what he has that I don't."

Olivia sighed. "There's no one else. I'm not dating. I'm simply here with my daughter to do a job. I don't have time for anything else right now."

"Then I'll wait until fall—once you're back here you'll be refreshed."

"No, Ted. It's *over.* I don't want to date you now. I don't want to date you in the fall." She didn't know how much more blunt she could be.

"You'll feel different then, so I won't argue with you now—but wow, it's good to hear your voice—I've missed you, Livie."

"Olivia. It's Olivia. I *hate* Livie. You *know* that,

Ted." "Olivia" had elegance; "Livie" was the woman who slaved away as mother to the Waltons.

"I also know that you like me even when you say that you don't."

Olivia wanted to pull out her hair. *"No,* Ted. I do *not* like you. So help me, if you keep calling, I'll contact the phone company. They have special departments now for harassing calls."

"I called *once*—and there was nothing harassing about it—that's a bogus charge. Do you know the trouble you could cause me if you use the word 'harassing'?"

"I know the trouble I could cause. The question is whether *you* do. If so, please think about it next time you pick up the phone and dial my number." She hung up.

OLIVIA CONTINUED TO ENJOY each dawn from her private window seat. Having set up a small coffeepot in her room, she brewed enough to fill a mug. She couldn't imagine a better way to start the day than with the mingling scents of mocha java and vineyard dew.

And watching Simon. She couldn't forget that. He was part of the scene, a segment of the still life that was fixed in her mind. Each day he appeared at the very same place at the very same time, a very much alive Marlboro Man minus the hat, the horse, the chaps, the hills, and the cigarette. That left just the rugged good looks, which Simon had in spades.

Not that Olivia was falling for them. She went out of her way to avoid the man during the day, and thankfully he hadn't yet joined them for dinner—something she would have found very awkward. But he was definitely part of her morning idyll.

He was the human part. She might not have used that word before the fiasco with Tess. Since then, though, it kept coming to her.

It came again now, when he looked up at her. He had looked up before with a brief glance over his shoulder, just enough to tell her that he knew she was there watching. This time, though, he turned around, faced the house, and met her gaze.

"Well, hel-lo," she whispered, hugging her knees, which suddenly felt odd and tingly. "What's with *you*, knees?"

She held her breath, wondering if he would wave, but he didn't. He just stood as he often did, with his weight on one hip, and he looked up at her.

Well, what could she do but look right back? She wasn't giving him the satisfaction of looking away. She had just as much a right to be here as he had to be there. And he was a fine one to call Tess out for not smiling. Olivia hadn't seen a smile on *him* yet. If he didn't have the courage to offer at least that—or to lift even one finger in greeting—that was his problem.

But it was her problem, too, because the weakness hadn't stopped at her knees. It had gone straight to the pit of her stomach, where it hummed a sexy little song.

Well, what did she *expect,* seeing him out there day after day, and her up here in her nightshirt, fresh from bed?

But she wasn't moving. On principle, she wasn't. She sipped her coffee, but otherwise kept her arms around her legs, holding in all those little wild threads of desire; and she looked right back at him, wondering if he felt any of it at all.

> Desire wasn't something we talked about when I was growing up. I would no more have mentioned sex to my mother than I would have robbed the local bank—and it wasn't that I didn't think my parents did it. Of course, they did. But they didn't talk about it.
>
> Quite different from today, huh? Today it's explicit. But I think you people are missing something. Sex is not as special when it's so blatant. There's something to be said for having to think about it and wait. There's something to be said for not talking it to death.
>
> Carl and I didn't talk about it either, but we felt it aplenty. I was twelve when I first got my period, and I swear he saw the difference the very next day. I'll

never forget it. It was the middle of winter, and though we didn't have much snow—we never do, being this close to the shore—it was cold, windy, and raw. We were all bundled up walking to school, me wearing a wool hat and scarf with little more than my face showing and him looking at me every few minutes with the tiniest furrow on his brow.

"What's wrong?" I finally asked.

"Nothing. You just look different."

"I don't know why," I answered, but my cheeks went from pink to red, and not from the cold. This red was pure heat.

It was a dead giveaway, of course. Carl and I talked about so much else that my not talking about this, plus the blush and what he later said was a purely feminine look, clued him in.

He was more solicitous of me that day and in the ones immediately following. He never asked how I was feeling, or whether I had cramps, but I swear he always knew when my body was doing its woman thing. His voice was a little softer, his eyes a little more gentle.

And me? I was totally in love. Half of it was still idol worship, with him being four years older, wiser, and more sexually mature than me, but there was enough of the other half to have me dreaming about the future. I had it all planned. We would marry as soon as I graduated from high school, and have one child a year until we felt we had enough. We would build a house on a hill overlooking the ocean, grow all the things Carl knew how to grow, and spend the rest of our lives doing things like dancing in little vine-covered huts.

I no longer thought about returning to New York. That life had faded to a distant memory, and a dark memory at that. Here at the farm, even in the midst of the Depression, there was light—at least, there was for me. By the time I was a teenager, I felt the rhythm of the growing season. I came to know the fertile scent of spring, the rich aroma of summer, the nutty smell of fall. When the fields grew bare and bleak, I understood that the earth was lying dormant, but I knew also that spring would return. Carl would still be there. I would be a year older. And we would be a year closer to being together.

"Was Carl in on the plans?" Olivia asked.

"I'm not sure I understand your question."

"Did you talk about the house and the kids with him?"

Natalie thought about that. "No. It was taken for granted."

"How do you know he felt the same?"

"The way he looked at me. The way he touched me."

"Touched you."

"It was innocent, but caring."

"Are we talking touching your hand, or touching something else?" Olivia asked, then caught herself. "Or shouldn't I ask?"

"You shouldn't ask," Natalie said, folding her hands in her lap. She looked away. Seeming to argue with herself, she raised a shoulder in a tiny shrug. She pursed her lips, then released them. Decision made, she looked back at Olivia and spoke quickly, as though she feared she would lose the nerve. "We touched. He taught me things."

"Were you kissing at the movies by then?"

There was a pause, then a soft, "Yes. I was sixteen, he was twenty. I was seventeen, he was twenty-one." She put a hand to her chest and raised tear-filled eyes to a point above Olivia's head. "Looking at him just took my *breath* away."

Apparently the memory still did. Olivia suddenly felt like an intruder. Like a voyeur. "I shouldn't have asked."

Natalie drew in a breath and blew it slowly out. Her eyes fell to her lap. She was quiet for a moment. Then she raised her head. "Yes. You should. This is what I hired you for."

"But these are private things. I'm . . . I'm embarrassed hearing you talk about them. It doesn't seem right."

"Because I'm seventy-six? Because you don't like to think of your own mother as being sexual, much less your grandmother?"

"I never knew my grandmother," Olivia said, "and I know that my mother is sexually active." She had grown up watching a stream of men come and go. "But you're different. You're a lady."

Natalie suddenly grew cross. "Is there some reason why a lady can't feel passion? Is there some reason why she can't love with her body as well as her heart?" With a convulsive little headshake, she erased her frown. "I'm not asking you to be graphic. I won't give you anything to be graphic about. But the whole point of this exercise is to let my family know that I felt things back then. Before they criticize me now, they should know how it was. Carl was my be-all and end-all. He was my first thought in the morning and my last one at night. Aside from when I was in school, we spent every waking hour together. He tried to shield me from work, always gave me the easier chore, but I was right out there with him. I was so in love I didn't know what to do with myself."

"So, what *happened?*" Olivia asked. "Why didn't you *marry* him?"

"Have you ever been in love?"

"Not like that."

"Did you love Tess's father?"

Olivia had met Jared in a coffee shop in Atlanta, where she was living at the time. He was there for a scientific symposium, looking adorably brilliant with his mussed hair and his glasses. He had a shy way of speaking that suggested vulnerability. Olivia had found that endearing, too.

"I thought I loved him," she told Natalie. "Listening to you, I'm not so sure. I know I liked him. He was a nice person. Yes, I guess I was in love." But Jared had been gone well before Tess was born, and though Olivia had felt his absence throughout the pregnancy, once she had the baby, she hadn't missed him at all.

So, had she loved him? Or had she simply loved the *idea* of loving him?

Natalie wore such a grandmotherly look that Olivia couldn't resist telling her more. "Jared was the kind of guy who could get so lost in his work that he didn't even know I was around. I wanted him to know. I wanted to be the distraction that he couldn't pass up. But I wasn't ever that." She smiled lopsidedly. "He did give me Tess. She was everything I wanted and more."

Natalie smiled. "She was all yours. She was a guaranteed love. She wasn't leaving. Not *ever.*"

Olivia weighed the words and slowly nodded. "That's it. That's what I felt."

"Then you do know what I felt with Carl. I never doubted that he loved me. I never feared that he would leave me. He was always there, and I was desperate for love."

"But you had your parents. You had your brother."

"You had those things, too."

Feeling like a fraud, Olivia sat back in the wing chair. She shouldn't have lied about her family, certainly not to the extent she had. "I wasn't completely honest about that. Having four brothers was a dream. I always thought it would be such fun. But . . . I only had one."

"One brother?"

Well, it wasn't *quite* as big a fib. "But he was protective. My parents were even worse. My brother was the boy. He could do whatever he wanted. I was the girl. I was coddled and kept close to home. There was a real double standard. I had to leave just to prove that I wasn't helpless." Feeling guilty, she stopped blabbering. "You didn't answer my question."

"Which question was that?" Natalie asked.

"About what happened with Carl. If you loved him so much, why didn't you marry him back then?"

My father wasn't doing well. When Prohibition ended, the black market went with it, which meant that our wine money dried up. But the Depression didn't end. Thanks to some of the New

Deal programs, farm production in other parts of the country picked up. Our market was local, and it was fine. We survived without federal help. We fed ourselves and clothed ourselves. But we couldn't get ahead. We couldn't get a leg up on the rest of the world, which was what my father needed to do. He was a businessman. He knew the importance of growth. That was why he bought up the farms around us. He had visions of building the whole thing up and selling it, recouping what he'd lost in the stock market crash, and returning to New York.

Funny, how quickly a person loses touch. There was no way he was going to do that. We didn't own nearly enough land, and the growing season here was nothing like it was in the Midwest or the South. Asquonset was never going to be worth enough to get him back to New York, not in the style in which he'd left. Little by little, that sank in. He worked the fields from dawn to dusk, pushing his body almost irrationally but getting nowhere.

He was depressed. He was delusional at times. Jeremiah and Carl covered for him when he wasn't functional.

He was still growing grapes, though there wasn't much of a market for the native varieties, and he was wasting precious money on vines from French stock that languished for a year or two and then died. But he wouldn't give up. When growing corn and potatoes and carrots and such didn't make us rich, he got it fixed in his mind that grapes were the answer. He kept at it, even when we were losing money that we couldn't afford to lose.

It was like gambling. After a while, you've lost so much that you have to keep going, because the jackpot is certainly around the next corner. You need the money so badly that you can't afford to stop.

Growing grapes was like that for my father. He was convinced that it was just a matter of hitting on the right varietal. It became an obsession.

Try to picture the situation. My father was physically depleted, a thin man with a bent back. He rarely talked and never smiled. He would sit with his paper and pencil at night and try to make the numbers come out so that there was a profit to show for the work that we'd done. He had high hopes that had nowhere to go.

At the same time, the world around us was going mad. Hitler was moving through Europe, annexing one country after another. First it was Austria. Then Czechoslovakia, then Poland. He made it clear from the start that his goal was world domination, but it was hard to take him seriously. To us, he was an awkward little man with a square black mustache and a penchant for invading the countries bordering his. There was nothing unusual about it. History is full of stories like that.

Then we started hearing the reports of what he was doing in those countries that he ruled. It was horrifying.

He took Poland, and soon after that, Norway, Finland, Denmark, Holland, and Belgium. That gave us greater pause. We sat around the radio at night listening to the reports.

But Hitler was there, and we were here. The Atlantic separated us from him. We were protected. Besides, it wasn't like we had nothing else to think about. We were barely recovering from the Depression.

Then Paris fell to the Third Reich, and Hitler began bombing England— and suddenly we didn't feel so far away. My God, it was in our living room every night, Edward R. Murrow with that inimitable voice saying, "This . . . is London." We heard air raid sirens just as they were sounding, and explosions when the bombs found their mark. You people grew up on live reporting, but we hadn't been exposed to it before, at least not this way. It was new to us, and terrifying.

Roosevelt agreed to supply the Allies with weapons and raw materials, but it wasn't until the Japanese bombed Pearl Harbor that we finally entered the war.

Your generation remembers where you were when you learned that Diana, Princess of Wales, had been killed. My daughter remembers where she was when she learned that President Kennedy had been killed. My friends and I, we remember where we were when we learned that Pearl Harbor had been bombed.

It was a Sunday. My parents and I had been to church in the morning and come home for dinner. I went to Carl's afterward. I always did that. His house was so much happier than mine. And he was there, of course. I was seventeen and in love.

Jeremiah and Brida had closely monitored Hitler's bombing of England.

They had friends and family in Ireland, and didn't want the bombing to spread. They applauded Lend-Lease and other promises of help in the battle against Hitler. This day, they listened raptly when Roosevelt went on the airwaves to report the bombing.

We were in their living room, Carl and I on the floor by the chairs where his parents sat. Our goal was to be as close as possible to the radio at the same time that we were as close as possible to each other. I remember hearing the president's voice that day and knowing right away that something was wrong. Carl and I looked at each other the whole time he talked. I think we knew even then that what had happened was going to change our lives.

Olivia's mind raced ahead, trying to guess exactly what had changed that would have come between Natalie and Carl. "He went into the army?" she asked.

"The navy."

"Even though he wasn't an American citizen?"

"Oh, he was an American citizen. He and his parents had been sworn in years before. They took pride in being American."

"But he was their only son. He was needed to

help run the farm. Couldn't he have gotten out of the draft?"

Natalie gave her a funny look. "Did I say he was drafted? He wasn't drafted. He enlisted. Don't look so surprised, Olivia. It makes a bad statement about your generation."

"It's just . . . if he loved you . . ."

"There were thousands and thousands and *thousands* of couples like us. But what good is being in love if your families and homes are threatened by a man who is carting people off to concentration camps and killing them in droves, or by a country that killed twenty-five hundred of our servicemen in a single horrible day of bombing?

"Your generation is fortunate. You haven't lived through a war, certainly not one that threatened your own soil. We had been convinced that Hitler would never make it out of Europe, but there he was, bombing England. We were next. The isolationists in the country were suddenly silent. We had a common enemy now.

"As for Carl," she went on, "there was never a doubt in his mind. He was hale and hardy. He wanted to fight for his country. It was a matter of pride. And he wasn't alone. Men enlisted, because it was the honorable thing to do. They didn't look for excuses to get out of the war and stay home. There was one fellow here in town—you know Sandy Adelson—I'm talking about her father. He was just Carl's age, the perfect age to enlist, but he was stone deaf. When the army turned him down, he was humiliated. Oh, there were other things he could do to help the war effort, and he did. But to the day he died, he insisted that the worst part of being deaf was not being able to fight in the war."

"Did your brother enlist?"

"Yes. He did it even before Pearl Harbor was bombed. He saw the war coming." Her eyes strayed. Beneath a soft sweep of white hair, that gentle brow of hers furrowed, and suddenly Olivia knew.

"He died in the war, didn't he?" It wasn't even a question, the answer was so obvious.

Natalie rose from the wing-back chair and went to the window. She would be looking out over rows of vines and down toward the ocean, Olivia knew—though from where she sat, all she could see was treetops. And clouds. It was another misty day at Asquonset. The health of the grapes was in doubt, as were the Fourth of July festivities.

Turning away from the window, Natalie came to stand behind the chair she had left. She put her hands on the wings. Her voice was quiet. "History talks about Pearl Harbor first. When we heard about the bombing there, we were appalled. We were also a little relieved. Brad wasn't at Pearl. He was at Midway."

Olivia was trying to remember every little thing she had ever read about the war when Natalie said, "Right about the time when we were sighing those sighs of relief, Japanese bombers were hitting other bases."

"Midway?"

"Among others. It was several days before we got word. The navy had been so startled by the speed and force of the attacks that things were chaotic. Understandably, the first efforts went toward getting medical help for the wounded. The dead couldn't be helped."

Olivia could barely begin to imagine it. She had been too young to know what was going on during the Vietnam War, much less have any friends who fought. Two of her high school classmates had fought in Desert Storm, but neither had been hurt, and for all the times she had imagined a father and brothers in the navy, not a one of them had died.

But she did have a daughter. It wasn't beyond the pale to imagine that if there was another war, Tess might be drafted under the premise of equal rights for women. As a mother, she would be worried sick.

"Your parents must have been devastated."

"Devastated," Natalie said with a stricken look. "Brad had been gone from home for a while by that point. He hadn't been back to visit more than a few weekends each year, but my father continued to hope. Suddenly hope was gone. Just . . . *gone.*" She rapped the top of the chair once, as though to cap the finality of it, and took a steadying breath.

"After that, even if Carl hadn't felt the patriotism, he would have gone. He had Brad's death to avenge."

"Patriotism," Olivia repeated. She conjured up a vision of the movie *The Music Man,* with Robert Preston and his band dressed in parade regalia, launching into "Seventy-six Trombones," all of which was a balm from Natalie's stricken look. That look had touched her. Olivia didn't want to live through a war. She didn't want to lose someone she loved. There wasn't anything remotely romantic about that.

Natalie smiled. "Patriotism is another thing that your generation doesn't see the same way we do."

"I do," Olivia argued.

"You do not. When I say 'patriotism,' you think of George C. Scott as General Patton or Mary Lou Retton winning Olympic gold. To you, it's an event. To us, it's a state of mind. When we fly the American flag in front of our homes, it's a matter of pride. When vets march in parades, it's a matter of pride. When we do things up red-white-and-blue, it's an expression of that same pride. Even tomorrow. The Fourth of July marks a different time in our history from the one I'm talking about here, but they're related. The War of Independence gave us freedom, and we rather like it. Your generation takes even that for granted. We didn't. We were children of the Depression. We don't take much for granted at all. We may not have had prosperity, but we wanted our freedom. That's what we fought for during World War Two."

"You, too?"

"Did I enlist? No. I was here through the war. That didn't mean I was idle, though. The mobilization on behalf of the war effort was pervasive. You didn't have to be in uniform to help the cause. I don't know anyone who didn't do something."

"What did you do?" Olivia asked. She pictured Natalie working on the assembly line in an armament plant, turning out bombers. There was a drama to that.

"Oh, lots of things."

Modesty didn't work for Olivia. "Such as?"

Natalie sighed. "I was a civil defense volunteer—a spotter. I had a circular chart with pictures and watched the sky for enemy planes. Being on the East Coast, I imagined I would be the first to see the *Luftwaffe*. Fortunately, of course, no German planes ever appeared."

"What else did you do?" Olivia asked. This time she pictured Natalie rolling bandages for the Red Cross or nursing the wounded who had returned home. It wasn't as dramatic as turning out bombers, but it would have been heartrending.

Natalie fished a photograph from the group on the desk. It showed people working the fields. "Asquonset became a great big victory garden. With so much of the produce from traditional suppliers going to feed the troops, small farms like ours filled the void locally."

"These are all women."

"That's all who was left. Jeremiah told us what to do, and we did it. Those are other local women you see. One of them would watch the children while the rest of us worked."

The children. Olivia did a little quick math as she rose and pulled another picture from those on the desk. It showed Natalie with a baby. "When was this taken?"

"Before this one," Natalie said, pointing to the women in the field. "That was my son Brad. He was born in '42, obviously named after my brother. Susanne was born in '44. Greg was born in '60."

"Brad hasn't called here since I've come," Olivia said.

"No. He wouldn't."

Olivia was thinking that Brad the son must have opted out the way Brad the brother had done, when Natalie's eyes went to the door.

Catching a little breath, the older woman broke into a surprised smile. "How *nice,*" she said and crossed the room to embrace a blonde-haired woman who wasn't much older than Olivia. A bit taller than Natalie, she wore slacks and a knit shell, chunky gold earrings, a matching necklace, and a pair of glittering diamond rings.

Ending the hug, Natalie held her back. "You look pale, daughter-in-law, but as beautiful as ever. Is everything all right?"

The woman hesitated a second too long.

Natalie frowned. "What is it?"

"Nothing." There was a forced smile. "Well, nothing *that* bad." She lowered her voice. "Greg and I are having some troubles. I thought I'd camp out here for a bit."

Natalie released a breath, taking mere seconds to absorb Jill Seebring's words and move on. "You thought right. Take your usual room, and stay as long as you want. There's a buffet at the yacht club tonight and a cookout here tomorrow. After that, you can rest, unless you feel like helping out at the office. First, though, come meet my assistant."

Fourteen

OLIVIA LIKED JILL SEEBRING on sight. She didn't know whether it was the woman's easy smile when they were introduced, the bruised look that she couldn't quite hide, the closeness of their ages, or the simple fact of Jill showing up in the driveway late that afternoon wearing a sundress much like Olivia's. But she and Jill easily wound up in the same car heading for the yacht club.

"I'm not sure I'm up for this," Jill said softly. "It's been a long day. I'm exhausted."

Olivia was driving. Tess was in the backseat, along with the new maid, who was barely eighteen. Natalie claimed the girl had ten times the enthusiasm of the closest competitor. Whether she could do the job remained to be seen.

"One of us can always drive you back early,"

Olivia told Jill. The buffet was called for five o'clock. "How long do these things last?"

Tess leaned forward between the seats. She wore a pair of white shorts with a blue Asquonset T-shirt. Her glasses were clean. Her hair was in a neat French braid. "There's a fireworks show. It won't start till dark."

"Have you met any of the local kids?" Jill asked her.

"Some are in my sailing class."

"Well, that'll be fun, then."

"I don't know. I don't really know them."

"It'll be fun," Jill insisted, and Olivia liked her for her confidence, too.

"Where do you live?" Tess asked Jill.

"Washington."

"How come your husband isn't here?"

Olivia was thinking that she should have told Tess something of the situation when Jill said a perfectly logical, "He's busy working. I always spend more time here than he does."

"Do you work?" Olivia asked. Everything about the woman was professional, from the sleek blonde hair tucked easily behind an ear to the simplicity of another pair of chunky earrings to the absence of a watch or anything else that might mess up her wrists and get in the way of papers or other work materials.

"Not officially."

"What does that mean?" Tess asked.

Jill smiled. "It means I don't get paid." To

Olivia, she said, "I do PR for charity fund-raisers. I help with the planning and the publicity."

"Why don't they pay you?" Tess asked.

"They don't have the money."

"Do you have any kids?"

"Not yet," Jill said.

They pulled into the yacht club parking lot beside Carl's car. A third Asquonset car pulled up moments later.

Olivia didn't see Simon among the occupants—which meant that either he hadn't felt anything at all that morning or he had and he refused to admit it. She had thought he might come. After all, eating in the dining room at the Great House was one thing—Olivia could understand that he might find that too cozy—but this was a larger group, with a hundred or more at the buffet. There was nothing personal about it.

He could be coming in his truck.

Not that she was asking Natalie and Carl about him. She didn't want to give encouragement to something that wasn't going to happen.

So she asked other people, starting with Donna Gomez, Simon's first in command and, as such, the one who might have been expected to drive over with the man. Donna was strong and slim, dark haired, olive skinned, very much Olivia's age, though she had two children in their late teens. Her husband and the kids had come with her, which Donna claimed was an Asquonset tradition.

"If it's a tradition," Olivia said, "where's your boss?"

"Simon?" Donna asked. "Most likely back home. He doesn't come out much."

"Since his wife died?"

"Even before. He's very private. She was a socializing force."

The wine maker, David Sperling, echoed that thought when Olivia talked with him a short time later. They were admiring the boats secured in slips. The sun was starting to lower. "See that one there?" he asked, pointing to a handsome cruiser with a cabin underneath. "That belongs to the vineyard. We used to have a sailboat, but, well, you heard about the accident."

"That was four years ago. I'm surprised they haven't bought another."

"Alexander wanted to, but he wanted something large." David pointed to another boat. It was a sailboat that was longer and wider than the cruiser. "There you have a mainsail and a jib. Alexander wanted even more than that."

"I can see why," Olivia said, recalling Carl's description of the accident. "A large boat wouldn't be as vulnerable."

"That wasn't why Alexander wanted it," David said with a fond smile. "He wanted an eye-catcher."

"Was he a good sailor?"

"Not particularly. Fortunately, he knew it. When he was taking people out, he put Simon at the helm. Simon was the best. He hasn't been in a boat since the accident, though. In fact, he hasn't been here to the *club* since the accident."

"So what does he do with himself? You know, in his free time?"

The answer to that came from Anne Marie Friar, the receptionist in the business office. Olivia talked with her daily. She was personable and chatty, perhaps more so than she should have been in this instance, but Olivia was, after all, Natalie's confidante.

"He reads," Anne Marie said. "He's constantly buying books, mostly on-line now. He must love that. He doesn't even have to show up in a bookstore. The packages are delivered to us. We give him a buzz, and he picks them up. His place must be stuffed."

"Where is his place?" Olivia asked. She knew that he lived on Asquonset land within walking distance of the grapes, but nothing designated as Simon's house was marked on any map she had seen. She had explored. During late afternoon runs, she had taken every well-trod path on the property and still didn't have a clue.

"It's on the southeast side."

"There's nothing there."

"There is, only you can't see it unless you're on top of it. There's a narrow road marked by a reflector on a tree. The house is half a mile up. It's on the same acre that Natalie's father gave to Carl's father when the Seebrings first came here to live."

Olivia knew that Carl had a place in town. She

had assumed that the house where he'd grown up had been torn down and the land cultivated. "Simon lives in his *parents'* house?"

"Not quite," Anne Marie said, seeming delighted to be able to impart some inside information. "It's been razed and rebuilt. Twice now, I believe."

Olivia was about to ask more when she spotted Tess. She was with a group from her class. Well, not with them. More like trailing after them, and she didn't look pleased.

Want friends? Simon had said. *Try a smile.*

He was right. Nothing about the girl that Olivia saw just then would appeal to other children.

Smile, Olivia mentally commanded, concentrating with all her strength, counting on brainwaves to convey the message, and incredibly, Tess looked her way. But her scowl only deepened. She made a hard motion with her hand, telling her mother not to look at her. Then she turned her back and followed the other children off the deck and into the club.

By then, Anne Marie was talking with someone else, and Natalie was waving at Olivia to join her. There were friends to meet, several of whom had lived in Asquonset longer than Natalie and might have been the mystery woman in those early pictures. All were in their seventies and eighties now, which made resemblances harder to spot. Olivia searched, but in vain. She was about to ask Natalie, when the buffet was served.

Olivia had never seen a spread like it. There were fish chowder and clam chowder, both creamy with beads of butter floating on top. There were lobster salad, lobster Newburg, and lobster tails. There was skewered shrimp. There were grilled steaks and steaming corn on the cob. There were hamburgers and hot dogs, cole slaw and potato salad. There were molasses-heavy Boston baked beans.

Olivia filled her plate and went to check on Tess. The child was eating a hamburger on the dock, at the very edge of the circle of children. She had her back to Olivia, which was probably good. Olivia's heart would have broken in two if she had seen turned-down lips or a woebegone expression.

In that instant, Olivia would have gladly turned back the clock to the time when Tess was a toddler. She might have rescued her then. She couldn't do it now. Tess was too old.

Struggling with the helplessness of that thought, Olivia found a seat on the deck with the Asquonset group, and it was everything she had hoped it would be. She liked these people. She fit right in. Natalie kept her close, making her feel wanted and needed.

But she kept feeling little bits of sadness, like a nagging ache in the back of her mind that she had to actively concentrate on to identify.

The first was the most obvious. It had to do with Tess.

The second was more surprising. It had to do

with what Natalie had told her that day. Something about this most recent part of the story had been more real than other parts. It was the fact that death had entered the picture, she supposed. There was nothing at all romantic about death.

She barely knew Brad. He hadn't played a major part in Natalie's teenage years. Olivia had certainly heard more about Carl than she had about Brad. Still, his death stuck with her.

Actually, what stuck with her was Natalie's stricken look. That was what nagged.

The third little bit of sadness was more dismaying. It had to do with Simon, who had lost a good part of his family to the sea and was off somewhere, sitting alone.

Well, that's his choice, she reminded herself, but it didn't make her feel better.

Nor did Tess's appearance right about the time when people were heading to the buffet for seconds. She leaned against Olivia's chair, appearing to settle in.

"How's it going, honey?" Olivia asked.

Tess shrugged.

"Did you eat?"

The child nodded.

"Where are the kids?"

She moved her head in a way that could have indicated any direction at all, but her eyes settled somewhere else. Following them, Olivia saw Sandy Adelson heading their way. She wore a long flowing dress and had a flower in her hair. She was holding the hand of a boy Olivia hadn't seen before. He was an inch or two taller than Tess, and had straight dark hair and serious eyes.

Tess murmured out of the side of her mouth, "If she's bringing him over here as a consolation prize, I'll never forgive her."

"Smile," Olivia whispered and rose from her seat. It was the most natural thing in the world for her to give Sandy a hug. Then she stood back and studied the boy. "This is the most gorgeous guy in this room." When his cheeks reddened, she held out a hand. "I'm Olivia."

"This is my grandson Seth," Sandy said proudly. "We thank you for the compliment." She tapped the boy's cheek and, when he looked at her, said, "Olivia works at Asquonset, and this is her daughter, Tess. They live in Cambridge. They're here for the summer."

Nodding his understanding, the boy gave them each a short wave.

"Seth and his parents live in Concord," Sandy said. "That's not far from Cambridge. They're down for the weekend. I'm hoping Seth will stay on for a while."

Seth was looking at Tess like he wanted to say something but didn't dare. It was only when he tapped Sandy's arm and signed something that Olivia realized he was deaf.

She didn't dare look at Tess, lest they make something of it.

"Seth wonders if you know the Border Café."

"I know it," Tess said.

Seth signed something.

Sandy interpreted. "It's his favorite restaurant." When the boy looked up at her and signed something else, she signed quickly back. "He's waiting for dessert," she explained. "I swear, that's the only reason for coming here, as far as Seth is concerned. They do make-your-own sundaes, with a dozen different ice creams and every topping imaginable. Want to make one with us?" she asked Tess.

Tess touched her stomach. "I don't think I can. I'm stuffed."

"How about later, then? My dad—Seth's great-grandpop—has a beautiful old Chris-Craft. He's taking it out so that we can watch the fireworks from the water."

Olivia was about to accept the invitation when a ruckus arose from the far side of the deck. A mime was there, balanced on a single foot on the top plank of the deck, looking for all the world as though he was on a thin wire suspended dozens of feet off the ground.

Sandy shot Olivia an excited smile and drew Seth in that direction.

Olivia was about to follow when Tess held her back.

"I'm not going with them," she said.

"Why not?" Olivia asked. "It sounds like great fun."

"Yeah? Well, he's deaf."

Olivia blinked. "What does that have to do with anything?"

"I can't talk with him. He's *deaf.*"

"Watching fireworks doesn't require talking. This isn't a fix-up, Tess. It's just a boat ride."

"Yeah, but the only reason she's inviting me is because the other kids didn't ask me to go with them."

"I don't think that's true. She's simply inviting us to do something that sounds like a lot of fun."

"It doesn't sound like it to me. It sounds like she's putting the dyslexic one with the deaf one. I'm not *that* desperate."

Olivia stared at her daughter. "I can't believe you said that."

Tess didn't take it back.

Olivia put a hand to her chest. "I can't *believe* you said that." Suddenly, she was rip-roaring mad. She had the good sense to take Tess by the hand and pull her outside to the parking lot, but that was where her consideration ended. Rounding on her, she said, "I am appalled at you, Tess. *Appalled.* What's wrong with that boy?"

Tess pushed up her glasses. "He's deaf."

"And you're dyslexic. And I'm a slow writer. And Sandy is free spirited. And Natalie is seventy-six. There's nothing wrong with that boy that lip-reading and signing don't fix. He's not *inferior* any more than *you* are. Isn't that what I've been trying to teach you all these months, all these *years?*

You're not inferior. You learn in a different way from most kids, but there's nothing inferior about it. The end result will be the same. You'll grow up just like they will and go to college and have a career. So that boy speaks in a different way from most kids. He'll grow up doing the same things as you. My God, Tess. You, of *all* people, should know better than to look down your nose at someone who isn't quite like you."

Tess didn't seem quite so cocky. Her arms were pressed to her sides. Her chin was lower.

"And what about compassion?" Olivia cried. "That little boy can't *hear*. He can't hear songs. He can't hear words. He can't hear the chirps of those baby birds in the vineyard. He can't hear Henri purring. He wakes up in the dark of night and has to rely on his eyes to tell him if there's someone in his room. He has to work twice as hard to get the same thing out of life that you do."

Tess's chin sank even lower. Her eyes were woeful through her glasses. "I wanted to be with the other kids."

"Because they're popular? That's not a good reason. Popularity is skin deep, Tess. It's substance that counts."

"Not at my age," Tess muttered.

"At *any* age!" Olivia argued. She pushed a hand through her hair, started to turn away, then came back and leaned into the argument. "Compared to that child, you're pretty lucky. Can't you *see* that? No, you can't, because you're too busy feeling sorry for yourself." She straightened. "Well, listen up, Tess. You have a choice. You can sit around feeling sorry for yourself and blaming every little problem you have on being a slow reader, or you can move on. It isn't the dyslexia that's causing you the trouble with these kids. They don't *know* you're dyslexic. What they *do* know is that you have a chip on your shoulder a mile wide."

She was suddenly exhausted. Taking a tired breath, she let her hands fall to her sides. "I love you, Tess. I love you with all my heart. If you were to tell me you don't like Seth because he's snobby or self-centered or . . . or even *geeky,* I could accept it. But to tell me you don't like him because he's deaf?" She shook her head slowly and definitively.

Then she closed her eyes and inhaled deeply. When she looked at Tess again, the child seemed contrite. "Does what I've said make any sense?"

She waited, staring, until Tess said a quiet "yes."

The victory was empty. Olivia felt drained. She inhaled again. Quietly, she said, "I think I've about had it. How about we go back?" She gestured for Tess to come. "Let's thank Natalie."

They had barely reached the clubhouse door when Jill appeared. She looked relieved to see them. "I was worried you'd left."

"We're about to. I was just going to let Natalie know. You look beat."

"Slightly," she said, easing down onto a wood bench. "I'll wait here."

"We won't be long."

Olivia went searching for Natalie. She was still upset enough with Tess not even to look at the child when they passed the lines of people waiting to make their own sundaes. Tess would have loved that. She deserved to miss it.

Natalie and Carl were sitting with friends on the outside deck. The sun spilled lower over the water now, but it would be another hour yet before dusk.

Olivia squatted beside Natalie's chair. "We're heading back," she said softly. "I just wanted to thank you. This has been lovely."

"Aren't you staying for the fireworks?"

Smiling, Olivia shook her head. "I'm tired. I'm taking Jill back with me. I guess it's been a long day for her."

"Want to drop her off and come back?" Natalie asked hopefully.

Olivia loved her for the genuine enthusiasm. It was so *nice* to feel wanted—so nice that she was tempted to change her mind. But Natalie was with her friends, and the others from the vineyard were with *their* friends, and maybe, just maybe, Olivia was still feeling a little like the outsider.

"Thanks, but no," she said gently and was rising when Sandy Adelson materialized.

"There you are," Sandy said. "Tess says you're heading home. Do you mind if she comes with us? I'll be glad to drop her home afterward."

Sure enough, there was Tess, standing on one side of Sandy. Seth was on the other.

Olivia's first instinct was to decline the invitation on behalf of her daughter. Tess didn't deserve to see the fireworks, much less from the deck of a boat belonging to these good people, not after what she had said.

But she did look contrite—a little shamefaced as she looked up at Olivia—not to mention unsure. And Seth had a hopeful look on his handsome face.

"I really want to go on the boat," Tess said, sounding as though she meant every word.

It did cross Olivia's mind, in a moment of cynicism, that given a choice between the boat and a furious mother, Tess was choosing the lesser of the evils. The bottom line, though, was that Olivia wanted Tess to go on that boat.

To Sandy, she said, "Will it be much out of your way to drop her at the house?"

"Nope." Grinning, Sandy hooked an elbow around each child's neck. "We're off."

Fifteen

"SO, WHAT DO YOU THINK about Natalie and Carl?" Olivia asked Jill as they drove back to the vineyard.

Jill's head lay against the headrest. "I think it's fine," she said, sounding exhausted. "It's not like she's cheating on Al. He died. She's free to remarry." She snorted. "Easy for me to say. He wasn't my father."

"What was he like?"

"He was fun, very social. A schmoozer, if you know what I mean. Had things been different, he might have been a politician." She spoke fondly. "He was good with names and faces. He could forget his own wedding anniversary, but if he had met a man five years before, he would go right up, call him by name, and shake hands."

"That's a remarkable skill."

"I saw him do it more than once. He used to visit Greg and me in Washington. We'd be at a restaurant; he'd see a familiar face across the room and leave us and go visit. If the man was a veteran, so much the better. Al could stand for hours talking about the war. Mind you, it'd be a one-way conversation. Most men who fought in the trenches didn't want to relive it. For Al, it was a thing of great pride. Not that he was in the trenches."

"No?" That had certainly been part of the image. Natalie hadn't discussed the war yet, but Olivia had seen pictures of Alexander in uniform. Yes, he looked proud—dashing and proud.

"He was in intelligence," Jill said, then went in a different direction. "He liked the grand gesture. If it'd been up to him, he'd have built a castle, rather than a mill, for the winery."

"Who decided on the mill?"

Jill turned her head on the headrest and looked at Olivia. "Natalie. She's the driving force behind the whole operation."

"Greg said it was Carl."

"Greg would," Jill muttered, facing forward again.

They had touched on a sensitive point. Olivia was dying to ask what had gone wrong with the marriage, but it wasn't her place. She didn't know Jill, so she said, "Natalie's seventy-six. What'll happen when she starts to slow down?"

Jill chuckled. "I'm not sure she ever will. The

vineyard is her life. But if you're wondering whether Greg will do it, he says not."

"He's called several times," Olivia ventured. "He's upset that she's marrying Carl."

"That's because he has no control over the situation. It stymies him when people go off and do their own thing with no regard for his wishes."

Another sensitive area. Again, Olivia steered away. "Maybe Susanne will take over the vineyard. What's she like?"

Jill smiled at that. "I like Susanne. Greg sees the difference in their ages and imagines a great distance because of it, but she's always been nice to me. She made me feel welcome, like she was really glad to have me in the family."

"Maybe she wants *you* to take over the vineyard."

"I doubt it." Jill looked at Olivia. The smile was gone now. "You seem concerned about who's taking over. Is Natalie all right?"

"Oh, yes, as far as I know. She has incredible energy. Incredible *strength*. It's just that I think of her as being middle-aged, then she starts talking about the thirties and I realize she's more than that."

"Greg is convinced that she isn't *of sound mind*. What do you think? Is she all there?"

"Totally. *Totally.*" So why did Olivia worry about her health? Because Natalie *wasn't* middle-aged, and because when it came to family, she was surprisingly alone. She had drawn Olivia in, made her a part of everything, like she was starved for companionship, and Olivia loved it. But Natalie had the potential of Susanne and Mark, Greg and Jill, and two grandchildren. "I saw her there at the yacht club with her friends and their families, and it's like for Natalie, without any family, there's a generation missing."

"Could be because Simon wasn't there," Jill said. "You've met Simon, haven't you?"

Olivia turned up the vineyard drive. "I have."

"Do you think he has designs on Asquonset?"

"No." She would put money on it. "I think he loves it here. He'd probably be happy to spend the rest of his life here. Does he want to own it?" She shook her head. "He wants to grow grapes. That's it."

NATURALLY, BECAUSE HE WAS the last thing she and Jill discussed before parting in the Great House foyer, Olivia had Simon on the brain. She kept picturing him alone in his house with everyone else celebrating the Fourth at the club. She kept thinking that no one should be so alone.

Changing into a singlet and shorts, she tied the laces of her running shoes and did stretches out by the car. Then she set off down the driveway, running into a setting sun. At the main road, she turned left and ran at a comfortable pace. A breeze came in off the ocean, cooling her skin when it started to heat, but the exertion felt good.

She had run this route before. She had made the entire circle around Asquonset, but she hadn't seen any reflector on a tree that was supposed to mark the way to Simon's house. She must not have been looking closely enough.

This time, she kept a sharp eye out, slowing at every possible spot where a road might be. She even turned in at one that proved to be only a parking spot for the house across the road.

Then a spark caught her eye. It was a last ray of sun glinting off a reflector on a tree at the start of what looked like a tractor path—two dirt ruts separated by grass. As camouflage went, it worked. There was a paved section thirty feet in, but it was barely visible under a forest of trees. This was definitely the road of a man who didn't want to be bothered.

Heart pounding, Olivia turned in. She ran to the start of the pavement, thought about the man who didn't want to be bothered, turned around, and ran back to the main road. But then she thought of the man who was totally alone. Jogging in place for a minute, she pictured him. Turning around again, she started up the path.

It was uphill most of the way, not the easiest run for a woman who dedicated her life to finding level ground. Breathing hard, Olivia actually stopped at one point, bent at the waist with her hands on her knees, and wondered if she was having a heart attack.

More like a panic attack, she decided. Simon was an imposing man.

But she wanted to see where he lived. And since it was getting dark, chances were he wouldn't even know she was there. And if he did see her, well, that was all right, too. She could handle it. Hadn't she handled him when it came to Tess? Hadn't she handled Tess when it came to Seth? She could handle people. She was tough.

She straightened and pushed on until the road abruptly ended. Sure enough, there was Simon's mud-spattered silver pickup. A small house stood nearby.

House? Cabin was more like it. It was gray-shingled, with windows suggesting no more than three or four rooms, and it was placed on the land in a way that came close to showing its backside to anyone who dared intrude. That was Simon's house, all right.

Her step slowed. She came to a halt.

Not that she'd have done differently if she'd been building this house, she decided with a ragged breath when she looked out past the edge of a front porch and saw the view. She hadn't realized she had climbed so high. From here, the ocean was distinct. Beneath a dusky sky, it was deep gray broken by patches of violet under clouds of similar hue.

Hands on her hips, breathing a little more evenly now, she wondered what she should do. There were no lights on in the house. Other than the rhythmic chirp of a cricket, there was no sound. Had it not been for the pickup, she would have thought Simon was away.

Something furry bumped her leg. With a frightened cry and visions of a weasel, a ferret, even a *bear* cub, she skipped back, but it was only Buck.

Hunkering down, she scratched the cat's head. Just because Buck was here didn't mean Simon was. He might have been picked up by a friend. He might have been picked up by a *woman*. Yeah, yeah, yeah, he had sworn off relationships—but men didn't necessarily consider sex a relationship. For all Olivia knew—for all *anyone* knew—he and some woman were going at it hot and heavy in a pretty little house near the center of town.

There was another scenario, of course. This one had Simon picking up his little sweetie and going at it hot and heavy right here. That would explain the presence of his truck, even the darkened house, with the poor cat exiled into the night.

And Olivia had been feeling *sorry* for the man?

She was nursing a potent sense of indignation when she heard noise from the porch that stopped her cold. The creak of a chair was followed by the unmistakable sound of bare feet on wood. She rose and held her breath.

"Are you looking for me?" Simon asked from

under the shadowed overhang at the edge of the porch.

Everything was difficult to make out, what with the trees blocking out the last rays of the setting sun. Simon's world was purple and deepening to black by the minute. Olivia, on the other hand, felt positively neon. She might as well have been spotlit. Denying her presence seemed pointless.

"I was," she said, "but I think I've come at a bad time. I'll see you tomorrow. Bye." She turned to go.

"Why aren't you at the club?" he asked.

She thought about that and turned around. If his talking to her was a diversion—if there was indeed a woman in the shadows pulling on clothes—it was too late to run. She had to look at the humor in the situation.

"That was supposed to be my line," she said. "I was there. Dinner was great. We missed you."

He snickered. "Not likely. In case you hadn't noticed, I'm not exactly the life of the party."

"Actually, I hadn't noticed. The only time I've seen you with other people was with Natalie that first day."

"And with Tess."

Unless she was mistaken, he was inviting comment on that. With a lover listening? Hard to believe.

"You did okay there," she said.

"She's forgiven me?"

"Well, I don't know if I'd go *that* far. The apology helped. She doesn't seem any worse for wear."

Olivia jumped again, this time at the sound of a boom. She looked toward the ocean in time to see a brilliant pink flower open and spread in the sky. She caught her breath as smaller yellow ones came to life around it.

"I had no idea she had a learning problem," Simon said when the color faded and fell.

"There's no reason you would have known," Olivia replied, but her eye was on the harbor. A second boom was followed by a third and a fourth. The sky was alternately lit with red-white-and-blue, then green, then yellow and pink.

"How serious is it?" he asked, seeming unmoved by the display of fireworks.

"Serious enough to be hurting her socially. Social things are important for a child her age. She's having a hard time."

"Getting along with kids."

"Oh yeah."

Another boom sounded. This time the fireworks were multicolored and squiggly, an army of little sperm swimming through a darkening sky.

Tess was under that sky, watching from the deck of a boat. Olivia wondered if she had done the right thing letting her stay. She would never forgive herself if Tess was rude to Seth. It struck her that maybe she should be near a phone, just in case.

She was thinking of leaving when a vivid cornucopia of patriotic colors exploded over the harbor. She whispered an involuntary "Ooooo."

Simon asked, "When did you learn she had the problem?"

The cornucopia broke up. Reasoning that staying another minute or two wouldn't hurt, and that he was the one encouraging conversation, Olivia looked at the porch. She saw the outline of a raised arm, a hand braced on the overhead beam, a lean body outlined in blue, thanks to the next display of the pyrotechnics.

When had Olivia learned that Tess was dyslexic? She remembered every detail of the nightmare. "When she got into school and couldn't do the work. There were stomachaches, and tears, and teacher conferences. I should have seen it sooner. If I had, they could have given her help right from the start. But it isn't easy spotting things like that. I knew she wasn't good with certain toys, but I didn't love puzzles either. So we played with the things she *was* good at."

"Did you read to her when she was little?"

Another boom came, but Olivia didn't look at the sky. Something in Simon's voice sparked a picture of him reading to his daughter, Liana. She opened her mouth to ask about it, then shut it abruptly, thinking, *Painful terrain—do not go there, Olivia Jones.*

Instead, she took his question at face value. "All the time. I still do. When she was little, I read her all the stories I'd missed myself. I hated reading when I was a child. Just couldn't do it. By the time I could, I was too old to read fairy tales, so I experienced them with Tess, and it was such fun—not to mention that it was a validation for me that I could do it." It still was. "I probably got more out of it than Tess. I should have been teaching her letters and words. If I'd done that, I might have realized she had a problem. But I wasn't about to teach her how to read. I was afraid I'd do it all wrong. And then I kept thinking she was learning it all on her own. We'd be reading one book or another, and she'd start doing a page herself. So we'd take turns. I'd read one page, she'd read the next. I thought she was brilliant. I mean, I still do. She *is* brilliant. But I thought she was just so far ahead of her age group. I mean, what parent doesn't want to think that? Then we were reading one night and I accidentally turned two pages at once, and Tess started reciting lines from the page I had skipped, and I realized she wasn't reading at all. She had the whole book memorized. Even then, I thought she was just so smart. I didn't grasp the implications."

Olivia scrubbed at the short strands of her hair, embarrassed even now to have been so obtuse then. She smiled. "Got more than you bargained for with that answer, huh?" Another boom came from the harbor, but there was no sound behind Simon. Apparently, there was no guest. She felt obtuse about that, too.

"I asked," he said.

Buck meowed. She made out his large, dark shape midway between Simon and her. Night was falling fast, the purple on Simon's hill deepening. Olivia knew that she was going to have to run down the road in the dark, and figured she ought to get started while there was even the last little bit of light. But she stood her ground and glanced at the cabin.

"So, this is your place?" she asked. She wondered what the inside was like.

"It isn't the one I lived in with my wife and daughter. I burned that one after they died."

"Burned it? Why did you do that?"

"I built it for them. They were gone."

"You *burned* it?"

"To the ground."

"And the forest didn't go with it?" The place was positively *surrounded* by trees.

He made a sputtering sound that might have been a laugh, a note of amazement that she wasn't freaked out about his burning down a house. She saw him shake his head in the dark. Buck meowed again.

"Are you trying to scare me off?" she asked.

"Am I succeeding?"

"No. I have no stake in you. There's no risk."

"You don't care that I have a violent side?"

Olivia saw herself yelling at Tess in the parking lot outside the yacht club. There had been violence

in that. Granted, it hadn't been physical. As cata-
lysts went, though, Simon's loss was far greater
than Olivia's momentary disappointment in Tess.
"I can't begin to imagine what I would do if I lost
just about everything, the way you did. If you can't
just pick up and move away, I suppose destroying a
painful reminder is the next best thing."

He didn't respond at first. His profile was a
dark silhouette when he looked out at the sea.
There were more fireworks, but she didn't think he
saw those. He seemed to be in a world of his own,
back at least four years.

Time to leave, Olivia thought.

Then he spoke, and the thought left her. His
voice was less sure, even pained. "I shouldn't have
done it. I was angry. I felt helpless. I needed to do
something. What I ended up doing was erasing
every trace of my life with them. The painful re-
minders went along with all the good stuff. I
burned it all to the ground. There were ashes.
That's it."

"There was nothing left at all? Not even any
pictures?"

"Carl had some. Natalie had some. They kept
trying to give them to me. It was awhile before I
could bear to look at them. I still have trouble. Part
of me says that all I need is my memories."

Well, he certainly did have those. And they
were like a moat around him, keeping Olivia at a
distance. She was here—and he was there, with his
dead wife and child.

Grateful now to the dark for hiding her ugly hair and sweaty body, she said, "Look, if Tess bothers you again, just tell her to get lost."

"That would be mean."

"Tell her you're busy. Tell her that you're spraying something dangerous and that she shouldn't be in the fields. I'll try to keep her from going out when you're there." Another meow came from Buck. "Is he all right?"

"He's fine."

"Aren't you worried about him being out here in the woods?"

"He's a tough guy."

"But aren't there tougher guys here?"

"Not many. You haven't been coming out mornings."

Olivia was a minute changing gears. She wrapped her arms around her middle. "No. That's your time. Your place."

"I was wondering if it was something else."

He was looking at her. She heard the directness of his voice, along with something of a challenge.

She threw the challenge right back at him. "Like what?"

"I see you sitting up there in your window. What are you thinking?"

"I'm thinking how lucky I am to be here."

"Anything else?"

"What else would there be?"

He didn't speak, but she felt his answer right there where it was every morning, in the pit of her stomach. It was a tiny ache, unwelcome and annoying, but *there*.

She took a step back and held up a hand. "Hey, if you're thinking there should be something else, that's your problem. Me? I'm free and clear. We agreed that if anyone thought there might be something, they were totally misguided. There's nothing. Absolutely nothing." She took a fast breath. "And even if there *were* something, I wouldn't act on it. In case you hadn't realized it yet, Tess is a handful." She began walking slowly back toward the road. "I'm a mother, first and foremost. That doesn't mean I don't *feel* things. Of *course* I feel things. But that's as far as it goes." She jogged backward now, adding breaks to the flow of her voice. "And even if I *was* attracted to you, it'd be a moot point. I may be a sucker for nice legs, but I'm no masochist."

She turned, accelerated gently from a jog to a run, and poured her concentration into staying on the road in the dark.

IT WASN'T OVER. The next morning at dawn, she was there on the window seat, having slept less than five hours. Tess hadn't come home until ten-thirty. Then they spent two hours talking about sensitivity, respect for others, and the endurance of motherly love. After that, Olivia had lain awake for a while before finally dropping off—and still she was up at first light.

It struck her that since today was the Fourth of July, Simon might be sleeping in.

But there he was, right on schedule, emerging from under the awning and walking to the edge of the patio. There was no coffee cup in his hand, though—that was a first. Curious, she watched him put his hands on his hips. He stared out over the vineyard as he had done so often before. His back was straight. Same with his legs. There was no casual one-hipped stance today. To her, his stance indicated that something was wrong, and she wondered what it was.

Then he looked up at her over his shoulder, hitched his head in the direction of the vines, and set off down the path.

Her heart began to thud. His gesture had been an invitation—no doubt about it.

Did he want to talk? Did he have something to show her?

She kept her eye on the path, thinking he might reappear and give her a clue. When he didn't, she made a snap decision. In two seconds, she had the nightshirt off and a T-shirt and shorts on. Snatching up flip-flops, she went barefooted through the bathroom to check on Tess, then returned through her room and ran quietly down the stairs.

It had rained not long before. The patio stones were still wet. She put on the flip-flops and set off.

Dampness was thick in the warm July air. Add that to the rain itself, and the grapes couldn't be pleased. Perhaps the unwanted rain was the cause of Simon's tension. What she had imagined to be the hitch of his head might have simply been a gesture of frustration.

But she reached the vineyard path and, with the slap of the flip-flops, strode on, looking down each row, wondering where she was supposed to find Simon. Suddenly it struck her that she was probably making a fool of herself coming out like this. She should have stayed in the window. She should have stayed in *bed*.

Still, she went on. She was at the very end of the block of vines when she saw him way off to the side. He was leaning against a fat old maple tree, arms and ankles crossed.

He was waiting for her. She approached more slowly, stopping when she was a dozen feet away, and tucked her hands in her pockets.

"You called?" she asked sweetly.

He grunted, shot a look to the side, and almost smiled.

Just as she was thinking that if an almost smile made her this weak, a full one would absolutely make her melt, he crooked a finger, inviting her closer.

Heart pounding, she took a single large step toward him and stopped. "Yes?"

Uncrossing his ankles, he pushed away from the tree and closed the distance between them. His eyes were serious as they searched hers. Seconds later, he took her head in both hands and tilted her face up for a kiss.

There was nothing gentle about it. It was a hard, open-mouthed thing that spoke of raw hunger.

Olivia felt that hunger right down to her toes. She had admired him once too often, had watched his lean-hipped walk and seen those biceps lift and pull. There was a mystery to him that increased the hunger. There was also about him an element of the forbidden. His kiss was all the more exciting for the fact that it wasn't supposed to happen.

He wasn't smooth. There was no finesse in the way he held her head or manipulated her mouth, but raw hunger didn't allow for finesse. Olivia didn't care, though—she craved hunger far more than style. Slipping her arms around his neck, she kissed him back. Suddenly she had an image of her daughter, and she smiled inwardly. Yes, Tess had been right saying that he smelled—he smelled wonderfully clean and totally male. His hair was damp and thick to the touch, his neck warm, his shoulders strong. She slid her palms over the swell of his chest, but they quickly returned to his neck. She had to hold on. Her legs wouldn't support her.

She had thought it was only her. She had thought the tingling she felt watching him each morning was one-sided, but it didn't feel that way now. His body was tensed, straining.

So maybe he had been without for so long that any woman would do. When he tore his mouth from hers, he pulled her into his body and held her there with an arm across her back and a hand on her bottom. He was fiercely aroused. It was an incredible thing for a woman to feel. Would any woman have caused it?

She didn't want that. She didn't do anonymous sex. She didn't do *surrogate* sex.

But that was her name she heard murmured by a hoarse, broken voice seconds before he drew his head back, and those were her eyes that his found and held. Looking into his eyes, she saw surprise and confusion. She saw heat. His breathing was rough, his brow damp. His jaw was square, newly shaved so that only the ghost of a dark beard remained. His mouth was lean, slightly ajar. His eyes were a deep, deep blue.

Those eyes were wide open and knowing. Yes, he knew it was her. Unbelievable, given that she was no blonde bombshell, but he did know it was her.

That made it more sweet when he kissed her again, gentler this time, tasting more than devouring. His tongue moved against hers, sliding up, slipping back. His movements became slow and arousing, tempting as all get-out. She ached inside.

She gave herself up to the ache, moving against his body for relief, searching his mouth for whatever she could find. But just as she didn't do anonymous sex, she didn't do one-night stands—or one-morning stands, which was where they seemed headed. It was totally exciting and utterly terrifying. And absolutely impossible.

Exerting a small pressure on his shoulders, she

broke the kiss and stepped back. Breathing hard, she stared at him.

Breathing equally hard, he stared right back.

This time, she didn't have the wherewithal to stare him down. Dropping her gaze, she flattened a fist on her thudding heart and took a breath that should have calmed her. But one wouldn't do. Her insides were wired. She took a second breath and then a third. Without looking at him again, she held up a hand.

She should have waited longer. Her legs were far from steady. But she feared she might change her mind and go back for more, which wouldn't do at all.

She was the woman. She was in control. She could say when she wanted to be kissed and when she didn't, and right now she didn't.

Turning in a way that sent her heel skidding off its flip-flop, she caught herself, raised her chin, and walked off with as much dignity as a woman on wobbly legs could muster.

Sixteen

"WHY DIDN'T YOU MARRY CARL in 1942?"

"Because I married Alexander."

Olivia looked at Natalie for a minute, then shook her head and smiled. "Why am I not surprised by that answer?"

Natalie was smiling, too. "Why aren't you? Tell me."

"Because you always see the cup as half full. And because you don't like talking about things that are painful."

"Or embarrassing."

"Embarrassing? The reason you married Alexander instead of Carl?" Olivia could only think of one embarrassing reason—her being pregnant with Alexander's child. But there was no way that would happen. No way. Natalie loved Carl.

"Yes, embarrassing."

"Why?"

Natalie rolled her eyes. When they returned to Olivia, they held a sheen of tears. Her smile was self-conscious now. "Because . . ." She started, but stopped. She rose from the wicker lounge chair and began gathering dirty paper plates and cups from the nearby table.

It was late afternoon on the Fourth of July. Waves of heat rose from the gas grill as it burned off remnants of hamburgers and hot dogs. Madalena and Joaquin had returned salads, rolls, and condiments to the kitchen. The dozen or so friends who had been there for lunch had departed. Carl had taken Tess and Jill for ice cream cones.

Simon hadn't showed. Carl had been asked about him, though it was more a query about how he fared than about where he was. Apparently no one had expected to see him—and while Olivia found that sad, she was profoundly relieved. She was still trying to decide exactly what had happened this morning out there under that tree.

It was much easier to focus on this.

Rising, she helped Natalie clean up. Beneath mustard and ketchup stains, and the occasional potato chip or hot dog bun scrap, the paperware was a patriotic red-white-and-blue.

"Why is it embarrassing?"

Natalie emptied fruit punch leftovers into a single cup and stacked the empties underneath. "Maybe 'embarrassing' is the wrong word. Maybe 'ashamed' is better." She quickly looked at Olivia. "Not that the decision I made was wrong, or that Alexander wasn't a good man. I don't want my children to think that, because it isn't true. He was a fine man. I liked him. I came to *love* him. We had a good life together. If I was in the same situation and was given the same choice, I'd do exactly the same thing now as I did then." The fire left her. She frowned and toyed with the cups.

"What?" Olivia prodded gently. "What did you do?"

"By today's standards, what I did sounds shallow. It sounds like a betrayal of the first order. It sounds materialistic."

Olivia could only think of one way that could be. "You married Alexander for *money?*"

The fires had barely been extinguished, the bodies removed, and the damage assessed at Pearl Harbor when every able-bodied man in town began to think about enlisting. Carl was one of the first, he felt that strongly about it. Before I could turn around and say that I thought we should be married before he left, there he was in uniform, ready to be shipped overseas.

It was early 1942. A raw February day. February 8—I won't ever forget the date. Carl and I had agreed that I wouldn't go to the train station. It would be too painful. We were in the tractor shed, awake all night holding each other. We didn't care that it was cold there. We had nowhere else to go.

The sun came up—cruel sun, on such a dismal day. The fields were barren. Ice coated all the little spikes of dead grasses and plants in a way that might have actually been beautiful, had the circumstances been different.

We didn't talk. There wasn't anything to say. He was doing what he had to do, and I supported him in it. But he was about to be sent God knew where and suffer God knew what. We had never been separated before.

Three times he went to the door to leave. Three times he came back. Then he couldn't put it off any longer. He went to the door a fourth time, stood there with one hand on the big iron latch and the other limp at his side, and looked back. I remember the details of it as clearly as I remember seeing him when I was five. The clothes were bigger, but with the exception of work pants for overalls, he was dressed much the same—similar hat and jacket, similar boots. His hair fell over his brow. We knew it would be shorter by the time the day was done. His shirt hung out of his pants, the last of that kind of thing, too. His eyes held me, touched me, loved me. Then he put his head down and slipped through the door.

My heart went with him. I ran to the door and watched him walk away. The farther he went, the smaller he grew, until he turned onto the path that led to his house and disappeared from my sight.

I slipped to the floor and cried. Just cried. Had I not known how strongly he felt about doing this, I would have run after him and begged. But that wouldn't have helped either of us. I just . . . sat there . . . sat . . . and cried.

No. I'm . . . all right. Give me a minute.

It was just . . . oh my . . . just a heart-wrenching time.

There. I'm fine. But that isn't what you really want to know. What you *really* want to know is why we didn't marry before he left.

Believe it or not, he didn't ask me. And I didn't think anything of it. Things happened so fast. It was like he was here one day and gone the next. I just assumed that we would get married when he came home. If he came home. Yes, I do see the cup as being half full, but the reality of those days made it harder. Hitler was a monster. We may not have known the details of it back then, like we do today, but we knew he was evil.

Who was Carl to fight that? He was a gentle man. A nonviolent man. I told myself he was strong and determined, and that those qualities would carry him through the war and let him come back in one piece. But there were bombs falling. We heard them on the radio each night. How could Carl protect himself from a bomb?

I was seventeen, and I was terrified for him. Yes, I wish he had proposed before he left. It might have given me an argument not to marry Alexander—and again, I don't want that misconstrued. Alexander was a *good man*."

But I loved Carl.

Was I angry that he hadn't proposed? No.

Actually, yes. The days that followed were so tumultuous for me that it's only natural anger should be one of the emotions I felt. However—and this is important, Olivia—I did *not* marry Alexander on the rebound. There were other reasons why I married him.

But I'm getting ahead of myself. Let's go back to my not marrying Carl. Like I said, I didn't think about it in the flurry of his departure. Once he was gone, though, I did. Other girls I knew were marrying their sweethearts. It struck me that we might have been married, too, and suddenly I was desperate for it. But Carl hadn't been. For years, I wondered why. I asked him about it only recently—it took me that long to get up the nerve.

His answer surprised me. I had thought that the timing was his only reservation—my age and the rush of his induction. But he had other reasons to pause. He was Catholic, we were Protestant. His parents were immigrants, mine were blue bloods. He wasn't educated. He wasn't rich. He wasn't a landowner. He felt inferior to the man my father had been in his prime. He said that in all the years my parents had known him, as kind as they had been to his parents and to him, they had never once taken him seriously as son-in-law material.

He was right. My parents made that clear to me when Alexander proposed.

I didn't see it at the time, though. I was so in love with Carl that I just assumed my parents knew how I felt and what I wanted. There was no reason to talk about it. I was only seventeen. I hadn't even finished high school.

My parents had been discussing my future between themselves, though. In the months leading up to Pearl Harbor, while I was dreaming my girlish dreams about marrying Carl, they were nurturing other thoughts. Alexander Seebring was the son of a successful businessman. His family had spent their summers in Newport way back when we did, so I knew who Al was. We hadn't been friends, though. He was ten years older than me.

That fall before Pearl Harbor, our families started getting together. I remember the preparations—the cleaning and polishing and sprucing up designed to impress guests. I was stunned that things could look so nice. My mother had been sick on and off, and hadn't put any effort into appearances, so I was accustomed to something simpler. When everything was done up, though, we didn't look quite so poor.

Even then, I didn't think anything of it when the Seebrings came to visit.

Alexander was giving my father a hand. The Seebring business was shoes, which meant that Al made regular trips to Europe. He was helping my father in his quest for the perfect grape.

I used to ask Al about those trips. He could talk for hours and be totally enchanting. It didn't occur to me that our parents were encouraging those talks for anything deeper.

I did know that my father was better when the Seebrings were around. As soon as they left, he would sink back into depression, and that was before war had been declared. After Pearl, after Brad died, the depression deepened. He would go for days without saying a word, leaving the work in the fields to Jeremiah and us while he sat and withered alongside his vines.

My mother was in a panic. She couldn't talk about Brad, because his death was painful and fresh, and my father was getting worse by the day. So was she. We later found out that what we had thought was chronic indigestion was a tumor. All I knew at the time was that she was painfully thin and growing more frail by the day.

Carl had barely been gone a month when my mother suggested I marry

Alexander. She was so desperate that she didn't even dress up the reasons. We needed money, she said. Alexander had it. She claimed that if I married him, he would pour untold resources into the vineyard. My father would be able to buy many more vines and make them grow this time. He needed this desperately. Otherwise, he would die.

Yes. That was what she said. If I didn't marry Alexander—if there was no infusion of funds—my father would die. For my part, I was thinking that my mother might die first, and that if this was her last request, how could I possibly deny it?

Alexander enlisted. He wanted to marry me before he went overseas. I had all of a week to make my decision.

"It must have been a *nightmare* for you," Olivia said, wondering for the first time if she would have liked to live through those days after all.

They had finished clearing the patio table and were wandering into the vineyard. It made sense that Natalie needed the vines around her when she told this part of the story. The vines were a major player—and beautiful ones they were. Olivia could see the change that moving from June to July had brought. The leaves were a richer green now, reaching the higher wire in greater numbers, and though the grapes remained small and hard, with this day's sun there was an air of promise.

"It happened so fast," Natalie said, sounding overwhelmed.

"Where was Carl at this point?"

"Guadalcanal."

"Did he know what was going on?"

Natalie didn't answer at first. She left the path and started down a row of vines, putting a hand out to graze a leaf here and there. "Not until after the wedding," she finally said.

"Did you try to reach him?"

Natalie looked at her then. "To what end? He hadn't mentioned a wedding—his and mine—either before he left or in the first letters he sent. My mother was pressuring me. My father was pressuring me. Alexander was pressuring me."

Ever the romantic, Olivia said, "But you loved Carl."

"I was seventeen. I was confused. And I was alone. When I most needed help, my best friend—my soul mate, my other half—was gone. My mother was saying that if I didn't marry Alexander, Asquonset would fail and my father would die. She was getting weaker by the day, and they had just lost Brad. I was all they had left. I was their only hope."

Olivia could see the anguish in her eyes even now. They were suddenly old eyes, bloodshot with misery, heavy with decades of private grief. For the very first time, Natalie looked her age.

Seeming to understand that, awkward with her own transparency, Natalie looked away. But she went on with her tale.

"I kept praying my mother would know why I was torn, but she was too tormented for that. I made the usual arguments—I barely knew Al, I was too young for marriage, Al was too old for me. Finally, when he wanted an answer and I was frantic, I told my mother that I loved Carl. I blurted it right out, and she didn't blink an eyelash. She asked where Carl was in our time of need and whether he could come up with enough money to save things. I had no answer. Alexander was pushing to get married within the week. I didn't know what to do."

"What about Jeremiah and Brida?" Olivia asked. "Didn't they speak up on Carl's behalf?"

Smiling sadly, Natalie cradled a bunch of baby grapes in her hand. "I talked with Brida, but they were in an untenable position. They worked for my father. He put the roof over their heads and food on their table. They were acutely aware of that—and grateful. Brida had a terrible case of arthritis. She wasn't old, but the damp air wreaked havoc with her joints. She couldn't do some of the things she used to, and no one complained. So Jeremiah and Brida felt a special loyalty to my parents for that."

"And not to their own son?" Olivia asked in dismay.

"Yes, to their own son." Natalie paused.

"And?"

"They loved me. But there was a girl in Ireland, the daughter of dear friends there. They had always dreamed that she and Carl would marry."

"Did he know her?"

"No."

"Then it was a bogus claim," Olivia decided.

Natalie smiled. "Is that so? How do you know?"

Olivia looked at her in a moment's pause and let out a breath. "I don't."

"For what it's worth," Natalie relented, "I had my own moments of wondering if Brida had contrived the story to make my decision easier. She was a bright woman. She knew I was between a rock and a hard place. She loved me, but she loved my parents, too. She was convinced that the money would help, and a healthy Asquonset was good for her family, too. Besides, her story wasn't bogus. There was a young woman in Ireland. But it was years after the war before Carl would even consider marriage, and then not to her."

"So," Olivia said, trying not to sound judgmental, "you agreed to marry Alexander."

Natalie grew defensive. "I tried to buy time. I said that we should let him go off and plan a wedding for when he came home on leave. I kept thinking that maybe Carl would show up and marry me first—and that my father would have found his dream vine in the meantime, so he wouldn't need the money. But I was bucking the tide. Young girls were getting married right and left. It became the patriotic thing to do—you know, send our boys off to war with one more reason to want to win. So, yes, I agreed to marry Alexander. And then it was like it was done. I had barely given the word and there I was, in the little church in town, promising to love Alexander forever, for better or for worse."

"What did you feel for him then?" Olivia asked.

Natalie didn't answer. She walked on through the rows of vines, murmuring gentle words of encouragement to the grapes. Simon was nowhere in sight. Olivia heard the distant drone of a machine that said he was in another field. He was shorthanded. He would work on the holiday. Olivia knew the type.

Not that he was like Ted. That kind of workaholism was bad. She couldn't say that Simon's was. His felt more like dedication.

Besides, here was Olivia, working on the holiday, too. Only this didn't feel like work.

"Natalie?"

The older woman stopped walking. She studied the clusters on the vines for a minute before asking Olivia, "Do you know what grapes these are?"

"Yes. They're Gewürztraminer."

"Bet you didn't know that name before you got here."

"No," Olivia confessed.

"Many people don't. The word *gewürzt* means 'spicy.' The wine we produce from these grapes is spicy and light. This was one of the first varietals that we grew successfully. Gewürztraminer loves a cool climate. It's commonly grown in Alsace, in France. That's where my father got the rootstock."

"With Alexander's money?"

Natalie made a mocking sound. "Not . . . quite."

"Uh-oh. Why not?"

She shot Olivia a crooked smile. "That's for another installment. We haven't finished with this one. I believe you were asking what I felt for Alexander." She frowned. "The answer is complex."

When she said nothing for a long minute, Olivia helped her out. "What was your wedding day like?"

I was numb. Out of breath. Have you ever been swept along by a powerful wave at the beach? Or by a crowd of people? It was like that. Once I said that I would marry Alexander, I was swept along by a powerful wave of events. Before I knew it, I was standing there at that altar in my white dress, with Alexander beside me in his brand-new uniform. We made a handsome couple. I say that without arrogance. I can do that, at my age.

You've seen the pictures. I was smiling, wasn't I? Didn't I look happy? And it wasn't an act. Every girl dreams of her wedding day. I was marrying a fine man from a fine family. I was marrying a *mature* man. He would take care of me—he would take care of all of us once he returned from the war. He was the answer to my family's woes.

Did I think about Carl that day? No. I couldn't. It would have been too painful. I didn't allow myself to think about him that whole week. Just . . . blotted him out.

What else could I do? The decision was made. My betrothal was a fait accompli. There was no purpose in wondering where Carl was and what he was thinking.

I'm not proud to admit that. It doesn't say much about my love for him that I could push him out of my mind and smile through my marriage to another man. I've often asked myself how I did it. Carl asked me, too, when we finally talked, but that wasn't for four years. He was overseas that long. Again, though, I'm getting ahead of myself.

My wedding that day in March of '42 wasn't elaborate. My parents couldn't afford it, and they had a perfect excuse for modesty, what with Brad's death and the war and such short notice. There was a ceremony at the church, followed by dinner at our house. Alexander and I drove to Boston for a two-day honeymoon, before he left for the front.

So. What did I feel for my new husband? I felt all the things that many a girl marrying in the early days of the war felt. I was young. I was advancing my wedding date because of the war, but I believed that I was doing the right thing. I was a bride, and I was excited about that. I bought into the role. I had a new husband and a new name. I had the highest hopes for the future, even with him heading off to war—and I was philosophical about that. My husband was fighting for our country. I was proud. I put a starred flag in our window to show that we had a boy at the front.

I stayed with my family in Asquonset. Many young girls did that when their new husbands went to war. Alexander wanted to settle in Asquonset. His family owned shoe factories in New Bedford and Fall River, both an easy drive from the farm. He promised to build us a house of our own when he returned. In the meantime, I had to finish high school, so I had to be close. Besides, my parents needed me.

At the beginning, I wrote a letter to Alexander each night. Each night, when that letter was addressed and sealed, I tried to write to Carl. Night after night I struggled with the words. Finally I realized that there weren't any right ones for what I had to say. So I simply wrote out my thoughts. It was an artless letter, blunt and without pretense. By that time, though, I was angry. The reality of the situation had begun to sink in. I was married. I was tied to another man for the rest of my life. It was legal. It was religious. It was permanent.

But it should have been Carl.

Because it wasn't, he became the bad guy in my mind. I decided that he had put his feeling for war before his feelings for me. I reasoned, selfishly, that in racing to enlist without a thought to *my* welfare, he had betrayed me as surely as I had betrayed him—and the letters I received from him each week reinforced that belief. They were newsy notes, telling about the men in his unit, the food, even the showers. They weren't personal. They weren't love letters.

He and I were talking about that just last week. He thought for sure that he must have said something about love, because he remembers that was what he was thinking and feeling. But I showed him. I took out the letters. There were no words to that effect. He frowned— legitimately puzzled, bless his soul— and said that he must have been afraid the censors would black out anything personal.

I'm not sure the Japanese were into collecting personal information about individual servicemen, but I gave him the benefit of the doubt.

Anyway, back in 1942, I sent my letter off. In the two months that Carl had been gone, I had received six letters from him. I never received another after that.

"Not *one?*" Olivia asked. They were heading back to the house now, walking slowly under an ominous gray sky. "Not even a little note of congratulations?"

Natalie had her hands linked behind her in a pose that suggested impotence. "Nothing. It was my punishment. He was angry and hurt. He destroyed every bit of evidence that he had with him of my existence."

"Like Simon burning his house?" Olivia asked.

Natalie shot her a curious look. "Who told you about that?"

"Simon," she said and realized her mistake when Natalie raised a brow. "You know me," she said with a wry grin. "Mention something about the past and I foam at the mouth with questions. I got him going about his wife and daughter. He wasn't pleased with me."

"He isn't pleased with many people. Keep at it."

"Uh-uh. Not me. A therapist could spend *years* getting Simon to talk. I'm only here for the summer, and I'm no therapist."

"He deserves happiness."

"Don't we all?" Olivia mused and changed the subject. "What was it like the first time you saw Carl?"

"After the war?" Natalie asked. "It was hard, but not as hard as I'd imagined it would be."

"Why not?"

"Because we needed him. All hell had broken loose here. Jeremiah was trying to run things himself, and desperately needed help."

"Where was your father?"

"In the house. He didn't get out of bed much after my mother died."

"When did *that* happen?"

"A year after my wedding. I had a baby by then, and, thanks to Alexander's leave time, two by the end of the war. I was running the house, raising children, nursing my father, working with Jere-

miah, who was in none too great spirits himself."
They reached the patio and stopped walking.
"Brida's arthritis was the crippling kind. She could
do less and less, though she tried. The more she
tried—and the more she failed—the more heartbreaking it was for those of us who watched. Jeremiah became her nurse, on top of everything else
that he had to do. He just couldn't—just couldn't
do it all."

"Where was Alexander?"

"England."

"I mean, after the war."

"England," Natalie repeated. "Then France. He
was gone for the better part of five years. To this
day, I think he loved intelligence work more than
anything else he ever did. V-E Day—V-J Day—
our boys started streaming home. Not Alexander.
He stayed on to gather evidence of war crimes for
the trials."

"But you needed him here," Olivia argued.

"Carl was back."

Carl was back. As though that said it all. But it
certainly didn't, in Olivia's opinion. "So what *was*
it like having him here?"

"Awkward at first," Natalie said after a moment's thought. "We didn't know what to say to
each other. We had to redefine our relationship."

Olivia tried to imagine how it was for Carl.
"I'm surprised he came back to Asquonset. Seeing
you must have been painful."

"He believed in the cause. That was the thing about Carl. To him, Asquonset wasn't a job. It was a way of life. He truly believed that one day we would be successful grape growers and wine makers. He wanted to help make it happen. Besides, he wanted to be near his parents."

"The romantic in me says he wanted to be near you, too."

Natalie glanced at the house just as Madalena and Joaquin came out the door. "There may have been some of that, too," she murmured distractedly. Then she paused and called out, her voice wary, "Madalena? Are you and Joaquin going somewhere?"

They were dressed in a way that Olivia, for one, had never seen them. Not dressed for work. Not dressed for church. They were dressed for . . . travel.

Madalena's face was covered with guilt.

In heavily accented English, Joaquin said, "My sister is ill. We go to Brazil now."

"Brazil," Natalie breathed in dismay as she crossed to where they stood. She took Madalena's hand. *"Brazil? For how long?"*

Madalena looked at her husband.

He said, "My sister, she has seven kids and twelve grandkids."

"I know that, Joaquin. I've been sending them clothes for years."

"She is ill now. She need help."

"Can't we hire someone? I'll gladly pay."

"She need family."

"For how *long?*" Natalie asked again. When neither of them answered, she said, "You're leaving me. You're leaving because of my marriage. That's it, isn't it?"

Again, Joaquin spoke for the two. "It's time. We're tired."

"Fine," Natalie said, nodding. "I can understand that. But at least wait until after the wedding."

Joaquin shook his head. "My sister."

"Then go for a week. Go for the rest of July. But come back in August." When neither of them said anything more, Natalie turned to Olivia. "Try to convince them, please."

Olivia did her best. She said that Madalena's roast duck was the best she'd ever eaten, and that Joaquin had an unrivaled way with the roses. She said that Tess had refused to eat salad until she tasted Madalena's garlic dressing, and that her old Toyota had never run as smoothly as it had since Joaquin had worked on it. She said that if ever the two of them were needed at Asquonset, it was now. She asked if money was the issue.

"No," they both said with such ferocity that Olivia sensed it was a lost cause. She sent Natalie a look that said as much.

But Natalie already knew, judging from the look of resignation on her face. She pressed several fingers to her forehead in a moment of gathering her wits. Then, ever the lady, she said, "Come. We'll go inside. I'll pay you what you're owed."

OLIVIA STAYED ON THE PATIO, not so much because she expected Natalie to return but because she felt unsettled.

Unsettled? No, that wasn't it. Disappointed. She understood why Natalie had married Alexander. Given the circumstances, she supposed she might have done the same thing. But without regrets? Without thinking of Carl day and night? Could she have done that? Did that kind of love just *end?*

Sinking back in her chair, Olivia rested her head, closed her eyes, and thought about the men who had passed through her life. She revisited each relationship, searching for something she may have missed at the time. Not a one came close to what Natalie and Carl had had.

Olivia would give her right arm for that kind of love. If she ever loved someone that way, she would never let go.

"I've let you down."

Olivia jumped. She hadn't heard Natalie return. "No, I was just thinking. Are Madalena and Joaquin gone?"

"Gone."

"I'm sorry I couldn't help. They seemed to have their minds made up."

"And their bags packed. It wasn't worth arguing. But if you're thinking that I accepted that as easily as I accepted losing Carl—that I just cave in and move on—you're wrong."

"I wasn't thinking that."

"But you were thinking something like it." Natalie lowered herself to the foot of the lounge chair. "My children are thinking it, too. They're thinking that I buried Alexander and moved on"—she snapped her fingers—"just like that. But it isn't just like that. It never was. What I feel here"—she touched her heart—"doesn't always jibe with this." She touched her head. "You can know, intellectually, that a course of action is the right one, even when you don't want it to be. In this instance, I know that Madalena and Joaquin have to leave. His sister really is sick. He needs to help her. The timing is suspicious, but truthfully, if they're unhappy with the prospect of my marrying Carl, then they shouldn't be here. Carl has given too much to this place to have people here who think less than the world of him."

"What about Susanne and Mark?" They certainly fell into that category.

"It's different with them. They're family. You would know, if you were closer to yours."

Olivia felt lower than low. Natalie was sharing private things, giving honest answers even when they didn't paint her in the best light—yet twice now, Olivia had told lies about her own situation. Suddenly that seemed very wrong.

"The truth," Olivia said quietly, "is that I would know, if I had family at all. It's only my mother and me. I wanted there to be a father. I wanted there to be brothers, even just one. But there aren't."

Natalie's features softened. Where there might have been anger at having been deceived, there was only compassion. "Do you see her often?"

Olivia shook her head.

"Do you see her at all?"

Olivia paused. She could tell a last little lie, just to put herself in a more lovable light. But she was tired of lying to Natalie—tired of lying to *herself*. Again, she shook her head.

"Where is she?" Natalie asked.

"I don't know."

"I can find out. I can put an investigator on it. People don't disappear from the face of the earth without leaving a clue."

"No, don't do that," Olivia said quickly. "I don't think she wants to be found. I was a difficult child. I tied her down for years. She deserves her freedom."

"But you want a mother, and you want a grand-mother for Tess."

"Not an unwilling one. What if we found her, and she resented it? That would be worse."

"Ah," Natalie said with a gentle smile. "It's a matter of weighing and balancing. You're ready to let her go, because knowing for sure may be worse than not knowing. The truth may be more painful than living without. Now you know what I felt. I was willing to pack up my love for Carl and put it in storage, because looking at it each day would have killed me."

"But you did have to look at him each day. He was right here after the war. How could you *help*-but think about all you'd given up?"

"What good would it have done?" Natalie cried with greater feeling. "I could have thought about it night and day, and nothing would have changed. Besides, I didn't have the *time* to think about it night and day. It wasn't like I was sitting in a hayloft all day drooling at the sight of the man that I had always thought I would marry. I had two children, a catatonic father, a house to clean, cooking to do, and a business to run. Try to find the romance in *that,* Olivia Jones. Morning to night, I was busy. I had the weight of the world on my shoulders. That didn't mean I didn't think about what I had lost. Of *course* I did. I'm human." She rose from the chair and strode to the far side of the patio, where she stood with her hands on her nape and her back to Olivia.

Olivia followed, feeling guilty. "I'm sorry. I shouldn't have pushed like that."

"It's not your pushing that I mind. It's your condemnation."

"Oh, no, I'm not doing that. How could I? You didn't condemn me when I lied about my family. How could I condemn you now?"

"Well, I condemn me," Natalie said. When she

turned her head, there were tears in her eyes. *"I condemn me. I betrayed Carl. I gave up something so beautiful that it takes my breath away even now. For what it's worth, I suffered. I suffered in ways that no one will ever know."*

She stopped and brushed at the corners of her eyes with the back of her hand. It appeared suddenly wrinkled and shaky, a hand that showed its age.

"I'm sorry," Olivia whispered.

"Oh, don't be," Natalie muttered, bracing that hand on Olivia's shoulder. "You're doing what I hired you to do. I don't like to talk about suffering. I don't feel that I deserve anyone's sympathy. The problem is that my children think my life has been a walk in the park."

"Wasn't it better once your husband got back?" Olivia asked.

Natalie gave her a look. "That was when, excuse my French, the shit hit the fan."

Seventeen

OLIVIA DIDN'T WANT TO SEE SIMON. She didn't know how to deal with what she felt. It was raw physical attraction with no emotional link, and it was totally wrong at this time in her life. But Natalie was right—a woman's mind wasn't always in sync with her body.

Actually, Natalie's analogy had to do with a woman's mind and her *heart,* but the result was the same. Olivia didn't trust herself. For the next few mornings, she stayed in bed until Tess came through the bathroom door with a cat or two in tow. By then, Simon was long gone from the patio.

Did she think about him?

She shouldn't have had time. When she wasn't on the phone in the loft, she was writing, staring at the computer screen, reading what she'd written, changing it all around. She talked the story aloud and typed as she talked in an attempt to make things flow, but flow was only part of it. Words could mean one thing in one context and another in another. She had to convey just the right feeling at each turn.

Natalie was correct. Olivia had no right to be judgmental, but the opposite was just as bad. If she sugar-coated the story, it would lose authenticity.

The key was to find a happy medium. To that end, she wrote, rewrote, and rewrote yet again. She worked in the loft after Tess was in bed, and kept a pad by her own bed to jot down thoughts that came to her through the night.

Did she think about Simon? Of course, she did. What red-blooded woman wouldn't? She might even have been seduced into doing something about it if he had showed any inclination. But he was as absent as ever. That made it easier to push him from her mind.

The chaos in the house also helped. One maid had been fired and another hired, which meant that a new person was in need of training—all of which would have been easier had Madalena been there to do it, but she and Joaquin were long gone. In their absence, the kitchen had become disorganized. Natalie was interviewing possible replacements, but she hadn't yet met one who appealed to her. In the meanwhile, it was catch-as-catch-can.

They ate dinner out. They brought lunch in. Break-fast was strictly help-yourself; at least, it was sup-posd to be, but Olivia liked breakfast. It was the only meal she was any good at making. So one day she whipped up a batch of pancakes; the next, omelettes; the next, French toast. She sliced a mean banana on cereal and brewed a full-bodied pot of coffee. She was having a grand time of it, until Jill came down the fourth morning wanting nothing but tea and toast.

Olivia's first thought was that something she had cooked hadn't gone down the right way. Her second thought was more intuitive. "Oh dear. You must have talked with Greg."

Jill smiled curiously. "How did you guess?"

"You're lookin' a mite pale."

It was actually an understatement. Jill's skin was nearly as colorless as the white robe she wore. Her blonde hair was limp, pushed behind her ears in a way that said she didn't have the strength to do anything more to it.

"Greg can be difficult," she said, dropping a tea bag into a mug. She filled the mug with water and put it in the microwave oven.

"Is he upset that you're here?"

"Oh, no. He likes my being here. If I'm here, he doesn't have to be." She set the time and started the microwave. "I wish he would come. I haven't seen him in over a month. It feels like a separation."

"Is it?" Olivia asked, venturing deeper into the

personal than she had done before with Jill, but she wanted to think that they were friends.

Jill must have agreed, because she answered without pause. "Not . . . formally. I spent some time with my mom. I wanted to talk with her. I wanted to give Greg a scare. Well, he does want me back in Washington with him." She opened the refrigerator. "But we need to talk about some heavy stuff first. I'm afraid that if I go back, we'll fall into the old routine." She took out a loaf of raisin bread and put a slice in the toaster.

"Is he willing to talk?"

"He says so." Leaning against the counter, she folded her arms. "The thing is, his definition of talk is different from mine. He has trouble with anything deep."

"Maybe it's a Seebring trait," Olivia mused, thinking of Natalie. "It's hard to talk about some things."

"Hard to *talk* about them?" The microwave beeped. "Try, hard to *think* about them," Jill said as she took out the mug and began dunking the bag. "Like father, like son. Alexander wasn't a deep thinker."

"Natalie is. She just doesn't like sharing those thoughts."

Dropping the tea bag into the disposal, Jill grasped the mug. Her eyes met Olivia's over the rim. "Is she really in love with Carl?"

"Has been since she was five," Olivia said. Natalie had given her permission to talk freely with Jill. She had actually seemed eager for it.

"Really?" Jill asked, sounding totally surprised.

"Truly."

"That's *so* interesting." She frowned. "It puts things in a new light. Raises a whole lot of other questions. Like about fidelity."

"Natalie was faithful to Alexander," Olivia said. She didn't know that for sure, of course. She hadn't ever asked, and Natalie hadn't put anything on the record, but she believed that a woman should be innocent until proven guilty.

"All those years?" Jill asked. Her toast popped up. "Loving someone else?" She pulled it from the toaster.

"Was he faithful to *her?*"

Jill nibbled on a corner of the toast. "I don't know."

"Guess."

"Between you and me?" She lowered her voice. "No. I think he had a little someone on the side. He loved to talk, loved to travel, loved being the center of attention. He spent more time down in our area than he ever needed to. I think he had a woman in the District."

Olivia was deeply offended. "What was wrong with his wife?"

"If you were to ask his kids, they would say she wasn't interesting enough. They would say she spent too much of her life here in Rhode Island. They would say she was too parochial."

"She's an *unbelievable* woman," Olivia argued.

"You and I can see that, but we're not See-brings. Amazing how family dynamics cause blindness. Susanne and Greg don't see what we do. Their own needs shape their vision. They wanted to be doted upon growing up, but Natalie was always busy. Susanne used to come here with her kids and expect Natalie to baby-sit, but she didn't have the time.

"The irony is that she did dote on Alexander. She satisfied all his little needs, and after all that, he just put her down. So much the better it if he did it in front of other people. He'd say things like, 'Don't those napkins look wonderful? Folding napkins is Natalie's specialty.' Hey"—Jill gestured with the toast in her hand—"I'm not putting down folding napkins, but Natalie does a lot more than that around here. Whenever I'm in for more than a weekend, she puts me to work, and it's not planning a party, it's doing PR for a multimillion-dollar business. The amazing thing is that when I'm not here, she does it herself."

"All of it?" Olivia asked. She knew that Natalie had her finger in more than one pie. Monitoring her telephone calls for a day made that clear. But running the entire show was something else.

Jill didn't quite answer. "Alexander put her down because he couldn't accept the fact that she's a capable woman. That threatened him. So he left Natalie here to see to the day-to-day running of things, billed himself as the face of Asquonset, and went off on the road like a hero. I wouldn't be the *least* bit surprised if along the way he found someone nonthreatening to build his ego a little." Her eyes grew pained. "Why is it that men have trouble with strong women? Are their egos that fragile? My husband is wary discussing substantive things with me, and that goes for political issues as well as things like love and responsibility. He always said he was talked out from work, and for the longest time I believed him. But it's an excuse. The truth is that he's threatened by my opinions. He doesn't want to think that they may be different from his, because there could be a chance that I'm right."

Olivia was fascinated. She hadn't counted on learning so much.

And Jill wasn't done. "I'm thirty-eight years old. Up until the time I married Greg, I always worked, but he didn't want me doing that, and I thought it was really sweet. Then I realized that it was a power thing. He was worried I might actually have a successful career. He's the man. He's the breadwinner. He's supposed to be right. He's supposed to lead. That's what his father did." She looked suddenly stricken. "So, does Greg have a little someone on the side who builds his ego while he's on the road?"

"Does he?" Olivia asked, ready to condemn the man in no uncertain terms if it was so.

Jill shot a glance skyward. "God, I hope not."

In the next instant she blew out a breath, put a hand to her throat, and swore softly. Closing her eyes, she inhaled through her nose. She swallowed once, then again. Her complexion seemed to go from pale to green.

Olivia went to her side. "Are you all right?"

It was a minute and a few more swallows before Jill opened her eyes and gave a wan smile. "That depends on what you call all right. If being pregnant by your insensitive, unknowing, beloved but estranged husband is okay, then I'm all right."

Olivia's eye went wide. "Pregnant. And he doesn't know?"

"Neither does Natalie. I'd like to keep it that way for now."

Delighted to be Jill's confidante, Olivia moved two fingers over her mouth. "My lips are sealed."

SIMON WANTED TO SEE OLIVIA. He didn't want to talk with her, didn't even want to kiss her again. Well, actually, he did. But that was secondary. For now, he just wanted to *see* her. He wanted to look at her. He wanted to know if she was refreshingly different or . . . just . . . odd.

When she didn't show in the window for three mornings running, when she wasn't sitting on the patio at dawn or wandering through the vineyard, not even once during any of those following days, he realized that she was avoiding him.

Not so Tess. He would be hand-leafing on his knees in the dirt, or riding the hedger with his work gloves on and a sharp eye on the vines, and suddenly there she would be, out of nowhere, a little ghost child watching him work.

He didn't have time to play. Without Paolo, he had to cover extra ground himself, and the weather didn't help. Thanks to the lack of sun, he had to do added hedging to control every last lateral shoot. Thanks to the rain, he had to aerate the cover crops yet again. He wanted to do an extra round of fertilization, and more spraying, but the dampness lingered. And there was always leaf pulling, vine by vine, row by row, block by block. He was too busy to interview replacements, much less train one.

But there was Tess, watching him with her glasses at half-mast.

Glasses at half-mast. His mother used to say that when he was a kid. He wore contacts now. But he remembered those days.

He remembered something else about his mother. She hated dogs. They'd had a yellow Lab once. It was supposed to be man's best friend, but it hung around his mother. None of them knew why. She didn't feed him or brush him or bathe him. She didn't even pet him. But the more she shooed him away, the closer he crept. She finally gave up and let him follow her around. He lost interest after a while.

Simon wondered if the same might happen

with Tess. He was up on the hedger when he saw her next. Putting the machine into neutral, he gestured her over. She shook her head and ran off.

But she was back the next day. Buck seemed to like her. He sat beside her, staring up at her while she stared at Simon.

Simon wasn't on a machine this time, but on his own two feet. "You can come closer," he called. "I won't bite."

"My mother said I shouldn't," she called back.

His guess was that Olivia had told the child not to go *anywhere* near him, meaning that she shouldn't be in the field where he worked at *all*. He guessed that she wouldn't be happy if she knew Tess was there. She would worry that he would hurt the child again.

He wouldn't. He still felt bad about the first time.

He was about to say that he wanted to show Tess what he was doing when she vanished.

It did occur to him that teaching the child something about the vines would lure the mother. But Tess came only so close, and what could he say to Olivia? *Come see my grapes? Isn't this a neat hedger? Want to hold a grub?*

He wasn't good at opening lines. He hadn't needed one with Laura. They had met at Cornell, and she had been intrigued with his work from the start. Before Laura, girls had just . . . been there. He hadn't needed any opening lines.

To a city girl like Olivia, his work would be boring as hell. Chores might change with the seasons, but it was a constant grind day after day, year after year. The beauty of it, to him, was that the routine was never the same. Bud break never occurred on the same date two years in a row. Waiting for it, watching for it, feeling the excitement when the vines suddenly burst into the palest of pale greens was . . . incredible. Same the critical few days when the buds burst into bloom. That was actually a little more hairy. He remembered seasons when they had lost an entire block of grapes because wind and cold had destroyed the petals before self-pollination could take place. A vintage was a precious thing, dependent on variables like the weather, the age of a particular vine, the size of the Japanese beetle population. Viticultural practices were changing so quickly that he was always trying out something new, but the overall picture stayed the same. He loved seeing the grapes grow and ripen, and never failed to feel a rush when the balance of sugar and acid was right and he made the decision to harvest the crop.

No, siree, there was nothing boring about what he did. It just didn't lend itself to opening lines.

So what to do instead? He could hang around the patio. But he wasn't the hanging-around type.

He could join them all for breakfast or lunch, or go out with them for dinner. But he hadn't done that in four years. Doing it now would be as good as waving a red flag in front of Natalie, because he didn't care *what* Olivia said, Natalie wanted the two of them together, and Carl was just as bad. He tried to be subtle. But he had made one Olivia comment too many to Simon.

Simon's only other thought was to ask her out. But that would be a date.

He wasn't going on a date. He just wanted to *look* at her. She was entertaining.

IN THE END, the solution that presented itself had nothing to do with any racking of brains on his part. It was all Buck's doing, and it came in the middle of the night. Simon had dozed off on the sofa with his glasses dangling from a hand and a book open on his chest when a strange noise brought him awake. Dropping his feet to the floor, he sat up, rubbed his eyes, and put on his glasses.

He heard the noise again. It was a plaintive meow the likes of which he had never heard from Buck before, and it was coming from the direction of the bedroom, but he didn't even have to go that far. Three wicker baskets were lined up in the short hall leading there. The first was filled with books waiting to be read. The third was filled with clothes waiting to be washed. Between them, the second held clean clothes waiting to be worn. Buck had wisely chosen this basket to do . . . what he was . . . doing.

Simon watched in disbelief for a minute. There was more plaintive meowing, and several positively heartrending looks from Buck that might have held bewilderment, pain, or pure panic. Then again, the poor cat might have been begging for help, but there wasn't a thing Simon could do.

Smiling in amazement now, he went to the phone—only to realize that the phone wouldn't help. It would disturb everyone he didn't want to disturb. Talk about raising a red flag.

Flashlight in hand, he jogged through the woods along the shortcut to the Great House. Letting himself in the patio door, he took the stairs to Olivia's wing two at a time, and went down the hall.

Her door was shut. There was no sliver of light underneath. She was sleeping.

But this event was worth waking her for. It was a once in a lifetime thing.

He knocked softly and waited with a shoulder to the door frame and the flashlight trained on the floor. After several seconds, Olivia appeared. He redirected the flashlight so that she could see that it was him, but the beam lit her, too. He saw a nightshirt, hair that stuck up at odd angles, a wrinkle mark on her cheek, and sleepy eyes that registered surprise.

"There's something you have to see," he whispered, gesturing at the next room. "Get Tess."

Olivia looked like she thought he was daft. "It's after one."

"I know. But this is incredible. Buck is giving birth."

She didn't say anything for a minute, just stared up at him. Then, cautiously, she asked, "Giving birth to what?"

"Kittens."

Another silence was followed by a confounded, *"Buck?"*

Simon shot a look at the wall. "Yeah, well, I guess we made a mistake."

"We?"

"Me. Come on. Do you want to see this, or not?"

"I didn't know you wore glasses."

"Only when my contacts are out. Listen, I watched him—her—have one of them, and she looked like she was ready to have another. I don't know how many there'll be, or whether you even want Tess to watch. But it's pretty remarkable, and she does love cats. But I don't think Buck's going to hold the show off too long. If you want Tess to see this, you'd better hurry."

"If I want her to see—Buck having *kittens?* Of course I do."

Without further comment, or promises to be fast, she shut the door in his face. But he heard sounds inside—the pad of running feet, muted voices, the click of the bathroom door—so he knew they were coming.

Buck, you devil, he thought, and wondered if he should have stayed with the cat in its time of need. Not that he would know what to do if he—if *she* ran into problems. But they were pals. His presence was a show of support.

Anxious to be back, he glanced at his watch. Ten minutes had passed since he had left his place. Leaning against the wall, he folded his arms and tried to be only as excited as having a cat that was having kittens warranted.

Eighteen

SIMON HAD TO GIVE OLIVIA points for speed. He couldn't have been waiting for her in the hall more than a minute or two. Not that it took long to pull on a T-shirt and shorts. She was safely dressed when she opened the door. One look at Tess, though, and it was all he could do not to laugh. If the mother's hair stuck up, the child's was worse. Her sleepy little face was nearly lost in the mess of it.

But maybe that was good. She actually looked sweet.

Unfortunately, she grew less sleepy and more wary when she saw him there. But it couldn't be helped—he wasn't letting them traipse through the woods alone in the dark.

Gesturing that they should follow, he focused the flashlight behind him and went down the stairs and out the door. He crossed the patio and led them along the forest path, glancing back from time to time to make sure they were all right.

There was no moon. Other than the beam of his flashlight, the forest was pitch black, at its most dense this time of year. They were nearly into the clearing before the light from the cabin appeared.

He opened the door and let them in, then moved ahead again to show them where Buck was. The hallway was dim, lit only by the spill of living room light, but it was appropriate for birthing and there was more than enough light to be able to see.

Tess gasped, gave a small cry of delight, and tiptoed closer to the basket. Olivia was right beside her, quickly crouching down, enthralled.

And Simon? All *he* saw was the pile of dirty clothes in the basket beside Buck. As unobtrusively as possible, he nudged it into the bedroom with his foot and shut the door. Then he took a closer look at the cat. Three kittens lay in the basket now, and judging from Buck's sudden resumption of meowing and another beseechful look, a fourth was on the way.

"Omigod, Mom," Tess cried softly, "they're so little!" She inched closer. "They don't even look like kittens." She put out a small hand, finger pointing in the general vicinity of one of the babies. "See those bumps? I think they're ears. And their eyes are still shut. How long before they'll be able to see?"

"Three days maybe," Olivia said and raised questioning eyes to Simon. "Right?"

He was less than an arm's length away, leaning forward as he watched. "Don't ask me," he replied. "I'm the one who thought she was a he."

"*Look,* Mom."

"She's licking them. Cleaning them up."

"No. There." She pointed to the other end. "She's having another one, I think."

"I think you're right."

"It's slimy."

"The whole process is actually pretty clean," Simon offered. "Buck eats everything."

"*G-ross,*" Tess said and sat back on her heels. "How many more do you think she'll have?"

"Don't know that," Olivia replied. "We'll have to wait and see."

Tess looked at Simon. He thought he saw a bit less distrust. "How did you know she was having babies?"

"I heard meowing and followed the sound."

"Did you put her in here?"

"No. But it's a great place. Lots of cotton. Warm and comfortable and clean. Sides that'll keep the babies in until she's ready to take them out."

"When's that?"

He shrugged. "A week or two? Maybe three. Maybe *four.*"

Olivia chuckled. "Good answer."

"Do *you* know?" he asked.

"Not me. He's not my cat."

"Who's the father?" Tess asked Simon.

"I don't know."

"I'll bet it's Bernard. No—Maxwell. He's more Buck's size. Why didn't you know he was a girl?"

"I never needed to know. It's not like he's been here—not like *she's* been here that long, not even a year. And it wasn't just me," he said, needing to share the blame so that he wouldn't feel so foolish. "Natalie was the one who named him Buck."

"This explains why he was so fat," Tess said.

Simon nodded. "I'd say so."

The child settled down on the floor and folded her legs. "Can I hold one?"

Simon was thinking that it was too soon for that but that he didn't want to be the one to tell Tess when Olivia said, "Not for a few days, sweetie. They're very fragile."

Tess was pensive. "Remember we saw a thing on TV about four little kittens that someone put in a plastic bag and tried to drown?" Her voice rose. "How could anyone do that? These are babies. They're *Buck's* babies. It'd be awful if someone did that to them."

Simon got the message. "I won't hurt them."

"What'll you do when they get big?"

"I don't know. I'll figure something out."

"Would you just let them loose in the woods?"

"No. They need a home." He stood. "I'm thirsty. Does anyone want anything?"

Tess must have found his last answer acceptable because she asked, "What do you have?"

He pictured the inside of his refrigerator. It wasn't exactly stocked for kids. "O.J. T.J. Water."

"No Coke?"

"No Coke."

"No Little Bunches?"

"Sorry."

"How can you do what you do and not have Little Bunches?"

"Tess," Olivia chided. "That's rude."

But Simon said, "She has a point. It's just that I'm not used to having kids in here. You're the first one."

Tess's brows went higher than her glasses. *"Ever?"*

"Ever."

"Where did your daughter live?"

"Tess," Olivia whispered.

"We all lived in another house," he said, wondering what the chances were of Tess leaving it at that. When it came to curiosity, she had the same overabundance as her mother, which was probably why Olivia was quiet now. Two of them couldn't chatter at once. Unless it was something else, like Olivia being tired. Or feeling awkward. Maybe she wasn't a night person.

She was good in the morning. He knew that.

"Don't you even have *wine?"* the child asked.

Relieved that she hadn't homed in on Liana, he smiled. "Not for you." He looked at Olivia. In the dim light, he could have sworn she was startled. "What?"

She stared at him for a minute, then shook her head and looked at the basket again.

"Would you like wine?"

"Water, please."

"I want O.J.," Tess said. "But not if it has pulp. I hate pulp."

"Hates pulp," he murmured, going to the galley kitchen at the end of the living room. He poured a glass of water and was in the process of pouring orange juice through a strainer when Olivia came up beside him.

"You don't need to do that," she said. Her voice was gentle.

He shook the strainer to let the juice through. "She hates pulp."

"She could have done without. Seeing Buck having kittens is treat enough. She's not budging from that basket."

He put the strainer into the sink and turned to Olivia. Her head just reached his shoulders. Her hair was a dozen different shades of dirty blonde. It actually looked natural.

"Something startled you before," he said.

She shot him the briefest glance and shrugged.

"What was it?"

She shrugged again. "You smiled. It changed your face."

He could have sworn she was suddenly shy,

then decided it was just that she seemed mellow. The night would cause that.

"Thank you for coming to get us," she said, and turned so that she was leaning against the counter, looking out. "This is a nice place."

He leaned against the counter beside her. "It's small. I couldn't see building a place that echoed."

"No chance of that with all these books. I've never seen so many. I'll bet there are none on raising kittens."

"Give me three days." He handed her the water and said quietly enough so that Tess wouldn't hear, "I haven't seen you in a while."

She took a drink. "I've been sleeping later."

"Deliberately?"

"I work at night. Sometimes pretty late." She studied the rim of her glass. Finally, she raised her eyes to meet his. Her face was bare in every sense. "I don't know how to deal with this. It's not why I'm in Asquonset."

Her honesty did something to his insides. "It was just a kiss."

She arched a brow and shot a look at his pants. "Sure felt like it could've been more."

And it did again. Just like that. One look caused a telltale rush of blood. Embarrassed, he bent his knee and put the sole of his foot against the cabinet door. So much for mellowness.

"The thing is," she whispered, looking out at the room again, "I meant what I said. I'm here for the summer, then I'm gone. This place . . . this vineyard . . . it's just an oasis for me."

"Bad analogy. With all this rain, it's more like a mud hole."

She looked up at him in concern. "Is there a chance the crop will be ruined?"

"There's always a chance. But it doesn't happen often. More likely, the wine is just better or worse."

Tess ran in, eyes wide. "She's having another one. That's *five*. Can you imagine having five babies?"

"Not me," Simon said.

Olivia sputtered out a laugh, but Tess was suddenly staring at him. "Why are you wearing glasses?"

"I've been wearing them all night."

"What do you do during the day? Do you wear contacts?"

"Yes."

"I'm getting contacts, but I have to wait until my eyes stop changing. When did you get yours?"

"When I was fourteen," he said and handed her the juice.

"I can't wait *that* long." She peered into the glass.

"No pulp," he assured her before she could ask. "The pulp went down the drain."

"Oh. Good." Holding the glass in her left hand, she did something with her right that might have been a wave, and set off.

Olivia's voice followed her. "Tess?"

"I *signed* it," Tess called.

"Ah," Olivia said and told Simon, "Sandy's grandson is deaf. I'm not sure she's doing that sign right, but the thought is there. Thank you for the juice."

Simon wandered into the living room and looked at Tess in the hall. He tried to picture Liana in her place, watching Buck have kittens, getting a drink, remembering a thank-you. "We were just beginning to get into that. You know, manners and all." He started to gesture Olivia into a chair, then realized she might want to watch Buck. Shifting the gesture, he pointed a thumb in that direction and raised his brows.

She shook her head and slipped into a deep, overstuffed easy chair. Moving herself all the way back, she pushed off her sneakers and folded up her legs. She looked about sixteen.

"Does it bother you having Tess here?" she asked.

He looked at Tess and the baskets in the hall, then looked behind him. Pushing the book aside, he sat on the edge of the sofa and considered the question. Did it bother him having Tess in his house? It hadn't been a premeditated thing. He hadn't anticipated bringing either of them here. But Buck had given him a golden opportunity, so here they were.

Did it bother him? He would have thought that it would. He had deliberately not invited Olivia in last time. This was his private place. There was no room here for women and children.

Funny, though. Olivia and Tess weren't just women and children. They weren't . . . generic. They were . . . Olivia and Tess, each with her own personality and looks. They were totally different from his wife and daughter.

"Or shouldn't I have asked?" Olivia said.

"No, it doesn't bother me having her here. I could try to imagine Liana at Tess's age, but the fact is that when I see her in my mind, she's the six-year-old she was when she died. She'll always be that. Tess is a different species—and I don't mean that in a negative way. I mean it timewise. She's older. She's more verbal. She's street-smart."

"Is that a euphemism for 'mouthy'?" Olivia asked with a half smile.

"She's that sometimes, but from what you say, there's good reason. Is she doing any better?"

Olivia nodded, but she didn't look convinced. "Sandy is great. Tess is starting to get the knack of the method she's teaching. It'd be neat if I could get her into a private school that specializes in it. We applied to one in Cambridge"—she dropped her voice to a whisper—"but they just sent me a letter saying that they don't have room, and I haven't had the courage to tell her."

"Does she have her heart set on the place?" he whispered back.

"She has her heart set on *not* going back to the

school she was at. I've applied to several more, but we may not know until the last minute. It's nerve-racking."

"Has she made any friends here?"

"None who call on the phone. That's the big indicator, in case you didn't know."

Oh, he knew. "Some things never change. Who's calling *you?*"

"Me?"

He hadn't planned on asking, but there it was. "I was at the office the other day when a guy called. Anne Marie was having trouble convincing him you weren't here."

Olivia grunted. "That would've been Ted. He swears he isn't calling, but there's no one else it could be. We dated in Cambridge. He's still interested. I'm not."

"Why not?"

"He's too uptight. He makes problems where none exist. I can't deal with that. I have enough *real* problems. Beside, he's up there in the city thinking that I'm lounging around down here at the shore eating grapes. If only . . ." she said with a tired sigh and laid her head against the back of the chair. "Natalie's book was supposed to be at the compilation stage by the first of August. She wanted her family to have it before the wedding, but she didn't count on having so many distractions."

"She's a busy lady."

"Well, I'm learning that. I suppose I should be

grateful. I was worried I wouldn't be able to keep up. I'm not the fastest writer."

"But you are keeping up."

She smiled then—and if his smile had startled her, hers did the same to him. It was hopeful and bright. It was happy. It was *contagious*. She was proud of herself, but without ego.

"I'm keeping up. Actually, I'm dying for more. Her story fascinates me. The question is whether it will fascinate Susanne and Greg. More to the point, the question is whether they'll read it."

"I think they will. They're not bad eggs."

"If that's true," she said, doubt clear in her voice, "where are they? Why haven't they been here? It's summer, and it's gorgeous. If this was my family place, I'd have a standing reservation for a room here." She lowered her voice. "Speaking of rooms, you knocked on the right door tonight. You knew which one was mine."

"No mystery there," he said, wanting to nip suspicion in the bud. He didn't want her thinking that he was dwelling on *her*. "Natalie always puts guests in the wing, so I knew you were there. You watch me from a window seat. Only one of those rooms has a window seat."

"So, who's in the main house?" Olivia asked without missing a beat, as though the main house had been her interest all along. "Natalie has one room. Jill has another. I assume the third room is for Susanne and her husband. What's behind the closed door?"

Simon wasn't sure how he felt playing second fiddle to a closed door. He did know what was there, but it was Natalie's job to tell Olivia. "Mementos. Trophies. Old books and stuff."

"Where's Brad?"

"Brother Brad?" he asked.

"Son Brad. He's the only one who hasn't called. Natalie says that he won't. I take it there was a mega-falling-out. That's so hard for someone like me to swallow. I'd give anything for family. These people have it, and throw it away. Why don't they want anything to do with Asquonset? Or is it just the wedding?"

"This summer, it's the wedding."

"But it's such an *incredible* love story. Do you know . . . has Carl told you . . . ?"

"That they were childhood sweethearts? Yes."

"Did you always know?"

"No. He loved my mother. He treated her well. He worked with Natalie, but he always came home to my mother."

Olivia grew pensive. "And he loved her."

"Yes."

"Then you think it's possible to love two women at once?"

"He loved them in different ways."

Olivia's face grew pensive as she thought about what he had said. He watched her as she leaned forward and hugged her knees. Finally she sat back, looking not at all eager to leave, though it was nearly two in the morning. She seemed content.

Simon found that fact gratifying. It said that he had been right in bringing them here. It was all well and good to build a house free of women and children, but some things were meant to be shared. Buck's babies were one. The quiet of the night was another.

Then it struck him that it might be a little *too* quiet. Frowning, he sat forward and looked down the hall. Tess had her head on the rim of the basket.

"Is she all right?" he asked.

Olivia smiled. "She's probably asleep. Usually is, when she's quiet this long."

Indeed, Tess was asleep. She came awake but barely when Olivia touched her shoulder. Olivia had started to scoop her up, as though she intended to carry her back to the house, when Simon took over.

"You get the flashlight," he whispered, slipping his arms under the child.

It was drizzling outside. Thinking first of his grapes, he swore softly.

"Should we drive?" Olivia asked, misinterpreting his displeasure.

"No. It's just as fast to walk, and she doesn't weigh much. This kind of rain won't saturate the trees for a while, so we'll be dry." He strode toward the path, pausing at its start to let Olivia go ahead. "The forecast said it would do this, but I'd been hoping we would be spared."

"It isn't cold or windy."

"Cold we don't need. Wind we do, as long as it's gentle. A gentle wind helps dry the grapes. Otherwise the dampness just sits."

The rain fell softly on the leaves high overhead, but they didn't feel the dampness themselves until they left the cover of the trees and made a dash for the house. Simon held Tess closer, shielding her body as he ran. When they were under the patio awning, he carefully transferred her to Olivia and opened the door.

No one spoke, and Olivia and Tess were gone before he could think of anything suitable to say. Walking back through the woods, though, he realized he felt satisfied.

He also felt horny as hell by the time he was in bed, but still he was satisfied.

Nineteen

SUSANNE HEARD THE PHONE RING while she was turning the key in the lock. Thinking she could use an interesting call, she hurriedly opened the door and disengaged the alarm. She dropped her things on the chair and caught up the receiver just before the call went to voice mail.

"Hello?"

"Hi, Susanne. It's Simon."

Well, it wasn't quite the want-to-have-lunch-at-Palio call she was hoping for, but it might yet be interesting. "Simon. My stepbrother-to-be. How are you?"

"Not bad. How about you?"

"Great. Couldn't be better. Hey, I haven't seen you since our parents broke the news. So, what do you think?"

"I think it's pretty nice."

Of course, he would. His father was marrying up. That enhanced his own standing, not to mention his job security.

But she was being unfair. Of her brother's childhood friends, she had always like Simon the best. He had been loyal to Greg—and loyal to her parents, too, if the hours he poured into the vineyard counted. She owed him the benefit of the doubt.

"Were you surprised?" she asked. "Or did you see it coming?" He should have. He was at Asquonset on a daily basis. He would have noticed a change in Natalie and Carl—would have seen little looks exchanged, hands held, kisses blown. He would have been taken into their confidence.

"No, I honestly didn't see it coming. But then, I wasn't looking for it. I've been a little preoccupied for the past few years."

Susanne was instantly contrite. More gently, she said, "I understand." Regardless of what role Simon may or may not have played in the joining of their families—whether innocent or not so—what he had suffered with his own family was tragic.

"Natalie and Carl seem happy," he said now. "That's what counts."

"Does that mean *you* aren't happy about it?" She hadn't considered that possibility. What was there not to like, from his point of view?

"I'm perfectly happy. I've always thought the world of Natalie."

"And she of you," Susanne said, envious of that. "She always wanted one of the family to take over the vineyard. Now she'll have her wish."

Simon was the voice of reason. "No. Her wish is for you or Greg to take over. She still wants that. Besides, I'm not taking over anything. I've been vineyard manager for six years. That won't change."

"Not now. Down the road, well, that's something else." It had to be said. It was what she believed.

Simon paused. His voice held caution. "I don't need that, Susanne."

"What? Owning Asquonset? Or my mention of it?"

"Either," he said with more feeling. "I'm working my butt off trying to get a good vintage, and the weather isn't cooperating. I don't have time to be making this phone call."

And she didn't particularly care to be *taking* it. "Then why are you?"

"Because Natalie needs you. She has a lot on her plate. I thought you should know that."

"Ah. You want me there." Mark thought she should be there, too. Her kids thought so, as well.

"I think it would be nice if someone from the family gave her a hand."

"But she has a new assistant," Susanne said sweetly. "Can't she help?"

"She does. But Natalie could use you."

"Like I have nothing else to do with my life?" It always came down to that.

Simon sighed. "I know you have things to do, but how can you worry about my taking over the vineyard when you and Greg won't come near it?"

"Have you called him? Have you told him he ought to be there?"

"No. I didn't think he'd appreciate that."

She bristled. "Because he works, while I sit around doing nothing? Is that what you think? I have things to do, Simon. I have *more* than enough to keep me busy. My mother has always done her own thing. She certainly didn't consult me before she decided to remarry. What could she possibly need me for now? And if she needs me, why can't she pick up the phone and tell me?"

"I don't know. Maybe it's not in her to ask for help. She's always just done for herself."

"Exactly. Natalie first."

"That wasn't what I meant, Susanne. I meant that she would rather do something herself than ask for help."

"So now you know her better than I do? That's *very* interesting, Simon. It's very *presumptuous.* Tell me, what *business* is all this of yours?"

There was a long pause before Simon spoke, his voice quiet. "None. You're right. It's not my business. She's your mother, not mine. Mine's dead. That must be clouding my vision. I miss her. If I could get her back, you can be damned sure I'd be doing everything I could to make her golden years easier."

TROTTING DOWN THE STAIRS from his office, Simon was furious. He didn't understand why people who had so much had to go and throw it away. He and Olivia were of like mind in that. Asquonset was the most beautiful place he had ever seen, and he had traveled some. There had been a time in his life—a brief period when he was in college and felt like a hick—when he had considered working elsewhere. Nothing he had seen in the search had come close to Asquonset, though, either in physical beauty or viticultural philosophy.

Not that he wanted Susanne or Greg around if they were going to treat his father and him like gold diggers. He wasn't after money. Money had its limits. It sure as hell couldn't bring back the dead.

In the supply room on the ground floor, he grabbed tools, a coil of wire, and work gloves. The top trellis needed repair on one of the Chenin Blanc rows. The leaves had already reached it. They had been hedged once and needed a second round. First, though, he needed to put up new wire. It was good, mindless work.

He had the gloves on and was using pliers to free the old wire from the one pin that still held it when he spotted Tess.

Last night was one thing. Today was another.

As sure as those spots on some of the grapes spelled trouble, he wasn't in the mood for a child.

Naturally, because he didn't want it, she approached, but she seemed more cautious than ornery. "Where's Buck?"

"Back at the house," he said and went on with his work. "She's staying pretty close to the kittens."

"Did she have any more after I left?"

"No. There are five in all."

"What are you doing?"

"Repairing the trellis."

"What does the trellis do?"

"It holds up the vines." That was the simplest answer. In an effort to be kinder than last time, he added, "It directs the vines vertically rather than horizontally. I want the vines to grow high, not wide."

"Why?"

"Because if they grow wide, they'll cover the grapes, which means that the grapes don't get sun or breeze. If they don't get sun, they don't ripen. If they don't get breeze, they don't dry out, and if they don't dry out, they get rot."

"Rrrrot," Tess echoed, seeming to like the sound of the word.

Simon did not. "It's also known as fungus, or mold. It's bad stuff." He glanced at his watch. She looked like she might just stand there awhile. He didn't have time to humor her. "Don't you have tutoring in the mornings?"

"Mrs. Adelson is sick. Can I go see Buck?"

"Not now. I have to work."

"That's all right. You can work while I go see Buck."

"But I don't have time to drive you there."

"I'll walk. Just tell me where the path starts."

"Where's your mother?"

"In the loft, but I don't have to ask her, if you say it's okay."

He looked her over. She was neat and clean, but then, the day was young. "Did she tell you not to?"

"She told me not to get in the way." Her face gentled. Either she momentarily forgot to be belligerent or she was being manipulative. In any case, she was convincing. "If you're here and I'm there, I'm not in the way. Do you really think Buck should be alone all day? He knows me. He likes me. I think he'd like to show off his babies. Besides, I want to see the kittens so I can tell everyone in my sailing class about it."

Ah. A bid for friends. "You have to smile."

"What?"

"You have to *smile* when you tell the people in your sailing class about the kittens. That lets them know you're genuinely excited and not just trying to one-up them."

"Well, I'll bet *they* don't have kittens."

"Neither do you," he said and regretted it when her face dropped. "You do," he relented and pulled off the gloves. "You were the first one who noticed how fat Buck was. Come on. I'll show you the path. But you have to stay on it. If you don't, you may get lost. There's bear in these woods."

"There is not," she scolded in a way that said she knew he was kidding. "There's mink and raccoon and deer and pheasant, but they're more afraid of me than I am of them." She jogged to keep up with him. "Aren't they?"

"Definitely. Okay. There it is. See the path beside the old maple tree?"

"I see." She ran toward it.

"Wait," he called. "What am I supposed to say if your mother comes looking for you?"

She turned, running backward now. "Tell her you invited me. You just did, y'know."

He could have argued about that, but let it go. "What time do you have to be back?"

"Sailing's at two."

"And what are you going to do when you tell the kids about the kittens?"

She bared her teeth in a spastic rendition of a smile, then turned and ran off.

SUSANNE SPENT AN HOUR wallowing under the burden of guilt for ruining her mother's golden years before she picked up the phone and called Greg at work.

"Bad time," he told her, but she wasn't being put off. Her time was as valuable as his. Her peace of mind was as valuable as his. Besides, for Greg, any time was a bad time.

"I just got a call from Simon," she said. "He claims that Mother needs help. Do you know anything about this?"

"What kind of help?"

"I don't know. All he said was that she could use a hand."

"She has a hand. Jill's there."

"Oh. I didn't know. Well, that's good. But why would Simon call me, then?"

"Listen, I have a meeting in twenty minutes and fifty pages of data to review beforehand."

"Are you joining Jill there?"

"Not if I can help it."

"Maybe one of us should go. You know, see for ourselves what's happening."

"You go. You have more time than me."

"But your wife is there. That gives you a good excuse to go."

"Why do you need an excuse? Just say that you're worried."

"You're the one who's worried," she argued. "You're the one who thinks the Burkes want the vineyard. You could talk with Carl if you went."

"Susanne, I don't have time for this."

"Neither do I," she cried, "and what if something happens? You're the man. You're attuned to business. You'll see right away if something's up."

"Susanne, my meeting is in . . . eighteen minutes."

"Oh, please," she said. She was tired of feeling insignificant. "Is your work more important than family? I'm asking for your help in this, Greg."

"I am *not* going to *Asquonset,*" he said with sudden force. "If Jill wants to talk, she knows where I am!"

Susanne was taken aback. She spoke more quietly. "Are you two having trouble?"

He grunted. "Nothing that a little time and space won't take care of. Look, Susanne, forget I mentioned it. I'm tired and I'm stressed. Jill wanted to visit Asquonset, and I couldn't get away. Give her a call. Ask what she sees. If that doesn't satisfy you, go on up there yourself. But I can't. Not now. I just can't."

Twenty

"THERE ARE TIMES," Natalie mused, "when I wonder about family." She stopped talking, apparently to muse a bit more.

Olivia gave her a minute before prodding gently. "In what sense?"

The older woman looked troubled. "The business about blood being thicker than water." She looked at the window. "I always thought it was meant in a positive way—you know, that ties to family are stronger and deeper. But one could, in theory, interpret it differently. One could, in theory, make the argument that thick blood slows down the functioning of the brain, so that reason lags behind when it comes to family matters." Her eyes sought Olivia's. "Take commitment. I wonder about it sometimes."

Sometimes? Olivia wondered about it more than that. Having an absentee mother was conducive to it. But Natalie had been there when her children were growing up, and she was still there.

"Maybe you should try calling again," Olivia suggested.

"No. They're still upset."

"They need to read what I've written."

"But you haven't written the best part. You haven't *heard* the best part."

The desk was covered with pictures that had been taken during and immediately after the war. She had repaired some—generally the more formal ones, showing the elegant life that had sparked her imaginings. Others—ones she was seeing for the first time—were work photos. It struck her that Natalie hadn't wanted these prettied up.

The older woman lifted one of the latter. It showed her holding the two children, one on each hip. Alexander had an arm around her shoulder and was grinning broadly. He was the only one in the picture who was.

What with Alexander staying overseas after the war ended, we were separated for nearly five years. Granted, he had leave time, but those days were too few and frantic for getting to know someone. Add to that the fact that I hadn't known him well when we married, and when he finally came home, I found I was living with a stranger. The children didn't know him and were leery, which made things all the harder. But at least he was home. Things were going to improve. Alexander was going to save Asquonset. That was why I had married him.

Alexander was going to save Asquonset. That was why I had married him.

How often I said that during the years when he was gone, years when I missed Carl far more than Alexander. It was a terrible time for me, and I did suffer. Once the novelty of being married wore off and the situation here worsened, I wanted Carl.

But Alexander was going to save Asquonset. That was why I had married him.

It became my mantra. It was the only thing that kept me going during the bleakest of those days.

Bleak?

Maybe that's the wrong word. They were hard. They were filled with work and worry. We were always hoping for letters. The mailmen gave priority to ones from the front and would deliver them whenever they arrived, which meant that we were always on the lookout. Of course, an unexpected visit could also be from the minister. We feared that kind. We'd been through it once. Each night we sat in front of the radio in the living room and listened to news from the front. We shuddered each time we learned that another local boy had died.

These were lonely days for me. My children were too young to offer companionship. I had no one to talk with, no one to complain to, no one to seek help from. I was on my own.

But Alexander was going to save Asquonset. That was why I had married him.

So, where was the money?

That was a very good question. Not that I did the asking. It wasn't my place. I was the woman. I was the daughter. It was my father's place. After all, he was the one who had negotiated the deal.

"Coming after the war," he said with an unhappy grunt the one time I dared ask. So I staked my hopes on that. Alexander would save Asquonset once the war was done. And in so doing, he would save my father's life. We just had to hold on long enough.

Well, we did hold on, Jeremiah and I. We kept things going until Carl returned and took over some of the responsibility. For me, it was both better and worse— better because there was someone to help, worse because that someone was Carl. I had to see him every day. I had to remember what might have been and, finally, explain to him why it wouldn't ever be.

Alexander was going to save Asquonset. Once he returned from the war, he was going to invest in the vines that would give my father a new lease on life. Asquonset would grow as a vineyard in ways it hadn't quite grown as a farm.

In theory, Alexander's promise wasn't empty. His family had two very successful shoe factories that, despite suffering during the Depression, remained very much alive and vital. Then war broke out, and instead of making shoes for a struggling population, the Seebring factories were suddenly making boots not only for American soldiers but for our allies as well. They couldn't make them fast enough, the demand was so great.

Well, the war did end the Depression. As awful as that sounds, it was true. The Seebring factories were only one of the beneficiaries. Not only did our fighting men have to be clothed, they had to be fed. They had to be armed. They had to be provided with vehicles for land, sea, and air combat. Many a business that had struggled was suddenly thriving. Alexander's certainly wasn't unique.

Then the war ended, and the same people who had squirreled away their pennies in the shadow of the Depression now had optimism and a nest egg. The same factories that had been turning out uniforms now turned out suits for men to wear in civilian life, or dresses for women to wear celebrating peace. The same factories that had been turning out combat boots began turning out shoes for pleasure.

That was what was supposed to have happened at the Seebring plants. Had things gone as planned, they would have converted to peacetime production and thrived.

What happened? Alexander's father had died midway through the war and was out of the managerial picture. Alexander named a trustee to oversee things until he returned. He was caught up playing spy and stayed in Europe longer than I would have liked.

No. No. It's unfair of me to say that. Don't write it, Olivia. Alexander wasn't playing spy. He was doing something that needed to be done. Collecting evidence for the war crimes trials was important. The atrocities of the Third Reich had to be answered.

But Alexander's being there created a void here. If he had come back at the end of the war, along with the rest of the servicemen, the factories might have been saved. By the time he did return, though, the damage was done. His trustee had absconded with the profits, and the conversion that would have cashed in on the postwar prosperity never took place. By the time Alexander returned, the factories were dark.

So. I told you about the first day I ever laid eyes on Carl. And about the day he left for the war and the day I married someone else. Now let me tell you about the day I learned that it had all been a waste and that I had given him up for nothing.

It was a Sunday. Alexander had been home for a month, but was gone most every day to see to his factories. We all thought they were fully operational and that he was simply fine-tuning what had been done in his absence. He didn't tell us about the trustee or about shutting down. He left with a smile in the morning and returned with a smile at night.

In fact, just then we were the least of his worries. He had lost his family business. It was gone. It took him a month of scrambling around trying to salvage something, anything, before he accepted that himself. Then he had to break the news to us. What better day to do it than on a Sunday? Sunday was the Sabbath. It was a day for going to church, a day of understanding and forgiveness.

So we went to church and came home for dinner. My father was too weak for church—by then he rarely left the house—but he did join us at the table that day. Alexander waited until we were done eating. The children had gone in for naps. I cleaned the kitchen.

Al was listening to the radio with my father. As soon as I joined them, he turned the radio off. He returned to his chair, leaned forward, hung his head just a little.

"I have some bad news," he said and proceeded to tell us what the trustee had done. He spent a long while talking about his attempts to reverse the damage. He repeated in detail conversations that he had had with local workers. He told about working with the police to no avail, and he acknowledged the anger and frustration he felt.

I listened closely, but it was awhile before I took in the words. After all, Alexander was going to save Asquonset. He was going to give my father what he most needed. That was why I had married him, rather than waiting for Carl.

Only, Alexander had no money. He couldn't save Asquonset.

My father was white as a sheet. After three tries, and then only with my help, he rose from his chair. He was pitifully thin and stooped, shaking so badly that I began talking off the top of my head just to reassure him.

"We'll find money," I said. "We'll get your vines. Don't you fret. We'll find a way. You just lie down now and get your strength, so that when the plants come, you'll be able to tell Jeremiah where you want them."

He didn't speak. His head was turned away, his eyes vacant. I could tell it was over; he had given up.

I ached for him. He was my father, I loved him, and he was dying right there before my eyes. I helped him to bed and sat with him until the children woke up. By then Alexander was his old ebullient self.

Not me. I needed to think. I needed to be alone.

I asked him to watch the children. But he was off to meet a wartime buddy in Newport.

So I bundled up the children. Brad was nearly five. He walked, usually ran on ahead. I carried Susanne. She was only two.

I headed for the water. We walked on and on. It was a brisk September day, sunny but cool. When we reached the ocean, we climbed up on the rocks to a spot where we could sit and watch the surf without being hit by the spume.

I remember being awed by the force of the waves hitting the rocks, by the thunder of the crash, awed by the beauty of it all. Of course, beauty was the last thing I felt inside. I felt empty and dark. I felt powerless. Sitting there on those rocks, I was overcome with despair.

I thought about jumping.

For the space of a minute, I did—I thought about jumping.

Then Brad wrapped his arms around my neck. The ocean frightened him. He needed reassurance.

It was enough to bring me to my senses.

Before I could think about it again, I scooped up the two of them and headed back. I don't know where I found the strength to carry them both, but I did it. By the time I was in the farmhouse again, I had found a new resolve.

It was an epiphanous experience.

IT WAS AN EPIPHANOUS EXPERIENCE, Olivia typed, and sat back in her chair. Natalie had always struck her as being an optimist. Optimists didn't contemplate suicide.

She rose and leaned toward the window. She could see Natalie in the distance, an elegant figure moving in and out of rows of vines. She was with the graphic designer who was creating new labels for the Estate wines. They had been out there for nearly an hour. Natalie was determined that the woman get the feel of the place before she made sketches.

An epiphanous experience. Olivia had looked up the word "epiphanous" for the correct spelling. At the same time, she checked out the meaning. An epiphanous experience was one that was deeply insightful. A simple event that carried great meaning could be considered epiphanous. Certainly, a life-changing experience was all that.

She wanted to hear more. Natalie had promised to be back, but there she was, still with the artist.

Tess would be wanting lunch before going to the yacht club. One cook had come and gone in a day, a sweet thing from a diner who was instantly overwhemed. Natalie was in the process of finding another. In the interim, after too many days of take-out from the sandwich shop at the crossroads, Olivia figured she could at least make tuna sandwiches. Natalie and Carl liked those.

She found cans of tuna on the pantry shelf and mayonnaise in the refrigerator, quickly mixed them together, and slathered the outcome on bread. She added lettuce and cut each sandwich in half. Nothing fancy. Nothing gourmet. Lunch wasn't her thing.

She was reading the newspaper, waiting for Tess, when Simon walked in. He paused for a minute when he saw her, then crossed to the refrigerator, uncapped a bottle of water, and drank the whole thing.

He was sweaty. His T-shirt was stained with moisture, his skin beaded. Damp, his hair looked darker than auburn now. His cheeks were flushed over a deep July tan.

Olivia's blood ran suddenly hot. She wondered why it was that chemistry worked with some men and not with others. She was certainly attracted to this one.

"It's warm out there," he said when he righted his head. He eyed the sandwiches. "Who made these?"

"Me," she said, setting down the paper. "Eat at your own risk. I'm not a very good cook." Although she wished that she was. She wished that she could put together incredible meals. Men loved home cooking. But then, they also loved long blonde hair, and she didn't have that either.

He peered under one slice of bread. "You can't go wrong with tuna."

"No, but there's a whole lot more you can do with it than I did. Madalena used to do something wonderful. She wouldn't tell me what it was."

"She added cilantro."

"Cilantro."

"Crushed into the mayo."

"Ah." Olivia self-consciously crossed her arms, then uncrossed them and folded her hands in her lap. Simon was watching her. All sweaty, he was gorgeous. Feeling decidedly *un*gorgeous herself, just then she would have settled for *collar*-length hair. "How are the kittens?" she asked, anxious to escape the awkward moment.

"Tiny." He hitched his chin toward the sandwiches. "May I?"

"Be my guest." Cilantro. She didn't know what cilantro looked like, but that was easily remedied. She could crush cilantro into mayo.

Still, with or without, Simon seemed to be enjoying her sandwich.

Desperate to fill the silence lest he think she wanted a compliment, she said, "Natalie loved Buck being a girl."

"Oh yes. She's told me that three times now. I may never live it down," he said, but he didn't look terribly upset. He actually seemed amused. And although he wasn't exactly smiling, he looked like he might.

She waited, hoping to see it.

Then his gaze touched her mouth, and she forgot about waiting for a smile.

"Where is Natalie?" she asked, needing a diversion. "Still outside?"

"Yeah." He took another sandwich half.

Olivia glanced at the clock. "Where's Tess?" It was a rhetorical question, so she was startled when he had the answer.

"At my place. She wanted to see the kittens. I showed her the path in the woods."

"Uh-oh. That might not have been a wise move. She's apt to be there more than you want. She's intrigued by those kittens. They were all she talked about at breakfast."

"Why don't you take one when they're ready to go? Better still, take two. Or five."

"Uh, I don't think we can. It's not like we own our own place. I'm not even sure where we'll be in the fall. Some landlords hate cats."

"Well," Simon said, "you have six weeks to decide." He held up the sandwich half as he made for the door. "This is good. Truth is, I never was a big cilantro fan myself. Thanks for lunch."

"IT WAS AN EPIPHANOUS EXPERIENCE," Olivia read aloud to remind Natalie where they had been. Turning away from the computer screen, she settled into one of the wing-back chairs with her paper and pen. She had fed Tess and dropped her off at the club. She had pushed Simon out of her mind. It was time to work. "Did you seriously consider suicide?"

Natalie smoothed her linen shorts at the same time that a crease appeared on her brow. "For a minute. Just a minute. I was feeling horrible pain, and emptiness, and loss. I was tired. I was frightened."

"Of what?"

"The future. The whole time Alexander had been away, I had built up a picture of what our lives would be like. Maybe it wasn't an overly pretty picture, but it was one of the ways I rationalized losing Carl. What I got would be worth the loss. Suddenly, it wasn't. The whole picture just . . . just . . ." She gestured frantically. "Just *broke apart.*"

Her hands fell. Her face reflected the memory of that long-ago pain.

Olivia's life hadn't been without pain. She had

felt emptiness and loss, tiredness and fear. Natalie must have felt them that much more, if she actually reached the point of having to consider suicide.

The difference, she realized, was in highs and lows. Natalie had felt the extremes. It made sense that someone who had known the kind of happiness she had with Carl would have found the low of total disillusionment unbearable.

"Anyway," the older woman said now, "it was just for that minute, and then it was done. During the walk home carrying the children that day, I revamped my view of life. Up until then, I had pinned my hopes on other people. I had relied on my father, then on Carl, then on Alexander. I had listened to my mother and made a decision I shouldn't have made. But it was my decision. I want that to be clear in what you write. My mother didn't force me to marry Alexander. It was my decision to do it." She paused.

"Yes?" Olivia coaxed.

"But the real decision came that day. Sitting up on those rocks, with the wind blowing hard and the waves exploding in the air, I was at a fork in the road. I chose life. But not just any life. I wanted a good life. I vowed to make it so."

Olivia saw the next part of the story opening up, but she held off going there. A major question lingered. "Did you consider divorce?"

"No. I had married Alexander of my own free will."

"But you did it based on false promises that he made."

"His promises weren't false at the time he made them. He fully intended to build the vineyard with shoe money. He hadn't lied to us."

"But he let you down," Olivia said. "Weren't you angry?"

"Angry? Maybe at the situation, but not at Alexander. How can you be angry with someone who acted in good faith? Someone who had suffered a great loss himself? I was disappointed. I had assumed that he was a smart businessman, and he wasn't, but his heart was in the right place."

"You said that he stayed longer than he should have in Europe."

"No," Natalie corrected patiently, "what I said was that things might have been different if he hadn't stayed so long. But he wasn't idle there. What he was doing was important."

"What about your father? Your mother said that without more money and new vines, your father would die. Didn't you blame Alexander for his death?"

Natalie smiled sadly. "Alexander had nothing to do with the money my father lost when the stock market crashed. That was the start of my father's decline, but it was his own doing. He was the president of the bank. He approved all major decisions. Alexander had nothing to do with my father's mistakes as a farmer, and as for buying rootstock in

Europe, he only bought what my father told him to buy. It wasn't his fault that those vines were ill-suited to the microclimate here. He wasn't the one telling my father to pour more and more money into it. Besides"—she took a gentle breath—"my father didn't die. He lingered for quite a few more years—probably because of Alexander."

Olivia was startled. "He lived?"

"He did. And Alexander was good to him. He used to sit with him and talk, and when Alexander talked, you listened—and smiled and believed. He would say that Asquonset was on the cusp of great-ness, and that the newest batch of vines were pro-ducing grapes to beat the band. He would point to a bottle of French wine and insist that it was only a matter of time before our wine was as much in de-mand as that one. I mean, most of it was baloney," she said with a fond smile, "but my father no longer went to the fields, so he didn't know the dif-ference. He listened and felt better. Alexander even took him into town, which I could never do because he was so frail, and Carl could never do because he was so busy. But Al had the time and the patience, and he could lift him and move him. He could help him out of the car and ease him into a chair at Pindman's. Granted, there was some-thing in it for Alexander. My father was a guaran-teed captive audience. Still, in his own way, Al did give the man a new lease on life."

"Well, I'm glad about that."

"But you're still upset that I didn't divorce him to marry Carl."

"No," Olivia said quickly, determined not to be judgmental. "You had your reasons. I'm just not sure I would have done the same thing."

"That's because times have changed. You people take divorce lightly. You see it all the time in the papers and on television, and you read about it in books. It's become commonplace. So, naturally, at the first sign of trouble, one of you moves out. My generation wasn't that way. Granted, it was harder to get divorced back then, but that wasn't why I stayed with Alexander. And it wasn't for the sake of the children, though had it not been for them, Al and I might have drifted apart. No, I stayed with him because he was my husband. Back then, we respected the institution of marriage. Maybe it had to do with the war. Our husbands had fought so that we could be free. They had risked their lives. They had seen horrors we could only imagine. We owed them our loyalty. Divorce was not a consideration."

"Even if he had been abusive?"

"Well, he wasn't. He didn't drink. He didn't gamble. He was a good man with no business sense."

"But didn't you even *think* about divorce?"

"Not as a viable option," Natalie insisted. "I loved Carl. Had I been able to turn back the clock, I would have chosen to be married to him. But I couldn't change things. I was married to Alexander. I had to live with that. I had to make the best of it. Look at you. Haven't you done the same thing?"

Olivia was puzzled by the shift in focus. "Me?"

"You wanted your mother to love you, but she took off for parts unknown. You wanted Tess's father to love you, but he didn't. So, there you were with no family backup, and you suddenly had a child who was totally dependent on you. You couldn't change things. You couldn't ask your mother to baby-sit when you were climbing the walls. You couldn't just . . . draft another man to put bread on the table and play father to Tess. So you went to work. You took care of Tess yourself. I respect that."

"You do?" Olivia asked with a smile.

"I do. That's one of the reasons I hired you. I might not have known the details, but I sensed an independence in you."

Olivia's smile faded. "It isn't always fun being independent. It seems that I've spent my life looking for someone to lean on."

"But you haven't fallen down without."

"No. I couldn't. I had Tess. She needed me."

"Just as I had Asquonset. It needed me, too.

I think that was what kept me going more than anything else. I loved my children, but I knew that they would grow up in spite of me. Children do that.

Regardless of what their parents want, they become adults with minds of their own. Asquonset was something else. It didn't have a brain. It couldn't function on its own. If we did nothing, it would fall fallow. If it was going to grow, someone had to take charge.

Who could do that? My father was frail and sick. Jeremiah was taking care of Brida. Alexander was paralyzed when it came to money, and Carl refused to upstage him.

That left me. I had worked the farm during the war and knew every aspect of the operation. So I had knowledge, and I had purpose—and the purpose had little to do with growing potatoes and corn. I wanted to grow grapes. Grapes were the underlying reason for my marrying Alexander. What better way to justify that marriage than to make a success of growing them?

Ah. But we couldn't buy vinifera vines. We had no money.

Well, we didn't have the kind of money we had expected, but we did have something. The Seebring factories were silent and dark, but they were solid structures sitting on solid land in the midst of a plentiful workforce. Someone had to want to take them off our hands.

Alexander was a hard sell. Those plants had the Seebring name on them. To this day, I believe that a part of him dreamed that somehow they would one day reopen and thrive. Don't ask me how he thought that would happen, but then, Alexander was never one for solutions. But he did dream. And he did have pride. As long as he owned those plants, he owned something.

I convinced him that owning Asquonset was something. I painted grand pictures of what the place might be if we put all our energy into it. I told him that he would be traveling to Europe to buy vines, just as he had for my father, only this time we would be more careful with our choices. I showed him a diagram of the farm with the fields that I thought could support grapes, and I told him why.

How did I know all this? My father had books. He had letters. He had handwritten treatises.

Unfortunately, he was a banker. He was a mathematician and was good with numbers, but he couldn't read that material and interpret it with regard to our land. Carl could, and he did. He passed the material on to me, and I saw it, too. It made sense that a grape that would

thrive in Napa Valley would not do well
here. Nor would a grape that would
thrive in the warmer regions of France or
Italy. Those are Mediterranean climates.
They are more stable, with long, hot, dry
summers and cool, rainy winters. Ours
isn't like that. Ours is a Continental climate, like that of the European growing
regions in Burgundy, Champagne, and
the Rhine, where the air is cooler and the
growing season shorter. We needed to
plant vines that had thrived in these regions, because their weather was com-
parable to ours.

I explained all this to Alexander, and
he understood. He saw the potential for
successfully growing grapes here. More
important, he liked the picture I painted
of his role in it.

So he gave in. We met with the local
bankers, and he made my arguments
about the buildings, the land, and the
workforce. He convinced them that
those two factories would be worth a
pretty penny to an entrepreneur wanting
to cash in on the prosperity that had
come with peace. He was passionate and
persuasive. But then, that was his forte.
He was also a poker player and knew
how to bluff.

We made fifty percent more on the sales of those buildings than we had thought we would get—which wasn't saying much, but it was a start. We borrowed the rest of what we needed from the bank.

We? No. Alexander handled that part on his own. He was a man. I was a woman. When it came to bank loans, that made a difference.

Did it bother me? No. The important thing was that we got the money. I wasn't doing this for the sake of pride. I was doing it for Asquonset.

Besides, I was lucky. Many women I knew were out of work. They had jumped into the workforce during the war, when men were few and jobs were plentiful. Suddenly the men were home, and the women were out of work. That was an injustice. What I experienced was merely an annoyance. There's a big difference.

Besides, Alexander needed to feel important. He put behind him the factory closings and latched on to the vineyard as though the first had been a deliberate move to facilitate the last. Yes, there was pride involved for him. He had a sizable ego.

Please, Olivia. Take care when you write that. It can sound critical, which is not how I feel. Susanne and Greg had the highest regard for their father, and he did deserve it. What he did, he did well. He was a powerful public relations instrument for Asquonset. I could never have been on the road the way he was. It didn't interest me. I was happiest when I was at home.

Why? Because of Carl? you ask.

No. Because of the vineyards. As my own children grew, the grapes took their place.

But back to Alexander. His ego wasn't unique. Many men need adulation. The trick is for us women to understand this and use it to our own benefit.

You look dismayed. Why? Ahhh, you think that sounds manipulative?

It isn't manipulative, Olivia. It is pure common sense. Alexander was good at certain things. He wanted to think he was good at others. If I let him think that, he felt better about himself. When he felt better about himself, not only did he do better at what he already did well, but he was easier to live with.

That made my life easier. It's as simple as that. Once his ego needs were met, he was comfortable letting me do what I wanted. When I did what I wanted, I felt in control. We supported each other.

"But that's playing a game," Olivia remarked. "Why do we have to do that?"

"We don't," Natalie answered. "But if we play, we stand to win. If we refuse, we don't have a chance."

"Then the women's movement was a waste of time?"

"Not at all. It taught women to aspire. It opened their eyes to possibilities. What it failed to do was to be realistic about getting there. In an ideal world, women have equal rights with men, but our world isn't ideal. Being realistic means working the system. It means understanding the psyches involved and using them. Take Simon."

Olivia shot her a puzzled smile. "What does Simon have to do with anything?"

"He's a complex person. Women want him to be warm and open, but he isn't. There are reasons for that. If we understand the reasons, we can work around them to find the openness and the warmth."

"I take it you're talking about his wife and daughter."

"In part. He was torn apart when they died. He doesn't want to be vulnerable to that kind of pain again, so he's put up a wall."

Olivia had seen that wall. He had all but planted it in front of her nose when she had first come to the vineyard. "What's the other part?"

"His childhood. His mother was a lovely person. Ana was a local woman who married later in life, but she knew what she wanted. She wanted a husband, and she wanted a child. I suspect that she knew how Carl felt about me, but she was wise enough to marry him anyway. She got a husband and a child, and they did love her. That said, I'm not sure she ever fully believed it. She always held a little something of herself back."

"So you think Simon is predisposed to hold back?"

"It's possible."

"Did he do it with Laura?"

"I suspect. She was quiet. It wasn't in her nature to push him." She looked at Olivia and smiled for a minute longer than necessary.

Olivia smiled right back. "And it is in mine?" Slowly, purposefully, she shook her head.

"Of course it is," Natalie insisted. "You push me all the time."

"That's not what I mean. If you're playing matchmaker—"

"I'm not. I'm just making a point about men."

"You were supposed to be making a point about women."

"Well, I am. The point is that women can do far better with men if they understand what they're about. I was fine once I understood that Alexander needed to be stroked. Simon doesn't need to be stroked. He needs to be *prodded*."

"Not by me," Olivia said and picked up her pen. "Do you want to do more now, or would you rather I get back to writing?"

Twenty-one

THE SUMMER WAS HALF DONE. Olivia kept thinking about it that night. How not to, with the direction that Tess's questions had taken? They had been reading *On the Banks of Plum Creek,* one of the Laura Ingalls Wilder books that were Tess's bedtime favorites, but her mind was on the kittens. Smack in the middle of a chapter, she looked up at Olivia and asked again if they could have one. Olivia repeated the argument about apartments and cats.

"But if we move," Tess reasoned, "we could get an apartment that would let us have one. When will we know if we're moving?"

"As soon as I know where I'm working."

"When will that be?"

"Soon."

"When will I hear about schools?"

Olivia didn't know. And suddenly, with no more provocation than Tess's few questions, she was worried. With more Asquonset time ahead than behind, she had coasted. She had assured herself that something would come through, that things always worked out, that come fall she would have a job and Tess would have a school.

Now summer was half gone, and she had nothing. She had to get cracking. If she didn't do it, it wouldn't get done.

To that end, she got up even before dawn the next morning and, taking care not to wake anyone along the way, went up to the loft. She turned on a light, then the computer. Within minutes, she was surfing the Internet. This time she wasn't going to put all her eggs in one basket. She wasn't even putting them in a dozen baskets. She printed out the names and addresses of every museum she could find, then did the same with art galleries. Inserting her own floppy disk, she printed out that many copies of her résumé. She was in the process of composing a new cover letter when the door opened. Her heart skipped a beat—largely in relief that she had gotten dressed—even before she saw who was there.

It was Simon. Quietly, she said, "Why did I know it was you?"

"Because," he answered, closing the door, "no

one else is crazy enough to be up so early. I saw the light. What are you doing?" He came up behind her and looked at the screen.

She nearly covered it with her hands, but stopped herself. That wouldn't have been very grown-up. "Don't read it. It's just a rough draft. I'm a lousy speller, totally spell check dependent. If you read that, you're going to wonder how in the world I'm writing Natalie's story, but the finished product is always—"

"Shh!" he said and put a hand on her shoulder.

She didn't say another word. His hand stayed where it was, even after he finished reading and had straightened.

"I need a job," she said softly. She kept her eyes on the screen. "Natalie signed me on only until Labor Day."

"Will your work for her be done by then?"

"Yes."

"Where do you want to go?"

"Wherever. Beggars can't be choosers."

His hand moved. Was it a caress—or simply a gesture of comfort? "Why do you say it that way? You have a skill. You're an artist."

"Artists have a knack for living on the verge of starvation. I need to feed, clothe, and educate Tess." Taking a breath, she put on a smile and rose from the chair. His hand fell away, which made it easier for her to talk. "I'll find a job. I may try something entirely different."

"Like what?"

"Being a concierge."

He looked bemused. "At a hotel?"

"Why not? I'm a people person. I can arrange for theater tickets and limos. I can tell people which sights to see and which ones to avoid. I can recommend restaurants and make reservations." She grinned, letting her imagination go. "Wouldn't *that* be fun, trying out all those restaurants so that I'd know which ones to recommend."

"I think most recommendations are bought and sold."

"Well, that's a cynical view. I wouldn't run my concierge station that way, and I'd let hotel patrons know it. We don't have payola on my shift. I'd tell them the truth."

"What if their taste in restaurants is different from yours?"

She shrugged. "That's bound to happen once in a while. You can't please all the people all the time. We could live right there at the hotel. Can you imagine? Tess would be another Eloise. Wow, did she love those stories. She wanted to go to Paris after she read *Eloise in Paris*. But I think she'd settle for New York. Wouldn't that be cool, living at the Plaza—"

Simon silenced her with a kiss, not altogether a surprise, given that seconds before he was looking at her mouth, but that didn't prepare her any. Nor did talk of moving to New York do anything to

dampen the feeling. It was warm and fuzzy, familiar in ways that it shouldn't have been with only
one prior kiss.

Olivia had always liked warm and fuzzy. Warm
and fuzzy was a sepia-toned print of an apple pie
hot from the oven, sitting with crockery that had
seen generations of use. It was a dancing fire drying a pair of wool mittens with her name knitted
into them—or a big mug of hot cocoa with a huge
glob of whipped cream on top. Warm and fuzzy
was the kind of kiss that was so gentle and sweet
you wanted to melt—the kind you leaned into and
curled up next to—the kind that just went on and
on and on without losing a drop of heat. It was the
kind that you clung to, that you didn't want to end,
that startled you when it did because you didn't
understand it at all.

Simon looked just as startled; not that that answered any questions.

"What *is* this?" she whispered.

"Beats me," he whispered back. Holding her
close with one arm, he moved his fingers slowly
through her hair. It was growing out, but not fast
enough.

"It used to be long, down below my shoulders,
right up until this past May. It was really pretty
neat, but too warm. I got impatient one night and
cut it all off. I'm like that—impatient and impulsive. Maybe that's what this is."

He ran his thumb over her mouth, again slowly,
and it didn't feel like an impulsive thing. It was

arousing in the deepest, most unbelievable way—
every bit as hot as his kiss—and then he did the
most incredible thing. Watching his own hand, he
slid it down her throat to her chest, turned it over,
and ran the back of it over her breast.

Olivia could barely breathe. She caught his
hand and pressed it tight against her, closed her
eyes, put her forehead to his chest. "What *is* this?"
she murmured.

"What is *this?*" came an echo, but not from
Simon.

Olivia looked up to find his eyes on the door,
and shot a look that way, fearing that Natalie had
found them out. But it wasn't Natalie standing
there. The resemblance was strong—same height,
same shapeliness, same remarkable posture and
dewy skin. The hairstyle was even the same,
though this woman's hair was a warm chestnut
color rather than white. Olivia felt she was seeing
Natalie as she had been twenty years before.

Susanne smiled in amusement. "And here I
thought Mother might be up early working on her
guest list. You're looking rosy cheeked, Simon."

"And you," he said with remarkable poise,
moving ahead of Olivia, as though to shield her. "I
didn't know you'd come."

"Neither does Mother. I arrived late last night. I
thought I'd come up here, open this door, and surprise her." Her eyes went to Olivia, brows raised in
question.

Olivia had already moved out from behind

Simon. She didn't want to be shielded—what an *arcane* male thing—though she did take example from his poise. Extending a hand, she said, "I'm Olivia."

Susanne said, "I figured you were." The dry tone notwithstanding, her handshake was warm. "It was either that or the new maid, new accountant, or new field hand." She paused and drew back. "Any other defections lately?"

"Madalena and Joaquin," Olivia said and watched Susanne's brows rise and her eyes fly to Simon.

He edged in front of Olivia again. "Natalie's already hired a replacement."

"A second replacement," Olivia corrected, coming even with Simon. "She starts next week. This one sounds promising. She worked in a restaurant in Pawtucket. The first one didn't know anything but fast food. She couldn't deal with a substantive dinner."

But Susanne didn't seem to hear. She was glaring at Simon. "You *rat. That's* why you called. Natalie needs my help, you said. She needs a *cook,* is more like it."

"You're the best," Simon said, "but that wasn't why I called. Another cook is on the way."

"I'll believe that when I see it," Susanne murmured. Slipping her hands in her pockets, just as Olivia had seen Natalie do dozens of times, she looked at her and said, "So. You and Simon."

"No," Olivia replied. *"Not* me and Simon."

He seconded that. "There's nothing going on."

"I'm just here for the summer."

"I can't handle anything deep."

"Sex doesn't have to be deep," Susanne remarked, but that hit Olivia the wrong way.

"It does. It should be."

Simon said, "What you just saw wasn't sex. It was—"

"A hug," Olivia proposed. "I was feeling discouraged because I don't have a job yet for the fall, which is why I was working before hours up here. Simon was trying to make me feel better."

"I'll bet he was," Susanne said. "I want to say that this is a novel use of this room, but for all I know it's been a little love nest for years. I need coffee." She backed out, shutting the door behind her.

FIVE MINUTES LATER, Olivia found Susanne in the kitchen with a pot of coffee already on. "I'm sorry," she said. "You shouldn't have to walk in on something like that in your own home."

Susanne opened the cabinet that contained baking supplies. "Then you admit it was something?"

"Yes," Olivia said, because it was absurd to deny it, "but I don't for the life of me know what, and I don't really want it to happen again." She touched her chin with a level hand. "I'm up to here with other things on my mind besides Simon. For what it's worth, he's never been in that office with me before, and I don't think your mother was there with Carl, at least, not fooling around."

"But you don't know for sure, do you?" Susanne said, holding the cabinet door. She made a face. "Fooling around. That's an absurd phrase for someone Mother's age."

"Oh, no," Olivia said, breaking into a smile. "It's not absurd at all. I hope when I'm her age I can do all sorts of things. Can you imagine the freedom of being seventy-six? Admittedly, you have to be healthy to enjoy most of it. But even if you aren't, there's a plus side to things. You don't have to worry about what people think. You can do what you want."

"That's a plus side?" Susanne asked. "What about the people you hurt in the process?" She pushed things around in the cabinet, removed flour, cornmeal, and sugar, and shut the door with more force than was necessary.

"I wasn't talking about Natalie," Olivia said. "I was talking about the idea of . . . wearing hot pink when you're eighty-five."

"Is that any different from a six-month turn-around in husbands?" Susanne was at the refrigerator now, assessing its contents. When Olivia didn't have an answer, she said, "Gotcha there," and pulled out milk and eggs.

Olivia rested against the edge of one of the counter stools. "You have to read Natalie's story.

Once you have, six months won't seem so fast. I can give you what I've written so far, if you'd like."

Susanne pulled mixing bowls from a cabinet under the counter. "Thanks, but I have plenty to read before that."

"It explains things."

"If my mother wants things explained, she can do it face-to-face."

"She has trouble talking about some of this. I've had to coax and prod." Olivia grinned. "She'll be so glad you're here. Is your husband here, too?"

Susanne took measuring cups from the drawer. "Nope. He's working."

"Are your kids coming?"

"Nope." She put shortening in the baking pan. "They're working. In case you haven't guessed, I'm the only one who isn't. Homemaking isn't considered work nowadays." She spread the shortening with a paper towel.

"Well, that shows how much *they* know," Olivia declared. "Homemaking is the oldest profession in the world."

"I thought prostitution was that."

"Nope, homemaking is. Think about it. Neanderthal men went out to hunt, while their women did . . . what? Kept the cave neat, cooked the meals, raised the kids. If they hadn't done that, their men would have starved to death. I mean, they couldn't very well eat raw meat, and if the kids didn't get raised, there wouldn't be any descendants, so that would be the end of the species, right there and then. Could those men have kids without us? No. Their bodies are *totally* ill-equipped. Us? We can do anything we want. We can clean and cook and raise kids. We can make clothes and sell clothes—and *market* clothes. Getting back to my analogy, we can also hunt—though I don't know about you, I think I'd *shatter* if I ever killed a deer. Of course, I've never had to make the choice between hunting and starving. I guess I could do it then. Your mother did."

Susanne paused, about to dip a measuring cup into the flour. "Choose between hunting and starving? *My* mother?"

"Well, not exactly between those two things, but there are correlations in her life. I didn't think so, either. I came here assuming that everything at Asquonset had always been elegant and posh, but it wasn't."

"I know that," Susanne said and went on with her work. "The vineyard was slow to grow, but I don't think Natalie was out in the wild killing grouse for dinner in the meanwhile."

"Are there grouse here?" Olivia asked, but before Susanne could answer, Natalie appeared at the door.

"I heard your voice," she said to her daughter, crossing the floor with a smile on her face and her arms open wide. She waited only until Susanne wiped her hands on a dish towel, then gave her a hug. "I'm *so* glad to see you." She held her back, suddenly accusatory. *"When* did you get here? You weren't driving in the wee hours, were you?"

"It was midnight when I pulled up. Your door was shut. I wasn't about to disturb you."

"I was sleeping alone," Natalie replied archly, but the tone held a ghost of humor, and she was quickly smiling again. "I see you've met Olivia."

"Oh, yes. She was in your office when I went up there to surprise you. She followed me down here and has me talking in a way that I should never do with a stranger."

Olivia was infinitely grateful that Susanne hadn't mentioned the scene in the office. She didn't want to have to explain.

"She's been a help to me that way," Natalie said and stood back to study her daughter. "You look beautiful, Susanne. Young, young, young. I love your hair. How are the children? Melissa? Brad?"

Olivia listened for only a minute. It wasn't that she didn't want to hear, only that this seemed like a private mother-daughter time. She left, marveling that things could sound so perfectly pleasant between two women who had such a major block between them.

Twenty-two

SIMON DIDN'T GO AWAY. He lurked in the back of Olivia's mind for the rest of the day, pulling her this way and that. It was a tug-of-war, with sex at one end and logic at the other.

Logic won. Regardless of the attraction, she couldn't afford to be sidetracked from where she was headed—which was what she told him the next morning. She went outside as soon as he appeared on the patio, and feeling the physical pull even then, launched into it with barely a hello. He listened to her without a blink and, in response, asked a calm, "Where are you headed?"

"I don't *know*. That's the problem. But I need maximum flexibility, which means no involvement. It means focusing on Tess and focusing on me. I'm at a crossroads in my career—a crossroads in my *life*. It's a crucial time."

They were walking down the path that divided Cabernet Sauvignon grapes from Chenin Blanc ones. The sun was starting to rise in a cloudless summer sky.

"What's your dream?" he asked.

"My dream? As in, my ideal job?"

"Other than living at the Plaza and being a concierge," he teased, and for a minute she didn't answer. Teasing was something she hadn't expected from a man who had been so cold at the start. He wore the gentleness well—which didn't help her cause any. She would have preferred that he do something crude, like scratch himself or burp. It would make her decision easier.

"My dream?" she repeated, mustering resolve. "Seriously?"

He nodded.

"I'd like a grant to do a photo essay on the elderly."

He gave a curious half smile. "The elderly?"

She nodded. "Our society is attuned to youth and beauty. Seniors don't rate on that scale, but they have a wealth of experience to impart. It's written all over their faces, if you have the patience to read between the lines. Their faces can be *the* most expressive. I could capture that on film." Self-conscious at having shown so much enthusiasm, she smiled. "Just a dream."

But Simon wasn't laughing. "Vines are like that too. The older they are, the more character they have. A vine has to grow for four years before it produces a steady yield; then, like wine, it gets better with age. We keep them hedged tightly during the growing season, so you don't get a feel for their individuality. That comes out during the winter months. Once the leaves fall, you see the uniqueness of each vine."

Olivia wanted him to keep talking, if only to hear the feeling in his voice. "Once the leaves fall, doesn't the place seem barren?"

"No, because it isn't. Dormancy is an important time. It's when the vines rest up from the work of one season and gain strength for the next. We prune them then, and that's crucial, too. The yield can be ruined if the pruning is wrong."

"Do you do it all yourself?"

"Donna helps. Paolo used to. I'll hire someone else in the fall, but I'll have to spend most of the first year training him. Or her." A distracted look came to his eyes, a small smile to his lips.

"What?" Olivia asked, intrigued by that smile.

"The sound is amazing."

"Sound?"

"The vineyard in winter. There's creaking in the wind. There's a woody cracking when we cut a limb, and a snap and echo when it falls on the pile. The air is crisp, your breath is white. The sun is weak, but fine for the vines." The gentleness that had been in his smile was in his eyes now, along with anticipation. "Then comes bud break. You wait for that, wondering when it'll happen, getting up each morning, looking outside, ready for it after winter"—his voice held suspense—"and then there it is. Just like that. It can happen at dawn, or at ten in the morning, even at two in the afternoon, that single moment when the buds emerge from their casements enough to be seen. It's like a pale, pale green mist creeps over the vines. The buds are so small, so pale, almost fragile—no, *entirely* fragile. A frost at that point can kill the vintage."

"Kill the *whole* thing?" Olivia asked.

"I know of cases where that's happened. We've never had it here. The ocean moderates things so that once it's warm enough for bud break, a frost is rare. Cold air sinks, though. We've lost a few rows low on the hill in a freak frost. A degree or two can make the difference. But we're careful where we plant things. Some varieties are more resistant to cold than others. Some do better higher or lower on a hill, some do better facing east than south, or south rather than west."

"How do you know what works where?"

"Trial and error."

"My God. That must be expensive."

"Not necessarily. When we wanted to produce a Chenin Blanc grape, we planted a few vines in different places." He tossed a glance at the rows beside them. "This was where they grew best, so we ordered more and planted a block. This block has been here a dozen years now."

"Did you have to uproot something else to make room?"

"Not in this instance. We had tried Gewürz here, and it hadn't worked, but it thrived off there to the side. What's good for one vine isn't necessarily good for another. It all evens out. There's still the weather to factor in. Weather patterns change. Something can work well in a spot for three years, then have an awful time for another two. When a vine withers and dies, you know you've planted it in the wrong place at the wrong time."

They walked on, more aimless than not. *The wrong place at the wrong time.* The words lingered.

"Like us," she said quietly.

He stopped walking and nodded.

"The wrong place at the wrong time," she mused.

"Yeah." He gazed off down the hill. Watching him, she thought him more handsome than ever with his auburn hair newly washed, his square jaw newly shaved, his broad, sinewy shoulders relaxed, ready for work.

"Maybe in another five years," she teased to break the moment, "when I'm a renowned concierge at the Plaza and my daughter has captivated the place to the point that publishers are beating down her door begging her to write about her experiences. She could be the next Eloise. Okay, she'd be fifteen then, but that wouldn't matter. There's a market for teenage adventure—or angst. She could write *Tessa Jones's Diary,* and I'd be her assistant. We'd get a big advance that would keep us in Starbucks mocha-latte-Rio-Grande-cappuccino-whatever for years, so I'd retire and we'd move here and I wouldn't have any worries about what work I should do and where Tess should go to school . . ."

She might have spun the vision even more if, chuckling, Simon hadn't hooked an arm around her neck, pulled her close, and started heading her back toward the house. It was the gesture of a fond friend, with nothing predatory in it—the kind of gesture Olivia could fall in love with in no time flat.

OLIVIA SHOWERED thinking of Romeo and Juliet, and dressed thinking of Antony and Cleopatra. She was thinking of Scarlett and Rhett while she helped herself to breakfast from the lavish spread Susanne had laid out, and headed for Natalie's office thinking of Gwyneth and Brad.

She and Simon weren't tragic, but she felt a certain sadness that morning. It didn't help that she was working alone, or that the work in question was the restoration of some of Natalie's newer photographs. Her brushes and inks were set up on the desk, and she did love the work, but it didn't require the concentration writing would have. Her mind wandered any number of times. The tug between what was and what might have been was strong.

Natalie saw it immediately when she joined Olivia at midday. "You look worried about something. Is it anything I can help with?"

Olivia capped her inks and sighed. "No. I'm just starting to think about where I'll be in the fall. Summer's passing too quickly." Wiping her brushes, she changed the subject. "I'm glad Susanne is here. She's lovely." Indeed, if Susanne had negative thoughts about Olivia and Simon—or about Olivia and Natalie—she didn't let it show. She was friendly each time Olivia saw her. "And she's a wonderful cook."

Natalie said, "Better than me, that's for sure. I cooked when the children were little, but my cuisine was more functional than gourmet. Preparing meals was just one more chore that I had to do in a busy day."

"But you had a cook," Olivia said, happily reimmersing herself in Natalie's life.

"Not when the children were young. Back then, it was me or nothing. I'm afraid I opened cans more than I should have. My children grew up on Franco-American spaghetti. The boys didn't care, as long as there was plenty of it, but I've always suspected that Susanne vowed early on to feed her own children better, and she did. She still does. For her, cooking is an art. For me, it's a nuisance. I hired a cook before we could truly afford it, but I was desperate. I had too many other things to do."

Those first years after the war weren't easy. We had money from the sale of the factories and from the bank, and we decided which vines we thought would grow here. Alexander made buying trips to Europe and returned with our order, but there was no profit in it yet. We were experimenting. We were living on dreams of future prosperity, selling corn and potatoes to pay for clothes and oil and machinery. In some respects, our existence was as meager as it had been during the Depression.

The difference was in attitude. During the Depression, the public mind-set was dark. During the war, the fragility of life had people holding their breath. Afterward, with victory fresh and money from the sale of military goods pouring into peacetime endeavors, there was optimism.

I lived and breathed it. I had to. I was the one pushing for a vineyard now. The responsibility of making it work was mine.

Did Alexander say that? No. He saw himself as the leader. He was more than ready to accept responsibility when we planted a vine and it failed. But Carl and I were the ones who felt each failure most deeply.

Alexander wanted to make a name for Asquonset. Carl and I simply wanted to make those grapes grow.

"Did Alexander ever wonder about your feelings for Carl?" Olivia asked.

"No."

"Then you hid it well."

"Hid it?" Natalie asked. "The reason for our being close was so legitimate that Alexander accepted it perfectly. Besides, there was nothing not to accept. By the mid-fifties, Carl was managing the farm. He was doing all those things that Alexander didn't want to do. Carl's being here allowed Alexander to run around Europe, go wine-tasting in New York, or spend time in Newport with friends. Alexander liked Carl. He trusted him. He wasn't suspicious. I didn't give him reason to be."

There it was. The big question.

"Ah-ha," Natalie crowed. "I can see there's something you don't want to ask."

Olivia raised a hand and shook her head. "I'm not goin' there."

"But you're wondering."

"I'm thinking that your children will be wondering." She didn't just think it. She knew it. Hadn't Susanne suggested hanky-panky right off the bat?

"The answer is no," Natalie said, raising her chin. "I never betrayed my husband. Not once in all those years. I may have spent more time with Carl than I did with Alexander, but it was work. Carl and I were on the same project, so to speak. My children may fault me for that, but I never betrayed the vows I took."

"Didn't you want to?" Olivia asked. She was thinking of Simon now, thinking of raw chemistry between them and guessing that it had been the same between Natalie and Carl.

Natalie pondered that. At one point she frowned and shook her head, but the frown faded and still she said nothing. Finally she sighed. "I didn't let myself want it. I acclimated myself to having Carl as a work partner."

"A chaste daytime marriage."

"No," Natalie said quickly, then paused, considering what Olivia had said. "Well, I suppose. I never really thought of it that way. But it was at least something—better than nothing. It grew to be satisfying." Her eyes found Olivia's. "But I never betrayed my vows," she repeated. "I was committed to making my marriage work."

"Did it?"

"Yes, but it wasn't easy. Alexander had been in

his element during the war. He talked about it whenever he could, and it was the espionage angle that I heard most. I just assumed that was what he had loved—the secrecy and excitement. Living with him, I realized there was more. He liked the neatness of it, the regimentation, the spit and polish. He liked being a senior officer." She sent Olivia a dry, woman-to-woman look.

"Oh, dear. He wanted the family run that way too. How did you handle it?"

"I humored him. I kept the house as clean as I could, and ordered our lives as neatly as possible. I served him breakfast in the dining room with the newspaper laid out just so. I gave him the first cut of meat at dinner, and made sure that the children didn't make noise when he was taking a nap. They'll remember that. They used to complain, like it was my doing, when I was only the messenger. I let Alexander issue directives, knowing full well that he would soon be off doing something else and forget. Yes, it was a game. But it worked. He was content, and I was able to work with Carl to shape the vineyard in the most promising way." She sat back with a smile. "The rest, as they say, is history."

Olivia waited out the silence for a minute, then laughed in surprise. "You're not stopping there, are you?"

Natalie's features were peaceful. "Well, you have the basics. I loved Carl, but Alexander never

knew it. I always respected his needs. He died believing that he was the center of my life. If my children know that, they'll perhaps find it in the
goodness of their hearts to accept my marriage to
Carl now."

"But you haven't talked about the fifties,"
Olivia argued.

"What do you want to know?"

"I want to know how the vineyard grew. I want
to know your part in it and Carl's part in it. I want
to know about the sixties. I want to know how the
Great House grew, and when you decided to build
the winery. I want to know whether the kids were
ever involved and if not, why. I want to know what
they thought about your working at a time when
women didn't work. I want to know what happened between you and Brad."

She stopped. Natalie was pressing a finger to
her lips, looking beseeching.

Softly, Olivia said, "I want to know why he
wasn't invited to the wedding."

Natalie's eyes grew moist, and Olivia almost
dropped the subject. But it was starting to feel
like something important. "What happened?" she
whispered.

Natalie didn't move for a minute. Nor did the
moisture in her eyes become actual tears. Then she
inhaled, straightened, and dropped her hand.
Studying a knuckle, she said, "It was a long time
ago."

The phone rang.

Olivia ignored it. "He isn't in any of the newer pictures. I used to think he was just away from home."

Natalie rose to look at the ones Olivia had been working on. When the phone rang again, she said, "Would you get that for me?"

Turning away, Olivia answered the phone. "Hello?"

"Olivia, it's Anne Marie. Your fellow just called here again. He insisted that he had something *very* important to tell you, and got *really* upset when I wouldn't put him through."

Olivia rubbed her forehead. She couldn't believe Ted was still at it, even after she had been so blunt. But who else could it be? "Are you sure it's the same man?"

"Yes. I know that voice."

"Did he threaten to come here?"

"No, but it's probably only a matter of time. If he has the phone number, he can get the address. Should I call the police?"

Olivia had threatened doing that once, and been hit with the ultimate guilt trip. But she wasn't ready to jeopardize Ted's career now, any more than she had been then. Not yet.

"Ted's a pest," she told Anne Marie. "But he isn't dangerous. If he calls again, hang up on him."

"Your secret admirer?" Natalie asked when she replaced the receiver.

"My *annoying* admirer. Poor Ted. Here he's taking the time to call from work, no doubt watching his clock—" Her eyes flew to the one on Natalie's desk. "Omigod. It's late! I have to get Tess to the yacht club." Appalled to have so lost track of the time, she turned in apology to Natalie.

Natalie waved her off. "I didn't want to talk more now anyway."

"We'll get back to this," Olivia warned on her way to the door.

Natalie didn't reply. She simply stood there looking beseeching again, making Olivia all the more curious. If she hadn't been so late, she would have pursued it. But Tess was her first priority. Responsible mothers didn't make their children late for lessons.

Guilt ridden, she ran down the stairs and out to the drive, wondering why Tess hadn't come to get her, thinking that the child would surely be at the car—unless the child had deliberately let the time pass. Tess liked sailing, but she remained wary of the class.

No Tess on the stone steps in front. No Tess at the car. No Tess in the rhododendrons.

Olivia searched the road. No Tess there. No Tess in the vineyard—not that she would be visible, with the vines so much higher and darker. No Simon, either, which was good.

"Susanne took her," Jill called, coming out the screen door to the porch and down the steps.

Olivia met her at the bottom. "Susanne? Good Lord, she shouldn't have had to do that."

"She was actually thrilled," Jill said, sitting down. "She had to go out for groceries anyway, and it gave her direction. 'Just like the old days,' she said. She's ready for grandkids."

"Tess must think I forgot her."

Jill smiled. "We blamed it on Natalie. We told Tess it was our job to do the shuttling, since Natalie was keeping you up there with her."

"Like you have nothing else to do," Olivia remarked, sitting beside her. "You're in the office all hours."

"My choice. It keeps me busy."

Olivia felt an affinity for Jill in that they were both non-Seebrings, both in their thirties, both grappling with man problems. "Have you talked with Greg?"

"Oh, we talk, but we don't, if you know what I mean."

"That's a very Seebring thing. I was with Susanne when Natalie first saw her. It was a perfectly friendly greeting. There was no mention of any disagreement or any hard feelings." More softly, she said, "How are you feeling?"

"Better, actually. I have my moments, but it's restful here."

"Even working at the office?"

"Even then." Her eyes went toward the vines flanking the road. "I've always loved this place."

"Doesn't Greg? Even the littlest bit?"

Jill was pensive. "He does, but in a love-hate kind of way. He felt pressure growing up."

"What kind of pressure?"

"To shine. To excel. You know how parents do that kind of thing."

"Actually not," Olivia said. "My mother knew I wouldn't shine. She didn't have any hope of taking great pride in her daughter. So she left."

"The message in *that* being that if you *had* excelled, she would have stayed. I'd call that pressure."

Olivia hadn't looked at it that way. "But it was different. My mother and I were nothing. This family has a big name. Big name, big pressure."

"I disagree. All of us want parental approval. Big name, little name, *no* name—it makes no difference. We want to please our parents. Greg wasn't unique in that. He says the expectations were out of line, especially from Natalie, but hell, he isn't the first son to have to live in the footsteps of an older brother."

"Brad?"

"Brad."

"Did you know him?"

"Me? *Greg* didn't know him. There was eighteen years between them. Brad was gone before Greg was even born. So, did that make it better or worse? I'd say worse. I'd say Natalie was holding Greg up to a fantasy model."

"Natalie? What about Alexander?"

Jill frowned. "No," she said slowly. "It was Natalie." She looked up at the sound of a car. "There's Susanne."

Olivia couldn't help but notice that Susanne was driving the vineyard SUV, well marked with the logo, rather than her BMW. That said something, she thought.

Leaving the steps, she was at the door when Susanne opened it. "I'm sorry, Susanne. I totally lost track of the time. Thanks for taking Tess."

Susanne gave an easy wave. "No problem. I was headed that way, anyway." She went to the back and opened the hatch. It was filled with groceries.

"Was she upset that I wasn't there?" Olivia asked, lifting a bag.

Susanne took one herself. "No. She was upset that I wouldn't let her go marketing with me. I take it sailing isn't her favorite thing."

"Oh, she loves sailing. She just hasn't settled in with the other kids."

Jill joined them and reached into the car, only to have Susanne swat at her arm. "Don't lift," she said under her breath and shot Olivia an unsure look.

"She knows," Jill said, testing bags until she found a light one. "She's sworn to secrecy. We were just talking about Brad."

"Ah," Susanne breathed. "Saint Brad." One-handed, she passed Olivia a second bag and took another herself. "He didn't walk on water, but he came close."

Olivia looked from sister to sister-in-law. "He isn't here, but he's here."

"Always has been," Susanne replied and led the group toward the house. "Not that it was as bad for me as it was for Greg. I was the girl. I wasn't expected to be like Brad—*or* him like me. He never had to wash dishes or make beds or iron shirts. Oh, boy, did we argue about that. Mother always kept him that little bit separate—that little bit superior. I hated it."

"But you named your son after him," Olivia reminded her as they climbed the steps.

Susanne didn't look at all sorry. "It was the right thing to do—you know, the firstborn in each of three generations—but you can be sure that my Brad knows how to wash dishes. He knows how to cook, too. If there was one thing I could teach him, it was that." Crossing the porch, she looked at Olivia. "Jill swears she can't taste food, so the choice is yours. What'll it be for dinner—marinated flank steak, garlic mashed potatoes, and salad, or grilled salmon, wild rice, and veggies?"

Olivia grinned. "Grilled salmon," she said, feeling like an almost-sister and loving it.

THE SALMON WAS WONDERFUL, cooked moist and flavorfully, beautifully presented on a bed of nutty wild rice surrounded by julienned zucchini and yellow squash. With it, Susanne served a fruity Chardonnay from the Asquonset Riverside White series. Dessert was a smooth chocolate mousse.

Olivia insisted that she and Tess do all the

cleanup by way of thanks for Susanne's help driving, but more was called for. When the counters had been wiped down and the kitchen lights turned low, she ran up to the loft, took a folder with the pages she had written to date, and ran back down. Susanne was using that low light in the kitchen to plot out the next day's meals.

Olivia set the folder on the counter beside her. "This is what I've written of your mother's story so far. It probably needs more editing, but it's readable. If you want to take a look."

She left before Susanne could say whether she would, but when she returned to the kitchen later for a glass of milk for Tess, Susanne and the folder were gone.

Twenty-three

THE WEATHER IMPROVED. With the coming of August, the sun shone more often, moderating the sea air and warming the days. The vines grew tall and a richer green, and Olivia's hair was long enough to look windblown rather than mussed.

"Sun and heat," she said, a bit self-conscious when Simon remarked on the latter one morning. "Good for the head, good for grapes."

"Don't you know it," he responded.

If she did, it was thanks to him. Natalie was knowledgeable, but she was busier than ever making do with a skeletal crew as the wedding approached, and when Olivia might have talked grapes with Carl, he was lobbing tennis balls to Tess. He seemed to love it as much as she did, particularly since she was catching on. She hit more balls than she missed now, occasionally making Carl run to return one. She even listened to his talk about form and was feeling good enough about herself to pay heed. The lessons went on beyond the hour and often resumed after sailing, even after dinner. The days were still long enough for that.

This one promised to be a scorcher, even at dawn.

And why, Olivia wondered, was she out here with Simon at a time of day when she was vulnerable? Because they were friends now, she decided, feeling safe with that thought. They had things to talk about, whether it was her job search, Tess's reading, or Buck's kittens. Their favorite topic, though, was always the grapes.

Not that temptation entirely vanished. With the return of sun, Simon's skin burned as it had in June. His nose peeled, his shoulders peeled—all of which was endearing in a macho way. He had his sunglasses on the top of his head, at the ready for work, but his eyes were nearly as deep a blue now as the sky in the west.

Oh, yes, the attraction was still there, sometimes so strongly that she had to close her eyes and consciously redirect her thoughts, but Simon cooperated. He didn't look at her mouth or at her breasts. He looked either at her eyes or at the ground.

"August and September are big growing times," he said now as they walked through the rows of vines. "If we get sun and warmth, we can make up for the rain and cold we had in June and July."

"Then that rain won't affect the wine?" Olivia asked, encouraging him to say more. She loved watching him when he talked about his work, because he so clearly loved it. His face was gentle, his dark blue eyes remarkably warm.

"Everything affects the wine. That's why each year's vintage is different. But the rain won't be a negative thing, as long as we do get the sun. If the grapes only half ripen, that's something else."

"What do you do then?"

"Make rosé. Or grape juice."

"What if you don't get another drop of rain between now and harvest?"

"Not another drop in two months? That'd be trouble. If the ground gets too dry, the leaves close their pores to conserve what water they have. But carbon dioxide has to enter through those pores if photosynthesis is going to take place. If the pores close, there's no photosynthesis, and without photosynthesis, the leaves won't produce sugar to pass on to the fruit." He stopped walking to gently move aside a patch of leaves. "See that pole?"

Olivia did, but only because he pointed it out. It was barely three feet tall, narrow, and so close to the post holding the trellis wires as to be nearly invisible.

"That's drip irrigation," he explained. "It draws

freshwater from the river. If things get too dry, we can water the soil in a way that won't soak the grapes. We haven't had to do it often, but given the market we've built, it pays to be safe."

"What about intense heat? Can that ruin a vintage?"

"It could. We've planted vines that thrive in the kind of cool weather climate we have here on the coast. Usually, it just means earlier ripening and an earlier harvest. I can handle that."

"What can't you handle?" Olivia asked, doubting there was much.

"Hurricanes," he said without missing a beat. "Word is this is going to be a bad season."

"Here?" In the seven years Olivia had been in Cambridge, there had been only a handful of mild blows. Granted, Rhode Island was on the coast. Still, New England was New England.

"The Caribbean's already had two."

"But you don't usually have trouble here, do you?"

"Oh, we have. Not that I'm looking for trouble"—he shot her a dry look—"but you asked."

"How do you protect the vines from a hurricane?"

"You don't. You just see that they're healthy, which means that you do what you normally do in August. You hedge. You layer leaves on the trellis. You monitor for pests. From this point on, I have to be careful about spraying. Some sprays aren't allowed within a certain number of days of harvest. If harvest comes early, and a spray is prohibited within sixty-six days of that, we're talking *now.*"

Olivia thought about the harvest, and briefly regretted that she wouldn't be here to see it, to be a part of it. "How do you know when to pick the grapes?"

"Taste and a refractor. That's a machine that registers the sugar and acid content. We harvest when the grapes have the optimal balance between the two. If it happens in one group of vines before another, we harvest only the block that's ripe."

"Do you use a machine?"

"If we're racing an early frost, we may, but I prefer to do it by hand. We hire extra workers for that. More this year, what with two of my staff gone." He shot her a look as they walked on. "Speaking of which, how's the new cook?"

"Susanne?" Olivia asked only half in jest.

"No. The *cook* cook."

"You mean Fiona." Olivia was a minute finding the right words. "Young . . . willful. She prides herself on knowing how to cook and doesn't like having Susanne there, but Susanne's far better at it. She's trying to teach her, but Fiona resists. The truth is, I don't think she's long for Asquonset life."

"Is Susanne?" Simon asked with caution.

"Well, she's not talking about leaving. I think she's having fun. Not that she would admit it."

"Barely a month till the wedding. Any word from Greg?"

"I TALKED WITH HIM LAST NIGHT," Jill told Susanne when she asked. Breakfast was done. They sat on the patio, lingering over coffee. "He's with a client in Dallas."

Susanne put her head back. She felt lazy in the heat. "Is he coming here?" It was no longer a matter of making him share the guilt. She wasn't feeling guilt now. She was here, she was busy, and if the truth were told, she was having a good time. Her days were filled doing what she loved most, and for once, she had an appreciative audience. But Jill wasn't quite as content.

"Not yet."

"Is he coming for the wedding?"

"He says no," Jill answered. "I think he's wrong, but when I dare suggest that, he gets defensive. How about you?"

Mark had asked her the same thing less than an hour ago. "If you're wondering whether I feel any better about the wedding seeing Mother with Carl, the answer is no. They're good together, and they're in love—all that is quite apparent. It also makes a mockery of her relationship with my father. No, I'm only staying until the cook business gets straightened out."

Jill leaned forward. "Fiona is *not* getting straightened out."

Susanne knew that. "But maybe her problem is with me. Maybe once I leave and she's in charge, she'll be fine."

"She may be happier, but will we? Where *does* she get some of those combinations? Rack of lamb dredged in cardamom? Shrimp on a bed of stewed figs? Kiwi sorbet with peanut brittle bits? I mean, innovation is one thing. Pushed too far, it's unpalatable. There may be good reason why her restaurant closed. I think you should stay awhile, Susanne."

A small part of Susanne could do just that. When the children were young, she had spent most of the summer at Asquonset. The kids had loved the open air, the warmth, the shore breeze. They had loved playing with their grandfather.

Playing with their grandfather. Not their grandmother, Susanne mused. Alexander was the one who gave piggyback rides and played ball. Granted, he did it on his own schedule, and he was ever the disciplinarian if the playfulness got out of hand, but he was the one who took them to the yacht club and bought them penny candy at Pindman's. The children would have continued spending summers here if Susanne hadn't balked. But she couldn't relax here—because her role model, Natalie, never relaxed. If Natalie wasn't gardening, she was cleaning closets with Marie, or nosing around the shed, or meeting with her accountant, or joining friends for lunch. She always seemed to have something to do that kept her from

Susanne and the children. That made Susanne feel superfluous.

Obviously, some things never changed. Natalie hadn't spent more than twenty minutes at a stretch with her since her arrival. True, she wasn't exactly meeting friends for lunch at the yacht club or planning prewedding soirees. When she wasn't in the loft, she was outside, often on a cell phone. Fine, she was arranging for people to clean the carpets or groom the rhododendrons. Still, Susanne was her daughter, here for Natalie's sake. If Natalie didn't spend time with her, where was the incentive to stay?

"I'm here only until Fiona shapes up," she said. "Mother can't help. She isn't focused enough."

"She's feeling pressure about the new label look. It's a major marketing move. She's very involved in that, Susanne."

Susanne grunted. "She certainly likes to think she is."

"She is," Jill insisted. "I'm at the office every day. She's instrumental in the marketing operation, and not only since Alexander's death. She has always been involved. Have you read anything of what Olivia's written?"

Susanne closed her eyes and lifted her face to the sun. "Nope."

"You should. It's enlightening."

"It's one-sided. My father isn't here to tell his side."

She was delighted when Jill had no answer for that—but her delight was short lived. When Jill finally responded, her voice was more reasonable than Susanne might have liked.

"This isn't adversarial. No one's taking sides. Natalie isn't denigrating Alexander. She's simply telling about her part in the growth of Asquonset. Why is it we always knew so much about Alexander and so little about her? And the truth is, it's because he talked and she didn't. Now she's opening up. I think you should read her story, Susanne."

We started slowly. For a while, it felt like we were spinning our wheels more than anything else. Wherever he went, Alexander created a vineyard in the minds of the people who listened, but back home, it was still largely experimentation and prayers.

Image was important. Alexander said that, and I agreed. We added the upper floors to the Great House in the early fifties, perhaps before we could comfortably afford it, but with two active children, we needed the space, and it did look good, I have to admit. We incorporated a picture of the house in our sales kit. Again, this was cultivating the image of success before we had a right to do it, but there was no harm done. It wasn't as though we weren't on our way. We did have grapes to sell.

Chardonnay were the first vines that took conclusively. We planted one acre, then two, then four in successive years. We weren't thinking of making wine ourselves. We weren't even thinking of supporting ourselves. Our goal was to add to the acreage at the same time that we found other varietals that would thrive here. To that end, we sold juice from our grapes to vineyards in Europe.

Why does that surprise you? European vineyards have good years and bad, too. Nowadays, we all have tricks up our sleeves to minimize the bad years, but back in the fifties, growing methods were less sophisticated. In a lean year, a vineyard could mix the juice from our grapes with their own and produce a wine that was actually quite respectable. And if the product of our work went into the lesser of their wines? That was fine. We were paid for what we sold them. That meant we had money to buy more vines.

How did we support ourselves? Corn and potatoes.

But you're right. That wasn't enough. Not to care for a growing family. Not to pay for Alexander's trips. Not for machinery and fertilizer and pesticides and fungicides.

How did we manage? I lost many a night's sleep until I found an answer, and then, when I acted, lost many a night's sleep worrying that it would fail. Fortunately, it didn't. Suburbia was an idea whose time had come.

Let me backtrack a bit. There was a fellow in town who had grown up with my brother and Carl. He visited us when Brad died, then went off to war himself, but he was injured and returned within the year. He had lost the sight in one eye, and though he swore that he could still fight, he was discharged. We used to see each other at Pindman's. I'd share my dreams about growing a vineyard, and he'd share his dreams about growing a town.

Yes, a town. He always thought big, Henry Selig did, and there were people who laughed. I never did, lest he laugh at *my* dream. Both were relatively far-fetched at that point.

I lost track of him when the war ended. I was so busy trying to hold my life together, and he moved down to New York. Next thing I knew, though, he was back, and suddenly his dream made a great deal of sense. He was looking around him, seeing all those soldiers back from war, many of them with college degrees thanks to the GI Bill, many with wives and growing families and jobs that paid good wages. Those men wanted to buy houses in places where their children could play outdoors and their wives could grow flowers.

Henry knew how to build houses. He knew how to plan a development that included hundreds of them, and he knew where he wanted to do it. There were small towns within an easy drive of Providence, and large tracts of land that were his for the buying. Suburbs were springing up in other states. He saw no reason why they shouldn't spring up in Rhode Island.

All he needed was the money to buy the land and to finance the purchase of building materials.

I had money. It wasn't much—I would be but one of many investors—but I had taken it out of the bank loan and set it aside. I didn't know why at the time. Security, I guess. I had lived through the Depression. I liked knowing I had something stashed away just in case.

No. Alexander didn't know I had it.

Why not?

Oh, dear. How to explain. Maybe I felt I deserved something, after having been let down so badly. Maybe I was worried that he would spend it and lose it. Yes, I suppose it was a matter of trust. I needed to know that I had something of my own.

I didn't tell Alexander about Henry Selig's business proposal. For what it's worth, I didn't even tell Carl. I was working as hard as any man at Asquonset to make the place a success. As I saw it, that money was mine.

It was a wise investment. Within a year, the first batch of houses were built and every single one sold. I saw a five-fold return on my investment. So I put the original amount, plus some, back in my account at the bank, and invested in the next phase of Henry's project. It was even more successful. Again, I added part to my account at the bank and reinvested the rest, and Henry never let me down. He went from building houses to building offices to building shopping malls. To this day, I get dividends on some of those investments.

Was I frightened? Terrified during that first phase. Logic said that it would be a success, but if it wasn't, my nest egg was gone. Once we saw how wildly successful real estate ventures could be, there was no fear.

Well, at one other point there was. During his time in New York, Henry mingled with the theater crowd—playwrights, directors, actors, and actresses. Henry was already in Rhode Island—with some of my money in hand—when Joe McCarthy and his committee were questioning members of that crowd for communist leanings. Henry's name came up. There was talk that he would be called to testify. He was never actually questioned. I guess they figured that even if he had left-leaning friends, he was such an utter capitalist that his presence would make mockery of their witch-hunt. But it was a scary few months. People were condemned by association. Henry was fingered because he was the friend of others who were fingered, and I was a friend of Henry's.

All's well that ends well, as they say. McCarthy got censured, Henry got rich, and I got the money to make the difference in our lifestyle while we were waiting for our grapevines to grow gold. We enlarged the Great House again, and decorated this time. We hired a cook and began to entertain. We hired a field hand, plowed new land, and planted triple the number of new vines. We bought modern machinery and enlarged the shed. We began bottling wine.

I'm not saying we couldn't have done it without my real estate earnings, but I do think it would have been harder, and surely would have taken longer. Those earnings made the difference. They were the little boost we needed. I'm pleased to have done that for Asquonset.

Natalie sat back, looking mystified. "Funny. I haven't thought about that in a long time. It wasn't ever something I dwelled on, wasn't something I discussed with Alexander, even so many years later."

"Because of his ego?" Olivia asked.

"Because it was *irrelevant*. I could have poured *ten* times what I did into the vineyard, but if we hadn't put backbreaking hours into planting and nursing those vines, into researching new methods of trellising and testing new pesticide programs, they wouldn't have amounted to much more than weeds." She fell silent.

Silence was part of their routine. Olivia had learned to use it to gather her thoughts. Doing so now, she felt something was missing. She flipped back through her notes, but couldn't put her finger on it. So she said, "Describe an average day."

Natalie smiled. "There was no average day, not when you were raising children and grapes, not when you were feeling your way along, building a business when you really knew nothing about building a business."

"And you were the one who did it, not Alexander."

Natalie thought for a minute. "I suppose that if you have to label things, you could say that I was the what-to-do person and Carl was the how-to-do-it one. Alexander was our front man. He traveled. He spread the word. By the time we were bottling wine in great enough quantity to market it, we knew just where to go. Alexander was wonderful that way. He wasn't good with money, and he wasn't good with plowing or plucking or grafting, but he was a powerful publicity tool."

"Was he good with children?" Olivia asked and suddenly realized that that was it. Natalie's story lacked that personal element.

"He was *wonderful* with children," Natalie said, but her smile quickly faded. "Oh, it was hard at first. I told you that. When he came home from the war, he was a stranger to them and they to him. After a year or two, as the children grew a little older and more familiar, that changed. I guess he found that they weren't any different from adults. If he played with them, they liked him. Mind you, he wanted the house rules followed, but I was the enforcer. I was the bad guy, he was the good guy. It probably helped that he traveled, because it was more of a novelty when he was home. He never took a trip without returning with some little toy or memento for them." She sighed, smiling again. "They adored him, which made him happy, and Alexander happy made my life easier."

"Was it a hard life?"

"Hard? *Physically* hard?"

"Living on a small farm on the coast."

"It got easier in the fifties. Suddenly we had washers and dryers. We had dishwashers. We had vacuum cleaners. We had oil heat and a thermostat. We had two cars. We had three televisions. It wasn't a bad life at all."

"Were you happy?"

"I was very happy."

"Were you *happy?*"

"I . . . was," Natalie replied, but more reflectively. "You're wondering what I was feeling about Carl all this time."

"About Carl. About Alexander. About the children. You've given me facts about the vineyard's growth. I want to hear the emotional side."

The older woman remained thoughtful. "I was thrilled about the vineyard. That was always a source of joy for me. To this day, I get a lift just walking among the vines."

"With Carl?"

"With or without," she said, then amended that. "With is better. He loves the place like I do. He put in the work and feels the pride."

"And you love him."

"Yes."

"What about Alexander? What was your marriage like?"

Natalie considered that for a moment, and when she began, she spoke slowly. "Hard work. Al and I had very different outlooks. I accepted that most of the time. On occasion, it bothered me. I sometimes grew frustrated with him. I wanted him to be . . . to be . . ."

"More like Carl?"

Her sigh was confirmation of it. "He wasn't, of course. Couldn't ever be. And if it suddenly happened, it would have thrown me for a loop. I had structured our lives in a way that made accommodation for his needs and mine." She paused, frowned, pressed her lips together. "There were times of strain. But they always passed. In the overall scheme of things, we had a good working marriage." She raised earnest eyes. "And I was happy, Olivia. Alexander wasn't Carl, but Carl was in my life. I had the best of both worlds. Yes, I was dutiful when it came to doing things Alexander liked, but I enjoyed many of them, too. I liked going to parties. I liked going out to dinner. I liked taking theater trips to New York. I am *not* making myself out to be a martyr in this book."

"Were you happy as a mother?" Olivia asked, because it struck her that Natalie hadn't once said that.

She didn't now either. She studied her lap for the longest time before finally raising her eyes. They held dismay. "I love my children. I suffer when they do." Her voice quivered. With a breath, she gathered her composure. "As the years went by, we drifted."

"Why?"

Natalie's eyes returned to her lap. Her brows rose. "Probably because I was doing so many other things. Our social life was more active in the fifties and sixties. We joined the yacht club and started giving parties. I was active with community groups. All that took time, on top of what I did at the vineyard. As the children grew older, there was less custodial work, so I focused on those other things."

"But you were here with them every morning and every night," Olivia argued. She would have given anything to have her mother do that. "You were physically present."

Natalie didn't let herself off the hook. "Physically present, mentally afield. I . . . I don't think I gave them the time or attention they needed. I think they resent that to this day."

Olivia agreed with her there. Susanne had actually talked about special treatment given to one child and not the rest. "What about Brad?"

Natalie shifted in the wing-back chair. When she settled again, she looked as though she had braced herself. "Brad was my oldest."

"I know."

"He was the first son."

"Yes."

"Greg was born eighteen years later. Our lives were very different then. We were more prosperous."

"Was Greg a surprise?"

"No. We wanted another child."

But there was something in the way she said it, a small hesitancy.

Seeming to sense it, too, she said quickly, "I love Greg. I loved him from the minute he was born. I've followed his career in ways he doesn't know about."

Olivia tried to read between the lines. "But you were conflicted about having a third child?"

It was a minute before Natalie continued. Nodding, she said, "I was thirty-six. My days were already full."

"Then why?"

"Alexander and I were going through one of those periods of strain that I mentioned."

"You had a baby to save the marriage?"

She came alive. "I know, I know. Folks your age think that's the worst reason to have a child, but it is not, Olivia. It is not. Alexander wanted another child. He said that he'd missed the early years with the others. He was happy when I got pregnant, which made me happy. And I did get Greg in the deal."

Greg, who never knew his older brother.

Olivia came forward. Quietly, she asked, "What *happened* to Brad?"

For a minute, Natalie was perfectly still. Then her mouth moved, lips pursing and releasing. She moistened one corner and the other, and raised her eyes to Olivia. The sadness there was breathtaking.

Brad was born during those early dark days after the men went off to war. Given the circumstances, the maternity ward was surprisingly upbeat. There were many of us in the same situation, young and a little frightened, giving birth to our babies with no daddies in sight. We were a sorority of sorts, actually kept in touch for years afterward.

I was in labor for nearly a day before Brad was born, but from that moment on, he was a delight. He was quiet and sweet. He smiled from the time he was a month old—and no, it was not gas. Those smiles were real. I swear he knew how badly I needed them during those days with so much worry and fear.

It was always like that—Brad being attuned to my moods and my needs.

When I was feeling lonely, he was at his most cuddly. When I was feeling blue, he would just grin with a mouth full of rice cereal. How not to laugh with him? How not to think that something was indeed right in the world? This child was a gift. Many a Sunday I sat in church giving thanks for him.

Susanne was born two years later. It was a much easier delivery, and I knew the routine of caring for an infant, so she just kind of fit into the family, and Brad was good. There were no jealous outbursts, no temper tantrums in a bid for attention. Of course, he got his share of that anyway.

Susanne would say he got more than his share. Perhaps she's right. Perhaps I did take her for granted. She wasn't demanding. She did what she had to do without a fuss—ate, slept, grew. I always saw her as being like me. I assumed she would grow up to do the same things I did.

Brad was something else. He was male. He had a world of opportunities. I wanted every option open to him—and he showed the promise of all that. He learned to read when he was four and excelled in school, but he knew how to handle it. He had an innate modesty and an outward gentleness, which made him popular. He was the captain of whatever team was on the playground. He had friends, friends, and more friends. He was kind. Other children gravitated toward him.

I have to say one thing here. I don't think Susanne looked at the whole picture. I may have favored Brad. I may have taken her for granted. But once their initial strangeness with each other disappeared, she was the apple of her father's eye. Alexander was far stricter with Brad than he ever was with her. If Brad were here today, he would vouch for that.

But he isn't here, and you want to know why.

Give me a minute. Losing a child has to be the most painful thing a parent can possibly experience. It's always difficult for me to discuss.

So unexpected. Brad was the picture of health. Always. He never had colic. He never had colds. He was strapping and strong, tall and confident for his age at nine and ten. Then he turned eleven, and barely a month later he developed a fever.

The fear was instant. All around us, polio had reached epidemic proportions. We sent Susanne to stay with friends who had no children. We prayed that we were wrong.

The fever went on for six days before we saw another symptom, and then it was terrifying, because we knew. We knew. Our healthy boy—our *strong* boy couldn't raise his head from the bed or lift his legs. It was a classic case. I was with him all hours of the day, putting warm towels on his legs when the muscles spasmed, but it wasn't enough. It wasn't enough. When he began to have trouble breathing, we brought him to the hospital.

I will never forget the sight of my child in an iron lung. I will never forget the helplessness I felt when he looked at me, silently begging me to make him better. He knew what was wrong with him. He knew what could happen. He was old enough for that.

Do you remember the horrible plane crash not long ago, the one in which the plane started to plunge for no apparent reason? All those people killed, after a death spiral during which they must have known, must have realized, what was happening? Consider what the families of those victims must endure thinking about their loved ones—knowing they were going to die, unable to help themselves.

I lived that with Brad. He grew weaker and weaker. He struggled to breathe, struggled to open his eyes, but the knowing was there right up to the end. His body gave out before his brain did. It was . . . the worst experience of my life.

Natalie finished speaking. She sat for several minutes, wearing the pain of that experience on her face. Then, without another word, she rose and left the office.

Olivia didn't move for a long time, and when she did, it wasn't to write down what she had heard. Leaving her paper and pencil on the computer desk, she went off in search of Tess.

Twenty-four

NATALIE LOSING BRAD was like Simon losing
Liana, all the more tragic with a child, such potential lost. No one went through life without knowing death. But a child—a child was all innocence
and hope.

Olivia felt a compelling need to hug Tess. It
wasn't until she was out beside the flagpole that
she realized Tess was sailing—and even then, the
need remained strong enough for her to consider
driving to the yacht club to wait at the dock. She
might have done just that if Susanne hadn't opened
the screen door and called, "Phone, Olivia!"

Given her frame of mind, Olivia's first thought
was that there had been a sailing accident. Rushing
back to the house and up the stone steps, she must

have looked terrified, because Susanne said a calming, "It's just Anne Marie."

Just? Olivia's thoughts turned to Ted, which wasn't a calming subject at all. If he was calling yet again, she might have to act.

Uneasy, she slipped past Susanne and picked up the phone in the front hall. "What's up?"

"There's a man here. He says he has to see you."

Olivia hung her head. She squeezed her eyes shut and pressed her brow. "Is he five ten and kind of wiry, with short dark hair?"

"No," Anne Marie said very quietly, "he's over six feet, heavyset, early sixties. He's the one who's been calling. I recognize his voice."

Olivia straightened. If not Ted, then a friend of his? "What's his name?"

"He won't say."

"Well, I'm not talking with him unless he does."

Anne Marie directed her voice to the man, who was clearly right there.

With his half of the conversation inaudible, Olivia raised her brows in bewilderment to Susanne, who stood nearby. They both looked up when Natalie started down the stairs, but Olivia had barely noted her pallor when Anne Marie returned to the line.

"He says you won't know his name. He says he has something for you from your mother."

Olivia's heart began to pound. And *this* was the

man who had been calling? "Ask where he's from. Ask for ID." Gnawing on her cheek, she glanced nervously from Susanne to Natalie, both of whom seemed to sense the import of the call.

"He's from Chicago," Anne Marie reported. "His name is Thomas Hope. I have his driver's license in my hand."

"I'll be right there," Olivia said in a shaky voice and hung up the phone. "He knows my mother," she told Susanne and Natalie on her way out, but by the time she reached her car, they were climbing in, too. She started to protest, then realized that it felt right to have them there. She had been privy to some of the most intimate aspects of Seebring history. It was fitting that they should be involved in this most intimate aspect of hers—not to mention the comfort she could find in having them there. Driver's license or not, Chicago or not, she had no idea if this man was legitimate. He could be a fraud or a scam artist. He could be a thief.

She knew how to protect herself. She was quite practiced, quite capable. But she was touched that these women cared enough to be with her.

None of them spoke during the short ride down the hill to the main road and east to the office. Olivia's hands shook. Gripping the steering wheel tightly, she tried to think what her mother might have sent. There was only one thing she wanted, but when she pulled into the office parking lot and homed in on a car with Illinois plates, she didn't see a woman inside.

She parked and went directly into the office. Thomas Hope was in the small reception area where Anne Marie sat. He turned from the window as soon as she entered.

He was indeed large, but his body carried no threat. He seemed more annoyed than angry, but even that faded when he took a look at her.

"I'm Olivia," she announced in something of a challenge.

"Hard to miss," he replied in a thin voice. "You look like her. You have her stubbornness, too, dragging me all the way out here, but you wouldn't take my calls, and I promised her I'd get you this." He held out a thick envelope.

Olivia stared at it. An envelope like that could hold a week's worth of vacation plans. Carol might want to meet them somewhere lovely, like San Francisco—or somewhere fun, like Disney World. An envelope like that could hold several chapters of a memoir like the one Olivia was writing for Natalie. Carol might be wanting to tell her things— things Olivia might have read weeks ago, if she hadn't been so *bullheadedly* sure that Ted was the one on the phone. An envelope like that could hold a large, multicreased family tree. It could hold names.

Fearful, unable to reach out, Olivia wrapped her arms around her middle. "Why didn't she bring it herself?"

"She died two months ago. It took me awhile to get your number—"

Olivia's heart stopped. *"Died?"*

"She had liver disease. I was calling two different apartments in Cambridge, and one didn't know where you were, and the other wouldn't tell."

"She's *dead?*" Olivia asked, disbelieving in spite of the fact that the man must have driven two days to give her the news.

Thomas Hope nudged the envelope toward her. "The obituary's inside, along with her bankbook and all. I have some cartons in the car." When she made no move to take the envelope, he set it down on Anne Marie's desk. Stepping around the women, he went out the door just as Simon came in.

"Who is that?" he asked, looking back, and suddenly Olivia wanted to know, too.

She ran past him, out to the parking lot. Thomas Hope was just opening the trunk of his car.

"How did you know her?" she asked, not caring that she sounded accusatory. She had a right, after the bomb he had dropped.

"We lived together."

"Were you married?"

He picked up a small box. "Not to Carol."

"To someone else?"

"My wife won't give me a divorce," he said, putting the small box on a larger one and lifting the two. "Carol knew that. I never lied about it. I was always up-front. Where do you want these?"

"Liver disease. What kind of liver disease?"

"The kind you get from too much drinking. You knew she drank?"

"I didn't. Did she get the letters I sent?"

"Whatever she got is in these boxes. Where do you want them?"

"I'll take them," Simon said, relieving him of the armload.

"Why didn't she write back?" Olivia asked.

Thomas Hope reached for another carton. "Probably because when she was sober, she didn't think she had the right."

Didn't have the right? Didn't have the *right?* A mother *always* had the right. "Did she know about Tess?"

"Yes. She knew."

Olivia was stunned. "How could she know and not want to *see* her?"

Simon took the second carton and disappeared.

The man closed the trunk. "That's it. She cleaned things out before she died. What you have in those boxes are some pictures and books. When she was sober, she knitted, so there's also a few of the things she made. I think she wanted you to have them." He fished his keys from his pocket. "She didn't make a will. You're gonna have to take my word that what's here is all she had."

He opened the door, got into the car, and started the engine.

Wait, Olivia wanted to cry, as she stood on wooden legs. *What was she like? What did she do?*

Did she work? Did she laugh? Did she mention me? Did you love her?

But the words didn't come. Numb, she watched him back around and drive off. Bewildered, she looked up at Simon, who stood beside her.

"Maybe it's a hoax," she said. "Maybe she wants me to react."

Natalie came up with the envelope in her hand. "He said there was an obituary notice."

Olivia hesitated before finally taking the envelope, and then held it for a long minute before looking inside. The newspaper clipping was at the very front of the papers, a small square, ineptly cut. The obituary was brief. The only survivors listed were Olivia and Tess.

Olivia reread the notice. Feeling suddenly empty and lost, the only thing she could think to say was, "I always thought there might be someone else."

Natalie put a consoling hand on her arm.

"Is there anything we can do?" Susanne asked.

Olivia tried to think, but it wasn't like there was a funeral to plan. There weren't even any phone calls to make. The only thing to do was to tell Tess, and how hard could that be? Tess had never met her grandmother. Carol had never been part of their lives. Olivia hadn't talked about her in anything but a passing way. She had never raised Tess's hopes, had never shared the dream that one day they would be reconciled, three generations of a family, together and happy.

But the dream was an impossibility now. As the reality of that sank in, Olivia felt a panicky need to do something . . . anything. Frantic, she looked at Simon, then at Susanne and Natalie.

"I think I . . . need to run." She went to her car.

Simon was there, bending down to the window when she slid inside. "Are you okay?" he asked with such gentleness that she teared up.

She forced a smile through the tears. "Yup. I am." She started the car and waited only until he stepped away before backing up and heading out. Minutes later she was at the house, running up the stone steps, through the foyer, up the stairs, and into the wing. Minutes after that she headed back down, wearing a singlet, shorts, and sneakers. She hit the front drive and, without bothering to stretch, broke into a jog.

She set a brisk pace going down the drive and picked it up when she turned onto the road. The air was warm, the afternoon sun strong. Heat radiated from the pavement, broken into waves by the occasional car that passed.

Her lungs hurt after a bit, then her legs, but she didn't care. Thinking that pain was more fitting than numbness, she quickened the pace again. She was sweating now, pushing it off the tip of her nose with the back of her hand.

Hitting the pavement with the rhythmic slap of her sneakers, she passed Simon's road and ran on, one mile, then another. When she reached a path on the right that led to the shore, she took it for a third mile. Here, on dirt, the slap of sneakers was duller. It faded the closer she came to water, and was completely drowned out by the sound of the surf when she left the path and emerged onto rocky headlands.

She ran from one boulder to the next until she reached a chasm too wide to cross, so she ran in place there, breathing hard, sweating profusely. Several sailboats were in sight. She wondered if Tess was in one—hoped that she was—hoped that she would stay out there awhile because Olivia wasn't ready to talk, to explain, to deal with her emotions. Waves thundered against the rocks, sending spume high enough to spray her with a sea salt. It was refreshingly cool, mixing all too soon with her own sweat and tears.

Her feet slowed, then finally she stopped. Gasping for breath, she lowered herself to the rock. When gasps turned to sobs, she put her face to her knees.

She couldn't remember the last time she had cried. The act felt foreign—or maybe what felt foreign was the depth of it. Those sobs started at the very bottom of her heart. They were deep and wrenching, reflecting a sentiment she shouldn't have felt but did.

"Olivia."

She turned away from Simon's voice but couldn't stop crying. Once they started, it seemed, she was helpless to control the tears, or the anguish that caused them.

He didn't say anything else, just sat down beside her, facing the opposite way, put an arm across her chest, and drew her close. She cried against his arm now, still those same wrenching sobs.

In time they slowed, but mostly it was due to exhaustion. The pain remained just as overwhelming. She wasn't in control here, but was at the whim of a powerfully raw emotion. Her breath came in ragged bursts. She was exhausted, emotionally and physically, infinitely grateful to be leaning on Simon.

"Christ, you run fast," he said, and she would have laughed if she hadn't been so spent. His arm was wet, though she had no idea whether from his sweat or her tears.

Her breath continued to come in broken bits. "She wasn't supposed—to die until—we talked."

He stroked her head, moving his fingers through her hair.

"I wanted Tess to meet her and to like her. I wanted to like her myself. I wanted her to see me as an adult—and like me, too."

"I know."

"There may have been—a whole other side of her. I didn't know she drank."

"It's done, Olivia. You can't torture yourself."

But she did. "What a *wasted* relationship!" she cried, feeling nearly as angry as she was bereft.

He didn't argue with her, just continued a gentle stroking. When she turned to face him, he supported the back of her head. She needed that support. It buffered her from the pain.

"She couldn't love me."

Simon said, "That's not it."

"How do you know?"

"No mother *can't* love her child. Sometimes she just won't."

"But why *not?*"

"Sometimes she has her own issues."

"My mother's issue was me. I came at the wrong time and did all the wrong things."

"It wasn't you."

"How do you *know?*"

He held her back, and gently conceded, "I don't. I didn't know your mother. What I do know is that mothers are made to love. Look at you and Tess. You love her, even though she isn't perfect or always easy, but you wouldn't trade her for the world. That's what mother love is about. Your mother loved you. If she couldn't show it, the problem was with her, not with you."

Olivia wanted to believe him. His eyes were the same blue as the skies at the end of night. She wanted to believe him *so badly.* "Maybe if she could have seen me now—seen the kind of mother I am, seen the kind of work I do and the kinds of people I work for—maybe she would have loved me *now* . . ."

But Carol Jones was dead. The obituary said it. Thomas Hope said it. Olivia had no reason to doubt either one. For once, she couldn't even pretend. Fantasies wouldn't help her here. She couldn't think up a single story that would make it not so.

The pain in her mind spread to her heart. Again, she felt a dire need to hold Tess.

"I have to get back," she whispered. Separating herself from Simon, she pushed both hands over her face to erase tear streaks. Her legs shook when she stood, but Simon was beside her, and much like having Susanne and Natalie in the car earlier, it was a comfort.

Grieving, she let it be that. Nothing more.

THAT EVENING, she and Tess opened the three boxes. They found pictures of Carol and Olivia, and pictures of Olivia alone. There were Olivia's school papers—the best of the bunch, Olivia decided, since they showed B's rather than D's. There was a hospital tag so tiny that it was hard to imagine it ever fitting around Olivia's ankle, and the cast that had been on Olivia's broken arm when she was seven.

There was a dried corsage. Olivia cried over that. She had worn it pinned to her senior prom dress—a dress that Carol had neither helped her shop for nor seen her wear, though Olivia didn't tell Tess that.

"I can't believe she saved it," the child breathed in awe. "That was *so sweet!*"

Olivia didn't argue. She thought about what

Simon had said—about Carol wanting to be there for her daughter but having issues that prevented it. Maybe it was true. If Carol had missed her own prom because she was pregnant with Olivia, she might have felt too much pain to be involved with Olivia's prom. If that was so, taking Olivia's corsage from the trash and saving it all these years was, as Tess said, sweet.

Was there any harm in believing that? Was there any harm in letting Tess believe it?

Olivia pulled Tess close and held her there. "Yes, it was sweet. It was very sweet."

"Don't cry, Mom. Please? I hate it when you're sad."

"I am so lucky to have you."

"Ow. You're squeezing too hard."

"Sorry," Olivia said and reluctantly loosened her grip. "What else do we have?"

They had a pair of afghans, one green and one blue. Olivia felt a chill when she pulled them out, wondering how Carol had known their favorite colors. She searched the bottom of the box for a note, but there was none.

They found a small zippered sack with jewelry inside, none of which was valuable but all of which Tess adored. She promptly put a small Timex watch on her wrist.

They found a diary with a discolored tin latch, and again, Tess was all eyes. "Open it, Mom."

Olivia wasn't about to do that in front of her

daughter. Fearing what Carol had to say, she tucked the diary under her thigh. Seconds later, though, her own curiosity won and she took it back out. The latch opened easily. She opened the book to a blank page. She turned to another, blank as well, as was a third. She fanned the pages, looking for writing on any of them.

"Nothing?" Tess asked in dismay.

Olivia fanned the pages again, then turned to the very first. A neat hand had written "Carol Jones" in clotted ink, but the name appeared to be the only words written in the entire book.

"Why would she have a diary," Tess asked, "if she didn't want to write in it?"

Olivia thought about that. It was a cruel hoax, offering them hope in one breath and taking it away in the next. She didn't want to think of Carol as cruel.

Simon's words echoed. *Your mother loved you. If she couldn't show it, the problem was with her, not you.*

"Maybe she was dyslexic," Olivia said. "You hate to write."

"I'd write in this."

Suddenly, the past was moot. There was sadness in a blank diary, but good could come of it. "Well, maybe that's why she put it in this box. Maybe she meant it for you."

Tess's eyes lit up. "Do you think so?"

Olivia couldn't imagine a better legacy. "Yes. I think so."

Smiling, Tess pressed the diary to her heart.

Warmed that this little bit of pleasure had come of such pain, Olivia removed the last item from the box. It was a small leather folder, barely big enough to hold a three-by-five print. The photographs inside were roughly half that size. There were two, one on each side.

Tess caught her breath. "Who are they?" she whispered.

Olivia had no idea. She hadn't seen either face before—not when she was growing up, not in any of Natalie's prints—but suddenly the idea that she was related to Natalie seemed silly. Time to face facts. "Maybe my grandmother?"

"And your grandfather? On their wedding day?"

It looked that way to Olivia, but more than the clothes, she was riveted to the faces. Both wore gentle smiles.

"They look very nice," Tess said.

Olivia nodded. Her throat was tight.

"Do you think they're still alive?"

Olivia swallowed and took a steadying breath. "Not according to your grandmother's death notice."

But Tess wasn't giving up hope. "Maybe there's an address in the envelope. If there is, we can go there and find them."

The envelope was the only thing left to explore. Olivia hadn't opened it since she had returned the obituary notice there that afternoon. There had been no personal note packed in with the other things. If Carol had written one, it would be here.

A personal note might hold explanations. It might hold words of love. It might hold the name of Olivia's father.

Olivia wanted those three things desperately, so much so that she was of half a mind to put the envelope in a safe deposit box unopened. That way she could always hope there was a note, even if there was not.

Reason won out, though, because finally Olivia was tired of pretending.

Opening the envelope, she pulled out Carol's driver's license and her Social Security card. She pulled out the bankbook from an account that had been closed out three years before. She pulled out several newspaper clippings. The first was the review of an art show that contained photographs "restored by Otis Thurman and Olivia Jones."

Olivia had barely recovered from seeing that when she found the death notices of Carol's parents, six years apart, though both within the last decade. That meant both had been alive when Tess was born.

Furious at Carol for this as well, Olivia reached for the final item in the envelope. It was a piece of typing paper folded in thirds, surely a note. But the paper was blank, used simply as wrapping around another bankbook.

This one wasn't for a closed account. The most

recent interest notation had been made three months before, which would have been a month before Carol died. But the date didn't hold Olivia's attention for long. What did was the bottom line of the account.

Tess was at her elbow. "One hundred and fifty-three dollars?"

Stunned, Olivia said a quiet, "No, sweetie. It's one hundred and fifty-three *thousand* dollars. Plus change."

Tess tipped up her head and pushed her glasses higher. "Whoa. That's a *lot.*"

"Yes, it is." Olivia put a hand to her chest. She blinked and looked at the numbers, but they didn't change. Setting down the bankbook, she wrapped her arms around Tess and pulled her close. She closed her eyes and breathed in the scent of aloe shampoo and warm child as she rocked back and forth. "Your grandmother gave us a cushion. This means you can get the best ed-ucation money can buy."

"How about the best clothes?"

"Clothes come from me. Schooling comes from her."

"Did she say that?"

"No. But she would want it."

"How about the best clothes for *you?*"

"This is school money."

"How about the best *vacation* for you?"

"No."

"Why not?" Tess asked, pulling back.

• • •

IT WASN'T UNTIL SEVERAL HOURS LATER, when Tess was asleep for the night and the rest of the house was quiet, that Olivia realized why she didn't want any part of the money Carol had left her. With the understanding came anger and an urgent need to vent.

Tucking the bankbook in the pocket of her shorts, she left the house and found the path through the woods. The moon was bright, lighting a sky that teemed with stars. She half walked, half ran toward Simon's cabin, building a fierce anger along the way. She was shaking with it by the time she arrived at his door.

Simon was sprawled on the sofa reading when she knocked. When he saw her through the screen, he was on his feet in an instant. He looked warm and almost sleepy with his hair mussed and his glasses below the bridge of his nose. Pushing them up with one hand, he opened the door with the other.

Slipping past him, she held out the bankbook and, arms folded tightly, watched his face while he looked inside. He read the contents impassively, and seemed about to say something when, wisely, he caught her expression. Closing his mouth, he gave an almost imperceptible nod.

It was all the permission she needed. "I am *furious*," she cried. "How could she *do* this to me? Did she think I wanted money? Was that all her life was about? Where has she *been* for the last twenty years? Didn't she hear all the talk about quality time? Didn't she see *Terms of Endearment* or . . . or *The Cosby Show?* Didn't she *get it?"*

Olivia looked around in bewilderment, then put her hands on her hips and stuck out her chin. "Where did she get that money? I want to know, but of course, she isn't here to say, so I can only *guess.* She didn't have a career, and she didn't win the lottery, and if she drank herself to death, she spent a shitload on booze. So where did *this* money come from?"

She held her forehead and looked at the floor. "Her parents? I doubt it." Her eyes found Simon's. "There was no lump-sum deposit in this account, just a whole lot of small ones over a dozen years, and that's only *this* bankbook. The opening balance is big enough to suggest there were bankbooks before this one, probably with a whole lot of *other* little deposits."

With an angry expulsion of breath, she went to the window. "She was probably stashing money away from the time I was a child—and that's all well and good and honorable and almost every other nice word you can say except 'insightful' and 'perceptive' and 'sensitive.' " She whirled around and cried, "I had to buy all my own clothes. I used to work in the local supermarket, seven days a week sometimes, over holidays and after school, because she said she didn't have extra money, and

I didn't have anything to wear. I'm talking basics. I bought my own jeans. I bought my own shirts. I bought my own underwear. The first time I bought a *bra,* I went out and did it myself. That was baby-sitting money. I mean, even back then!"

Olivia remembered being acutely embarrassed, buying that bra without quite looking the salesclerk in the eye. The hurt was acute only now, looking back from the perspective of a mother with a daughter of her own. Olivia would never, *never* send a child of hers off to do something like that alone. It was a female thing—a milestone meant to be shared. She wouldn't miss it with Tess for the world!

Pushing a hand into her hair, she walked off toward the hall. Buck was in her basket, but the kittens were playing around it on the floor. She barely saw.

"Okay." She turned back to Simon, trying to reason things out. "Kids need to be taught the value of money, but hell, I was out there on my own. Do you know what it would have meant if she'd handed me a ten-dollar bill to put toward the sweater I wanted because every other girl in the class had one? Do you know what it would have meant if she had *come* with me to buy that bra? Do you know what a little help would have meant? I had to get a new apartment after Tess was born because the one I was in didn't want kids. So here I am with a newborn, and the first apartment I take doesn't have a refrigerator. I mean, how many apartments don't have refrigerators? Well, I didn't have the time to fight, and I didn't have the strength to move to another place, and Tess needed formula stored because I couldn't produce enough milk to feed her myself, so I bought a refrigerator, and paid twenty-five dollars a month for nearly two years because, of course, the interest from buying on time nearly doubled the cost of the thing."

Her eyes filled with tears. The aloneness hurt. "Was that a lesson I needed to learn? Would it have killed her to help me out a little? Would it have killed her to send baby clothes? There we are, me pushing Tess in her secondhand stroller through the nicest parts of Atlanta that we could find, and we're surrounded by mothers pushing state-of-the-art prams with their kids looking oh-so-cute in their Baby Gaps. I wanted that for my child, too, but I couldn't afford it. Would it have killed her to send one little sweatshirt? Would it have killed her to buy a cheapo plane ticket and come *visit?*

"But no," Olivia raced on with a snort. "She was too busy making her little trips to the bank to stash her money away. And then," she drawled derisively, "it comes back again to how she got the money in the first place. Did she take it out of her paycheck? Did she steal it? Or was it money for sex, left on a sleazy nightstand by a sleazy John when he finished doing his *sleazy thing?*" She shuddered.

Simon was in front of her then. "Olivia . . ."

She looked up into eyes that would understand. "I don't want it, Simon. I don't want her money. It wasn't about money then, and it isn't about money now. I wanted her time. I wanted to have a mother with me at Girl Scout meetings, just like my friends did. It's lovely to think she collected articles about my work with Otis, but would it have killed her to call me? My number was listed. All those years I kept it listed so that she could find me if she wanted to, but no. She didn't. She couldn't get herself to tell me I was doing good, not now, not when I was a kid. I tell it to Tess all the time, even when she's doing lousy, but if she's trying hard, she deserves the praise. Didn't I deserve something?" She exhaled shakily. "It wasn't about money. It was about love."

He pulled her close, pressing her cheek to his chest. "Oh, baby, she did love you. She just didn't show it the way you wanted her to."

Olivia tried to shake her head, but there was no room to move between his hand and his chest.

His voice was deep, but soft as warm flannel. "Yes. She did love you. Forget money. Think about Thomas Hope. She made him promise to get her things to you. Made him *promise*. And it wasn't easy for him. It wasn't like a trip across town. Chicago's a long drive, but he did it, because it was her dying wish. Her *dying wish*. Deathbed confessions are admissible in court. They're considered sacrosanct. Well, your mother's deathbed confession was that she wanted you to have her personal effects."

"That's not a confession," Olivia murmured, but her resistance was fading.

"From a woman who refused to open her life to her daughter and granddaughter? I'd say it is. She could have thrown everything out. But she wanted you to have something of her. She could have given the money to charity, but she wanted you to have it. Does it matter how she got it? Does it really?"

"Yes," Olivia said, but she knew he was right. It didn't matter.

"We think we have the answers," he said quietly. "We think we know a better way. I've spent four years cursing Laura for not seeing that boat coming and getting the hell out of the way, but I wasn't at the tiller. I wasn't in control. I don't know the time factor, or what I would have done. Since I don't like the outcome, I say I would have acted differently if I'd been there, but I wasn't there." His voice grew raspy. "I wasn't there, Olivia, and Laura wasn't me. She did what she could. Same with your mother. We can second-guess them all we want, but what good does it do? It only sullies their memory." He exhaled deeply and murmured a guttural, "Let it go, Simon, let it go."

Olivia slid her arms around him. He was solid physically and, while still feeling a pain of his own, solid mentally. He understood what she felt and steadied her at a time when she might otherwise have crumbled. Emptiness did that to a person. Her insides were a big black hole where dreams of her mother had been. She was hollow now. There was nothing of substance to keep her intact, except Simon.

He was substance. The beat of his heart in her ear was strong. His body exuded strength and warmth. He was perhaps just another dream, certainly one she had no business entertaining, but in this place, at this moment, he filled the emptiness.

She wasn't sure whether she raised her head, or whether it was his hand at her nape that did it, but their mouths met with exact precision, their thoughts apparently alike. She touched his back and his shoulders, touched his jaw and his throat. He was real, such an incredible comfort that she let herself go. He tasted of coffee and smelled of man. He felt like a lover, if the tremor she felt in his lean muscles were an indication.

He whispered her name. She caught the sound in another deep kiss. When he called her a second time, though, there was urgency in his voice.

"We shouldn't do this," he whispered, looking down at her with something akin to desperation in his eyes. "It's not fair. Not tonight. You're vulnerable."

"But I need *help*," she whispered back and waited, praying that he wouldn't leave her, because that was part of the dream. She had been left alone too many times. For once, just once, she wanted someone to stay.

He did. He stayed. He pulled her close and held

her as though he was into the dream himself, as though he would stay forever. He held her and kissed her. He undressed her with steady caresses in a way that made her feel round and full, made her feel desirable, and when he slipped out of his own clothes and put her hands on him, he was breathing so hard, was so clearly aroused that she felt all the more feminine and strong.

He carried her to his bed and came down over her, pausing only to ask if she was protected, then taking the responsibility himself—and even that was a gift. Loving him just then, trusting him just then, she opened to him as she had rarely done. He rewarded her with a climax that went right through his and beyond, and though she should have felt sad when it was done, the only thing she was aware of was a sense of completeness.

They didn't speak. Words didn't seem fitting in the shadow of her mother's death, but they made love twice more before he walked her back to the house.

SIMON WAS LEANING against the old maple tree the next night when she came out. He hadn't known if she would come, hadn't known if he really wanted her to—but his body did. He didn't understand it. She was unlike any other woman he had known, more spritelike than feminine. He could only guess that sprites had a special way with men.

Taking her hand, he led her back to the cabin and made love to her again, and it was just as good as he remembered, just as exciting—and perhaps just as wrong. But then, it was just for the moment, and he deserved a little pleasure in life. He had no expectations, no plans for the future. He had stopped making those four years ago. But there was pleasure in learning what she liked, and pure male pride in the moment when she cried his name and arched off the bed. There was the utter satiation that intercourse brought and the faint tremor in his muscles that no other physical act caused. He even liked the shared silence of the predawn walk back to the house.

How not to return in hope the next night? They didn't even make it back to the cabin this time. She was naked under her nightshirt, and hungry, if the hands that freed him from his pants meant anything. Just like that, he was ready. All he had to do was to put his back to a tree. She was easily lifted, easily held even when the going got hot and heavy. He had never had sex like that—and would have told her so, if it hadn't been too revealing.

Besides, what they shared in the darkness wasn't talk—it was sensation. When the sun came up, reality set in.

Reality for Simon this August came in the form of a hurricane brewing in the Atlantic basin. It wasn't the first of the season, and it surely wouldn't be the last, but it showed signs of becoming one of the strongest. Though it was still a ways off, Simon kept a close eye on its projected track, which at the moment showed it coming perilously close to Rhode Island.

Thinking about a hurricane hitting the vineyard was better than thinking about Olivia leaving Asquonset.

Twenty-five

SUSANNE HADN'T BEEN APART FROM MARK for this long since the summers she had spent at Asquonset with the children, and then he had joined them at least for a weekend or two. This summer, he was taking advantage of her time in Rhode Island to do business traveling that would otherwise have to wait until fall. Though they talked daily, Susanne was starting to think about flying home to see him between trips.

Then she conjured him up. She was in the chilly wine cellar under the Great House, searching for just the right vintage Pinot Noir to go with the tenderloin she was baking for dinner that night, when she heard a sound on the stairs and looked up. The light was dim but there was no mistaking the vision. He stood there with his hand on the rail, smiling at her.

"What's a gorgeous woman like you doing in a cold, dark place like this?" he asked.

She laughed. This was no apparition. Forgetting the wine, she went to the stairs and wound her arms around his neck. "Waiting to be rescued," she said, kissing him soundly. "You read my mind."

"I missed you."

"Is this Detroit?"

He grinned. "Nope. Canceled Detroit right at the airport. Best impulse I've ever had." He hugged her and said with mock sternness, "I don't like it when you're here so long."

"I can tell," she answered, warming her hands against his middle. "You feel thinner. I left you tons of food, but you're not eating."

He held her back. "You were supposed to say that you don't like it when you're here so long, either."

"Well, I don't. You always came sooner."

"That's still not what you're supposed to say," he teased. "You're supposed to say that you hate this place, that your mother drives you up a tree, that you don't care *what* she says, you're not interested in joining the team."

"I'm not. But I don't hate this place. The truth is, I've kind of been enjoying myself."

He touched her cheek with the back of his hand. "It would have been easy to say the other, though I'd hardly have believed it. You look too good, all golden and rested."

"Golden is from the sun. It's been a perfect August. As for rested, that's a dream. I fired mother's second new cook."

"Fired her?"

"She was impossible—bad-attitude Fiona. This time, I'll do the interviewing. Mother is such a noncook that she just doesn't know what it takes. It'll take me a week to find someone good."

"And in the meantime?"

"I can cook for another week. It's easy."

"And you love it."

"I always have."

"I wish you'd do something with it."

Susanne humored him. "Like what?"

"You tell me. In an ideal world, what would you do?"

She thought for a minute. "In an ideal world, I'd open a restaurant—but in an ideal world, I'd be thirty-four years old."

"You can open a restaurant," he said in a confident tone.

But Susanne was a realist. "I cannot. Owning a restaurant is a major commitment. It takes huge amounts of time and effort. I'm fifty-six."

"That isn't exactly ancient."

"No, but why would I want to work like that at my age?"

"Then open a little restaurant. Or a B-and-B.

You could offer breakfast every morning and dinner a night or two a week. You could do it right here in town. Then it'd be a seasonal crowd. You could close for the winter, and we could do something fun."

Susanne drew in her chin. He sounded serious. "And live here? Come on, Mark. We're New Yorkers."

"We never had a summer place. This could be it."

"Uh-huh. Right. We could live here and watch mother play with Carl."

Mark's arms slid from her waist. "You've been here for weeks. Has nothing improved on that score?"

"The wedding's still on. Thank heavens, she has a caterer for that. There's no way I'd do the cooking."

"Come on, Susanne."

"I mean it. I still think it's wrong."

"Have you read her story?"

Susanne sighed. She was sorry she had told Mark about that bit of drivel. He asked about it every time they talked. "No," she said now. "I have other reading."

He drew his teeth over his lower lip in a gesture she knew well. He was preparing to say something she wasn't going to like.

Before he could, she warned, "Do *not* say that the other reading can wait."

"It can," he said gently. "This is more important."

"To Mother. Not to me."

"It should be to you, too. She isn't exactly a
stranger."

"She's making a big mistake."

"How?" he asked. "Marrying Carl? What'll
change, other than the fact that she won't be sleeping alone? Why does that bother you so much?"

Susanne frowned. Mark had always been her
greatest supporter, which was why she found his
questions now unsettling. "Why does it bother you
that it bothers me?"

"Because I love you. Because I know what a
generous, giving, loving person you are. Because
this is out of character."

"This is my *mother*," Susanne reminded him.
"Rules change when it comes to mothers."

He nodded. "That's fine. I understand that. But
they shouldn't preclude common sense."

"Are you saying I don't have that?"

"No. Well, maybe. But only when it comes to
your mother. Then again, it may not be a matter of
common sense, so much as open-mindedness.
That scares me a little."

"Why should it scare you?" Susanne asked.
His tone was making her uneasy. "This has to do
with my mother and me, not with *you* and me."

"In a way it does," Mark said, suddenly gentle,
even beseeching. "I think a lot about aging. I think

about the things I'd like to do when I don't have the pressure of work. I could be like my parents and sit around waiting for death, but it comes faster when you do that. I want to live, Susanne. I want to try new things."

He hadn't ever said *that* before. "Like what?"

"I don't know. Maybe teach. Maybe learn to paint. Maybe travel somewhere far off the beaten path. I don't *know,* Susanne. The point is that I want to be open to different things, but you have to be open to them, too, if it's going to work. I'd never make you do something you don't want. But there are things both of us like. There's a whole *world* waiting for us if we have the guts to take advantage of it. Coming in here just now, I saw Carl on the tennis court with that little girl, and he didn't look a day older than seventy. That's because he's active. That's how I want us to be." He touched his head. "But it starts up here. If you can't accept this change in your mother's life, how will you ever accept a change in *our* lives?"

Susanne swallowed. "There's change, and there's *change.*"

"Right," Mark said, "and we don't know which kind will fall into our laps. Our kids may hate what we decide to do, but does that mean it's wrong? Does that mean we shouldn't do it? What's right for us isn't necessarily right for them, any more than what's right for Natalie is right for you. She's not asking *you* to marry Carl." He paused, then hurried on before she could argue. "I may well die before you. If I do, and if you had a shot at happiness with another man, I'd be the first one to tell you to take it. If the kids have trouble with that, they're just being narrow minded."

Susanne wrapped her arms around her middle. "Like me?"

He started to deny it and stopped. "Talk to her, Susanne. And if you can't talk, read her book. You owe her that."

SIMON WAS IN AN ODD PLACE, neither here nor there on several counts.

Take the weather. On the one hand, it was ideal. The sun was working its magic on the leaves, which were feeding sugar to the grapes, which were growing larger now and were fungus free. On the other hand, the tropical depression in the Atlantic had worked its way into a tropical storm and continued to grow.

Take Susanne. On the one hand, she relied on him to run the vineyard the way her father would have wanted. On the other hand, she refused to discuss anything *but* the vineyard with him, lest he forget his place and think he was family.

Take Olivia. On the one hand, she brought passion to his life in ways he hadn't ever known, which wasn't taking anything away from Laura, simply saying that Olivia was different. On the other hand, she was leaving, gone in three weeks max.

Take Tess. She was a pest, albeit a sweet one.

She was lurking down the next row of vines even then.

"I know you're there," he called, not particularly loudly. "Are you following me for a reason?"

There was a pause, then a faceless, "How did you know I was here?"

"Your sneakers are orange and huge. Is that the style?"

"These are *last* year's," she said, crouching down to peer at him under the grapes. "This year's are more clunky, but my mom wouldn't let me buy any." She started to crawl under the vine.

He stopped her with a quick, "Hey. The grapes are right there. Walk around."

She ran, but he could live with that. He looked up when she rounded the end of the row and came toward him. She had a hand in her pocket and looked innocuous enough.

"Now, *those* look like grapes," she said. "What do they taste like?"

"You tell me." He picked one from the back of a bunch.

She put it in her mouth and made a face. "Sour."

"Not as sour as they were yesterday. More sour than they'll be tomorrow."

She looked up at the vines, which were significantly taller than she was. "Are you pruning again?"

"Nope. Just checking around. I want to know if birds are eating my grapes."

"What do you do if they are?"

"Fire a cannon."

"You *shoot* them?" she asked in horror.

"No. I just scare them away with the noise. It's not really a cannon, just a machine that makes a boom every few minutes."

Her hand moved in her pocket. With her free hand, she pushed curly wisps of hair from her face. She looked up at him through her glasses in a way that magnified her eyes and tugged at his heart. For once, she seemed to be hesitant about asking a question.

"What?" he asked, not wanting to be tugged.

"Did you decide what to do with the kittens?"

"Not yet."

"You won't just drive down a highway and leave them on the side of the road somewhere, will you?"

"I told you I wouldn't."

She gasped and yanked her hand from her pocket. Seconds later, it was back in, and she was trying to look nonchalant.

He cleared his throat. "How many do you have in there?"

"How many what?" she asked innocently.

He rolled his eyes, sighed, squatted down. A conspirator now, he asked, "Is it Bruce?" Tess had named each of the kittens, claiming that even if it was too early to know the sex, Buck had managed just fine as Buck.

She whispered, "Tyrone."

"Lemme see."

She pulled the kitten out of her pocket and kissed the top of its furry little head. "His nails are sharp, but he's the sweetest thing," she said and smiled.

Simon was dazzled, and not by the kitten. "Did anyone ever tell you how pretty your smile is?"

He could have sworn she blushed. "Kids don't say things like that. And I don't smile for them."

"Not even when you told them about these guys?"

She tucked Tyrone under her chin. "One of the other kids has a cat who just had kittens. Hers had *six*."

"Ah. So her story was better."

"*Everything* she does is better," Tess said, solemn now. "Everything they *all* do is better. They won't miss me when I'm gone."

"Sure, they will."

"If they do, it's because I make *them* look good. I'm the one who doesn't get things."

"What don't you get?"

"The tiller. I always push it in the wrong direction. I make the sail luff. I forget which way the wind is coming from, so I jibe instead of coming about. Last time, the boom nearly hit one of the other kids."

"Well, you sure have the lingo."

"I'm not *stupid*," she said in a defensive reflex, but softened in the next breath. "It just isn't easy.

There's so much thinking to do. I like tennis better. The ball comes over the net, and you hit it."

Simon knew both sports. If he had to choose between them, there was no contest at all. "Yup. The ball comes, and you hit it. Always the same. And that flat, hard court? Nah, the ocean's much more interesting. It has different moods and different sounds. And it's not that you have to think so much, once you've been out sailing enough. Tennis is easier for you just because you've done it more."

"I'll be able to play tennis wherever we live. I won't be able to sail."

"That depends on where you live."

Under her breath, she mumbled, "Don't know where *that's* gonna be."

It struck him that moving around had to take a toll on the child. "Wherever it is, you'll have skills you didn't have before this summer. Your friends will be impressed."

"Maybe about tennis. Not about sailing."

"Sailing, too. You just need more time on the water. I could take you out."

The words bounced between the rows of vines. He couldn't believe he'd said them.

Tess was nearly as incredulous. "Do you mean it? Really? Will you?"

"Well, I could," he said, suddenly hemming and hawing. "I mean, you'd have to get your mother's permission, and she might not want it."

"She will," Tess said excitedly. "I know she will."

"There's . . . there's also the problem of getting a boat. We don't have one that's like what you're used to."

"Mrs. Adelson does. Seth showed me." She started walking backward. "He could come, too. I mean, he can't hear the waves, and you have to poke his arm to let him know when the boom is going to change sides, but he's *so* cool." She was trotting backward now.

"Where are you going?" Simon called, suddenly frightened.

Still trotting, she turned and called over her shoulder, "I'm asking my mom. If she says yes, I'll ask Mrs. Adelson. If she says yes, can we go today?"

He raised his voice. "No. Not today. I can't do it today."

"Then tomorrow," she called.

"I don't know—there's a hurricane brewing—and that kitten needs to go *home!*"

He might as well have saved his breath. She was gone.

OLIVIA HAD ACCIDENTALLY DROPPED one of Tess's Asquonset T-shirts into a load of laundry with bleach, which meant that what had been burgundy in the afternoon was bright orange by night.

It wasn't a unique occurrence. Tess had long since learned to find at least one thing good about a color gone bad. In this instance, the good thing was that the shirt matched her sneakers.

She had promptly put both on that morning, which was why Olivia knew she was in the vineyard with Simon. The vines were tall and as lush as a plant that was kept plucked could be, but bright orange still stuck out. And Simon? Simon was tall enough to stand out on his own.

Besides, Olivia had the advantage of height. She was at the window of Natalie's office, watching Simon in his fields, when she caught sight of Tess. She couldn't hear what they were saying, but she didn't hurry down to referee. She trusted Simon now. When Tess left him and headed here, her run was of the excited variety. Olivia figured she had two minutes before the child burst into the room.

Olivia studied the envelopes in her hand. They had come for her with the morning mail, three letters in all. Two were school acceptances for Tess. One was a job offer for her.

The schools were in Hartford and Providence. The job offer was in Pittsburgh.

Life was never simple.

"Are you Olivia?"

She glanced at the door. Other than updated clothes, a tired look around the eyes, and tension at the mouth, the man standing there was the image of Alexander.

She smiled. "You're Greg."

"How'd you guess," he said. It wasn't a question; he didn't wait for an answer. "I'm looking for my wife. Do you know where she is?"

"She was at the office an hour ago."

He hitched his chin in thanks, and had to step aside when Tess barreled through the door, but seconds later he was gone.

"Simon's taking me sailing," Tess cried. Her eyes were wide, her freckles bright, her mouth sweetly curved. "Seth can come, but we need to use Mrs. Adelson's boat. Will you call her, Mom? Please? Will you do it now?" She put her hands together in front of her nose, as though that would keep her excitement in check. "He promised to teach me everything I don't know. This means *so* much to me I can't *tell* you!"

Olivia was startled—and it had nothing to do with the fact that Achmed had risen from Natalie's desk chair and was growling softly. Olivia knew how long it had been since Simon had gone anywhere near the yacht club, and she knew why that was so. "He's taking you sailing?"

"Maybe not today, but tomorrow, for sure."

"Did he say that?"

"Well, I'm not making it up." She softened. "I know about the accident. One of the kids told me, but he had nothing to do with it. He wasn't there. I'm not afraid to go out with him."

No. Olivia figured she wasn't. But that wasn't

what gave her pause. She was wondering if there was any significance in Simon's ending his exile from the sea for Tess's sake—or whether she was imagining something that had no deeper meaning at all.

Achmed was making an uncharacteristically wary circle around Tess, and suddenly Olivia understood why.

"Will you call?" the child asked.

"As soon as you take the kitten in your pocket back to its mother."

Tess rolled her eyes. "He is fine."

"Take him back and I'll call."

"All right. I'm doing it now." She ran to the door, then returned to Olivia and gave her an exuberant hug.

When she left, Olivia was still holding the three letters. Quietly, she put them on the desk to be dealt with later.

"UPSTAIRS, SECOND DOOR ON THE RIGHT," Anne Marie told Greg.

He nodded, took the stairs two at a time, and strode down the hall over dove gray carpeting that was new since he had been there last. Same with the walls, which were sponged a compatible soft gray, and the furniture, a surprisingly high-tech burgundy and slate. Asquonset had come a long way, he thought in passing. Had he been any more tired, he would be convinced he was in the office of any one of his last three clients.

The second door on the right was open. Jill was seated at a desk there, but his view of her was obstructed by the man leaning over whatever it was they were studying. Greg patted the doorjamb just enough to get their attention.

When Jill's eyes met his and widened, he felt the same surge of pleasure as when he had first met her eight years before. She had been running a fund-raiser that he was attending, and the connection was instant. He would have thought the thread would be weaker now, especially with all that had gone on between them of late, but it wasn't. At least, not on his part. He wasn't sure about her. Wide eyes could mean a dozen things.

He gave her shoulder an intimate squeeze and extended his free hand to Asquonset's head of sales. "How are you, Chris?"

"Fine, thanks to your wife. She's been a godsend." To Jill, he said, "You didn't tell me Greg was coming."

"I didn't know," Jill said in a way that could have reflected surprise, or pleasure—or indignation, for all Greg knew. Once, he had thought he could read her, but he wasn't sure anymore. That writer had it right; she was Venus to his Mars.

"We can finish this later," Chris told Jill. "Visit with your husband." He closed the door on his way out.

Jill's eyes fell to the papers on the desk. Her shoulder was tense under his hand, as though she resented his touch. Feeling rebuffed, he put the hand in his pocket and asked quietly, "What are you working on?"

She moistened her lips. "Getting our wines into new markets. Natalie's been working with an ad agency on a new campaign. The slogan is 'Truly Asquonset.' This is the marketing and sales side. We need name recognition. We're trying to edge our way west—creep up on California wine territory." She sipped from a water bottle and shot him a fleeting glance. "What brings you here?"

"What do you think?"

"You could be here to nix Natalie's wedding plans."

"I might try that on the side, but the main course is you."

She made a face. "That's a disgusting analogy."

"You were supposed to laugh at it. Before that, you were supposed to throw your arms around my neck and tell me how sweet it was of me to come and how thrilled you are to see me."

She looked away. "It was sweet of you to come."

"But you're not thrilled to see me."

"I am. I'm just . . . unprepared."

"I'm your husband. Since when do you have to be prepared?"

She met his gaze. "Since I realized that while I

need to be with you, I also need to work. I'm loving what I do here, and I'm feeling satisfied and challenged and tired at night in ways I haven't been since I quit work to marry you. But I realize also that if it's going to be even remotely possible for me to work in the next few years, it'll mean major cooperation and compromise on both of our parts."

Greg was right back where he'd been before she had gone to see her mother—totally confused. But right now he was too tired to work his way through a verbal maze. "Please repeat that in five words or less."

"I'm pregnant." She didn't blink, just stared at him with her brows raised the smallest bit. Her words hit him as though he'd had a whiff of smelling salts.

"Pregnant." It was the last thing he had expected. Jill had left him. They hadn't seen each other in two months. *"Pregnant?"*

"As in having a baby."

Oh, he knew what pregnant was, but he was still having trouble dealing with the concept. Their having children had always been something for the future, something vague; suddenly, it wasn't. In that instant, he could picture a baby of theirs in living color. It was . . . startlingly, brilliantly gold.

He wanted to hug Jill. But she didn't look like she wanted it, and he wasn't risking rejection. So he simply said, "When?"

"February. I conceived in May."

Greg thought back quickly. May had been a nightmare of a travel month for him. There had been only one time—a short weekend—when they had been together long enough to make love. "At the Delaware shore?"

She nodded. "You were bored to death."

"Not bored. Antsy. I was stressed about a poll that had come out all wrong." He pushed a hand through his hair. Pregnant. Whoa. She was having his baby. "How long have you known?"

"Since right before I came here."

He was a minute taking that in. "Since early *July?* And you're only telling me now?"

"I didn't want to tell you on the phone."

"You could have flown to Washington."

"No. I couldn't. I needed time to think."

He recoiled. "If you're thinking about getting an abortion, forget it. I want that baby."

She smiled for the first time. "Well, at least *that's* good to know."

"Not an abortion. A formal separation then? Forget it. If you'd wanted that, you shouldn't have gotten pregnant!"

That quickly, her smile became tears. "You jerk!" she cried, pushing herself out of the chair and past him. *"I shouldn't have gotten pregnant? Did I do this alone? Do you think this was immac-ulate conception? Did you use a condom? Did you ever use a condom? No. You never once offered,* even though your sperm were the little things that caused the risk." Throwing the door open, she stormed out of the room, but she was back seconds later, slamming the door shut again. "And there is no law that says a pregnant woman can't divorce her husband. Get with the program, Greg. I'm not dependent on you."

"You want a *divorce?*" he cried.

"No! I don't! I don't really know *what* I want. I just want our lives to be different!"

Well, that was something, at least, he thought. Different was better than *done*.

His neck ached, tense to the extreme. He kneaded the muscles there. "Different how?"

"I've told you," she said. She was leaning against the door, looking at him with those same wide eyes. This time, though, he saw a dare. "I don't want to be ignored. I don't want to play second fiddle to your work all the time. I don't want to feel like an appendage."

She wanted attention, he thought. Like he had all the time in the world. Like he was sitting around doing nothing. "How am I going to earn a living, if I don't do what I do?"

"There are ways, Greg. There are ways. Look at you. It's the middle of the summer, and you're pale. You have shadows under your eyes and grimace lines around your mouth. You're exhausted. Is that how you want to live?"

"I'm exhausted because my wife isn't around to make life a little easier for me."

"Oh please. You were exhausted before I left."

"Well, it's worse now. I need you home, Jill."

"I'm thinking of staying here."

"Here? Why?"

"Because they need me. I fill a role. I'm a somebody here. I like being a somebody, Greg."

He put his head back and closed his eyes. "Oh, God," he said. "This is going nowhere." His head came forward. His wife stood there, so close yet so far—a beautiful blonde with class written all over her. That was the very first thing he had loved about her. She had class without arrogance. That hadn't changed.

"You don't look pregnant," he said quietly.

"Not dressed."

"Take off your clothes. Let me see."

Her eyes took on something else, then—a hardness that might have been hatred—and he was suddenly, thoroughly unsettled.

"That was the worst thing you could have possibly said," she said tightly, her voice low.

"I'm sorry. I didn't mean it negatively. I meant . . . it's something so different . . . my child . . . our child. Is it wrong for me to want to see the changes it's made?"

"Intimacy is for people who love each other."

"We love each other." Hadn't she said it on the phone not so long ago? But there was that look in her eye now, and the set of her jaw. It couldn't be hatred. Surely, it was just anger. "At least, I love you."

"No, Greg. You love *you*." She opened the

door, with a gesture inviting him to leave. "I have work to do."

Greg wasn't used to being dismissed. His first instinct was to challenge her on it. Hell, she was the only reason he'd come here, and the trip was a pain in the butt on such short notice—driving to Baltimore for the only flight he could book to Providence, then renting a car. As it was, he couldn't stay more than a couple of days. He had clients waiting. He didn't have time to play these games.

But something told him that wasn't the right approach. Her anger needed diffusing. He could give her a day or two for that. One question remained, though. "What am I supposed to do while you work?"

It was like she'd been waiting for him to ask her that, her answer came so fast and direct. "Go see your mother. Talk with her. Ask *her* what love means. Better still, read her book. It'll tell you about the sacrifices people are capable of making when they care about others enough."

Greg rubbed the back of his neck. He felt cold and alone, separate from Jill, when what he wanted was to take her in his arms, hold her close, and tell her things would work out. But for the first time, he wondered if they would.

She hung her head, denying him even that visual contact.

Not knowing what else to do, he left.

Twenty-six

SIMON JOINED THE FAMILY for dinner that night. He wanted his presence felt. With the arrival of Mark and Greg, the deck was stacked heavily against Carl. He wanted to be there if his father needed help. Same with Olivia. If the rising family numbers made her feel like an outsider, he wanted her to have an ally.

There were nine of them at the table, though Susanne was up more than she was seated. Simon had known she was a great cook, but this night she outdid herself. She started the meal with a light corn chowder with clams, then served a tenderloin stuffed with herbs and beautifully rare, baked stuffed sweet potatoes, and a warm spinach salad with bits of pear and blue cheese. Dessert was a crème brûlée.

They talked about the food and how good it was. They talked about the body and bouquet of the two-year-old Cabernet Sauvignon that Carl uncorked. They talked about the Napa Valley Cabernet that this wine was most often compared with. They talked about the storm named Chloe, now crossing the North Atlantic and gaining strength.

Greg didn't talk directly to Jill. Mark didn't talk directly to Susanne. Neither Greg nor Susanne talked directly to Carl.

But Simon needn't have worried about Olivia. Since she was viewed as the most neutral person at the table, everyone talked with her, and she held her own without fault. He actually got a kick out of watching her handle the Seebrings in her own inimitable way. Pride didn't hang her up. She was happy to claim ignorance and ask questions, and Tess was the same. They were two of the most curious people he'd ever met, that was for sure.

It worked beautifully with this group, but then, they were on all on good behavior. No one picked a fight. No one was snide. No one said anything that could be remotely construed as criticism. Everything was civil and polite.

The tension was so thick, however, that Simon was delighted when the meal ended and he could excuse himself and go out to the porch.

Carl joined him there wearing a look of the same relief, but rather than talk about it, he broached the issue of Chloe. "She's a bad one, then?"

"Could be," Simon said. "She's feeding on the low pressure left by Beau. He petered out. Unfortunately, it doesn't look like she will. She isn't a threat to Florida or the Carolinas unless she takes a turn, but the air currents don't predict that. They say she'll move north just west of Bermuda and gain strength until she makes landfall."

"Where?"

"Here." That was what the latest bulletin from the National Hurricane Center had said. "But who knows. Hurricanes can be fickle. Air currents change. She could get hung up around Bermuda and die." He skimmed the rows of vines that spilled down either side of the road in the waning light of day. They were healthy now, but silent and still. Not even the distant trees moved. Even the birds were quiet.

It sure sounded to him like the calm before the storm, although he knew it was too early for that. At this stage, there was little to do but pray and wait.

His thoughts strayed. With a hand on the porch beam, he glanced at his father. "Do you still miss Mom?"

Carl kept his eyes on the fields. "She wasn't only my wife. She was my friend."

"Do you feel guilty remarrying?"

"Guilty?" He gave a small headshake. "No. I tried to be a good husband to Ana. I think she was happy. But she's been dead four years."

Simon knew those four years well. He had ticked them off day by day, month by month.

"Maybe the thing to do is not *care* so much. Then you don't lose so much if things go wrong."

Carl lowered a hip to the wide wood rail. Quietly, he said, "You can stop caring? I never could. As for loss, it's part of life. I learned that early on."

"When Natalie married Al?"

Carl looked out through the gathering dark. "I shut down emotionally during the war years. I got medals for bravery that wasn't bravery at all. It was recklessness. I just didn't care what happened to me, because she wasn't waiting here anymore."

"What changed your mind?"

He inhaled slowly. "All that death. All those bodies. I wasn't there when they liberated the camps, but I saw pictures. I heard stories. Look in the eyes of any one of those who witnessed it first-hand, and you know the horror."

It struck Simon that his father had rarely talked about the war and that when he did, it was of lighter things, like the bars in Marseilles. His voice was calm then. He was stating fact. Interpreting it now, he sounded tortured.

"I always wondered what was worse—having an entire family wiped out, or having every member wiped out except one." He was lost in the tragedy of it for a minute, before looking at Simon. "Suddenly my losing Natalie wasn't the end of the world. Same with losing your mother. It hurts. You never get used to the pain. But at some point, you put it in perspective with the rest of your life."

"At what point?"

Carl shrugged. "It's different with different people. Like a cold. Some people shake it in two days. Some sniffle for a week. All you know is at some point you start to feel better. You breathe freer. You sleep the night. You start wanting to do things."

"Yeah, but you sure as hell steer clear of the neighbor who's just been diagnosed with strep throat. You're not looking for trouble."

Carl smiled. "If that neighbor passes out on his front steps, are you just going to let him lie there?"

"That's carrying the example to the extreme," Simon argued.

"No. It's just carrying it to the point where taking the risk is preferable to playing it safe. If I'd protected my heart and never married, I wouldn't have had those good years with Ana, and I wouldn't have had you. So I lost Ana, and there was pain, and the temptation is to swear off anything that can cause it again." His voice was gruff with feeling. "Only I am so, so lucky to have another chance. Do you see that? Do you?"

JUST INSIDE THE SCREEN DOOR, Susanne leaned against the wall in the dark. Forget fatigue. Dinner had been *stifling*. Her face ached from forcing a smile, her heart from pretending nothing was wrong.

She had thought to get a breath of fresh air, when she had come upon Simon and Carl, and her first instinct was to turn right around and go back to the kitchen. Then she heard Carl's voice and something about his tone kept her there.

She didn't want to listen, didn't want to hear what he said, but she found that she couldn't move. She listened to every last word, and when she did return to the kitchen, she was subdued, preoccupied as she cleaned up, unable to shake what he'd said.

No. Not what he'd said. How he'd said it. He hadn't been loud or defensive. He hadn't mentioned Alexander or the vineyard, only Simon, Ana, and Natalie. They were clearly what mattered to him. And the something she had heard in his voice wasn't new, she realized when she finished up and turned out the lights. It was there in her memory, a given of Asquonset life.

Carl Burke had never been overly talkative, but when he did speak, his words held a ring of truth.

Climbing the stairs, she let herself into the bedroom that had been hers since the upper floor was added to the Great House. A hand squeezed her heart at the sight of Mark's things there. Disagreements between them always upset her. He was a remarkable person—far more so than she. He was a kinder person, a more compassionate person, a *bigger* person, and she wasn't talking about physical size.

Disappointed in herself, she went to the dresser. Natalie's book was there, a thick wad of manuscript pages tucked into an envelope. Sandwiching it between two glossy issues of *Food and Wine,* she brought it downstairs. Mark was reading in the parlor. He glanced up when she passed on her way to the den, but neither of them spoke.

Settling into a corner of the long leather sofa that had fit her father so well, remembering Nancy Drew nights with him there and feeling cushioned by her very own view of the past, she set aside the magazines, pulled the manuscript from its envelope, and began to read.

MUCH LATER Greg slipped out of bed. If Jill was awake and aware, she didn't let on, and he couldn't tell. She was on the far side of the bed with her back to him.

Her breathing was steady. He had been lying awake, listening to it for hours, realizing that the only thing worse than not having Jill with him at night was having her with him but out of reach— and she was definitely that. From the nightgown that went from her throat to her toes, to the sheet pulled up to her neck, to the fact that she hadn't once turned or spoken the slightest word of encouragement—everything about her said *Do Not Touch*.

He was a glutton for punishment, staying in

Asquonset. He didn't know why he didn't just turn around and go back home.

Yes, he did. If he went back home, he wanted Jill with him. Life without her in Washington was lonely and dry—and life on the road, without knowing she would be there at the end of the trip, was just as bad. It would be even worse now that he knew about the baby. He couldn't just leave her here.

But he couldn't sleep, either, and trying was only making it worse. Slipping on a robe, he pushed through his bag looking for something to read. All he came up with was reports, but he didn't want to read reports. He wouldn't be able to do them justice, given his frame of mind.

His eye moved through the darkness to the dresser, where the moon lit a large manila envelope. He knew what it was and didn't care to read that any more than the reports. But he picked it up anyway and found himself carrying it down to the kitchen.

Setting it aside, thinking that his own refrigerator was as barren as he was without Jill in the house, he fixed himself a snack from the leftovers of dinner. He had a bowl of ice cream and a handful of cookies. He warmed a glass of milk and drank it slowly, thinking that it might make him drowsy and spare him this chore.

But he remained wide awake.

Figuring that there was no one to see, and that

he had absolutely nothing better to do, he pulled the pages from the envelope there on the kitchen table and started to read.

OLIVIA WAS UP AT FIRST LIGHT. She knelt by the window only until she saw Simon, then ran softly down the stairs and outside. He was already making his way through the vines by the time she reached him.

Catching her hand, he pulled her into a half run. They were well under the cover of the trees before he stopped and, grinning, scooped her up in his arms. He carried her deeper into the woods before laying her down on a pad of moss.

What with his presence in her dreams, and the sight, smell, sound of him now in the flesh, Olivia was fully aroused. She helped him out of his shorts and cried out when he entered her, not in pain but in awe. Same with the moment when he pushed aside her nightshirt and took her breast in his mouth. No matter how often they made love, he startled her with the wholeness she felt, and the amazing thing was that it kept getting better. She should have been used to him by now. She should have been used to the scent of dewy grape leaves one day and cool forest the next. She should have been starting to get bored, but there was always something new when they came together, always something different, deeper, more enlightening.

Today, it was words. They had a tacit understanding not to talk about the future—and he did
stick to it, but only until they had both climaxed
and were lying side by side, slowly cooling, re-
claiming their breath.

Then, in a quiet voice, he said, "Stay longer."

She turned her head on the moss. He was looking up at the sky, his profile strong, his expression uncharacteristically vulnerable. "Here?" she
asked. "At Asquonset?"

"You have money in the bank. You don't need
to rush off."

"I do," she said quickly, because staying would
only make things worse. "Tess has to go to school.
I have to get her set up somewhere."

"Why not in Providence? She could commute
with Sandy."

"But I don't have a job in Providence. I have
one in Pittsburgh."

His head came around, eyes meeting hers.
"You didn't tell me."

She felt guilty, torn, and determined, in that
order. "I haven't decided whether to take it."

"Is it a good job?"

"Yes. I'd be working in-house at a museum.
There's a good school for Tess nearby. They can't
take her now—the class is filled—but they say
there may be a spot at midyear. They'd want to interview her and test her once we move. She could
go to a public school in the meanwhile."

"Pittsburgh."

Olivia had said the name dozens of times, and it still sounded foreign. "Like I say, I haven't decided."

"What are you waiting for?"

"A better offer," she said and sat up. She buttoned her nightshirt. "Something closer would make moving easier. I want Tess to be able to start right in at the best school for her. I'll give it another week. If nothing comes up, Pittsburgh is it. I've actually never been to Pittsburgh, but I've heard good things."

"LIKE WHAT?" Tess asked.

"Like nice places to live and pretty places to shop. Like restaurants on the water. Did you know that three rivers meet in the middle of Pittsburgh? So there's Three Rivers Stadium, and the Pittsburgh Pirates. There's the Steelers and the Penguins. There's an aircraft museum and the national aviary. There's all sorts of Carnegie stuff, and Frank Lloyd Wright, and the Tower of Learning. There's a *zoo*."

They were on Olivia's bed, where Olivia had found Tess on her return. Tess had been sketching in her book, but set it aside quickly and wanted to know where her mother had been. Out walking, Olivia said. Thinking, she added, and told Tess about the job offer.

"Is there a Gap in Pittsburgh?"

"More than one."

"McDonald's?"

"Definitely."

"Pindman's?"

"No. Pindman's is one of a kind."

"They know us there already. It feels good."

"That's the difference between small town and big city. It takes longer to get to know people in the city. But remember the Seven-Eleven in Cambridge? We got to know the manager. And the yogurt shop?"

"Why can't we stay here?" Tess said, and Olivia's heart ached.

"Because I don't have a job here."

"You can get one."

"Not the kind I want. No one here needs a photo restorer."

"You're a writer."

Barely. Winging it. Sweating it out. "Only for this summer." And possibly never again. Olivia had no idea whether Natalie was pleased or not. She hadn't said a thing about the pages Olivia had written. Olivia wasn't sure she had even read them.

"I want to go to Braemont with Mrs. Adelson," Tess said. "She's the best tutor I've ever had."

"You'll always have the skills she's taught you. You'll take them wherever we go."

Tess looked like she didn't believe it. When her brows knit and her chin went out, Olivia steeled herself for an argument.

In the next breath, the child softened. The eyes she raised to Olivia were soulful. "I do like it here, Mom. I wish we could stay."

"So do I, sweetie," Olivia began, but when she reached for her, Tess slipped off the bed. In seconds she was through the connecting bathroom and into her own room. "So do I," Olivia repeated, whispering to herself as she put Tess's sketchbook aside and shook out the bedsheets with more force than was necessary. "But I can't pretend." She yanked up the sheets. "This is not my family." She hauled the comforter up in a single fierce billow. "My job is nearly done." The pillows went on top, knocked this way and that. "I have to *leave.*"

She took up the sketchbook and was about to return it when she found herself drawn to the window seat. She spent several minutes feeling sorry for herself for not being a Seebring, for not having a permanent job here, for not being so important to Simon Burke that he would rather die than let her move away.

Then she thought of her mother. She was getting used to the idea that Carol was dead—not liking it, but accepting of what couldn't be changed. She was even getting used to the idea that maybe, just maybe Simon was right. Maybe Carol had loved her in her way. The money would certainly come in handy for Tess for private school, then college, perhaps even an advanced degree in art. The child was that talented.

Smiling, feeling pleasure and pride, Olivia

opened the sketchbook. It contained drawings of the vineyard and the Great House, and drawings of the cats, and of Buck with her kittens. It contained sketches of Olivia, alternately depicting her as an angel and a witch. It contained a sketch of Carl with his tennis racket and a regal sketch of Natalie. It contained a drawing of Simon on his haunches plucking leaves from a vine, Simon sitting high on the hedger, Simon wearing heavy work gloves as he repaired the trellis, Simon holding a kitten, Simon reading a book with his glasses halfway down his nose.

The sketches of Simon were greater in number near the back of the book, clearly more recent, and there were far too many of them for Olivia's peace of mind. She didn't need a college degree to realize that Tess was growing attached to him. And right there was the very best reason for them to move to Pittsburgh. Attachments could be nipped in the bud. Out of sight, out of mind.

They were better on their own, she and Tess. They were safer on their own. She could guarantee Tess love. No one else could do that.

SIMON WALKED THROUGH the rows of vines, looking for trouble, looking for *hints* of trouble, trying to distract himself with busywork in one block or another so that he wouldn't spend the entire day in his office waiting for updates on the storm. But the vines were all well. The canopies were trim, the soil aerated and comfortably moist, the cover crops adding nutrients, the grapes growing round and full. Sweetness would come. That was what the next few weeks would be about—assuming a hurricane didn't mess them up.

He had a bad feeling about Chloe, and it wasn't a mystical thing. She was real, she was growing, and she was headed their way. According to the bulletins he received by fax, she had been upgraded to a category-three hurricane, packing winds upward of 115 miles an hour. She was traveling north at a rate that would have her making landfall in less than forty-eight hours, and she was showing no signs of turning away or petering out.

While Carl and Natalie followed the storm's path on the television in the Great House, Simon pulled up satellite pictures on his computer. He studied radar maps forwarded from the National Hurricane Center. He got e-mail from friends wishing him luck. His contact at the NOAA had nothing to suggest but that they board up the house.

He would have boarded up the vines if it had been possible, but the vines—the very same that had survived a too-wet spring and were now thriving—would have to be on their own.

Twenty-seven

DETERMINED TO START separating from Simon, Olivia did not go out to the patio to meet him the next morning. She didn't even look to see if he was there, but stayed in her room making a chart of the places she had applied for jobs. Follow-up calls were in order, a paring down of the list by deleting definite nos and concentrating on the rest.

She went downstairs with Tess only when she knew that others would be awake, and indeed, they all were, strewn about the kitchen, each watching the small television set on the counter from a chosen spot. Olivia didn't have to ask whether Chloe had changed course. Clearly, she hadn't.

Just as clearly, they were praying she would. With little talk and a perfunctory downing of poached eggs over hash made from dinner left-overs, the group dispersed.

Olivia wanted to rave about the hash. She had never had hash as good. Of course, she had never before had hash made from tenderloin. But Susanne was as distracted as the others, so she let it go.

Same with talk about the storm. Apparently, the thing to do was to maintain a semblance of normalcy for as long as possible.

Jill went to the office to work. Susanne went to the market to shop. Tess went to the den with Sandy to read. Olivia went to the loft to organize photographs.

Natalie joined her there a short time later. She had no news of the storm and, like the others, seemed content to ignore it a bit longer. She did an effective job of it. This morning, in a single hour with Olivia, she identified every face in the photographs that Olivia didn't know, including that of Olivia's mystery woman.

Her name was June Ellenbaum. She had been a friend of Natalie's brother, more so than of Natalie herself, and had died of pneumonia in the early forties.

Olivia smiled sadly on hearing that. She stroked Achmed's elegant neck, soothed enough by the gentle purr under her hand to confess, "I used to look at her when I was working for Otis and imagine that she was my long-lost grand-mother or great-aunt or whatever."

Natalie was silent for a long moment. "And now?"

Olivia moved her hand over Achmed's silky head. "Can't do it anymore. Maybe I'm finally growing up. Pretending can be counterproductive. It keeps you from accepting things you can't change."

There was another silence. Then Natalie said, "Stay on here, Olivia. Stay on after the wedding."

Olivia looked up. "Excuse me?"

"Tess can go to Braemont, and you can be my assistant."

Pretending can be counterproductive. "You don't need an assistant. Not after the wedding, not once the book is done." Olivia still hadn't gotten Natalie's verdict on the work so far. She was almost afraid to ask.

"But I want an assistant. I can find plenty to keep you busy."

"You don't need me here."

"That's not the point. I *want* you here."

Olivia should have been ecstatic. Not so long ago she had dreamed something like this would happen. But now she was trying not to get embroiled in dreams. That was what her mother's death had taught her.

"I've been offered a job in Pittsburgh." She told Natalie about the museum job.

Unfazed, Natalie smiled. "Now you've been offered one here, too."

"But the one in Pittsburgh involves restoration work. I'm good at that."

"The one here is handling people. You're good at that, too." The older woman's smile faded, her expression grew earnest. "I need you, Olivia. I like knowing you're here. I've never had a personal assistant before. Not a *personal* one. But look what you've done for me."

"I didn't do much. I'm not really the best writer."

"Excuse me? I've read what you've written."

Olivia tried to be casual. "You have?"

"Of course. Did you think I wouldn't? I've read it at every stage of the writing."

"I didn't know that." She held her breath, searching Natalie's face for approval.

All she saw was surprise. "I didn't tell you? I thought I had. I guess I've been busy. I've had a lot on my mind."

It occurred to Olivia that this was what Susanne and Greg had experienced. But she wasn't blood kin, and she wasn't waiting a minute longer. "Well? What do you think?"

"I think it's *wonderful,*" Natalie said, still seeming surprised. "Did you doubt that?"

"Yes, I doubted it. I've never written anything like this before, never even come close!"

Natalie smiled. "Well, I love it. It's clear and eminently readable. It captures the time and captures the emotion. I can't imagine anyone doing a better job."

Olivia felt giddy. "Really? Thank you. You're no doubt being kind, but I like hearing it anyway."

"I am not being kind. I'm being honest. No one could have done better, not with my book, and not with all the other things you've done for me. I'm not getting younger. I like having someone to keep track of the details, and you're *good* at it. You could work here or over at the office. We always need help there. Or at the winery. We actually need a liaison between the winery and the office."

Aching to believe and fighting not to, Olivia tried to make light of the offer. "Now that's a stretch."

"Not at all. Your problem is that you don't understand your worth. You don't realize what you've done, how much easier you've made things for me. I'm seventy-six. I want help. You give it without making me feel like I'm halfway to the grave."

"You're not. Anyone with half a brain can see that."

"I'm serious about this, Olivia." Her face showed it. "I wanted my children to be involved with Asquonset, but although they ought to care about the place, they don't. Neither do their children, as you can see from the number of times my grandchildren have visited this summer, which is exactly none. You've been here, and you care. I want you to stay."

"I can't," Olivia said.

"Why *not?*"

She couldn't explain it. How to explain being terrified of something that sounded *ideal?*

Natalie sighed. "Well, think about it. I have to go over to the office, but I won't let this go. You've been good for me. You've poked and prodded. You've made me talk about hard things. I needed to do that."

"The door to Brad's room is still closed," Olivia said, and Natalie drew back.

"I don't follow."

"Nothing's changed. So I haven't done much after all. Susanne and Greg are still upset, and that door is still closed."

Natalie looked away.

"Why is it closed?" Olivia asked. She had never been quite so bold before, and wasn't sure whether she wanted to hurt Natalie, or anger her into withdrawing her offer, or simply put her approval to the test.

Whatever, Olivia would rather talk about Natalie than herself any day, and Brad was unfinished business. "Is everything inside the way it was before he died?"

Natalie nodded.

"Do you go in there much?"

Natalie pursed her lips. The gesture accentuated wrinkles that were usually camouflaged by optimism. "Once in a while."

"Is there more to his story than you've told me?"

The older woman put a hand to her mouth, moving her fingertips over those wrinkles as though she would iron them out, and indeed, when she lowered her hand to allow for a sad smile, they were gone. "There's always more to the story of a child whose life was cut short. But that story isn't for this book."

BY LUNCHTIME, everyone in the kitchen ringed the television more closely. The time for procrastination had passed.

A reporter was standing on a beach in nearby Newport. "As you can see," she said with a glance over her shoulder, "the surf looks normal, but every indication is that this will shortly change. Chloe is battering Bermuda and holding to a north-northwest path. As of this hour, a hurricane watch is in effect for the southern New England coast. Latest estimates have her making landfall by noon tomorrow. She is a large storm. We expect to see the first of the cloud cover moving into this area by later today. Those of you who remember hurricanes Gloria in 1985 or Donna in 1960 know the drill. For others of you who are wondering how to prepare for this storm, we take you now to the headquarters of the local Red Cross . . ."

Natalie lowered the sound and turned to the others. "I remember Gloria. I remember Donna. I also remember Carol and Edna in '54, one right after the other. Typically, we lose electricity. We do have flashlights and hurricane lamps, but we need to make sure they're working. Greg, we'll need spare batteries and lamp fuel. Will you handle that? If there's flooding, it may contaminate our wells, so we'll need plenty of bottled water. Susanne? And powdered and canned goods, if the refrigerator goes—and speaking of the refrigerator, turn the settings to the coldest and open the doors as little as possible. The windows have shutters, so we don't have to board up, but the furniture has to come in from the patio. Mark?"

"Done," Mark said with the ease that was his way.

Neither Susanne nor Greg had that ease, at least, not around Natalie. Olivia half expected one of them to accuse her of blowing the storm out of proportion. When neither did, she was unsettled. Apparently, they knew what it meant to be hit by a hurricane here. Either that or they were tired. Neither reacted with anything but nods. Susanne busied herself making chicken sandwiches. Greg and Mark left the room.

"What can I do?" Jill asked Natalie.

Natalie wrapped her arms around her daughter-in-law. "You," she murmured, apparently having been brought into the loop regarding the baby-to-be, "can take care of yourself. Sit. Eat lunch. Watch television and tell us if anything changes."

"What about me?" Tess asked. "I want to help."

Natalie cocked her head and frowned. "You can be the runner between Simon and us. He'll be monitoring the storm in his office. He gets bulletins on his computer. You can relay any new information."

Olivia wouldn't have given Tess that particular job. She would have kept her as far from Simon as possible, and it wasn't Simon she was worried about.

"Simon's taking me sailing," Tess told Natalie.

Natalie looked momentarily startled. Then she smiled. "Not today, he isn't."

"Why are hurricanes named after girls?"

"They aren't always. Not anymore. Beau was the one right before Chloe. They started using men's names in the seventies. Now they alternate, boy, girl, boy, girl."

"Who is 'they'?"

"I don't know. Simon would. Ask him."

"*I* know," Carl said, catching the question as he came in from outside. "There's a committee of people from the Caribbean islands. They have names ready to go for an entire year. The list repeats itself every six years, unless there's a bad hurricane. Then they retire the name."

"Hel-lo," Natalie sang with a smile and put up her cheek for a kiss.

When Carl gave it and slid a gentle hand around her waist, Olivia nearly sighed aloud. They were a wonderful couple to watch.

"I stopped at the club," he said. "The boat's as

secure as possible, short of taking it out of the water."

Tess was at his elbow. "Why do people in the Caribbean get to name the hurricanes?"

Carl put a gentle hand on her head. "Because hurricanes in the Atlantic basin most often hit there, so the people there get first dibs on names."

"Do hurricanes hit the vineyards in California?"

"No. They don't usually hit California at all."

"Why not?"

"Because they move east to west. We get hurricanes here that come from storms off Africa. They have a whole ocean to build over. California only has land to its east. A hurricane won't build over land."

"Why not?"

"Because it needs water, preferably warm. That's why most of our hurricanes hit in August and September. The Atlantic is warmest then."

"What's the word from town?" Natalie asked him.

"They're battening down the hatches."

"What does that mean?" Tess asked.

Olivia stepped in. "Nailing things down so they won't blow around. Come on, sweetie. Time for lunch." She turned to Natalie. "How about me? What can I do?"

Closing one eye, Natalie looked to be running down a list in her mind. "You can call the land-scapers. I want our name at the top of the list for cleanup after the storm." She made a tiny sound. "I do miss Joaquin. This service, that service—they'll all be swamped with calls, but I can't have leaves and whatever strewn about for the wedding. Get a promise, get a *guarantee* that they'll be here. Oh, and please call the caterer and the florist, just to make sure they don't mess something up in the to-do with Chloe. And the calligrapher."

"I faxed her the seating plan yesterday," Olivia said. "She'll have the place cards done in a week."

"Good." Natalie pressed her forehead. "Now, have I forgotten anything?"

BY MIDAFTERNOON, the surf had kicked up. Tess's sailing class was canceled, along with everything else at the yacht club. A lecture at Pindman's on canning vegetables that was supposed to be held that night was postponed so that people could prepare for the storm. Same with a potluck supper at the church.

The television reporter, at Narragansett pier this time, was holding her blowing hair off her face. "The hurricane watch has now been upgraded to a hurricane warning, with Chloe expected to make landfall in less than twenty-four hours. The governor has announced that state offices will be closed tomorrow for all but emergency personnel. The national guard has been put on alert. Many businesses have also closed. We will be running through a full list of cancellations later in this broadcast."

The screen door closed noisily. Tess ran into the kitchen, leaned against the counter, and breathless, reported, "Simon says the eye will just miss us. He isn't happy about that."

Carl grunted. "No. He wouldn't be. If you're sitting in the path of the eye of the storm, you get a small breather between blows. The point of greatest force is often sixty-some miles from the eye. If you happen to be sitting in *that* path, you get hit bad."

Tess pushed up her glasses and looked up at him. "Will we be hit bad?"

"Nothing we can't handle," he assured her.

"Simon says some people are evacuating."

"Those'd be the ones who live right by the sea. A hurricane like this, you worry about the storm surge."

"What's the storm surge?"

"Seawater that rises because of the hurricane blowing on the ocean."

"How high does it get?"

"That depends on the storm. Simon'd know about the predictions for this one."

"I'll go ask," Tess declared, but Olivia pointed her to a chair. The child had been back and forth to Simon's office more times than she could count. The poor guy deserved a break.

"Susanne needs corn shucked." Olivia took a

big brown paper bag from the counter and set it down in front of Tess. "You are *the* best at that. I'll go ask Simon."

Olivia let herself out the kitchen door into a late afternoon that was eerily dark. The air felt dense and heavy, filled with moisture. Cutting behind the house, she jogged along the path to the shed. A second-floor light was on, glowing as it wouldn't do on a sunny day. Slipping inside, she ran up the stairs and followed the light to the room at the end of the hall.

Simon sat at his computer with his chair tipped back as far as it could go. His hands were folded behind his head, and one knee was crossed. He was waiting, not necessarily for her.

"Hi," she said and went up to the computer screen. "Whatcha got there?"

"Radar pictures." Unfolding his hands, he lowered one to her back. "The National Hurricane Center posts them. It doesn't look good."

Olivia studied his face. She knew his features well enough now to see that his eyes were more deep-set than usual. "You're exhausted."

Snorting, he shot her a look. "This is only the start."

His hand moved the smallest bit on her back. She wanted to think she brought comfort. That was why she was here. She was a friend. "What kind of damage can she do?"

He shrugged. "That depends on her strength when she hits. If she weakens between now and then, the damage could be negligible—a few leaves, a vine or two. Anything more and the cost rises."

"Worst-case scenario?"

"She hits us with winds greater than one-fifty an hour and wipes us out."

"Wipes us out?"

"Snaps vines in two. That kind of wind is ferocious. Vines aren't made of steel."

"But I thought hurricanes lose strength over land."

"Yeah. After a few *hours* over land. We'll be getting her straight off the water. That's full force. And it isn't only the wind, it's the rain. Torrential rains soak soil. If the vines absorb too much too fast, the grapes swell and split. If they split, they rot. If they absorb too much water, the juice is diluted and the vintage is weak. Either case sucks."

Grasping at straws, Olivia said a weak, "She may still veer away from the coast."

Simon didn't look hopeful. "She may, but if she doesn't do it soon, we'll still feel her winds. She's a big fat thing. Look at this." Tapping a few keys, he brought another image to his screen. This one showed Chloe looking like a typical hurricane—windmill-like, with a hole in the middle.

He pointed to her width. "This mama is nearly three hundred miles wide."

Olivia had no basis for comparison. "That's big?"

"It's big."

His computer made a small dinging sound. Taking his hand from her back, he sat forward and clicked on his e-mail icon. Seconds later he had a new message on the screen.

Olivia read along. "Who is Pete G.?"

"A friend with the National Oceanic and Atmospheric Administration." He typed a fast answer and sent it.

"What did he mean, the right-left differential?"

"The winds on the right side of the eye are stronger. Right now, Chloe is blowing at one twenty right and one ten left." He shot her a dry look. "Any way you cut it, that's a powerful storm."

Olivia leaned against the desk. She wished there were something to be done. "I'm sorry, Simon."

He smiled. "Not your fault."

"It isn't fair. The vineyard had finally dried out. The sun was shining. Things were looking so good."

"Things were looking *great*," he corrected. "The sun's been making the grapes sweat. It's like boiling down syrup. The more excess fluid you lose, the more intense the remaining flavor. But hey, this is old hat. The crucial part of the ripening season always coincides with hurricane season. Happens every year."

"Is there *nothing* you can do?"

"Nothing."

"We've put men on the moon. Why can't we tame a hurricane?"

"Oh, we've tried. We've dropped silver iodide into the eye—there's a whole scientific theory why it should work, but it didn't. We developed a liquid cover to put on the ocean under a storm so that it can't feed off the water, but the damn cover comes apart in the waves. We've talked about dropping nuclear weapons into the eye, but forget that. Can you imagine the fallout?"

He let out a breath and, seeming calmer, caught her hand. "That's what this life is about. Farmers are gamblers. Didn't you know?"

She shook her head, lost—positively lost—in his eyes. Cold and hard? Is that what she had thought once? There was nothing cold and hard about them. They were the deepest blue imaginable. They were rich and knowledgeable, warm and compassionate. They were gentle, kind, worried, and she was nearly in over her head.

She felt terrified, just as she had when Natalie offered her a job.

He gave her hand a little shake. "Don't look at me that way."

"I'm not looking *at* you," she said, rising to the challenge. "I'm looking *through* you. Know what I see?"

He smiled, shook his head. "What do you see?"

"The reflection of a computer screen. That's what happens when you sit in front of one of these things too long. It starts to glow on the back of your skull. I mean, there's a reason why we use screen savers. Come on over to the Great House. You need a break from this."

He arched a brow. "That's a break? There's a cold war going on there, or hadn't you noticed?"

She had to laugh. "It isn't that bad."

"No one's talking to anybody."

"Well, they're talking about the storm." She tightened her fingers around his and gave a little tug. "Come on. Come with me. You know more than any of them do. You can tell us what's happening while we sit around and wait."

SIMON CAME, but he didn't have to tell anyone anything. Television coverage of the storm had preempted all regular programming. An army of reporters, experts, and would-be experts were on hand to answer every question imaginable.

Three sets were on in the Great House—the small one in the kitchen, a medium-sized one in the parlor, and a big one in the den. Dinner was served buffet style in the dining room, but no one actually sat. There was a lot of wandering—eating some here, walking to another room, eating some there. There was little chitchat, little closeness between couples who should have been close.

No big deal, Olivia told herself. *A storm's com-*

*ing. They're moving around, trying to keep every-
one calm.*

But there was more to it than that. Susanne ex-
cused herself and went to her room as soon as the
last of dinner was done. Greg was already gone by
then. Natalie stayed for a while but looked distracted, and finally, pleading exhaustion, went up
to bed. Simon shot Olivia a dry look and left. Jill
stretched out on the den sofa with her arms folded
on her chest and her eyes everywhere but on the
television. Mark sprawled out in a nearby chair
with his chin on a fist.

The tension rose, and still they waited.

SUSANNE WAS LYING AWAKE in the dark when
Mark finally came to bed. On her side, facing
away, she listened to the pad of his footsteps and
the rustle of clothing, felt the dip of the mattress
and the pull of the sheet.

All was quiet for a minute. Then came the soft-
est whisper. "Susanne?"

She wanted to pretend that she was sleeping,
but she was too unsettled. She needed to talk with
someone. "I'm awake," she said and rolled to her
back.

"Thinking about the storm?"

"No. About Mother. I'm in the middle of her
book. She makes herself out to be quite something."

"She is."

"No, I mean, *quite* something," she drawled. "To hear her tell it, Asquonset would have been lost years ago if it weren't for her."

Mark turned to his side and came up on an elbow. "Is that so?" he asked, as though it wasn't an absurd thought at all.

"I don't *know*. It's what she *says*. Or implies. Did you ever hear anything about real estate holdings?"

"Your dad's?"

"No. Mother's."

It was a minute before he answered. "I remember talking with her once and being impressed with how much she knew about real estate. She didn't mention specific holdings, but it wouldn't surprise me if she had them. She knew what she was talking about."

That was news to Susanne. "She never talked to me about real estate."

"Did you ever ask her about it?"

Susanne looked at him sharply. His face was a warm blur in the dark, but there was a distinct glint in his eyes. "Why would I do that?"

"You wouldn't. That's my point. But I *did* have reason. I invest in real estate. I must have mentioned something that started a discussion."

She wanted to argue. But if Mark was anything, he was logical.

"Okay," she said, coming at Natalie's premise from a different angle. "If you were to attribute the success of this vineyard to one person only, who would that be?"

Mark returned to his back and looked at the ceiling. "The vineyard itself?" He turned his head on the pillow. "Carl."

"Not my mother?"

"I give her the business. I give Carl the vines."

"What about my dad? What would you give him?"

He thought for a minute. "A Clio. For best ad. He did wonders spreading the name. Mention Asquonset, and people in the know mention Al."

"Do you think he was smart? You know, intelligent. Shrewd. A good businessman."

"He was definitely smart. I always thought he should have been a playwright. He had a flair for drama and a way with words."

"But was he a good *businessman?*"

Mark spoke lightly, fondly. "Oh, I don't know. The investment leads he gave me never worked out. But hey, I'm not speaking ill of the dead. He'd be the first one to laugh about those, and I certainly survived."

Susanne stared at him in the dark. "Why did I not know about *that?*"

"That I survived?"

"That Dad's leads didn't work out."

Mark paused, but briefly. "Why would I have told you?" he asked. "What point was there? Why would I knock the man down in front of his daughter?"

"Because I should have known the truth."

"The truth was that he was a great guy."

"The truth was," Susanne argued, feeling hurt at having been kept out of the loop by her husband as well as her mother, "that he didn't do much of anything around here."

"Did Natalie say that?"

"NATALIE DID *not* SAY THAT," Jill argued. She was lying on her back, about as far from Greg as she could get without falling off the bed.

Bothered by the separateness of it, he sat up. "She sure as hell came close. She all but castrates the guy."

"Greg, I read her book. She does not. She simply makes a point that people thought he ran the vineyard, when he didn't. I mean, you were here growing up. Did you see him making daily decisions?"

"I saw him promoting the vineyard wherever he went."

"That's right. He was wonderful at that. But he didn't know much about the grapes themselves. He didn't balance the books."

"Neither did my mother. An accountant did it."

"Okay," Jill said slowly. "Let me rephrase that. He didn't read the books that the accountant balanced."

"Did Natalie?"

"*Yes.* If you're reading *her* book closely enough, you'll see that."

Greg looked off toward the window. The sheers

billowed gently, but the air in the room remained warm. Suddenly needing to breathe, he jumped off the bed and opened the window as far as it would go. With his forearm on the upper sill, he put his face to the wind. It was instantly soothing, storm smell and all.

More quietly, he said, "She tells it like she personally made this place."

"And you can't accept that," Jill said, but her edge, too, had softened. That made what she said less of a challenge and more of an observation, even a bit of a question.

The wind continued to feel good. It carried the scent of earth and leaves, and dredged up memories that had been buried for years. Greg had helped plant many a vine. He had helped prune and harvest. Those memories were good.

He searched them for his father, but came up empty-handed.

"All right," he conceded. "I can accept some of it. I can buy the part about his losing the shoe business, but he wasn't the only soldier who came home from the war and found nothing. I can buy into Natalie making money in real estate, and into her letting Carl make decisions about the vineyard itself. Hell, she'd been in love with the guy. It'd be only natural for her to favor him."

Jill's head came off the pillow. "She didn't favor him. She let him run the vineyard because he knew what he was doing." Her head fell back.

"Love didn't have anything to do with that. It was pure pragmatism."

Greg put his forehead on his arm. "Maybe she wanted to punish my father for losing the factories. Maybe she pushed him aside to make Carl look good. Maybe she pushed him aside to make herself look good."

"She didn't push Alexander aside," Jill insisted. "She put her finger on what he was good at and let him do that."

Greg straightened. "Let him. See? She *let him* do it. Like he was an idiot who had to be spoon-fed."

Jill turned away. "This is pointless. You are hopelessly bullheaded."

He approached the bed, suddenly desperate. "I'm trying not to be. I'm trying to share my thoughts. Isn't that what you want? Isn't that what this is all about, my sharing myself with you?" When she didn't move, he gentled his tone. "Look, I'm trying to see my mother's point of view, but it's at odds with everything I was taught growing up. I was taught that my father was strong. I've always identified with that strength—always tried to emulate it. Now she's saying he wasn't strong at all."

Jill turned back. "No, she's not. She's not saying that. What she's saying is that *she* was stronger than any of you thought. Is that so awful?"

"No," Greg said. "No. It's fine. Maybe it explains some things. If she was running this place, if she was consumed by the work, it explains why she didn't have strength left for us. I used to take trips with my dad. He'd have business to do in New York or Philly, and he made it fun for me, made me feel like he wanted me there. I always felt like . . . like I was a *chore* for Natalie. He showed me more love than she ever did."

And he missed that. He missed Alexander's warm smile, his slap on the back, the hugs that father had given son long into adulthood. He also missed Jill's warm smile, her hand on his chest, the way she used to look at him as though there was no one in the world who mattered more.

He wanted that again. But he couldn't bring himself to reach out. Couldn't risk rejection. Didn't have the guts.

When a gust of wind whipped into the room and rattled the drapery swag, he lowered the window. Then, feeling helpless—feeling *impotent*— he sank into the chair on the far side of the room and waited for drowsiness.

AN HOUR LATER, he was still waiting. Caving in, he scooped up Natalie's manuscript and went downstairs to read. By the time he finished, the wind was whistling around the corners of the house, swishing through trees, creaking through vines. The sun was barely up, and the full force of the storm had yet to hit.

Twenty-eight

SIMON SPENT MOST OF THE NIGHT in his office. He wanted to monitor fax updates and study the latest satellite pictures of the storm. E-mail flew from his computer to ones in Miami, Atlanta, and Charleston, but the words coming back held more sympathy than advice. There was little to say and even less to do.

So he worried. He worried about the vines. He worried about the vintage. He worried about Asquonset ten years down the road. He worried about Olivia.

He slept for an hour or two on the sofa in the office, and returned to his cabin in the wee hours to close the shutters and take a shower. The kittens were all over the place now. When he made coffee, he nearly tripped on a pair playing in the kitchen. He held one—Oliver, the smallest of the litter—so warm and soft, so silly with too-big ears, and so trusting with too-big eyes that he would have been tempted to keep the little bugger.

But kittens grew into cats, and cats died. It was enough that he was attached to Buck. He didn't want to get attached to the babies.

Correct that. He didn't want to get *more* attached to the babies.

Attachment seemed to be a problem for him lately. He wondered about the message in that. Carl had said that he would know when the time came, but it wasn't so simple. Fine. If he wanted to keep a kitten or two, he could. But he couldn't keep Olivia and Tess, not if they were determined to leave.

Outside again, the wind blew away all thoughts but those of Chloe. She was moving in on schedule. The difference was noticeable, even in the hour since he had walked this way. Overhead, the tree boughs were more agitated than they had been such a short while before. Dawn had come and gone, but the skies remained dark.

Back in his office, he read the most recent fax with growing dismay. Quickly he pulled up radar pictures. He read two waiting e-mails.

His sources were in agreement, and the news wasn't good.

• • •

"SHE'S DRY," he announced in disbelief when he was barely into the kitchen. He had to close the door by hand against the rising wind.

Olivia had been scooping cantaloupe into balls. She stopped, unsettled by the frantic look in his eye. "Who's dry?"

"Chloe. She hit another storm system and lost most of her rain."

Susanne stopped whisking pancake batter. "Did she lose wind?"

"Nope. She's strong as ever." Swearing softly, he pushed a hand through his hair. "Dry hurricane. Hard to believe. They're part of the local folklore, but this is a first for me. Some people call them hundred-year hurricanes, which tells you how rare they are."

"Is a dry hurricane better, or worse?" Olivia asked.

"Neither. It just introduces a whole other problem. We won't have to worry about torrential rains flooding the vines and swelling the grapes. We'll just have to worry about the leaves suffocating."

"Suffocating?"

"In a dry hurricane," he explained in a voice with a panicky edge, "the wind whips up the ocean. Without significant rainfall to keep the salt water in place, it blows along with the wind. By the time the wind dies, our leaves will be coated with salt. Their pores will clog. They won't be able to breathe. They'll close up and die. But the leaves are the lifeblood of the vine. Without them, the grapes won't get an ounce more sugar than they have right now. They won't ripen. The growing season ends, just like that."

"But harvest is still a month off," Susanne said in an echo of his panic.

"Tell me about it," he muttered.

"What can you do?" Olivia asked. "There has to be something. You can't just let it all end."

"We'll have to wash the grapes," he said and reached for the phone. He punched out a number. "As soon as the wind dies enough for the ocean to settle, we'll get out there with hoses and wash every blessed leaf."

Olivia and Susanne exchanged looks. There was no doubt about the scope of the job.

"Who are you calling?" Susanne asked.

"Fire department," Simon answered, then bent his head and spoke into the phone. "Jack? It's Simon Burke. They tell me the hurricane's coming in dry. As soon as she passes, we'll need hoses up here. Can you help?"

THE FIRE DEPARTMENT was only one of the resources Simon tapped. While he ate pancakes as fast as Susanne could cook them, he called everyone he knew who had a four-wheel-drive vehicle, a strong back, and a hose.

He seemed to gain strength with each call, or

maybe it was the food. Olivia refilled his orange juice glass, refilled his coffee cup, even put butter and syrup on the last batch of pancakes he ate when he was too busy talking to do it. And then he was gone.

By then, everyone else was awake, the television was on, and the wind was rattling the shutters, which were closed against flying debris.

Tess, who was frightened by the sound and the unnatural darkness, stayed close to Olivia.

Natalie, who was worried about Carl, who was helping Simon line up volunteers to help wash the vines once the storm passed, stayed close to the phone.

Greg remained on the outside of the group, studying his laptop, brooding and aloof.

Susanne cooked with a fever—and everyone ate. Breakfast was hardly over when she put out a coffee cake to tide them over until lunch, which was a Portuguese fish stew with hard-crusted bread. The dishes had barely been washed, dried, and put away when she put a chicken in the oven to roast. The smell of garlic and thyme was just beginning to waft through the house when, with a howling wind at their backs, Carl and Simon barreled in the door.

Olivia understood the relief she saw on Natalie's face. She'd had her own little nightmare image of the two of them out in the wind—a tree crushing the truck, an electrical wire tearing loose and frying them as they crossed a wind-whipped street in town, a ferocious wind blowing them right off the road into God knew what. With Chloe fully upon them now, she felt better knowing that they were home. She felt safer being able to *see* Simon here, and when she felt safer, she could more easily convey calmness to Tess.

Susanne brewed a fresh pot of coffee and put out a plate of oatmeal cookies that had been baked somewhere in between the fish stew and the chicken. The television screen held images of arcing trees, a wild surf, and brimming shelters. The occasional thud of a branch against the outer walls of the house sent the cats into hiding and everyone else into upstairs rooms to check for damage.

The lights flickered and steadied. A few minutes later, they flickered again. Shortly before dinner, they flickered and died. Along with sudden darkness came the abrupt cessation of all sound but the rattle of the shutters and the howl of the wind.

Within minutes, flashlights were distributed and the hurricane lamps lit. The kitchen became the sole gathering place then, with its battery-powered radio and its warm smells—and there was a familiarity to it for Olivia. She conjured up the photograph she had restored for Otis, the one of the Dust Bowl family whose faces she had touched, whose shack she had explored, whose closeness she had envied.

Time and circumstance were different, but there was the same unity of spirit. The lamp flames cast a sepia glow, the smells were of sustenance and comfort. She was with people she cared about, gathered around a beautiful wood table with a small radio at its hub. Tess leaned back against her. She looped an arm around the child's chest. Behind her, hidden by the dim light, Simon slipped a hand in hers.

Her camera couldn't have captured it. Only the mind could, saving it for eternity as a special memory in a gilt-edged frame. It was a moment out of time, a moment when this small slice of reality was seductive.

But reality had more slices than this, none half as idyllic. For one thing, there was the vineyard. The wind that battered the house was doing untold damage in the fields. The fate of the grapes lay in the balance. No one in this family could forget that for long.

For another thing, more than just Chloe was brewing here. Greg remained withdrawn. He stayed in the same room as the others but by himself, despite the fact that he could no longer use his laptop. And Susanne continued cooking with intensity, but without a drop of visible pleasure.

Was it concern for Asquonset? Was that likely from the two people in the world who had most shaped their lives to exclude anything to do with grapes and wine?

Olivia didn't think so. She guessed that they had read Natalie's book.

Natalie's face said she guessed the same thing. As upbeat as she tried to be facing the storm, when she looked at her children, there was doubt.

Did either of them look back? Not once, that Olivia could see. Not even when Natalie said something and everyone else looked her way. If ever there was a tip-off of trouble, that was it.

Worry, tension, undercurrents of something personal and explosive—all grew as the afternoon dragged on.

Olivia tried to stay out of the way. Whatever was happening was Seebring business, and she was just a transient here. She read to Tess in the den. They played games in the parlor and took bathroom trips together for moral support. But Natalie came looking for her when she was gone for long, Susanne was grateful for cleanup help, Tess freaked out each time a shingle broke free from the roof and flew back against the house, and Olivia wanted to be near Simon. The kitchen, with the others, was definitely the place to be.

Radio voices dominated the talk, filling airtime with stories that often had little relevance to Chloe but were a welcome distraction. Simon went outside once, only to return moments later windblown, soaked with sea spray, and discouraged at not having reached the vines.

"You were smart to turn around and come

back," Natalie said, and he nodded, but Olivia sensed that he wasn't so sure. The vines were his children. It was painful for him, sitting inside, safe and dry, while they suffered.

She peered through the shutters, but the world was a medley of impenetrable gray. When dusk fell, even that bit of gray was gone.

Dinner was a silent affair, more a way to pass the time than anything else. No one was particularly hungry. They had been eating all day. Confined for yet another hour, they were edgier than ever. The house felt close and stifling. Wine went untouched. The sound of silver on china grated. The shutters rattled. The wind howled without stop.

Shortly after ten, the emotional storm crested.

Tess had fallen asleep in the den, wrapped in an afghan. Jill was reading in the parlor. Mark was doing a crossword puzzle in the living room. Simon was outside, trying again to see how the vines were faring.

Olivia sat at the kitchen table listening to the radio with Natalie, while Susanne put plastic wrap around a plate of newly baked biscotti. When Greg came in for water, she offered him one. He shook his head and went to the refrigerator.

Setting the plate down, Susanne leaned against the counter and said to no one in particular, "That's it for here, I guess. Everything is done. What to do now?"

Olivia knew the dilemma. They could go to

bed, but radio reports said the storm was starting to move off, and the minute the winds had died enough to allow for hosing, all hands were needed in the vineyard. That could be in thirty minutes, or it could be in two hours. In either case, going to bed seemed an exercise in futility.

"You could read," Natalie said innocently enough, but it was the drop of water that broke the dam.

Susanne looked directly at her. "I have. I've done that. I read every last page, every last word of what Olivia wrote."

Greg turned back from the refrigerator, silent but alert.

Olivia started to rise, but Natalie put a hand on her arm and gave a tiny head shake. "Stay. I need an ally."

"Why would you need that," Susanne asked, "if you told the truth in your book? Wouldn't it stand by itself, if it was the truth?"

"It is the truth."

Greg took up position near his sister. "Truth or not, it doesn't really matter. You're damned either way."

Natalie held steady. "Why is that?"

"Because if what you say in the book is true, it's an admission that you lied about your life."

"Have you read it?"

"Every page. It tells of a life built on lies."

Natalie shook her head. "No. I never lied."

"Then it's about omission," Susanne argued. "You didn't tell the whole truth."

"Which is the same as lying," Greg said.

"You kept secrets."

"You kept Dad in the dark."

Olivia rose. "I shouldn't be here. This is between the three of you."

"*Sit,* Olivia," Natalie said, her voice quiet but firm.

Olivia sat.

Natalie addressed her son. "What would you have had me tell your father? That I only married him for money? That I loved someone else? That if it hadn't been for my mother begging me to marry him, I would have waited and married Carl? What would have been the point of that?"

"Honesty," Greg said.

"Would it have been kinder? More productive? Would it have made your father feel better?" Natalie shook her head. "I don't think so. It would have caused irreparable harm to a marriage that went on to become quite good."

"Good? But it was based on lies," Greg insisted. "Lies to us, too. You kept *us* in the dark about what was going on here."

Natalie's voice rose. "What would you have had me tell you? That your father wasn't a businessman? That his zest for war blinded him to what was happening here? That he had *absolutely* no idea what to do when he got back and learned we were penniless?"

"You weren't penniless," Susanne scoffed. "The factories were worth something."

"Your father didn't see that until I pointed it out. He was paralyzed."

Susanne went on. "You could have told us. Why did we have to learn all this through a book?"

"Because I couldn't talk about it," Natalie said with what sounded as much like self-reproach as regret. "Because telling one's children some things is . . . *difficult*. Because I feel bad talking about it. Because the only reason I *am* is that you both need to see where I'm coming from in my relationship to Carl." She softened. "Why would I have told you negative things about your father? You loved him. That thrilled me. Why would I have talked about what he didn't do, when he did accomplish so much? What was *so wrong* with building him up in your eyes? He was a wonderful man. That's a totally honest statement. What he did, he did well."

"You manipulated him," Greg charged. "You ran his life."

"You manipulated *us*," Susanne chimed in. "You gave and withheld information based on a master plan that only you knew."

Natalie smiled sadly. "There was no master plan. There never is, when it comes to farming. I wanted Asquonset to thrive. That was my goal. I just did what I had to do."

"To save the vineyard. Was the vineyard all that mattered?"

"No, Susanne. Alexander mattered. My marriage mattered. You children mattered."

"Could have fooled us," Greg muttered, crossing ankles and arms.

Natalie was still.

"You were never here," he said.

Susanne nodded. "You were always off somewhere, doing something more important."

Olivia felt a dire need to flee. Softly, she murmured, "I should not be here. Really, Natalie."

Natalie shot her a hard look. "You wanted to be part of a family. Well, this is what family is about. It's about crossed wires and lack of communication. It's about making accommodation for things you would *never* allow in a friend. With a friend, you just say good-bye and that's it. With family, you're stuck."

Olivia was too startled to speak, much less move.

Natalie turned to Susanne. "Not more important. What I was doing was never more important, just more demanding. I was working."

"Well, I never knew that," Susanne cried. "I thought it was social. How could you let me think that? I wanted your approval. I did what I thought *you* did. I did what I thought you *wanted* me to do. You must have thought I was a total . . . *nothing* all these years."

"Never," Natalie said with the shake of her head. "Not once. I wanted you to have an easier life. What I did was hard."

"You weren't the first woman to work," Greg argued. "You certainly didn't have to do it. Dad would have found a way to support us. Maybe if you hadn't jumped right in, he'd have had more reason to do it."

Natalie sagged a little. "Maybe. Maybe he would have. Maybe you or Susanne would have done things differently from me. Maybe I was wrong. But the *truth* is that I believed I had to do what I did, or it wouldn't be done. Fault me for it if you want, but I did believe that. And I'm not complaining about working hard. I'm simply saying I did it."

"You took a whole lot upon yourself," Greg accused. "It could have all gone the other way. The real estate deal could have bombed. The vines could have failed. Dad could have realized what you were doing."

"What I was doing?" Natalie echoed, sitting straight again. "What *was* I doing? I was trying to build Asquonset into a profitable vineyard."

"You took risks without even consulting Dad."

Natalie sighed. "Dad was not *interested* in real estate. He was not interested in vinifera rootstock, either. He was interested in talking war with anyone who would listen—and I'm not the only one who took risks. He took risks aplenty over there."

"That's what war is about."

"That's what *life* is about," Natalie countered. "Everything good involves risk. Even now. We could sit back and rest on our laurels. We could tell ourselves that we've built a fine name and that we're in the black. Instead, we're launching a new ad campaign, and yes, it's costing a lot, and yes, it involves risk, but isn't the point to grow? When all is said and done, isn't growth the bottom line of life?"

"Mother," Susanne said. "You're seventy-six."

"So?"

"When does it *stop?*"

"When I die. Until that day, I'm here."

"Taking risks," Susanne said, but more quietly now.

Natalie gave a small smile. "Well, goodness, sweetheart, that's what keeps me young. Risk—challenge—it's what keeps me alive. Everyone needs new things to look forward to. Not that I wouldn't find others—not that I wouldn't back off here in a minute if one of you wanted to take over, but you don't."

"You don't need us," Greg said. "You have Simon."

Olivia pushed her chair back and stood. "I'm outta here. This is going places that I don't—that I don't—"

"That you don't *what?*" Natalie asked, frowning. "Don't want to hear? I'd say that if we're talking about Simon you have a stake here, yet you'd run off into the other room. For goodness' sake, stop *running,* Olivia. Isn't it time?"

Olivia was so stunned that she couldn't find a

retort. Shaky now, she returned to her seat, but she sat on its edge.

Natalie readdressed Greg. "Simon isn't taking over anything," she said with a fierceness that made Olivia feel not so singled out. "He's filling the role that his father filled, but the vineyard was never Carl's. It was mine."

Greg didn't give an inch. "If what you say in your book is true, for all practical purposes Carl was an equal player. It was you and Carl. Dad was in the dark. Did the two of you laugh at that?"

"If Carl had ever laughed at your father," Natalie said in a steely voice, "I'd have asked him to leave. Alexander was my husband. I wasn't having *anyone* laugh at him, and I never, *never* did it myself. I loved him. If I could have made him into a vineyardist, I would have, but he wasn't interested in that part of the business. He didn't have the patience to hang around here nurturing crops. He was a social creature, far more than me, so I gave him the responsibility of the side of the business that required social skills. And he was happy. He felt important. He *was* important. He had a good life. I gave him all the satisfaction I could."

Greg was suddenly indignant. "*He* gave you a name, when Carl wouldn't. *He* gave you a reason to keep this place alive, when Carl just walked off without you. He deserved more than just . . . satisfaction. He was *entitled* to more."

Natalie came alive then. Her face was tight,

every wrinkle distinct. Her head moved in an infinitesimal wobble. "Entitled? *Entitled?* That's a dangerous word, Greg. Be careful how you use it. People aren't entitled to things. They have to earn them. That goes for money and respect and love. It goes for a house and a car. It goes for a vineyard." Her eyes filled with fire. "Entitled? Your father let me down. He nearly destroyed me. But I stayed with him. I worked to make things right, even when that meant taking time away from you and Susanne. I worked because he didn't. I gave him more than another person in my position might have. Entitled to more? I don't think so. If he thought so, he was wrong, and if he passed that— that *horrible* concept—on to you, he was *doubly* wrong. You aren't *entitled* to anything that you haven't earned, starting with your wife!"

Oh, boy, Olivia thought. They were really getting into it. She had no business listening, but she didn't dare move. Better to sit so still that they forgot she was there.

Hands pressing down on the table, Natalie lit into Greg on this even more personal level. "You seem to think Jill belongs to you, like she's a possession. What have you done to deserve her? Given her your name? Given her a place to stay while you're off on the road? Given her money for clothes or food? Wake *up,* Greg. Times have changed. She doesn't need any of those things. She can provide for herself. The only thing you're *enti-*

tled to, where Jill is concerned, is a fair hearing and
a second chance, because she took vows when she
married you, and she owes you that. From what I
can see, you haven't earned a drop more. You never
will, if you think the world owes you. No one owes
you, Greg, least of all Jill. If you want her, you'll
have to go after her. Fight for her. *Earn* her."

Something of what she said must have registered, because Greg looked stricken. He swallowed, but made no attempt to speak.

Quietly, Susanne said, "Where did that come
from?"

Scowling, Natalie put her hands in her lap.
"I'm not sorry. It needed to be said."

Olivia agreed with that. She wanted to stand up
and cheer. She had half a mind to write down every
word Natalie had said and print it up for Jill to see,
and *then* she would describe that stricken look on
Greg's face. It was so deserved.

Greg found his voice, but he remained shaken.
"Okay. I hear what you're saying. But something
else needs to be said."

"What?" Natalie asked.

"Brad. Why was he so special?"

Olivia's eyes flew to Natalie, who suddenly
looked to be barely breathing.

"He was my firstborn."

Susanne asked a skeptical, "Is that all?"

Natalie started to speak, but stopped. She
frowned, seeming bewildered.

Trapped, Olivia thought and held her breath.

Susanne turned beseeching. "He was always your shining light. He could do no wrong. Not in life, not in death. We didn't have a chance against that."

"I always knew that Dad loved me," Greg said. "I was never sure about you."

"Ohh," Natalie breathed, suddenly tearful, "I loved you. I loved you both."

"But you loved Brad more," Greg put in with an element of defeat.

Natalie struggled. "No. No—it's just—he died." She frowned and studied the table. "That loss was almost unbearable."

Quietly, Susanne asked, "Because he was Carl's son?"

Olivia went stock-still. She didn't hear the wind or the rattle of shutters. There was utter silence in the room. Natalie didn't say a word.

"The timing would work," Greg said, sounding more as though he was solving a puzzle than making an accusation. "If you were with Carl that way before he left, it would have been a month before you married Dad. You could have pulled it off."

If you were with Carl that way. It was the million-dollar question. Olivia hadn't had the courage to ask Natalie herself. She waited, wondered.

Susanne, too, seemed to be reasoning aloud. "Remember Barbie Apgar, my friend growing up? Her mother always said that her actual birth date was three weeks before the date on all the records. She claimed that record keeping was totally messed up during the war, because the offices were all shorthanded and everyone was focused on Europe. The Apgars never knew when to celebrate Barbie's birthday. It was a standing joke."

"Brad looked just like you," Greg told Natalie. "It's in all the pictures. Your face, your coloring. Who'd have known if his father wasn't Dad?"

"Jeremiah and Brida," Susanne answered. "They were here. They would have known if there was a discrepancy in the dates, but according to what you wrote, they told you to marry Dad. They wanted Carl to marry someone from Ireland. And your father was ill, so he wouldn't have kept track of the dates, and besides, he wanted the Seebring shoe money. And your mother died before the war was over, which meant that she wasn't here to spill the beans."

"No one was around those first few years after Brad was born," Greg said. "Dad was gone. Carl was gone. Who'd have *known?"*

All eyes were on Natalie. Olivia's heart went out to her, but she wanted to hear the answer as much as the others.

Natalie didn't deny it. She wore a beseeching look, but she didn't say a word. Olivia was reaching her own conclusions when a sound broke the silence. It came from the door to the hall.

There, in the shadows on the outer fringe of the

light cast by the lamps, stood Carl. He was staring at Natalie, looking stunned. "Is it true?" he asked in a crusty voice, coming forward a single slow step.

Natalie put a hand to her mouth. She remained mute.

"You didn't know?" Susanne asked Carl, who shook his head, but the gesture went on longer than it would have for a simple negative reply. He seemed dazed. "You had to have known it was possible," she pushed. "Didn't you *guess?*"

Carl kept looking at Natalie. He started to speak, then stopped. He frowned, tipped his head, winced at whatever cut through his mind. It was so painful watching such a kind, gentle, good-hearted man suffer that Olivia would have called a time-out, had this been a game. She looked at Susanne, then Greg, thinking that one or the other would take pity on him. To their credit, at least, neither of them seemed angry with him. Carl had been kept in the dark about this, just as Alexander had been kept in the dark about so much else.

Carl ran a hand over his mouth. His eyes fell to the floor. Then, seeming puzzled still, he looked at Susanne. "I learned to distance myself," he said, sounding faraway even then. "I had to. When I learned that your mother had married someone else, I—my whole world fell through. For a while, all I did was fight. Helped the country in the war effort, that's for sure," he added, but without any hint of a smile. Rather, frowning again, he put a hand on the back of his head. "Then I came back here and had to see that ring on her finger every day. Had to see Brad and you every day. I learned to tell myself that that's just the way it was. Couldn't change it. All done."

"How could you stay here?" Greg asked with what Olivia was relieved to call compassion.

Carl's eyes cleared. "How could I stay? you ask. How could I *leave?* She was alone. Her husband was still over there, and she had two children, a sick father, and a farm that needed tending. I told myself I'd stay until Alexander got home, but it was clear right from the start that farming wasn't his thing, and then I couldn't leave Natalie alone with the work any more than I could before."

"How could you look my father in the eye?" Susanne asked.

Carl stood straighter, seeming challenged now. "Why would that have been a problem? I never compromised his wife. Any romantic involvement I had with her ended with her marriage. I had nothing to hide, nothing to be ashamed of." His gaze went to Natalie. "I had no idea Brad was mine. Maybe if I'd known it, I'd have done something. Maybe I'd have had trouble looking Al in the eye then, but I didn't know a damn thing. I was off in Europe fighting a war, catching what little sleep I could by dreaming about coming back here and marrying the love of my life. Then I was cut off cold. I was the last one to know about the marriage.

And about Brad?" The pain was in his eyes again. He blew out a sharp puff of air.

It was followed by a sharper sound, though, when the outer door flew open and Simon came in from the storm. He was windblown and wet, but there was a look of relief on his face.

"The wind is down. Let's go."

Twenty-nine

SIMON WAS VAGUELY AWARE that the tension in the kitchen was too intense to be caused by the storm alone, but that wasn't his worry just then. The grape leaves were. Every minute counted.

"Is anyone helping?" he asked in dismay when five pairs of eyes regarded him dumbly.

Natalie was the first to react, rising quickly from her seat. "Oh my God, yes. Where do you want us to start?"

"We'll work from top to bottom, starting with the Cabs. Donna's already out there. She'll set everyone up." He pulled a piece of paper from his pocket. It was damp and wrinkled, but ballpoint pen ink didn't smudge. He would rather Natalie stay inside making calls. It was gentler work.

"These people are waiting to help. They need to be called."

"Olivia will make the calls. I'm going outside."

Carl was suddenly there with a gruff, "Let Olivia do the physical work."

Natalie rounded on him. "I may have made other mistakes in my life, but giving the vineyard my all was never one of them. I'm going out there, Carl, and if I die washing those leaves, it's God's will." She passed Simon and went out the door.

"What was that about?" Simon asked Carl.

Looking cross, Carl merely followed Natalie out. Greg left seconds later.

"I'll get Mark," Susanne murmured and went in the other direction.

That left Simon and Olivia.

He pushed both hands through his hair, then wiped them on his shorts—but shorts, hands, hair were all as salty and wet as the vines. "Did I miss something?"

"Nothing you can't hear about later," Olivia said. "Are you okay?"

He felt a tiny pang in his chest. It had been awhile since anyone had asked him that. "Just tired," he said, managing a slight smile. "I didn't sleep much last night."

"How long will it take tonight?"

"Can't take more than a few hours, or the damage is done. Adrenaline will keep me going that long." He handed her the list. "Start with the fire department. They'll bring lights. Where's Tess?"

"In the den. I'll wake her when I go out, so she won't panic if she finds no one here."

"Bring her," Simon said, and suddenly, it was as important as the vines. The vineyard was his baby, but Tess was Olivia's, and Olivia mattered. They both mattered.

The doubt on Olivia's face reminded him what a bastard he'd been when they had first arrived. He still needed to absolve himself for that.

"She can help," he said. "It isn't dangerous, just tedious, but she's smart and she's strong. Every helping hand gives the grapes a better chance." When Olivia remained unsure, he said, "I'll keep her close."

Close to the house? Close to the others? Close to me? The words were vague, even to Simon.

Whichever Olivia chose, it was apparently enough to convince her. When she nodded, he smiled, feeling pleased for the first time that night.

"I'll get her," Olivia said.

But Simon wanted to do it himself. He remembered what it was to give to a child and see glee in return. Tess wasn't six, and it wasn't Christmas morning, but if he had learned anything about her this summer, he suspected she would be pleased to be asked. He wanted to be there to see.

"I will," he said, heading for the den. "You start on that list."

• • •

NATURALLY, OLIVIA FOLLOWED HIM to the den. If she hadn't already been in love with him, she would have fallen the rest of the way when she saw how gently he freed Tess's head from the afghan and brought her awake. Thinking that, realizing it, *admitting* it for the very first time, she felt hard palpitations in her chest. Well, she did love him. There was no point in denying it. Everything about him appealed to her—body, mind, and manner. And now there was Tess. That was a vital part of it. Tess was the center of her life. Olivia could never love a man who didn't understand that, or agree, or feel the same, and it looked from where she stood at the door to the den that Simon did. She couldn't make out distinct words in the low murmur of his voice, but she could have sworn she heard an element of excitement. She certainly saw it on Tess's face when the girl pushed the afghan aside and came to her feet—wide awake in an instant, looking more enthused than she had for anything in months.

Actually, that wasn't so. She had been just as eager to go sailing with Simon, but this was a more realistic activity. If the vines were saved, Olivia wanted Tess to know she had helped. It would bring closure to the summer.

The danger, of course, was that Tess would grow more attached to Simon. Olivia's heart was already lost, but she would have liked to spare Tess that. How to do it, though, with Simon taking

Tess's hand and leading her back to the kitchen, snatching a dry dish towel from the drawer and making her tuck it in the waistband of her shorts? *For your glasses,* he said. *I know how this is.* If Olivia might have custom-ordered a father for Tess, it would have been Simon.

Clutching the phone list, she watched them together. Her heart followed them right out the door, leaving a hole in her chest that would take a long time healing, she knew. But she could handle it. She would have to. She had no choice.

And Tess? If the connection with Simon strengthened after this, what then?

Reasoning as only a mother could who wanted her child to aim high, Olivia decided that given the choices, she would rather Tess know that men like Simon did exist than not.

SUSANNE'S NATURAL INSTINCT was to stay in the kitchen perking pot after pot of coffee on the gas stove, since the big electric urn wouldn't work. Her instinct was to make sandwiches and other goodies, and put out a spread for the people who would be coming to help.

But she had to get out of the house, for a little while at least. She had to breathe fresh air, had to stretch her arms and legs. Once Donna had set her up on a row of vines with a hose attached to the irrigation pipes, little concentration was required beyond keeping the wind at her back. More than anything else, she needed time to air out her mind.

Mark worked on the next row. She couldn't see him at first in the dark, not until the fire trucks arrived and set up huge floodlights, and then there was more to see than just Mark. The vineyard was suddenly a world of sparkle that could give Fifth Avenue at Christmas a run for its money. Spray from gently pressed nozzles arced softly over the uppermost leaves, shimmering and refracting in the light. The wind was gentle now, more a breeze than anything. With so much spray around, she inevitably grew wet, but the air wasn't cool enough to chill her, and the sight of the vineyard was compensation enough.

Working this way, fighting to save something that mattered more to her than she wanted to admit, she felt energized. It struck her, though, that much of the energy came from the thought of her mother working out there in the mist. Something had happened back in the kitchen. Susanne had read Natalie's book and managed not to be touched, but seeing Natalie in pain, with Carl angry and the spectre of Brad hovering and Greg needing answers as much as Susanne did—something had opened up inside her. For the first time in her life, she saw that Natalie was human. She was human, and she was flawed. That realization diffused Susanne's anger, allowing her to look back over the story of Natalie's life with the same honesty they had demanded of her, and acknowledge that the woman had been quite remarkable, faults and all.

Susanne wanted to reread that book. She wanted to get to know this other woman her mother had been, wanted to get to know the person who had made her share of mistakes but had surely built something of value.

Asquonset really was a beautiful place. Susanne had forgotten just how much so. Standing here now, smelling the wet earth and the fresh river water that came through the pipes and washed the leaves, thinking about her mother, who was seventy-six and vital in ways Susanne wanted to be when she was that age, she felt inspired.

GREG FELT LIKE he was holding three hoses. Only one sprayed water. The other two sprayed thoughts—one of Natalie, one of Jill—and they kept crossing each other, spilling back on him, flooding his mind. Then a rescue truck arrived from Huffington and set up a floodlight beside the Gewürztraminer vines, where he was. He caught sight of his wife in the next row, and suddenly the flooding eased and clear thought returned. Yes, he felt possessive; that wouldn't change soon. But he also felt protective, which seemed a far more honorable trait.

Dragging the hose with him, he shimmied

under the vines on his stomach, as Carl had taught him to do to keep from hurting the grapes, so many years before. Coming up near Jill, he continued spraying his row from her side. He had to speak loudly to be heard above the water's sibilance. "Want me to take your hose for a while?"

"No," she called back. "I'm fine."

"Are you sure this is all right for you to do?"

"Do you think I'd do anything to harm my child?" she asked sharply.

He pulled back. No. She wouldn't do anything to harm her child. He knew that. He also knew not to state the obvious and say that the child was his child, too. As angry as he was at Natalie for telling him how to handle his wife, he knew that things had to change if he was going to be any kind of a father to the child.

He could be a good one. He could be as good a father as Alexander had been—no, a *better* one, because he could be the breadwinner. That would allow Jill to be around for their kids as Natalie hadn't been around for hers.

Granted, Jill said she wanted to work. That would take some figuring out. Same with Greg's time. He couldn't be much of a father if he continued to travel the way he'd been doing. Couldn't be much of a husband, either—though he wasn't telling his mother that. If he cut back his hours and traveled less, it would be because he wanted to be with Jill, not because his mother had told him what to do. Natalie had no right to do that. She was no saint. He had to confess that he'd found satisfaction in her discomfort there at the end.

That said, he still felt the sting of her rebuke. She hadn't ever talked to him that way. Hadn't ever criticized him like that. When he had been growing up, her distraction had been disapproval enough.

He wondered if he'd been wrong, wondered if it hadn't been disapproval at all, if she had just been . . . *busy* . . . like she'd said.

In the spirit of the honesty he had accused her of lacking, he did have to concede that she had built something quite nice here at Asquonset. There were many more vines now than there had been ten years before. The scope of the current cleanup attested to that.

"Have you seen the front drive?" he called to Jill. "It's lined with cars. It looks like half the town's come to help."

"That's a tribute to your parents," she called back, surely assuming it would annoy him, but it didn't. It just made him think, again on an honest vein. He had been wrong about some things.

"It may be a tribute to Natalie. And to Carl. Not to my dad, though," he said. "Sounds like he didn't do as much as I thought."

"Of *course* he did," Jill scolded. "He just did *different* things from what you thought. If someone wasn't out there selling our wine, Asquonset would have gone right down the drain!"

She moved down the row to spray more vines.

He followed, taking strength from what she said. They were side to side, facing in opposite directions, and he paid attention to what he was doing, but his thoughts were back in Washington, back nearly eight years to the Jill he had first met. The one here now, in Asquonset, was like that old one. She was assertive. She wasn't afraid to speak up to him.

Marriage had muted Jill.

No. *He* had muted her. He had cut her short and put her down. He had taken their differences personally. He had wanted her love to be unconditional in ways that his mother's hadn't been.

Ohh, I loved you. I loved you both. Natalie's words came back at him along with a light spray from the dying breeze. He heard the breathy way she'd said them and saw, again, the tears in her eyes. He had never seen his mother quite that way before. It made him want to believe her—made him wonder whether he would view her as a parent differently once he was a parent himself. The issue of Brad was now put in a whole new context. He wondered what he would have felt had he been in Natalie's shoes.

He wanted to talk with Jill about that. He wanted to talk about how *they* would be as parents, because that suddenly seemed more important than any professional polling he might do. But talking wasn't easy, not when it was about substantive stuff, not when it was about *personal* stuff. In the end, he might not like what Jill said. There was that risk.

Everything good involves risk. Natalie had said that, too, and he couldn't rule it out.

He took risks at work. He had fought to make the business succeed and had earned the respect of his clients and peers.

The question was whether he could take those skills and direct them homeward.

OLIVIA WOULD HAVE SENT Tess to bed at two in the morning if she had thought the child would go, but Tess was totally into the mission. Somehow, in the jungle of grapevines, river spray, and flood-lights, she had found Seth and a boy from her sailing class, both of whom had come with their families to help. The three were taking turns with the nozzle, relieving one another when their hands tired, moving down one row and on to the next, keeping right up with the adults, even with the occasional squeal of laughter.

It wasn't until shortly before dawn that Olivia knew things were working. She saw the relief in Simon's tired eyes, saw the vigor of the handshakes he gave the friends who, one by one, coiled their hoses and returned to their cars. Floodlights were shut down. Fire hoses were disconnected. Simon and Donna sprayed the last of the vines themselves, then Donna and her family left, too.

By the time the sun had risen enough for its

first long rays to expose the damage Chloe had
done, the only ones not in bed were Olivia, Simon,
and Carl. They stood on the porch of the Great
House taking in the scene. The front drive was
strewn with debris, and though much of it had
come from the peripheral maples, oaks, hemlocks,
and pines, there were more than a few vinifera
limbs in the mess.

Not knowing where he found the energy,
Olivia watched Simon trot down the steps and jog
toward the Riesling block. Random blank spots
marred the perfect order that had existed there the
day before.

"How bad is it?" she asked Carl.

He drew in a tired breath. "We've lost some. It
was inevitable, with a wind like that. But we didn't
lose anything to the salt. All said, it could have
been worse. We'll replant. We've done it before."
He barely paused. "Can I ask you something,
Olivia?"

Simon turned down a row. Only then did Olivia
turn to find Carl studying her. His eyes were
Simon's, plus forty years, brimming with exhaustion and hurt.

"Did Natalie tell you about Brad?" he asked in
a voice that was more gritty than ever. "While you
were writing. Did she say that he was . . . mine?"

Olivia's heart ached for the man. "No. She
didn't."

He looked out toward the vines. "Did you
guess it?"

"No. I knew there was something about Brad that wasn't being said. But I didn't guess that." She paused. "Did you guess it? Did you ever wonder?"

Carl didn't answer. Olivia wasn't even sure he had heard the question. He continued to look out over the field, but blindly now. Even from the side, she could see tears in his eyes when he finally turned and entered the house.

CARL WANTED TO BE ANGRY. He wanted to lash out at Natalie for the years he'd had to live without her, the years when he'd had to play second fiddle to Alexander in her life, the years when he had truly believed that Brad was another man's son.

But his heart lurched when he reached the top of the stairs. Natalie stood in a beautiful long nightgown, arms bare and elegant, head bowed. She had her back to the wall beside the closed door to Brad's room, and looked so sad and vulnerable that he couldn't sustain disappointment, much less anger. He had loved her for more than seventy years. He had believed in her that long. Even through the dark days after her marriage to Alexander, he had known she had done it in good faith.

Now there was this.

His clothing was damp, and he was tired. Every bone in his body ached, but it was the ache inside that propelled him over the carpet to where she stood.

He leaned against the door by her side, staring

at the baseboard on the opposite wall while he faced a personal truth, made a soft confession. "I used to dream he was mine. After the war, I used to look at him and see if there was anything of me in him, but I only saw you."

Her voice was broken. "There was a chemistry between you two that was never there with Al."

"Did Al know?"

"No. He resented my favoring Brad, but he never guessed why." She wrapped her arms around her middle, and whispered a fierce, "Of course, I favored him. He was all I had of you. Then I lost him, too."

A tear slipped down her cheek. Carl turned to her in time to catch it. He left his finger on her jaw, needing to comfort her as surely as he needed to breathe. "You never lost me. I was always yours."

When she looked at him, he saw that the tears weren't new. She had been crying before he had come. "I wanted to tell you about him, Carl. You can't imagine how many times I came this close"—she gestured—"*this* close to it, but stopped because I thought it would only cause more pain." She pressed a tissue to her nose. It was a minute before she lowered it. "I used to look at the two of you and see the pleasure he gave you, and I said that it didn't matter if you didn't know the whole truth, that telling you everything would change our lives and that would only hurt Brad. I loved him. The world allowed me to do that. I loved him with all my being, because the world wouldn't let me love you." The tissue went to her nose again.

Hearing her reasoning, Carl wondered if he would have had her do differently. She was right. Things would have changed, perhaps her marriage would have fallen apart, but would that have made Carl happy? Or Brad? Would Brad have felt responsible for the breakup? Would he have lived any longer if he had known that Carl was his father?

In the end, the questions were moot. The only thing that mattered—the only thing that learning about Brad proved to Carl—was that Natalie had loved him for the same seventy years that he had loved her.

Pulling her close, he held her while she cried. When she quieted, he kissed her brow and murmured against her skin, "It's done. So, so long done. We can't change it. We can only go on."

Drawing back, he searched her eyes. Along with the love there, he saw understanding. She stayed where she was for another minute, he hoped drawing strength from his closeness. Then, holding his hand, she quietly opened the door to Brad's room, pushed it all the way back, and led him inside.

OLIVIA SAW THE OPEN DOOR as soon as she turned down the hall. Glancing inside as she passed, she saw Natalie and Carl, with their backs to her. They stood at one of the bookshelves that held all the things an eleven-year-old boy had loved. She went quickly on. Of all the angst she had witnessed tonight, this seemed the most private.

In the wing, she checked on Tess, who was sound asleep. She pulled draperies shut to darken the room, took a brief shower, and returned to her own room to find Simon there. He was propped on the edge of the window seat with his elbows on his knees, looking disheveled and needy, tugging at her heart like there was no tomorrow.

Trying to make light of the way she felt, she said, "Why do I get the impression that if I were to push one of your elbows, you'd fall on the floor?"

"I would," he said without a smile. "I'm that tired. I can't sleep for long, just an hour or two. There's cleanup to do." His heavy eyes held hers. "I can't . . . do anything. I just want to hold you."

She could barely breathe. No man—not a one—had ever said that to her. It was a profoundly beautiful thing to say.

Wondering what in the world she was going to do about the things he did to her heart, she turned away to pull back the sheets, but by the time that was done he was in the bathroom. The shower went on for barely two minutes. He returned with his hair damp and a towel around his hips. Dropping his clothes by the door, he climbed into bed and pulled her close—and it was exactly as he'd said. He didn't remove the towel. There was no sex. He just held her cupped snug to his body and was asleep within minutes.

Olivia had a harder time of it. She didn't want to sleep, if sleeping meant missing a minute of this. So she lay awake, aware of every spot where they touched, every sound, every smell. Inevitably, she dozed, only to waken a short time later when he rolled the other way.

She sat up then, wrapped her arms around her knees, and watched him. He was so very real lying there, the kind of man she had spent a lifetime fantasizing about.

But he wasn't the only thing she had been fantasizing about, and much of the rest was real now, too. She had found her mother. She had found a degree of financial security. She had found options for Tess. She had found a job, even a family of sorts.

So many changes this summer, so much of it unexpected. She could deal with the money, the school, and the job. Simon was the problem.

His back was broad and bare, freckled at the shoulders and lightly tanned, tapering in a virile way to his hips. From rounded biceps on down, his arms were darker than his back. One hand lay palm up. She studied it, mapping calluses and scars. She held her own hand inches above it and compared the size and shape of the two.

His hand was larger and stronger than hers. His

body was larger and stronger than hers. Perhaps his will was larger and stronger, too, if he could keep up his widower's wall, because she knew one thing right then. She was tired of that wall and wanted it down.

Not knowing how to deal with that, she did what she did best. Slipping quietly into clothes, she ran—but only as far as Natalie's office. She took refuge in one of the wing-back chairs.

Achmed lay on the other. Normally when she was there he sat tall, as befitted royalty of the Persian type. This day, like the rest of the household, he slept. His body was an elegant curve of sleekness, all ivory and gray. Even resting on a lean shoulder, his head had a dignified bent. His front paws were extended. She reached out to touch, wavered, pulled back.

It was all she could do not to pick up the cat and hug him to her. She wanted—needed—softness and warmth. But she knew just what would happen if she tried to hold him. He would pull free and run off.

"Fortunately, cats aren't men," Natalie remarked from the door. "Men can be tamed."

Olivia burrowed into the chair. "Do you think?"

"I do." She came to the chair where Olivia sat and put a hand on its wing. "If I was short with you yesterday, it was because I care. I do care, Olivia. I care about you and I care about Tess. You add something to this place. I knew you would, right from the minute I saw your picture."

Olivia's breath caught. "What picture?"

There was a moment's silence. Then she looked up into a sweet, sweet face full of guilt. "What picture, Natalie?"

"Of you and Tess. You were dressed as dance hall girls."

"I had that in Otis's studio. When were you there?"

"When I first hired him. I stopped at his house one weekend, and he showed me around the studio. That was when I saw the picture. The two of you were just so full of spirit and spunk."

Olivia had a sudden horrible thought. Dismay must have been written all over her face, because Natalie said with force, "No, Olivia, no. I did not make up this job for your sake. The job came first. Then I thought of you, because I knew Otis was retiring, but I doubted you'd be interested. I honestly didn't. After all, it was only for the summer."

"Did you think of me with Simon?"

"No," Natalie said a bit too quickly.

"Oh, *Natalie,*" Olivia cried in dismay.

"Well, what if I did? Do you think it would have made a bit of difference if you hadn't liked him, or vice versa? I couldn't make things happen between you. All I could do was to put you in the same general vicinity, and that was all I did, Olivia. That was all. You and Simon did the rest."

Olivia wanted to argue, but to what end? That things had gone as far as they had was her own responsibility. Hers and Simon's.

Natalie came around to the front of the chair. "Forget about Simon right now. My wanting you to stay has nothing to do with him. It has to do with me. You did exactly what I wanted when it came to my book. I couldn't have hired anyone better."

"You could have hired an English major."

"And gotten a book that might have been letter perfect but probably would have had none of the love and emotion you've put into it. You wrote that book the way I would have done it. You've been the backbone behind the details of this wedding. You've made my life easier just knowing that you're here, not to mention your daughter getting old Carl out there on the tennis court."

She pulled out Olivia's computer chair and sat. "So. Let's look at the slate. On the plus side, you have a job. You have a school for Tess. You have people who care. On the minus side, you have risk, because something could go wrong with one of those things and that would hurt."

Olivia nodded. "Big time."

"You can eliminate the risk if you want."

"How?"

"You can leave. Take the job in Pittsburgh. Start over. No risk there." She pushed herself out of the chair and walked to the door.

Olivia turned to follow her. "And?"

"That's it."

"No. We're in the middle of the conversation."

"I've said my part. You know how I feel."

"Convince me," Olivia begged, but Natalie was gone—and rightly so. Natalie couldn't convince her to stay. No one could, not even Simon. The decision was Olivia's.

Same with the risk.

Stay. Go. Stay. Go. She went back and forth until her head buzzed with indecision. This was reality as she had rarely known it. On top of a night without sleep, it was exhausting.

Thinking to slip back into bed with Simon, she returned to her room, but the bed was empty.

Just as well, she told herself. Tess would be getting up soon. No sense her seeing them sleeping together. No sense getting her hopes up.

Then again, maybe it wouldn't be getting Tess's hopes up at all. Tess had started off hating Simon. Maybe a part of her still did. Maybe she would be relieved to know they were leaving. After all, Tess had had Olivia to herself for ten years. What child wanted to share?

Climbing into bed in the exact spot where Simon had lain, Olivia put her head in the hollow his had left on the pillow and pulled up the sheets. His smell surrounded her.

She was just tired enough—just imaginative enough—to pretend that he was there in the flesh. Comforted by that thought, she fell asleep.

• • •

OLIVIA SLEPT until the middle of the afternoon. She came awake slowly, then bolted up when she realized how late it was.

Tess was gone from her bed, though certainly safe. If Susanne hadn't kepts tabs on her, Jill or Carl or Natalie would.

Feeling guilty even thinking that—Tess was *her* responsibility—she opened her bedroom door to go looking and and saw a note half over the threshold.

It was from Tess—no mistaking that handwriting.

"Gone sailing with Simon," it said, and her heart began to thud.

BY THE TIME Olivia pulled up at the yacht club and ran around to the back deck and out onto the dock, she had analyzed Simon's taking Tess sailing from most every angle.

One said he was procrastinating, that the vineyard was a mess and he wasn't ready to tackle it.

Another said he was fulfilling a duty. He had promised Tess he would take her out. Once it was done, he was free.

The therapy angle said that he hadn't been sailing in four years, but that the ocean was calm after the storm, and it was time.

Bribery was a possibility. He might be taking

Tess out in exchange for leaving him alone when he worked. Or for not talking back. Or for helping find homes for the kittens.

His taking her sailing might be a way of saying good-bye.

Olivia didn't want it to be that. Standing there on the dock, looking out at a sea filled with sailboats, any one of which might hold Simon and Tess, she realized that she didn't want it to be that.

Gnawing on her cheek, she walked back down the dock. Cleanup crews were removing boards from the clubhouse windows and sweeping driftwood, stones, and sand from the deck. Several boats lay askew in their slips. Others had lost masts, windows, or seats.

Olivia did *not* want it to be good-bye.

Turning on her heel, she went up the dock again. At the very end, she sat down and waited.

Several boats returned, but Simon and Tess weren't in them.

Another boat tacked toward the dock, then another, and she knew the people in these. They were locals. When they waved, she waved back.

Finally, she spotted Simon and Tess, and came to her feet. Their heads were close together, though she could have sworn that Tess was holding the lines. Then they spotted her and waved, both of them with jubilant smiles, and she started to cry—started to cry, just like that, for no good reason she could think of.

"Hi, Mom!" Tess yelled, but her eyes quickly

returned to the sails. When Simon said something, she pushed the tiller and pulled in the lines, and the sailboat sidled up to the dock as smoothly as if she had been docking boats for years. The sail went slack and lowered. Olivia caught the line they tossed.

"Did you *see* us, Mom?" Tess cried, ebullient. "Did you see how far out we went? We were heeling all the way, it was *so* cool!" She would have climbed out then and there if Simon hadn't insisted that she help fold and tie and put things away.

By the time that was done, she had spotted a friend on one of the other docks. Putting her small hands on Simon's shoulders, she said a very grown-up, "You were wonderful, Simon. Thank you." Then, like a switch flipped, she was a ten-year-old again, hopping onto the dock, giving Olivia a positively beatific smile before taking off at a run.

Olivia sat down on the dock with her feet hanging in the boat.

Simon leaned against her knees. "Why were you crying?"

Her eyes filled again. She coiled her arms around his neck and locked her hands. "Don't leave."

"Me? I'm not going anywhere."

"But will you? Will you get tired of things one day and just walk out?"

He smoothed back the hair that blew toward her eyes. "Not from you."

"That frightens me so much."

"And you don't think it frightens me? I lost everything once. I know that pain." He frowned and watched his thumb stroke her arm. "On my way to your room this morning, I saw Natalie and my dad. They were in Brad's room. It couldn't have been easy for either of them. I admire their courage." His eyes met hers. "I want to admire ours, too."

Olivia wanted it, too. She wanted it more than anything. "Do we have it?"

"I think we do." He swallowed, and while she watched his lips, he mouthed the magic words.

Thirty

"SHIFT THE LIGHT, SWEETHEART?" Simon asked around the nails clamped between his teeth.

Tess jumped up and adjusted the floodlight so that it was aimed at the spot where they worked. Seconds later, she was back, taking another handful of nails, handing him a few at a time. They were putting down the floor in what would be a family room with a cathedral ceiling and skylights. It was half of the addition Simon was adding to the cabin. The other half, already livable thanks to friends from town, held bedrooms.

"The cord is stretched to the limit," Olivia remarked from the door. She was leaning against the newly raised wood, with her hands in the pockets of her jeans and three cats at her feet. Buck was there with the two of her litter that they had kept, Oliver and Tyrone. Both were growing into their ears and eyes, but none of the three was venturing past Olivia until the hammering was done. "It's a message that you're supposed to quit for the night."

"Just another couple of feet," Simon said and put out a hand toward the pile of maple planks. "A short one now, Tess." She picked one out. He fitted it in beside the last piece laid, tongue to groove, and hammered in two well-placed nails.

Olivia should have insisted that they stop. It was getting late, and it was November raw. Though the walls were closed in and insulated, there was no heat here yet, which was fine for nestling under goose down in the bedrooms, but barnlike under high ceilings. On top of that, Tess still had homework to do. She was settling in at Braemont, far happier than she'd been in years, but the school didn't coddle its students. No excuses were made for learning disabilities. The teachers knew exactly what they were dealing with and how to do it in the best possible way. That meant work.

But then there was this—Tess feeling like she was a vital part of the building process, and Simon delighted to have her help. And it wasn't an empty gesture. He made her work, whether they were spraying vines, harvesting grapes, sailing, or building a room.

Olivia couldn't have asked for more for her

child. If ever there was a man who captured the work ethic of the past, Simon was it.

She fingered the ring in her pocket, then pulled out her hand to see it again. As engagement rings went, it was more beautiful than anything her wildest dreams might have forged. A single perfect diamond was flanked by matching pairs of baguettes, set in platinum with a simplicity that highlighted the sparkle of the stones. It was exquisite in every sense, not the least of which was that the gems were from a brooch that Carl had given Ana at the time of Simon's birth. It had belonged to Carl's mother before that.

To own a family heirloom—to be part of a family tradition—was more than Olivia had ever expected. She'd had the ring for two months and still found herself touching it often, just to make sure that it was there, that it was real. And there was another to come. The remaining baguettes from the brooch were being set in a platinum band to match the one she wore. That would be her wedding band.

Her wedding band. *Wedding* band. *So* hard to believe.

The wedding was planned for the Thanksgiving weekend. Olivia had needed that much time to accept that the whole of what she had with Simon was real. She couldn't pull their relationship out of her pocket and look at it, the way she could a ring. Love was intangible. For someone like Olivia, who had spent a lifetime thinking herself unworthy, believing came hard. But it did come.

Take sharing Simon with the vineyard. With harvest done, he had to aerate the soil, apply fertilizer, replace vines that Chloe had destroyed, and weed out others that were too old to be fruitful. On occasion something tied him up and he was delayed coming home. The first time it happened, Olivia convinced herself that he had changed his mind about them and was hiding behind work. The second time, she was merely alert. The third time, she was relaxed enough to use the delay for a little quality time with Tess.

There hadn't been a fourth time. As much as anything else, that told her how badly Simon wanted to be with her. Not even the most distrustful soul could hold out against his kind of devotion for long. They grew closer, best of friends now. They saw things the same way, be it designing an addition or parenting Tess. They talked. They laughed. They fell further in love.

Natalie lobbied for a large wedding, but Olivia and Simon were of like mind about that, as well. They wanted something small and intimate, so there weren't even any formal invitations sent. They had made phone calls inviting those people about whom they cared most.

Susanne and Mark would come. They even had their own place to stay, having just bought a house on the ocean, several miles down the road from the vineyard. It was a sprawling Cape with an endless porch, and a carriage house that Susanne would turn into either an apartment for their children or several rooms for B-and-B guests. Visiting every few weeks from New York, she was weighing her options while she fixed up the main house.

Susanne and Natalie were starting to open up with each other. It was an effort at times, what with old habits nearly as sticky as old gripes. But Susanne and her family had come to Natalie and Carl's wedding. Given Susanne's initial resistance to that, it was a big step forward.

Greg's steps were smaller. He came to the wedding and was pleasant enough, but Olivia suspected Jill was the force behind that. As though it was part of the bargain, she returned to Washington with him the next day, and while she continued to do marketing work for Asquonset from there, several weeks passed before anyone heard from Greg. Then he called Carl, perhaps finding that easier. He reported that things were better between Jill and him, that they were seeing a counselor and shopping for baby furniture. He told Carl to tell Natalie that they would be up for the Fall Harvest Feast, and indeed they did come. There was lingering tension, but the pleasantry interspersed with it was more genuine. He and Natalie talked some— about Alexander, about Jill and the baby, about the changes that he might make in his business so that he could be in Washington more with Jill.

Jill had promised Olivia that they would be up for the wedding. Olivia was honored to call her a friend.

"Okay," Simon announced. "That's it."

Tess pointed past him. "I thought we were going *that* far."

"It was a hope. We'll reach it tomorrow." He sat back on his heels. "In the meantime, look at what we've done. It's spectacular."

But Tess had caught sight of the cats. She crawled over to them, then sat and folded her legs. Oliver immediately leaped into the hole in the middle, climbed up her front, and began batting at a long strand of curly hair.

"Homework?" Olivia reminded her, while Simon began gathering tools.

"This baby is just *so cute,*" Tess cooed.

"Homework?" Olivia repeated.

Tess shot her what might have been a dirty look if the light had been better and her glasses cleaner. Seeming to realize that, she scrambled to her feet, went back to Simon, and gave him a kiss before breezing out past Olivia.

Simon pushed himself to his feet and came toward her, wiping his hands on his jeans. "Sorry about that."

Olivia smiled. "Don't be." She tipped up her face, slid her arms around his waist. "I don't mind being the bad guy. I'd rather she like you."

"She's playing us against each other."

"I think this is only the start. Wait till she drives. Wait till she *dates.*"

"We'll deal," he said. Bracing his hands wide

on either side of her, he leaned in. When he took a deep breath, she felt the strength of his body. "Do you know," he said on the exhalation, as much a satisfied sigh as anything else, "how happy I am?"

Olivia couldn't answer. She never could when he said things like that. The words were too real, too honest, too clearly heartfelt. She always choked up.

So she smiled.

He smiled back. "Nothing to say to that?"

She shook her head.

"The woman who had a comeback for everything I tossed at her when we first met—*nothing* to say?"

She shook her head, smiling wider to compensate for her tears.

"Want to go in and warm up?"

Thinking that the stony grouch *he* had been when they first met had developed a certain way with words, that he was absolutely, unequivocally perfect, and that she didn't deserve him but would surely take him anyway, she nodded.

LARGE
PRINT

LP
F
DEL   Delinsky, Barbara

           The vineyard

DUE DATE		OG10	25.00

JUN 2 2 2000